Vincent Van Gogh

Art, Life, and Letters

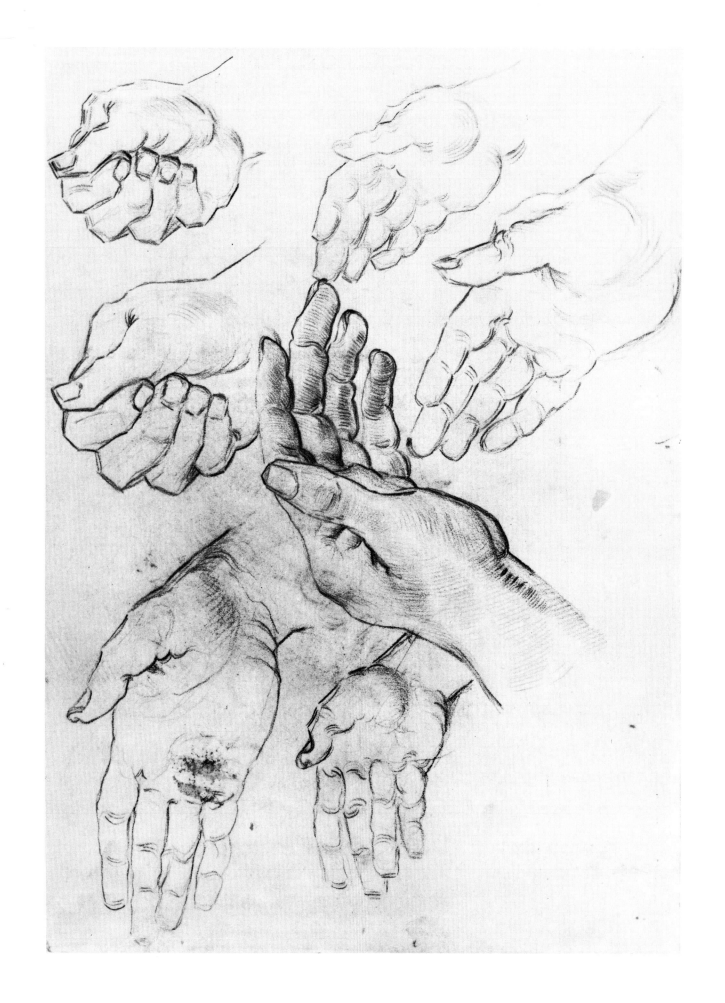

Bernard Zurcher

Vincent Van Gogh

Art, Life, and Letters

Greenwich Editions

This edition published in 1994 by
Greenwich Editions
Unit 7
202 New North Road
London N1 7BJ, UK

Greenwich Editions is part of The Ramboro Group of Companies.

ISBN: 0-86288-005-X

Van Gogh — Vie et oeuvre
Copyright © 1985 by Office du Livre S.A., Fribourg, Switzerland

English translation:
Copyright © 1985 by Office du Livre S.A., Fribourg, Switzerland

Translation from the French by Helga Harrison

This edition is published by special arrangement with William S. Konecky Associates.

Printed and bound in Italy

Letter excerpts from *The Complete Letters of Vincent Van Gogh* by New York Graphic Society Books/
Little, Brown and Company are reprinted by permission of Little, Brown and Company.

Frontispiece: *Study of Hands*, Nuenen, January 1885, Black chalk, 32x24 cm.
F 1360. Rijksmuseum Vincent van Gogh, Amsterdam.

Contents

Foreword   7

Introduction   9

I   Apprenticeship in Drawing   11
    In the Art Trade   11
    From Teaching to Preaching   13
    The Temptation to Draw   15
    A New Vocation   17
    Exercices for a Self-Taught Man   20
    An Irrevocable Decision   26

II Realist Painting   33
    A Fresh Start   33
    A Tragicomedy   35
    Lessons of Mauve   39
    Vincent's Point of View   43
    His Painting Takes Shape   55
    Drenthe   58
    The Brabant Weavers   59
    A Realist Palette   67
    Lies More Truthful than Truth   71
    The Potato Eaters   82
    Transcending Color   93

III A New Palette   97
    From Light to Color   97
    "In Color Seeking Life"   115

IV Between Africa and Japan   141
    First Cloisonnist Experiments   141
    Expressing the Essence   144
    Precursor of the Fauvists   154
    Starry Night   162
    "To Express Hope by Some Star"   170
    The Painter of the Future   171

V   The Studio in the South   183
    Waiting   183
    Face to Face   192
    The Drama of the Severed Ear   200

VI Mad about Painting   215
    Adrift   215
    The Splash of Black   222
    Dormant Sensibility   236
    "We Can Only Make Our Pictures Speak"   261
    "There Is No End to Sorrow"   277

Appendix   285
Notes   287
Vincent's Distinctive Hand   293
Chronology   303
Family Tree of Vincent Van Gogh   309
Bibliography   311
Index   315
Index of Vincent Van Gogh's Works   319

Foreword

Since the death of Vincent Van Gogh, there have been numerous commentaries on his life and work. Nevertheless, certain aspects that gave rise to misunderstanding and hostility among his contemporaries still arouse our curiosity today. Not the least of these is the intensity of the relationship between his life and his work. This led him to commit acts that were condemned as senseless—but that make perfect sense when viewed in their proper context.

The questions, reflections, and advice with which he filled his letters day after day constitute a veritable diary. His correspondence weaves a tissue of sometimes unconscious associations linking the events that shaped his life to their resolution on canvas as his work developed. Thus, in its approach this book is guided by his letters, and even in its form it strives to follow the letters in their emotional twists and turns.

Introduction

During his life Vincent Van Gogh was called accursed by the parish priest of Auvers, for example, who refused to lend his hearse for Vincent's funeral. Even in our time the now-famous painter remains an enigma: How can we truly understand the nature of his artistic commitment, so uncompromising, and of the passions that drove him to the final sacrifice, his suicide at the age of thirty-seven?

Van Gogh, who was so modest that he signed himself as merely "Vincent," always knew that his life on earth would be short. Seven years before his death, he wrote a prophetic postscript in a letter to his brother Theo: "Without any definite motive, I can't help adding a thought which often occurs to me. Not only did I begin painting late in life, but it may also be that I shall not live for so very many years [...] I think I may safely presume: that my body will keep a certain number of years 'quand bien même'—a certain number, between six and ten, for instance [...] So I go on like an ignoramus who knows only this one thing: in a few years I must finish a certain work [...] So this work is my aim [...] *Something must be done* in those few years, this thought dominates all my plans for my work. You will understand better my desire to push on. At the same time I am certainly resolved to use simple means. And perhaps you will also understand that I do not consider my studies things made for their own sake, but am always thinking of my work as a whole."[1]

Vincent's work exerts a twofold fascination: The more than 2,000 drawings and paintings that he produced over a span of only ten years (1880–1890) are matched by his magnificent correspondence—over 800 letters, most of them to Theo. These letters reveal how Vincent gradually became caught up in his work, carried away by its unremitting demands. As he had been unable to enter the ministry, he went into painting, seeking through it another way to the truth. In the very depths of his soul he felt "the positive consciousness of the fact that art is something greater and higher than our own adroitness or accomplishments or knowledge."[2]

Vincent's work deeply expresses the anguish of a man struggling against the "sadness" of the human predicament—struggling with his sole weapon, painting, after the failure of his other efforts in education, preaching, and evangelizing. As a painter, the only means of expression at his disposal was the use of light—a light created by color contrasts, a light only just restored to color by the Impressionists after two centuries of "halftones."

In the heart of the pallid Drenthe dawns, in the burnished dusks of Nuenen, in the dark houses of the weavers, Vincent kindled the "yellow spark" of a small flame, a lamp lighting—in the manner of Honthorst or Rembrandt—the peasant supper of the *Potato Eaters* (F82). From that moment on, the flame increased in intensity until its blaze rivalled that of the sun of the Arles country, the place that was called the "Provençal Japan," where that "devil of a question of yellow" had its roots. There Vincent rediscovered the glow of a childhood memory—of a day when he was seized by an irresistible desire to run through a burning forest.[a]

But although the "brilliant yellow note" sounded from one canvas to the next, a "black note" also appeared suddenly in the blue of the sky. It came from a myriad of sources, whether natural or artificial, sunlit or nocturnal. Vincent had not escaped the wounds of battle: Struck first by a "black ray" at the death of his pastor father, he was then to be seared by the heat of his Promethean talent. The "black note" rapidly became a blot—the black blot of cypresses standing like candles, the black flight of ravens blotting out the fiery yellow of the cornfields. The eclipse of the *Starry Night* (F474) of St.-Rémy enshrines this conflict between the "yellow note" and the "black note," a conflict that Vincent created even at the risk of tearing himself apart.

"You must *get your eyes accustomed* first and gradually to the different light," he told his brother on 10 September 1889.[3] We intend to follow that advice in this book so that we may unveil, bit by bit, the path of Vincent's evolution from natural light to that "different light" that shines from his work.

Chapter I   Apprenticeship in Drawing

In the Art Trade

In the summer of 1880 Vincent decided, at the age of twenty-seven, to devote himself entirely to drawing and took up a career as an artist. He had already undergone some cruel trials, although his first five working years as an employee of the Goupil Gallery at The Hague (1869-1874) had begun happily enough. On 1 August 1869 he had been taken on by the firm on the recommendation of Uncle "Cent," who was a founder and shareholder; and H.G. Tersteeg, Vincent's young boss, had nothing but praise for him. It was Vincent's particular task to sell the *Galerie photographique* (Gallery of Photographs) published by the art gallery, and he was enthusiastic about the contemporary artists whose works he had gotten to know. Business was good, he wrote: "We sell the Musée Goupil & Co. photographs only en papillottes, on an average of a hundred a day."[1] There were also the painters of the school of The Hague, especially his cousin Anton Mauve who, we shall subsequently see, played an important part in Vincent's life; and the brothers Jacob and Wilhelm Maris; also Jongkind and the French landscape painters of the Barbizon school, among them Diaz and Daubigny.

The cheerful letters Vincent wrote at this time to his brother Theo and to his friends testified to his happiness. Everything seemed set fair for a career in the art trade. When Theo in his turn joined the Brussels branch of the firm in January 1873, Vincent encouraged him. "The New Year began well: my salary was raised 10 guilders, so that I now earn 50 guilders a month, and in addition I got 50 guilders as a present. Isn't that splendid? I hope now to be able to shift for myself. I am so glad that you are in the same firm. It is such a splendid house; the longer you are in it, the more ambition it gives you."[2]

In June Vincent was transferred to the London branch to complete his training, and a few months later Theo replaced him at The Hague, working with Tersteeg. In London, Vincent lodged with the widow Loyer. He soon fell in love with her daughter Eugénie, but when he declared his passion she rejected him. Undoubtedly she preferred one of the German boarders "who are very fond of music and play the piano and sing,"[3] and what was more, who were financially much better off than Vincent. In fact, he added: "These gentlemen spent a great deal of money and I shall not go out with them in the future."

An unhappy first romance at the end of adolescence is not an unusual event in a man's life. And indeed Vincent's letters did not explicitly reflect his disappointment except through in a sudden change in mood. In July 1873 he had written: "All is well with me. I see much that is new and beautiful and have been fortunate in finding a good boarding-house, so that on the whole I feel quite at home already."[4] In October of the same year, however, upset by his love affair, he was surprised to find himself writing "without considering that one must take care a letter is intelligible."[5] Previously, in the grip of his romantic fervor, he had avidly devoured

L'Amour (Love) by Michelet, whose *Les Aspirations de l'Automne* (Aspirations of Fall) he urged Theo to read: "Such a book teaches us that there is much more in love than people generally suppose. To me the book has been a revelation and a Gospel at the same time."[6] But in a letter of 31 July 1874, his tone changed abruptly: "Since I have been back in England, my love for drawing has stopped...." Enthusiasm gave way to coldness. In October, Uncle Vincent, who had been alerted by the young man's parents, intervened with Goupil to have him moved for a short time to the head office in Paris, "for a change of air." But Vincent, obsessed by the thought of Eugénie, returned to London in December. He lived on his own and withdrew into himself. The tone of his letters became frankly sinister, and they were not without an occasional indulgence in histrionics: "As you see, it is sketched on the title page of *Poems* by Edmond Roche. There are some very fine ones among them, grave and sad; one begins and ends thus: 'J'ai gravi, triste et seul, la dune triste et nue...' (I have climbed, sad and alone, the sad and barren dune...)."[7]

At first Vincent sought refuge in his work, but his heart was no longer in it. Finally even his employers became dissatisfied with him. He was overcome by a profound lethargy. "I hope and trust that I am not what many people think I am just now. We shall see, some time must pass."[8] In fact, what has usually been called his "crisis of mysticism" was not so much an emotional aberration, which would have been natural enough in a sensitive young man like Vincent. Rather it was a new state of mind— triggered by his unhappy love affair—that I would readily call existentialist: a state of mind in which Renan replaced Michelet. "Pour agir dans le monde, il faut mourir à soi-même"—"to act well in this world one must sacrifice all personal desire." Jotted on the bottom of the aforementioned letter, this quotation strikes me as fundamentally significant: It both predicts and summarizes the whole course of Vincent's spiritual and artistic life. It reveals the meaning and the deep coherence of his future

work, and rebuts the facile charge of "madness" that has been accepted so unquestioningly. And it points to the way that Vincent would take as a man who "sets out on his life, gives it its shape, and beyond that shape there is nothing."[a]

The people in Vincent's circle in London found him increasingly "odd," so much so that he was sent back to Paris at the end of May 1875. Already Vincent had begun to "sacrifice all personal desire." His job no longer interested him. He still loved paintings, visited the Louvre and the Luxembourg Museum, and collected engravings, but his view of things was no longer quite the same. He was less impressed by the "beauty" of works than by their "effect." Thus, during an auction of Millet's drawings at the Hôtel Drouot, he said: "I felt something like: 'Take off your shoes, the place you are standing on is holy.'" His favorite expression, "That's it," held a new meaning. "Power" and "poetry" became a "sense of the sacred." Vincent came to realize that every successful work of art imitates the Creation. He advised Theo to read no other book in future than the Bible. "I am going to destroy all my books by Michelet, etc. I wish you would do the same."[9] He submerged himself in the Bible with fervor and copied out the Psalms, through which he asked God to help him. "'I dare not choose my lot; ... Choose Thou for me...'"[10]

In Paris, Vincent lived in a small room in Montmartre overlooking "a little garden full of ivy and wild vines."[11] He shared it with an eighteen-year-old English boy, Gladwell, who also worked at Goupil's. Unconsciously, Vincent experienced a "dissociation" phenomenon in which, through Gladwell, he saw himself as he had been a few years earlier. The severe portrait of his companion that he sketched for Theo is a disturbing echo of his own image: "He had never been away from home before, and, especially the first week he was here, he was very uncouth; for instance, every morning, afternoon and evening he ate four or six pieces of bread (bread is very cheap here), in addition to several pounds of apples and pears, etc. Notwithstanding, he is as thin as a stick, with two rows of strong teeth, full red lips, glittering eyes, a pair of large, generally red, projecting ears.... He has a wholly ingenuous, unspoilt heart, and is very good at his work."[12] Gladwell embodied the memory of the happy Vincent, the Vincent he had been before his catastrophic romance. "At first everybody laughed at him, even I. Later on I grew to like him, and now, I assure you, I am very glad to have his company in the evening." A scapegoat in the literal sense, Gladwell nonetheless helped Vincent to forget what he called his "Icarus adventure."

Vincent was vaguely aware that the future held something else for him other than the life of an art dealer; he longed with all his heart to free himself from the professional ties that no longer held any interest for him. So on 1 April 1876, when M. Boussod seized the first opportunity to ask him to resign, Vincent left his job. "When the apple is ripe, a soft breeze makes it fall from the tree.... And now, boy, I am not yet sure what I should do...."[13]

From Teaching to Preaching

Despair plunged Vincent into a twilight landscape. In mid-April he returned to England, where he contemplated the view from a window of his Ramsgate school and thought it beautiful, "especially in the twilight when the lamps were lit and their light was reflected in the wet street."[14] In Amsterdam a harbor fire at night had shown him "the black row of people standing there, watching; and the little boats hovering around the blaze also looked black in the water, which reflected the flames."[15] He wished he could walk with Harry Gladwell "in the twilight, along the Seine...."[16]

But the emotional wounds Vincent bore also brought forth his remarkable gifts of perception. He saw powerfully what others did not see at all: the absurdity of a world plunged into the gloom of its daily poverty. Such a vision was his prerogative as an artist, but he did not yet realize that. "Sad but always

2   *View from the School Window.* Ramsgate, 31 May 1876. Pen. Drawing in Letter 67. Rijksmuseum Vincent van Gogh, Amsterdam.

cheerful," as he described himself on several occasions, he hoped to find the remedy for his anxieties in the study of Holy Scriptures: "Wings over grave and death!"

The reassuring image of his pastor father suggested a solution to his quandary. All Vincent had to do was to follow him "by prayer and the fruit thereof—patience and faith—and ... the Bible that was a light unto his path and a lamp unto his feet."[17] That was the path Vincent wanted to follow, the path taken by the pilgrim in Christina Rossetti's poem:[18]

Does the road go uphill all the way?
Yes, to the very end.
Will the journey take the whole long day?
From morn till night, my friend.

His secret ambition, which he hardly dared admit even to himself, was to be a minister, like his father.

At Ramsgate the teacher, Mr. Stokes, gave him a job in his small school. There were only twenty-four pupils, boys from ages ten to fourteen. Vincent taught French, spelling, and even arithmetic, but in his spare time he liked to linger on the beach and watch the sea. He seemed to have regained a measure of serenity, tempered with caution: "These are really very happy days I spend here day by day, but still *it is a happiness and quiet which I do not quite trust.*"[19] In the course of his letters, new preoccupations arose. No longer content with only a brief mention of the countryside he loved, he began to dwell on it in his letters, describing the natural shapes and colors with precision: "The sea was yellowish, especially near the shore; on the horizon a strip of light, and above it immense dark gray clouds...."[20] Vincent was on the move, but his destination was still uncertain. What was going on inside of him? He had at least broken away from the narrow world of the Goupils, Boussods, and Valadons; when a former colleague, van Iterson, came to see him, it was like the visit of "a person from another world."[21] His own world he saw more as *The Wide, Wide World* of Elizabeth Wetherall, from whose work he read frequently to his pupils. In June Vincent revealed his plan: "If I should find anything, it will probably be a position between clergyman and missionary among the working people in the suburbs of London. Do not speak of it to anybody yet."[22] For Vincent, teaching was obviously a first step towards evangelizing, and with this in mind he wrote to a London clergyman whose sermons he had gone to hear. In essence, his letter was a call for help that, unconsciously, he actually meant for his father: "I think your fatherly eye will do me good."[23]

When Mr. Stokes moved his school to Isleworth, Vincent went too. But as the former had great difficulty in paying him (and the salary in any case was extremely low), he took the opportunity of looking for another job. To his delight, the Reverend Jones, a Methodist minister, took him on as an assistant. Reverend Jones also ran a school, and Vincent helped him as best as he could, coming very close through this work to achieving his ideal in which he identified with his father.

Vincent's admiration for his father reached its peak during this period, and unconsciously he came to endow him with the attributes of a mother figure as well: "But men like our father are more beautiful than the sea." In his anxiety and his obsession with his father, Vincent devised a trinity that

had the power to take him away from the world—the deceitful world, the world of the traders whom Jesus had driven from the Temple: a trinity that would lead him to the *true peace* of the blessed angels. "Our father and those in heaven are separated by the same stretch of life that separates our father from ourselves. God in heaven can make us our father's brethren and unite us both more and more strongly together."[24]

We must not underrate the influence of such an unconscious image on the process of artistic creation. Through their intimate and detailed correspondence, Vincent and Theo were bound to each other. The trinitarian connection between the father and his sons was fragile, however, for it failed to include Vincent's mother who, he unconsciously felt, blamed him for having "failed" her. In fact, in terms of salvation, the "successful" Vincent was he who was already with the blessed angels—the "first Vincent," who had been stillborn a year to the day before Vincent's birth. In making himself a part of this trinity Vincent could become his father's equal and thereby obliterate his mother's disappointment in him. If he did not draw much during this time, it was because he did not feel the urge, absorbed as he was in the wish to identify with his father. We shall see how, later on, he came to feel that drawing would enable him to fulfill that desire.

For the time being, Vincent was happy. The Reverend Jones permitted him to preach: His father could be proud of him! He felt that he was at last following the road taken by his father and several generations of ancestors before him, a straight road similar to those he later delighted in drawing: "When I was standing in the pulpit, I felt like somebody who, emerging from a dark cave underground, comes back to the friendly daylight...."[25]

Filled with the joy of reaching, he saw life through rose-colored spectacles. "In the morning it was so beautiful on the road to Turnham Green—the chestnut trees and the clear blue sky and the morning sun mirrored in the water of the Thames; the grass was sparkling green and one heard the

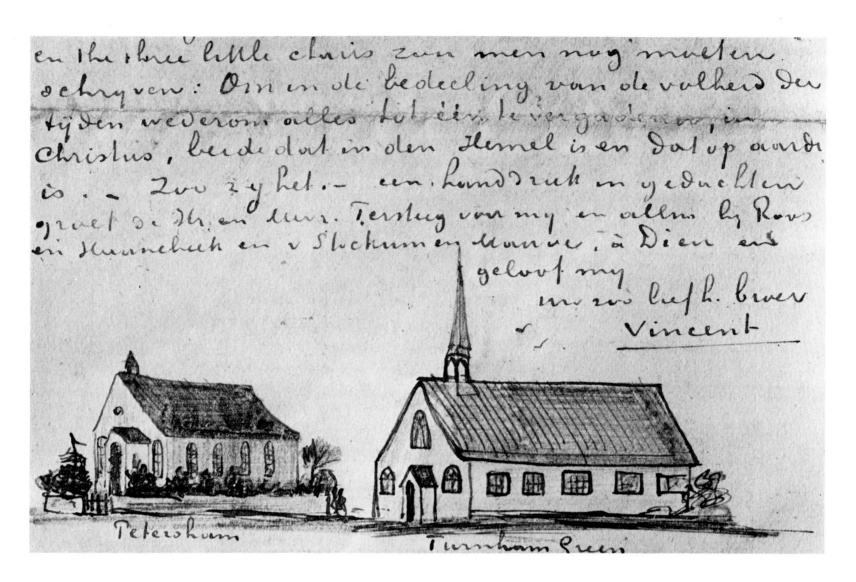

3 *The Churches of Petersham and Turnham Green*. Isleworth, 25 November 1876. Pen. Drawing in Letter 82. Rijksmuseum Vincent van Gogh, Amsterdam.

sound of church bells all around."[26] But the work Jones expected of him soon outstripped his strength. Often he had to collect school fees from parents who were sunk in dismal poverty. Vincent discovered a world of squalor worse than he had ever suspected. Suddenly he felt that his sermons were merely self-indulgent. This bitter experience inspired him with a new purpose: to live in the service of the most destitute. He had to respond to that call from God in order to teach his message of charity, and his response was evident in this phrase from his first sermon: "I shall be more and more tired but also nearer and nearer to Thee."

The Temptation to Draw

Vincent went home to his parents in Etten for the Christmas holidays. The whole family was gathered together, and they discussed his future. His job with the Reverend Jones paid very badly, and there was no hope that this would improve. His parents rightly felt that at the age of twenty-four he ought to be able to find a profession by which he could live. They persuaded him to leave Isleworth for good, Uncle Cent was approached once more, and thanks to his recommendation Vincent was taken on at the end of January 1877 as a clerk with Blussé & Van Braam, booksellers in Dordrecht. But his work in that "other world," into which he once more felt himself thrust, could never again satisfy him. More than ever his overriding wish was to become a clergyman like his father. He wanted to learn the Bible by heart, and spent most of his time at the bookshop translating biblical passages into English, French, and German. In his free time, however, he made long trips into the depths of the country, where he felt at peace. "This peculiar landscape and sourrounding is so expressive, it seems to say, 'Be of good courage, fear not.'"[27] He was hatching a new plan to achieve the goal he had set himself: He would go to Amsterdam to study theology. He took Theo into his confidence: "I suppose that for a 'sower of God's word,' as I hope to be, as well as for a sower of the seed in the fields, each day will bring enough of its own evil, and the earth will produce many thorns and thistles."[28] The image of the sower to whom Vincent compared himself would later become a recurrent theme in his work; one of his first "professional" drawings features a sower copied after Millet.

Realizing what little interest Vincent was taking in his work, his parents finally agreed to help him carry out his plan. His uncle Johan, a vice-admiral at the Amsterdam shipyards, made him welcome in his large house, while Uncle Stricker, a well-known clergyman, took charge of his studies. He arranged for Vincent to be coached in Latin and Greek by a young teacher, Dr. Mendes da Costa, who soon became Vincent's friend. But in spite of his parents' help and the encouragement of his teachers, in spite of the zeal that led him to punish himself if he felt dissatisfied with his own industry, Vincent failed after fifteen months of effort. The aridity of the subjects he had to study for his entrance examination so disheartened him that he could not master them. The Greek lessons "make one feel more oppressed than the Brabant cornfields, which are beautiful on such a day."[29] He preferred to waste precious time on long walks during which he was already looking at the landscape and street scenes with the eyes of a painter. "This morning I got up very early. It had been raining overnight, but very soon the sun broke through the clouds; the ground and the piles of wood and beams in the yard were drenched, and in the pools the sky's reflection was quite golden from the rising sun. At five o'clock I saw those hundreds of workmen scatter like little black figures."[30] His vague forebodings of failure were coupled with attempts to evade his anxiety about the possibility: "Yesterday Uncle Cor sent me a lot of old paper, like the sheet on which I am writing now; isn't it delightful for writing exercises on?"[31] Vincent greatly appreciated the quality of the paper. What a waste, he must have thought, to do Latin exercises on it! Under the pretext of doing geography, he copied maps untiringly and even sent some to his brother so that he could put them up on the wall with his drawings. And, of course, numerous prints hung above Vincent's desk. "Today while I was working I had in front of me a page from *Cours de dessin Bargue* (Bargue's Drawing Examples), II, part I, No. 39, 'Anne of Brittany.' It was hanging in my room in London with No. 53; 'A Young Citizen' was hanging in between. What I liked and admired in the beginning, I like and admire still."[32] In fact, that sheet of the *Cours de dessin Bargue*[b] was simply a drawing example for students.

Vincent soon went on to act. "Now and then when I am writing, I instinctively make a little drawing, like the one I sent you lately: this morning, for instance, Elijah in the desert, with the stormy sky, and in the foreground a few thorn bushes. It is nothing special, but I see it all so vividly before me, and I think that at such moments I could speak about it enthusiastically—may it be given to me to do so later on."[33] Vincent did not speak about it, he drew "instinctively," as he said—that is, from the images in his unconscious. This well-known phenomenon of "acting out" was a liberating process: It relieved the growing stress of his fear of failure, the failure to identify with his father.

His choice of subject for the drawing, Elijah in the desert, is particularly significant in this context. If we reread the relevant passage in Kings I, we can see how much Elijah resembles Vincent himself—one might even say the choice was a prophetic one! The passage about Elijah recounts that at the brook

Cherith, "the ravens brought him bread and flesh in the morning and bread and flesh in the evening." We cannot fail to recall the picture that preceded Vincent's death, *Crows over the Cornfields* (F 779), and the reproduction of Van der Maten's *Funeral Procession through the Cornfields*, which hung above his father's desk. Finally, consider the episode of the resurrection of the widow's son: "And it came to pass after these things, that the son of the woman, the mistress of the house, fell sick; and his sickness was so sore that there was no breath left in him. And she said to Elijah, 'What have I to do with thee, O thou man of God? Art thou come unto me to call my sin to remembrance and to slay my son?' Then Elijah raised her son from the dead. 'See, thy son liveth.'" From this, we might well believe that the "second Vincent" desired nothing more ardently than to wipe the "first" forever from his mother's memory.

A New Vocation

Along with Vincent's increasing sense of failure regarding his studies, which in turn grew more formidable as they advanced, he felt a quickening artistic awareness. A change was taking place in him. He began to refer more and more often to the works of Rembrandt, Ruysdael, Corot, Daubigny, Maris, Israëls, Ary Scheffer, Millais and Weissenbruch. Until then, he had seen only one way to fulfill his ambition to become a clergyman like his father—study. Now he was beginning to feel that there might be another way to win his father's approval. A significant phrase appears in his first letter to Theo from Amsterdam: "A great deal of study is needed for the work of men like Father, Uncle Stricker, and so many others, just as for painting."[34] Marc E. Tralbaut has already noticed it: "We might say that a repressed ambition—to paint—rises irresistibly to the surface although he was not aware of it."[c]

Vincent began to think that since he drew instinctively, he must have some "aptitude": at least he enjoyed drawing, in contrast to his dislike of his studies. He would certainly find drawing an easier kind of work and—who knew?—someday he might become an artist of whom his family would be proud, like his cousin Mauve, for instance, whom he mentioned more and more frequently in his letters. Besides, didn't a picture of which one could say, "that's beautiful, indescribably beautiful, unforgettable" have "something of the spirit of the resurrection and the life?"[35] In the same letter, however, Vincent showed that he dared not pursue the thought any further: " ...in fact, I need not wish it so much, for all things are in the word of Christ—more perfect and more beautiful than in any other book."

Although he was unable to continue his studies, Vincent did not abandon his plan. If he could not enter the ministry, he could at least become an evangelist. At Laeken, near Brussels, an evangelical training school had just been founded which awarded a diploma of evangelist after a course of only one term. Moreover, that school would help him to that intermediary "position between clergyman and missionary"[36] of which he had already been dreaming in Isleworth. While waiting to enroll he spent a few weeks with his parents at Etten, where he continued to draw furiously. "The other day I made a little drawing after Emile Breton's 'A Sunday Morning,' in pen and ink and pencil."[37] He was at Laeken by the end of August 1878, but his first letter to his brother, not written until 15 November, says nothing about his studies. Its reflections are mingled with undeniably picturesque descriptions and philosophical and religious thoughts: "Some of these old white horses resemble a certain old aquatint which you perhaps know, an engraving of no great artistic value, it is true, but which struck me and made a deep impression on me[...]. It is a sad and very melancholy scene which must affect everyone who knows and feels that one day we too have to pass through the valley of the shadow of death...."[38] Vincent believed in the power of art. To him, a work of art, whether drawing or painting, had as striking an "effect" as a live sermon or a letter.

4 *At the Coalmines* (Au charbonnage). Laeken, November 1879. Crayon and pen, 14 × 14 cm. Letter 126. Rijksmuseum Vincent van Gogh, Amsterdam.

5 *Miner Shouldering a Spade.* Borinage, July – August 1879. Black chalk, crayon, pen, brush, wash and white highlights, 49.5 × 27.5 cm. F 827. Rijksmuseum Kröller-Müller, Otterlo.

Thus more and more often he sent Theo some of his "scribbles," such as *Au Charbonnage* (At the Coalmines),[39] which he admitted he had done "mechanically," as he had previously drawn Elijah "instinctively." He confessed that the wish to draw was a perpetual temptation to him, constantly threatening to distract him from his proper work; and he was always succumbing to it.

Gradually he came to see that drawing, which demands a keen sense of observation, led him to a better understanding of the subject; and above all, it helped others to a better understanding, since a work of art speaks for all of mankind.

Ever since he had seen the poverty of the London suburbs Vincent had yearned to go back to the poor and to preach in that spiritual barrenness. "You know how one of the roots or foundations, not only of the Gospel, but of the whole Bible is 'Light that rises in the darkness,'" he wrote to his brother. "Well, who needs this most, who will be receptive to it? Experience has shown that the people who walk in the darkness, in the center of the earth, like the miners in the black coal mines, for instance, are

6 *Men and Women Going to the Mines.* Borinage, August 1880. Graphite and light aquarelle highlights, 44.5 × 54 cm. F 831. Rijksmuseum Kröller-Müller, Otterlo.

very much impressed by the words of the Gospel, and believe them, too."[40] So he decided to set off for the Borinage, in the south of Belgium near Mons, to live among the miners. At first the governing body of the school refused him the post for which he applied, so he settled in a small village, Pâturages, at

his own expense, cared for the miners, and taught the Scriptures. Finally, in January 1879, after his father's intervention, he was appointed lay preacher at Wasmes for one term at a derisory salary. The life he lived there among the miners, which has been   5, 6 compared with that of St. Francis of Assisi, has always appealed to popular imagination. In particular, Vincent's great charity, which drove him to such extremes as sleeping on the floor because he had given his bed to someone poorer than himself, has been "explained" as a symptom of his "narcissistic" bent—his yearning for the mortification of the flesh. In fact, Vincent was simply eager to follow the true teachings of Christ. For him there was no seperation between the truth of Christ and the truth of the Church, but the religious authorities soon were outraged by his conduct and reproached him with actually wanting to live according to the Word! In July 1879 Vincent was forced to resign. Despite this fresh setback, he decided to continue his ministry at Cuesmes.

Exercises for a Self-Taught Man

Vincent was drawing almost every day now, thanks partly to a present from his former employer Mr. Tersteeg, who had sent him a box of paints and a sketchbook. "Often I draw far into the night, to keep some souvenir and to strengthen the thoughts raised involuntarily by the aspect of things here."[41] What was Vincent drawing? "Local types" to begin with, either portraits or scenes from everyday life, like "the return of the miners," which he admitted was "very difficult, being an effect of brown silhouettes, just touched by light, against a mottled sky at sunset."[42] He also sketched weavers during an excursion to the Courrières (Pas-de-Calais) region, where the painter Jules Breton—who also used the everyday life of the workers as his subject matter—had his studio. Now Vincent stated his aim clearly: "The miners and weavers still constitute a race apart from other laborers and artisans, and I feel a great sympathy for them. I should be very happy if someday I could draw them, so that those unknown or little-known types would be brought before the eyes of the people.."[43] But "to bring them before the eyes of the people," which to Vincent meant transcending their squalid lives through art, his drawing would have to have the necessary artistry: "The thing for me is to learn to draw well, to be master of my pencil or my crayon or my brush; this gained, I shall make good things anywhere...."

Vincent needed to learn his craft. From his professional experience at the Goupil art gallery he had already gained a sound knowledge of old and contemporary masters. What he lacked was technique, but how could he obtain it in the depth of the Borinage, where "they do not even know what a picture is?"[44] Of course he must have dreamt of going to Paris, as his brother vaguely suggested (plagued, no doubt, by feelings of guilt): "It would certainly be my great and ardent wish to go to Paris or to Barbizon, or elsewhere. But how could I, when I do not earn a cent?"[45] Meanwhile, for want of something better to do, he continued his studies after Millet, especially the *Travaux des Champs* (Work in the Fields), which he knew well. "I have already drawn 'The Sower' five times, twice in small size, three times in large, and I will take it up again, I am so entirely absorbed in that figure."[46] For models he used the prints he had sold at Goupil: Charles Bargue's *Exercices au fusain* (Exercises for charcoal), studies from the nude, and the *Cours de dessin*, also by Bargue, reproductions of which (especially of the portraits after Holbein) he had already pinned up in his room in Amsterdam. He also copied etchings after Michel, and even photographs after Jules Breton and Bingham. To assess his progress more accurately, he worked on sheets of paper with the same dimensions as the examples in the *Cours de dessin*: "I hope that after having copied the other two series by Bargue, I shall be able to draw miners, male and female, more or less well, if by chance I can have a model with some character; and as to that, there are plenty of them."[47]

Vincent devoted more and more time to drawing, for it gave him the strength not to succumb to discouragement. He confided to Theo: "Everything has seemed transformed for me[...]I cannot tell you how happy I am to have taken up drawing again."[48] But model prints cannot take the place of a good teacher. Increasingly, Vincent felt the need to be in touch with other artists. At the beginning of October 1880 he decided to go to Brussels. There he met Mr. Schmidt, the manager of the Goupil branch, and the painter Roelofs, who advised him to attend the free courses at the Académie de Dessin. This prospect did not appeal to him, for he feared that he would once more be judged according to criteria that were alien to him. Although he went through the formalities of putting his name down for the courses, he did not mention the fact to anyone, which suggests that he was not very enthusiastic about them. At the same time, however, he studied Anatomy from John's *Sketches of the Anatomy for Artists' Use* in order to master the principles of proportion, and he read passages from *Physiognomy and Phrenology*, the famous work by Lavater and Gall, to learn "how character is expressed in the features and in the shape of the skull."[49]

In Brussels Vincent got to know the painter Anton Van Rappard, with whom he formed a lasting friendship. Whereas Vincent lived in a small room at 72 boulevard du Midi, Rappard was rather luxuriously settled in a large studio in Rue Traversière. Van Rappard took an interest in his compatriot, and "He impressed me as one who takes things seriously," wrote Vincent, who felt more than ever that he needed someone to advise him. On several occasions Van Rappard invited him to work in his studio. And when Van Rappard decided to return to the Netherlands at the end of April, Vincent, daunted by the prospect of being left alone in his small room, followed suit. In Brussels he took up drawing from life: "I have a model almost every day, an old porter, or some working man, or some boy, who poses for

7   *Diggers* (after Millet). Brussels, November 1880. Crayon and charcoal, 37 × 62 cm. F 829. Rijksmuseum Kröller-Müller, Otterlo.

me. Next Sunday perhaps one or two soldiers will sit for me."[50] His immediate aim was to follow in the footsteps of caricaturists such as Gavarni or Daumier, whom he admired greatly: "Now without the least pretending to compare myself with these artists.... I hope to arrive at the point of being able to illustrate papers and books."[51] But the two drawings that accompanied that letter were still rather clumsy, as he himself recognized: "I am sending you two small ones, 'En Route' and 'Devant les Tisons' [In Front of the Wood Fire]. I see perfectly well that they are not good, but they are beginning to look like something."

In the middle of April, Vincent returned to Etten. He hoped he would "somehow have the necessary models to finish them [the drawings] and then I trust the result will be good."[52] During the period from spring to winter 1881, he drew intensively. He longed to make swift progress, but to evaluate it, he had to be able to draw regularly from life, using either landscapes or live models. Then he would be

8 *Miners Returning Home.* Brussels, April 1881. Pen, crayon, and brush, 43 × 60 cm. F 832. Rijksmuseum Kröller-Müller, Otterlo.

9 *The Barn with the Mossy Roof.* Etten, May 1881. Black chalk, crayon, pen, highlighted with white and gray, 45.5 × 61 cm. F 842. Museum Boymans-van Beuningen, Rotterdam.

able to judge whether his copying exercises had been productive. He knew that when he was staying with his parents—as long as he made a few concessions (especially in his mode of dress)—he would not have to worry about his keep and so would be free to draw all day long. Moreover, he would have no difficulty in finding the subjects he wanted in the surrounding countryside, and as models for figure drawing he would have his sisters and the peasants he met during his walks through the fields.

No sooner said than done! "Every day that it does not rain, I go out in the fields, generally to the heath. I make my studies on a rather large scale, like the few you saw at the time of your visit; so I have done, among other things, a cottage on the heath, and also the barn with a thatched roof on the road to Roozendaal, which locally they call the Protestant barn."[53] Few of his drawings of that period have survived. The *Barn with the Mossy Roof* (F 842), in the

9

Boymans Museum, enables us to appreciate the rapid progress Vincent was making; he made even greater strides during the month of June, when his friend Van Rappard came to stay in Etten. "We have taken many long walks together—have been, for instance, several times to the heath, near Seppe, to the so-called Passievaart, a big swamp."[54] On these occasions they would work side by side, Van Rappard painting while Vincent "made a drawing in pen and ink of another spot in the swamp, where all the water lilies grow (near the road to Rozendaal)." Van Rappard taught him the technique of washes with a brush which was better suited than line drawing for creating an "aerial" perspective. Under his influence Vincent borrowed Cassagne's *Traité d'aquarelle*: "…even if I should not make any water colors, I shall probably find many things in it, for instance about sepia and ink. For until now I have drawn exclusively in pencil accented and worked up by the pen, sometimes a reed pen, which has a broader stroke. What I have been doing lately demanded that way of working, because the subjects required much *drawing*—drawing in perspective, too, for instance, a few workshops in the village here, a forge, a carpenter's shop and the workshop of a maker of wooden shoes."[55]

Vincent liked working on Ingres paper, "as it is very well suited to pen drawing, especially for a reed pen."[56] This detail, which at first might seem unimportant, is an indication of his rapid artistic evolution. In fact, in the same letter Vincent asked his brother for white Ingres paper, whereas in a letter barely two months later he asked for Ingres paper "the color of unbleached linen;"[57] the reason being that while white paper is suitable for line drawing, it is ill adapted for a technique of color wash or stump drawing, which are art forms using values.

10   *Road with a Row of Willows and a Roadsweeper.* Etten, October 1881. Charcoal, highlighted with aquarelle, 39.5 × 60.5 cm. F 1678. The Metropolitan Museum of Art, New York (Robert Lehmann Collection, 1975).

During that period (October 1881), Vincent was using pictorial effects more readily than before, as can be seen from a rather elaborate charcoal drawing, accented with white chalk and aquarelle, of 10 *Road with a Row of Willows and a Roadsweeper* (F1678). To the influence of Van Rappard was added that of Mauve, whom Vincent visited in August: "... I can assure you that when I went to Mauve for the first time with my pen drawing and Mauve said, You must try it now with charcoal and crayon and brush and stump, I had a deuced lot of trouble working with that new material. I was patient and it did not seem to help; then at times I became so impatient that I stamped on the charcoal and was utterly discouraged. And yet after a while I sent you a drawing made in crayon and charcoal and with the brush...."[58] Vincent continued his studies of figures. Here, too, his progress can be easily discerned if we 11 compare various drawings he did in 1881. *En Route*[59] (January) is a rather crude charcoal drawing 12 of a figure, in a black manner without relief. *The Sower* (F830) (April-May), copied after an engraving by Millet, is still very stiff in outline and rather stere-13, 14 otyped; the drawings of September (F856 and F862) were done from life, but as Van Rappard remarked, their movements still lack naturalness, and indeed Vincent himself admitted it: "Your remark about the figure of the Sower—that he is not a man who is sowing, but one who is posing as a sower—is very true."[60] Mauve actively encouraged Vincent to work from life. "Also, as result of some things Mauve told me, I have begun to work from a live model again."[61] This enabled him to put Bargue's *Exercices au fusain* into practice: "Studying the *Exercices au Fusain* by Bargue carefully and copying them over and over again have given me a better insight into drawing the figure. I have learned to measure and to observe and to seek for broad lines, so what seemed to be impossible before is becoming gradually possible now, thank God [...]. Diggers, sowers, plowers, male and female, they are what I must draw continally. I have to observe and draw everything that belongs to country life—like many others have

done before, and are doing now. I no longer stand helpless before nature as I used to."[62] This progress is noticeable when we compare, for instance, the *Peasant Seated by the Fire*, executed in September,[63] 16 and another drawing on the same subject done two 15 months later (F 868). The first peasant is shown in profile, his head buried in his hands; the outline is continuous, to the detriment of the modeling. The second peasant sits facing the viewer, and the figure is no longer isolated against a neutral background: on the contrary, Vincent used wash and aquarelle with red and white highlights to describe the surrounding space carefully, so that an integrated atmosphere is created. Here Vincent's new mastery in expressing values is clearly demonstrated. By now he had acquired a harmonious treatment of expression that enabled him, like the masters of the Barbizon school, to treat the figure and the landscape in the same manner : " now that I have begun drawing the figure, I will continue it until I am more advanced; and when I work in the open air, it is to make studies of trees, viewing trees like real figures."[64]

An Irrevocable Decision

Vincent was now ready to move from black and white to color—from drawing to painting. His first attempts were encouraging, but still tentative, as is shown by his urgent appeal to Theo for advice: "He [Mauve] thinks I should start painting now."[65] "Before long I hope to be able to pay another visit to Mauve to discuss with him the question of whether I should start painting or not. But I want to talk it over with some people before starting."[66] Beyond the technical problems that painting posed to him, there was also the question of the basic psychological commitment that a switch to painting represented. Until then he had always confined himself to drawing and had never attempted to paint. Was it only from the fear that he might not be sufficiently skillful? After all, he had not yet fully mastered

26

drawing. I believe that the real reason lay deeper: Vincent felt that if he committed himself totally to this road, he risked being relegated to the fringe of society and jeopardizing his chances of marrying a girl from among his own circle.

He had fallen in love with his cousin Kee Vos, the young widowed daughter of the Reverend Stricker who was spending her holidays at Etten with her four-year-old son. Unfortunately, Vincent took her kindness and interest in him as a sign of affection, and this emboldened him to open his heart to her. He was met with the most unyielding rejection. "No, never, never..." was the reply he reported to Theo on November 3.[67] Vincent seemed unable to accept the refusal and even tried to see Kee in Amsterdam a month later, but without success. I say "seemed" because there are some clues in the correspondence which show that deep down, in spite of his ardent passion, he felt an ambivalent sense of relief at Kee's rejection. "When it happened this summer, though I was not unprepared for it, it was at first as terrible a blow as a death sentence."[68] The admission that he was not unprepared for it is strange: Vincent was expecting to be rejected! The fierce insistence with which he repeated that "No, never, never" and the complacency with which he explained it clearly show that he wanted to perpetuate his love ("never" means "always") and thus to idealize it. That impression is confirmed by the manner in which he described his unsuccessful attempt to see Kee again. His account is clear, and pertinent, his tone matter-of-fact: "I ... remained very calm," he wrote.[69] Here was no poetic outpouring to express his despair, as there had been on the occasion of his earlier unhappy love affair. Oddly enough, Vincent did not breathe a word about the famous episode of burning his hand that has been so eagerly taken up by commentators; he did not tell Theo about it until several months later. "I put my hand in the flame of the lamp and said, 'Let me see her for as long as I can keep my hand in the flame'—no wonder that Tersteeg perhaps noticed my hand afterwards. But I think they blew out the lamp and said, '*You will not*

11 *En route*. Brussels, January 1881. Black chalk, 9.5 × 5.4 cm. Letter 140. Rijksmuseum Vincent van Gogh, Amsterdam.

see her'.... Then, not at once, but very soon, I felt that love die within me; a void, an infinite void, came in its stead."[70]

That "infinite void," as we can see from the letters, was quickly filled. Although Vincent would not admit it, Kee was the ideal woman of whom he had

◁ 12 *Sower* (after Millet). Etten, April 1881. Pen and wash with aquarelle highlights, 48 × 36.5 cm. F 830. Rijksmuseum Vincent van Gogh, Amsterdam.

13 *Sower*. Etten, September 1881. Crayon, charcoal and black chalk, 56 × 34 cm. F 856. Rijksmuseum Kröller-Müller, Otterlo.

14 *Sower*. Etten, September 1881. Crayon and black chalk, highlighted with white, 61 × 45 cm. F 862. Rijksmuseum Kröller-Müller, Otterlo.

been dreaming since his adolescence,[d] and he was always sublimating his wish to have her: "Just listen, dear Uncle: if Kee were an angel, she would be too high for me..."[71] For Vincent the best way to sublimate his desires was to paint. In the same letter in which he told Theo about his visit to Kee's home, Vincent said that he went on to see his cousin, the painter Anton Mauve, who gave him his first true painting lesson. "'This is the way to keep your palette.' And since then I've made a few painted studies, and then later, two watercolors." Vincent had

15 *Peasant Seated by the Fire.* Etten, November 1881. Charcoal and wash with white and red highlights, 56 × 45 cm. F 868. Rijksmuseum Kröller-Müller, Otterlo.

16 *Peasant Seated by the Fire.* ("Worn Out"). Etten, September 1881. Pen and wash. Drawing in Letter 150. Rijksmuseum Vincent van Gogh, Amsterdam.

actually made his decision before his final attempt: "Well, at present I begin to feel that I have a draftsman's fist' and I am very glad to possess such an instrument, though it may still be unwieldy."[72]

Kee, the ideal woman, was immediately replaced by the "practical" woman, the painter's model, who reminded him "of some curious figure by Chardin or Frère, or perhaps Jan Steen."[73] This woman, called Christine or Sien, "was perhaps as old as Kee, and she had a child—yes, she had had some experience of life, and her youth was gone; gone?—'il n'y a point de vieille femme' [there *is* no old woman]." Vincent remained true to the feeling he had experienced earlier, after his first unhappy love: "Uncle Cor then asked me if I should feel no attraction for a beautiful woman or girl. I answered that I would feel more attraction for, and would rather come into contact with, one who was ugly or old or poor or in some way unhappy, but who, through experience and sorrow, had gained a mind and a soul."[74]

With the arrival of a box of oil paints that Mauve had sent him in the middle of December, Vincent forgot, for a time, his recent disappointments: "I shall begin to paint, and I am glad things have gone so far."[75] He was all the more anxious to work since the atmosphere at home had been deteriorating gradually since the start of fall, to the point where his father threatened to throw him out if he continued to write to Kee. Vincent soon returned to The Hague to stay with Mauve, who was willing to have him. "On Christmas Day I had a violent scene with Father, and it went so far that Father told me I had better leave the house. Well, he said it so decidedly that I actually left the same day."[76] This quarrel, provoked by Vincent's refusal to go to church, shows how far he had come from his earlier ambition to follow in his father's footsteps. It completed the breach and forced him to choose one way or the other. But the thought of a new life devoted wholly to painting sustained him in spite of the extra expense this would involve: "though the path may be difficult, I now see it clearly before me."[77]

31

Chapter II   Realist Painting

A Fresh Start

Vincent left for The Hague to look for help. Inexorably the values in which he hitherto had believed failed him one by one. Considered a "drop-out" by his family, and deeply disappointed in his professional, emotional, and spiritual experiences, he felt that he had made a series of false starts. He was obsessed by an intense sense of guilt, which was carefully nurtured by his family and exacerbated by his inability to earn a living. Drawing, which had become his sole refuge against his anxiety, now seemed the only means of breaking the deadlock. His first attempts were promising, and he was now receiving financial help from his brother Theo: "I hear from Father that without my knowing it you have been sending me money for a long time, in this way effectively helping me to get on."[1] Moreover, Vincent could console himself with the thought that he was following a family tradition; so much so that he practically regarded Theo's help as his due: "But when I think it over, I cannot help wondering, isn't it right that in a family like ours—in which two Messrs. Van Gogh are very rich, and both in the art field, Uncle Cor and our uncle of Prinsenhage, and in which you and I of the younger generation have chosen the same line, though in different spheres—isn't it right, I wonder, that, this being so, I should be able to count in some way on 100 fr. a month during the time which must necessarily elapse before I can get regular work as a draftsman?"[2] As balm to his conscience Vincent persuaded himself that his situation was only temporary. In fact, it endured until his death barely ten years later. An infernal countdown had begun.

Vincent felt so sure of himself that he did not hesitate to leave his parents suddenly at the end of December—even at the risk of falling out with Theo, who reproached him bitterly for "contriving to leave Father and Mother" but did not threaten to withdraw the monthly subsidy. Vincent did not leave on a sudden impulse; he had thought his plan over carefully before coming to a decision. Hadn't he already confided to Theo a year earlier: "On the whole I can say I have made progress, but I ought to be able to get along more quickly. The principal motive for writing you now is to ask you if you know of any reason why I should not go to see Mr. Tersteeg and Mauve."[3]

From then on it was no longer the path of the ministry that he felt could lead him to salvation, but rather the practice of painting. His obsession with the father image faded away: "Father cannot understand or sympathize with me, and I cannot be reconciled to Father's system—it oppresses me, it would choke me."[4] It was replaced by the image of the painter, embodied by Mauve; a substitution, but still in the family, as Mauve was in fact Vincent's cousin on his mother's side.

At The Hague, Vincent hoped to find an environment that would favor the realization of his new plan: "For, Theo, with painting my real career begins. Don't you think I am right to consider it so?"[5] Besides the friendly advice of Mauve, he could also rely on the goodwill of Tersteeg, his former boss at Goupil's, who was now Theo's colleague. But he was not eager to get involved with his fellow artists. "I do not wish to associate much with other painters."[6]

On 1 January 1882, Vincent rented a "studio ..., that is, a room and an alcove which can be arranged for the purpose, cheap enough, on the outskirts of the town, in Schenkweg, ten minutes from Mauve."[7] Mauve helped him to settle in and lent him a hundred florins. Thus established, Vincent regained his cheerfulness. Proud of his studio, he was impatient for Theo to come and see the fruits of his own generosity: "Still, I enjoy [life], and especially my having a studio of my own is inexpressibly delightful. When will you come to have lunch with me, or tea? Soon, I hope. You can even stay overnight; that will be fine, and you will be quite comfortable."[8] In the same letter he told Theo that he had just acquired from the bookseller Blok "some beautiful wood engravings [...] the best from an enormous pile of *Graphics* and *London News* [....] among them [...] 'The Houseless and Homeless' by Fildès, (poor people waiting in front of a free overnight shelter); and two large Herkomers, and many small ones; and 'The Irish Emigrants' by Frank Hol; and 'The Old Gate' by Walker; and especially 'A Girls' School' by Frank Hol; and another large Herkomer, 'The Invalids.'"

These prints illustrate Vincent's intention "to make something myself that is realistic and yet done with sentiment," an aim he explained more fully later, quoting Dickens. "Dickens tells us a few good things about the painters of *his* time and their wrong working methods, namely, their following the model servilely, yet only halfway. He says: 'Fellows, try to understand that your model is *not* your final aim, but *the means of giving form and strength to your thought and inspiration*.' .... In my opinion two things which remain eternally true and which complement each other are, Do not quench your inspiration and your imagination, do not become a slave

of your model; and, Take the model and study it, otherwise your inspiration will never get plastic solidity."[9]

The whole history of realism in painting is contained in this apparent contradiction, which Vincent grasped with amazing lucidity for a "beginner." His choice of subject matter, too, is revealing: "I see drawings and pictures in the poorest huts, in the dirtiest corner. And my mind is drawn toward these things by an irresistible force."[10] For Vincent the only possible subjects were those of everyday life, such as "scenes in the street, the third-class waiting room, on the beach, in a hospital...."[11] He admitted no hierarchical distinction between these scenes, no kind of preference, and if at the beginning of his career the human figure attracted him more than landscape, to the point where "a row of pollard willows sometimes resembles a procession of almshouse men,"[12,a] that was simply because it embodied that aspect of the human predicament he called "resignation."

Marked from his youth by the material and spiritual poverty around him, Vincent had gradually discovered in his work as an evangelist that the mere mention of these subjects remained totally taboo among the very people whose duty it was to fight against them. Thus he felt a special admiration for the artists who dared to choose resignation as the theme of their work, even when they presented it under a more or less allegorical guise, as did Millet.

Speaking about a canvas by Mauve "of a fishing smack drawn up to the dunes," Vincent wrote to Theo: "I never heard a good sermon on resignation, nor can I imagine a good one, except that picture by Mauve and the work of Millet. That is *the* resignation—the real kind, not that of the clergymen. Those nags, those poor, ill-treated old nags, black, white and brown; they are standing there, patient, submissive, willing, resigned and quiet.... I find such a mighty, deep, practical, silent philosophy in this picture—it seems to say, 'Savoir souffrir sans se plaindre, ça c'est la seule chose pratique, c'est la grande science, la leçon à apprendre, la solution du problème de la vie' [knowing how to suffer without complaining, that is the only practical thing, it is the great science, the lesson to learn, the solution to the problem of life]."[13]

Vincent no longer looked for quotations in the Bible, but rather in Sensier's *Millet*: "L'art, c'est un combat—dans l'art il faut y mettre sa peau [Art is a fight—one must put one's hide (i.e., one's utmost) into art]."[14] He would remember this admonition until the end of his life, as is shown in his last letter, found on his body on 29 July 1890: "Well, my own work, I am risking my life for it and my reason has half foundered because of it...."[15] His interest in caricature and in the illustrations of the *Graphic*, quite apart from their possible usefulness as artistic models, showed his intention: to break the isolation of those who were trapped in poverty, as he himself might have been during his stay in the Borinage, the "black country" of the miners. He had a profound faith in the efficacy of art, its power of communication as long as its subject matter did not disguise or obscure its purpose. "It is the painter's duty to be entirely absorbed by nature and to use all his intelligence to express sentiment in his work so that it becomes intelligible to other people."[16] Faithful to this view, he hit on "the idea of making figures *from the people for the people* [...] not commercially but as a matter of public service and duty."[17] That utopian undertaking, which had no money-making purpose, never saw the light of day; but the project led him to make numerous attempts at lithography.

A Tragicomedy

Vincent devoted himself mainly to figure drawing, not only for its "moral" effect but also because its "technical" intricacies enabled him to tackle flaws in proportion better than the study of landscapes would have. "I am so glad I have worked on the figure up to now," he wrote on 13 February 1882. "If I had done only landscapes, yes, then I would probably do something that would sell at a small price

now, but then later I would be stranded. The figure takes more time and is more complicated, but I think in the long run it is more worth while."[18]

During his stay at The Hague he did numerous studies from life. He had great difficulties in finding and paying models. Nevertheless, he was able to progress from life studies as such to portraits proper; the first examples appeared during the Nuenen period and many more followed. His progress was greatly facilitated by his meeting with a young woman of thirty-two, Clasina Maria Hoornik, nicknamed Sien, who came regularly to pose for him, sometimes accompanied by her mother and younger sister. The first mention Vincent made of the woman who was to share his life for two years was in a letter dated Friday, 3 March: "The younger woman is not handsome, as she is marked by smallpox, but the figure is very graceful and has some charm for me."[19] Sien took on the features of The *Great Lady*[20] and also embodied that "resignation" that Vincent called *Sorrow* (F 1655)—a feeling that remained with him to the end of his short life. On his deathbed, he replied to Theo, who was trying to reassure him, "It's no use, there'll never be an end to sorrow." His experiences in England had first opened his eyes to this, which undoubtedly was why he gave these two drawings English titles.

Sien, a former prostitute—that "cesspit," as Gustave Coquiot meanly called her in 1923—was frail despite her apparently solid build. For Vincent she held the attraction of having been a streetwalker; she was the model *par excellence*. This time he did not have to go down into the depths of the mines or tramp through the slums. All he had to do was to undertake the "in-house" rescue of Sien. As he had not been able to win Kee's love, he needed another woman, a woman who provided affection, a woman he could desire, in whom he could sense "the body with its long undulating lines under the folds of a ... dress." But the attraction she held for him went further than the promise of mere physical satisfaction: "What I mean is, one feels best what love is when sitting by a sickbed, sometimes without any money in one's pocket."[21] If he asked Sien to marry him, knowing that this would make him a social outcast, it was because for him the word *love* kept all its meaning of "charity"—*agape*—as he plainly told Theo: "...I am not ashamed to say (though I know quite well that the word *benevolence* is in bad repute) that for my part I have always felt and will feel the need to love some fellow creature. Preferably, I don't know why, an unhappy, forsaken or lonely creature. Once I nursed for six weeks or two months a poor miserable miner who had been burned. I shared my food for a whole winter with a poor old man, and heaven knows what else, and now there is Sien."[22]

A passionate admirer of Zola (whom he called Balzac the Second), Vincent acribed to Sien the role of Florent in *Le Ventre de Paris*, while he cast himself as the helpful Madame François. But behind that "human comedy" Vincent's own tragedy showed through, a tragedy in which Sien was transformed into Lady Macbeth (*The Great Lady*): "...the form of her head, the line of her profile, is exactly like that figure by Landelle, 'L'Ange de la Passion,' so it is far from ordinary; it is decidedly noble, but it does not always strike the eye at once."[23] Like Shakespeare's original tale, Vincent's tragedy ended even in double suicide, since Sien threw herself into a canal in 1904.

Theo, alarmed at the turn things were taking, put a stop to Vincent's matrimonial plans. No doubt he was motivated not so much by the fear of what people would say—tongues had been wagging for a long time—as by the fear that he might lose the special bond he felt with his brother if the situation were allowed to continue. Very cleverly, Theo did not make any overt attack on Vincent himself: He merely did nothing (he may even have intervened behind the scenes in a negative way) to facilitate Vincent's relationship with Tersteeg, who suddenly considered him a good-for-nothing. Mauve, too, changed: "Mauve's attitude toward me changed suddenly—became as unfriendly as it had been friendly before.[...] I asked him, Mauve, have you seen Tersteeg lately? 'No,' said Mauve, and we

17 *The Great Lady.* The Hague, April 1882. Graphite and pen, 19 × 10.5 cm. Letter 185. Rijksmuseum Vincent van Gogh, Amsterdam.

18 *Sorrow.* The Hague, November 1882. Lithograph after a ▷ drawing executed in April. F 1655. Rijksmuseum Vincent van Gogh, Amsterdam.

Sorrow

talked on, but about ten minutes later he remarked that Tersteeg had been to see him that same day."[24] Everything suggests a conspiracy in which Mauve was involved as well as Tersteeg, who threatened: "Mauve and I will see to it that you don't receive any more money from Theo."[25] Then there was Uncle Cornelius (C.M.), who "seems to have spoken with Tersteeg before he came to see me, at least he began by saying the same things about 'earning my bread,'"[26] as well as Uncle Cent, "Our venerable Uncle Cent also has a way of gathering 'information' which I consider anything but fair."[27] Sien's mother may have been involved too, for she advised Sien to leave Vincent. Finally Theo, the moving spirit behind it all (although carefully entrenched behind the authority of Pa and the family), tried to frighten Vincent with the threat that "only a few witnesses (and even false ones) would have to declare that you are unable to manage your own financial affairs; this would be sufficient to entitle Father to take away your civil rights and put you under guardianship."[28]

On this occasion Theo came out in his true colors for the first time, as a rather Machiavellian "false brother." He agreed at first to Vincent's request for an increase in his subsidy: "If it is possible for me to receive 150 fr. a month this year (though my work is not salable at present, but it is the foundation on which I can build), then I shall undertake the thing with much animation and good courage, because then at least I know: I shall not lack what's strictly necessary for work." But Theo did not do so without a hint of doubt, for Vincent added: "If I know for certain that you are withdrawing your help, then I am powerless; my hand is paralyzed in spite of all my good will—yes, then it is all misery, then it is terrible." These were precisely the words Theo wanted to hear, for they showed the strength of his hold on Vincent. And Vincent, playing out his tragic role to the end, even showed himself a willing victim to his executioner brother: "*If this terrible lot must befall me—so be it.* Adieu, brother, sleep on it again before you strike the blow and cut off my head (and

Christine's and the child's too.)."[29] Living as a dependent, in daily fear of the morrow and on the defensive, Vincent tried to ensure his livelihood by bringing pressure to bear on Theo. By linking his fate with Sien's—to the point of wanting to marry her—he was trying, more or less consciously, to blackmail Theo: "Know it well, the life of the woman, of the children, of me, depends on that little thread of 150 fr. a month until my work begins to sell. If that little thread breaks before that time, then 'morituri te salutant.'"[30] Vincent was dreaming of a *ménage à trois*—himself, Sien, and Theo—a new trinity in which he now took the place of his fallen Pa, and Sien took his own former role. He expressed this wish in a barely veiled manner: "But we are happy this way because love binds us so closely."[31]

Theo did not see things in that light. He felt it was his duty to help Vincent, although he was not at all convinced that his brother would ever become a "recognized" artist (but you never knew!), but it was certainly not for the sake of seeing the firstborn of the Van Goghs tarnish the family's reputation by marrying a prostitute. Moreover, he was anxious to preserve his "exclusive rights" to Vincent, not only to Vincent's work (which Theo did very little to promote), but to his actual life. Vincent's failure in the social sense and his acknowledged lack of responsibility meant that Theo was the true head of the family now that Pa, grown old, suddenly seemed diminished in the eyes of his wife and children. Willy-nilly, Vincent had to cede his place to Theo, who had succeeded where Vincent had so unaccountably failed (and after such a good start...) as an art dealer; to Theo, who, on Tersteeg's orders, had taken Vincent's own place with Goupil and who had to bow, however reluctantly, to the summary judgment Tersteeg pronounced on his brother: "A nonentity, or an eccentric and disagreeable man—somebody who has no position in society and never will have, in short, the lowest of the low."[32] So Theo was hardly the man to stand up for Vincent's work. Yet he admired his brother's tenacity and courage, and he realized that Vincent's determination proved that his vocation was genuine even if it did not yield immediate results.

Theo's reaction to Vincent's affair with Sien gives us an insight into his real feelings for his brother, which at first seem contradictory. He felt "betrayed" because Vincent had called Sien a helpmate (as his model), whereas he felt that he alone deserved that title, not only for his material help, but chiefly because Vincent had, on several occasions, seen in him a potential painter. "Say, Theo, won't you think about the idea that there is a famous landscape painter hidden inside you? We both must become painters, we will earn our crust anyhow."[33] Here lies the true "knot" of the Vincent-Theo relationship. If Theo "kept" Vincent it was because he believed firmly that "it is even better to be a painter"[34] than an art dealer; and as he lacked his brother's courage to leave the art business (and remained deaf to his repeated appeals to do so), he was able by such means to become a painter by proxy.

To Theo, Vincent was still the older brother to whom he had looked up as a child, as his sister Elisabeth testified: "None of the children would ever have thought of laughing at him: no, he was held in the deepest respect; [...] But they sensed instinctively, with the fine perception of their age, that their brother preferred to be alone when he was home for the holidays from boarding school, where his father had sent him."[b] Theo was also greatly affected by the series of failures that had gradually brought Vincent to destitution. He felt that he was being dragged along with him. His role as "protector" suited him only insofar as he hoped it would sooner or later bring back the mysterious Vincent of his youth. As a painter Vincent gained a new magic that captivated Theo, so much so that it was now Theo's turn to ask Vincent's advice about a woman whose story was strangely like Sien's. Vincent now took on Theo's former role. "Then you said to me, 'Do not marry her,' and I admitted then that circumstances were such that it was better not to talk about it for the time being. And you know that since then I have not mentioned it again, but she and I have re-

mained true to each other. And just because I cannot think you were wrong in saying then, 'Do not marry her,' I give you your own words to consider; and besides, you will think of it yourself, for it is not I who say so, but you yourself."[35]

Theo realized that Vincent had the painter's gift of "double" vision, for his pictures showed another vision of reality. Thus when the two brothers had a similar experience, Vincent analyzed it effectively in his drawing, entitled simply *Sorrow*, of a faceless woman, whose suffering could only be expressed through art. "Generally speaking (apart from the difference of the two persons in question), to you and to me there appeared on the cold, cruel pavement a sad, pitiful woman's figure, and neither you nor I passed it by—we both stopped and followed the human impulse of our hearts. Such an encounter has the quality of an apparition about it, at least when one recalls it; one sees a pale face, a sorrowful look like an Ecce Homo on a dark background—all the rest disappears. That is the sentiment of an Ecce Homo, and there is the same expression in reality, but in this case it is on a woman's face. Later it certainly becomes different—but one never forgets that first expression.... Underneath the figure of an English woman (by Patterson) is written the name Dolorosa; that expresses it well. I was thinking of the two women now, and at the same time I thought of a drawing by Pinwell, 'The Sisters,' in which I find that Dolorosa expression.... Perhaps I express myself too vaguely, but I cannot say it differently."[36] He could not say it, but he could paint it.

Lessons from Mauve

"Yesterday I had a lesson from Mauve on drawing hands and faces so as to keep the color transparent. Mauve knows things so thoroughly, and when he tells you something, he exerts himself and doesn't just say it to hear himself talk; and I exert myself to listen carefully and to put it into practice.[...] When you were in Etten last summer, you spoke about my working in water colors. At that point I didn't even know how to start it. Now the light is beginning to dawn, and in spite of everything, the sun is rising."[37] Vincent never forgot what he owed Mauve, although the "lessons" lasted only two weeks. But Mauve was the only well known painter who openly encouraged him, even saying, "You need money, I will help you earn money, you may be sure that now your hard years are over and the sun is rising for you."[38]

In his first watercolors, Vincent tried to convey the effect of the paints directly with the brush in the traditional Dutch way. His habit of drawing in ink, charcoal, and chalk led him primarily to seek contrasts of light, as in the *Woman of Scheveningen* (F 871), for example. Mauve tried to soften what he called Vincent's "yellow soap mood", in which he showed "a head or a little hand which has light and life in it, and which stands out against the drowsy dusk of the background, and then boldly against it all that part of the chimney and stove—iron and stone—and a wooden floor."[39] He also encouraged him to do more landscapes because he knew that these usually sold rather well. In the company of the painter Breitner, Vincent did numerous sketches in the streets of The Hague—scenes of everyday life, passersby, and *Workmen at Their Task*[40] in order to use them later for compositions in the studio.

This type of drawing makes up a large portion of his work; but Vincent's drawing progress was sporadic, the most prolific outbursts occurring at both the beginning and end of his creative life, during a period between the Borinage (1880–1881) and Nuenen (1885), and during his stay at St.-Rémy (1890). Remarkably enough, Vincent tried to show most of the figures "in motion," which added to his difficulties. He wrote: "These fellows are all in action, and this fact especially must be kept in mind in the choice of subjects, I think. You know yourself how beautiful the numerous figures in repose, which are done so very, very often, are. They are done more often than figures in action. It is always very tempting to draw a figure at rest; it is very diffi-

cult to express action, and in many people's eyes the former effect is more 'pleasant' than anything else. But this 'pleasant' aspect must not detract from the truth, and the truth is that there is more drudgery than rest in life. So you see my main idea about it all is this—that for my part I try to work for the truth. It seems to me that the drawings themselves are even more urgent than their reproduction."[41]

Let us make no mistake: Even if he hoped—vainly, as it turned out—to find work with such magazines as *La Vie Moderne*, even if he greatly admired Gavarni and Daumier, Vincent was interested in caricature only insofar as it was an instrument of truth, not as a vehicle of social criticism. He was closer to the painter of *La Blanchisseuse* (The Washerwoman) (Louvre, Paris) than to the *Charivari* journalist. If he followed in Daumier's footsteps, it was as a painter of contemporary life fascinated by the eloquence with which a gesture could convey activity, whether his model was a workman, a peasant, or a weaver. His scenes with many characters, juxtaposed on superimposed parallel planes, constitute a kind of "comic strip." Each character is himself the synthesis of a large number of preparatory studies; as Vincent said: "For instance, for the drawing of three seamstresses one must draw at least ninety seamstresses."[42]

In his early works, Vincent drew gasometers, factories, and looms. Nevertheless, his "modernity" was not based on an interest in "modern" subjects but in conveying the feeling inherent in the most banal of scenes, such as the *National Lottery* (F 970). "For the most part they were old women and the kind of people of whom one cannot say what they are doing or how they live, but who evidently have a great deal of drudgery and trouble and care."[43] And this was quite incomprehensible to men like Tersteeg (and perhaps to Theo as well). What attraction could there be in this collection of faceless figures, with no narrative or picturesque meaning? Wasn't it almost indecent to want to express blind suffering in this manner? Well, the ugliness might pass. It might contribute to the "realism." But who

19 *Woman of Scheveningen*. Etten, December 1881. Aquarelle, 23.5 × 9.5 cm. F 871. Rijksmuseum Vincent van Gogh, Amsterdam.

would be crazy enough to buy a drawing that would literally give them the creeps?

Such compositions create a deep sense of unease—in fact the kind of malaise that was demolishing Vincent himself. It expressed itself in the amorphous figures of those anonymous characters, reproduced in series, flattened between the earth and the sky. Crushed by their heavy burdens, the women in *Women Repairing Nets in the Dunes* (F 7) or in *Miners' Wives* (F 994) are images of the same human misery. At St.-Rémy, the figures in *Peasants at Table* (F l588) are all so alike that their identities, even the difference between the sexes, are completely obliterated. Their bodies are interchangeable, their blank faces resigned, blotted out, their limbs deformed by the extreme abstraction of the sinuous lines and reduced to a "basic sign," as Matisse said later,[c] to a cipher of anguish; they all derive from *Sorrow*, the matrix of the human misery that spreads like a plague through the world and from which Vincent himself, despite Theo's help, could not be saved.

The lack of understanding that Vincent's work encountered, following Mauve's sudden change in attitude, is not really difficult to explain. Mauve was narrowly attached to academic teaching—for instance, he drew from plaster models, a practice Vincent absolutely detested— and he naturally was irritated by his pupil's behavior, although Vincent clearly was talented and hard-working. Mauve was dumbfounded when, after Vincent had done dozens of promising studies such as the *Old Almshouse Man*, he saw the formless compositions to which they led. In fact, these compositions seemed less finished than their preparatory studies, almost as if Vincent did not give a fig for all the trouble Mauve had taken—and free of charge at that—to teach him the "tricks of the trade." So it is hardly surprising that Mauve was annoyed. It was precisely the aforementioned plaster models that triggered the rupture between Vincent and Mauve. Vincent kept Theo informed: "I had to draw from casts, that was the principal thing, he said. I hate drawing from casts,

20 *Workmen at Their Task.* The Hague, April 1882. Graphite. Drawing in Letter 190. Rijksmuseum Vincent van Gogh, Amsterdam.

but I had a few plaster hands and feet hanging in my studio, though not for drawing purposes. Once he spoke to me about drawing from casts in a way such as the worst teacher at the academy would not have spoken; I kept quiet, but when I got home I was so angry that I threw those poor plaster casts into the coalbin, and they were smashed to pieces.... Then I said to Mauve, Man, don't mention plaster to me again, because I can't stand it. That was followed by a note from Mauve, telling me that he would not have anything to do with me for two months."[44] The breach was final in spite of Vincent's attempts at a reconciliation, which were thwarted by Mauve's violent hostility. Tersteeg's baneful influence cannot be held entirely accountable for this episode, although it hastened the final breach. The two estranged men met suddenly by chance, walking on the dunes, and Mauve rejected Vincent's final appeal. "You have a vicious character," he told him. "Mauve takes offense at my having said, 'I am an artist,'" Vincent wrote; but that was not due to pride: "As far as I know, that word means, 'I am seeking, I am striving, I am in it with all my heart.'"[45] Then he wondered if his affair with Sien might not be at the root of the trouble. "Vicious"—the word was aimed at the work rather than the man. Mauve reproached Vincent for defying his advice, for "perverting" it by applying it to a totally different kind of painting, which undermined the principle of imitating nature in order to achieve personal expression. At this point the parallel between the disagreement between Vincent and Mauve and that between Vincent and Gauguin at Arles six years later is especially significant. We shall return to that later. Here we shall simply point out that, though the outward reasons for the disputes may have been appreciably different, at heart they were of a kind: the main disagreement in both cases was over a specific concept of painting.

Vincent's Point of View

"I shall go my own way without paying much attention to the present school,"[46] Vincent told his friend Van Rappard, and if he sometimes remembered, not without emotion, the lessons Mauve had given him —he even dedicated one of his *Peach Trees in Blossom* (F 394) to him in March 1888 at Arles—it was because of such counsels as "Don't talk to me about Dupré; but talk about the bank of that ditch, or something like it."[47] "Realist" advice, no doubt. But where did it lead Vincent? To understand fully the originality of the options Vincent pursued, we must first compare them to those of the Impressionists, and of the Nabis in particular, for these were the two new trends in painting at that time, and at that propitious moment when the emergence of Vincent's own style was making his stylistic exercises pointless.

"It may take a longer or a shorter time, but the surest way is to penetrate deep into nature."[48] This basic principle animated Vincent's work from the beginning to the end. It seems banal enough. Until the Paris period (1886–1887), Vincent followed "naturalist" rules of painting. In droves, landscapists were now planting their easels "on site," especially in Holland where the tradition of landscape painting went back to the seventeenth century. During that period Vincent actually did landscapes in the manner of the school of The Hague to which Mauve subscribed. The *Bleaching-Ground at Scheveningen*[49] 25 is a perfect illustration of this style: The line of the horizon is above the median so as to achieve a perspective to infinity at a point displaced by a third to the left. But that kind of landscape is rare among Vincent's works, and he greatly preferred scenes such as *The Garden of the Carpenter and the Laundry* 26 (F 939) or the *Fish Drying Barn* (F 938), which en- 28 abled him to express a more human feeling. Vincent realized his own natural preferences: "Theo, I am definitely not a landscape painter; when I make landscapes, *there will always be something of the figure in them.*"[50] In his early work, figures—more or less blended into the landscape—are ever present, like actors in a perpetual silent drama. Vincent painted nature, admittedly, but chiefly *human* nature, doomed to suffering and privation: "I want to do drawings which *touch* some people. 'Sorrow' is a small beginning, perhaps such little landscapes as 'Laan van Meerdervoort,' 'Rijswijk Meadows,' and

21 *The National Lottery.* The Hague, September 1882.
Aquarelle, 38 × 57 cm. F 970. Rijksmuseum Vincent van
Gogh, Amsterdam.

22 *Miners' Wives.* The Hague, November 1882. Aquarelle highlighted with white, 32 × 50 cm. F 994. Rijksmuseum Kröller-Müller, Otterlo.

'Fish Drying Barn' are also a small beginning. In those there is at least something straight from my own heart. In either figure or landscape I should wish to express, not sentimental melancholy, but serious sorrow."[51] It was these drawings, which he saw when he visited his nephew's studio, that made Uncle Cornelius Marinus commission from Vincent a dozen crayon-and-pen views of The Hague, at two and a half florins apiece, with the prospect of another commission of a dozen drawings, this time of views of Amsterdam.

Vincent's "inhabited" landscapes, which were rare before the Paris period, constituted the main theme of his later work. The figures in his early works, however, outwardly so unobtrusive, only *seemed* to fade into the landscape. It was as if by

23 *Peasants at Table.* St.-Rémy, March–April 1890. Black chalk, 34 × 50 cm. F. 1588. Rijksmuseum Vincent van Gogh, Amsterdam.

some mysterious mechanism what the actual representation lost in "humanity" served to nurture the painting itself, a phenomenon demonstrated by the new liveliness in the treatment of form and the sturdiness of the color harmonies, tangible signs—no longer mere foreshadowings—of Vincent's emerging individual style.

The development of his own style at the expense of traditional notions of illusionism had its origin in Vincent's stay at The Hague. From there he wrote: "It is the painter's duty to be entirely absorbed by nature and to use all his intelligence to express sen-

24 *Old Almshouse Man*. The Hague, September 1882. Crayon, 50 × 30.5 cm. F 962. Rijksmuseum Vincent van Gogh, Amsterdam.

25 *The Bleaching-Ground at Scheveningen.* The Hague, July 1882. Pen and wash. Drawing in Letter 220. Rijksmuseum Vincent van Gogh, Amsterdam.

26 *The Garden of the Carpenter and the Laundry.* The Hague, May 1882. Crayon, pen and brush with white highlights, 28.5 × 47 cm. F 939. Rijksmuseum Kröller-Müller, Otterlo.

27 *On the Beach.* The Hague, August 1882. Oil on canvas,
pasted on cardboard, 34.5 × 51 cm. F 4. Stedelijk Museum,
Amsterdam.

timent in his work so that it becomes intelligible to other people."[52] Although in the early 1880s he had not yet discovered Impressionism, his own experiments were taking him along a path parallel to those that Gauguin and Cézanne followed during the same period. We shall come back to the special relationship between Gauguin and Van Gogh later on. The parallels between Vincent's work and that of Cézanne are compellingly obvious. Vincent did not yet know either of these men and yet, like them, he was trying to link figures to landscape, and the solutions he applied were similar to theirs.

Painters have always been faced with the problem of integrating the human figure in landscapes, and this cannot be done easily in a "realist" manner. The precarious balance of emphasis in a picture either tips in favor of the figures and thus reduces the landscape to a backdrop, or else shifts in favor of the landscape and renders the figures insignificant, as with several of Poussin's landscapes after 1650. Vincent chose the latter option when he painted the numerous small figures in *On the Beach* (F 4): They are stiff and anonymous, like plaster saints. His *Girl in a Forest* (F 8), on the other hand, executed at the same time as Cézanne's *Baigneurs* and *Baigneuse* (Men Bathing and Woman Bathing [1882]), approaches the problem in a manner similar to Cézanne's. In such works as *The Spring* (Louvre, Paris) Courbet was already heading in the same direction when he planted a generously proportioned woman bather against a rock, but showed her from the back. This unflattering pose was meant to reduce the "allegorical" impact of the figure and thus make it more "natural." Vincent planted his *Girl in a Forest* like a flower. He let her take root, making her lean against a thick tree trunk, just as Cézanne set his bathers among pine trunks. Both came up against the same difficulties.

Vincent explained them: " I try to work quickly, for that is necessary, but a study that is of any use requires at least half an hour, for instance, so one always has to fall back on real posing."[53] This is echoed by Cézanne in one of his *Conversations with*

Emile Bernard: "As you know, I have often done figures of men and women bathing, which I would have liked to do full size and from life; the lack of models forced me to confine myself to these outlines. I am up against a lot of obstacles, such as finding the site where to set the scene, a place that would not be too different from the one I have chosen mentally, or finding several people at one and the same time who are willing to undress and hold the poses I have fixed. Finally, there is the problem of the dimensions of the canvas I have to transport, a thousand difficulties in having fine weather, etc. ... Thus I have been obliged to put off my project of redoing Poussin entirely from life; and not built up from notes, drawings, and fragments of sketches; a real open-air Poussin, a Poussin of color and light instead of one whose works are thought up in the studio where everything has the brown color of poor light and lacks the hues of the sky and the sun."[d]

Cézanne's idea of "joining the curves of the women with the slopes of the hills" is found also in Van Gogh's view of the landscape proper: "Sometimes I have such a longing to do landscape, just as I crave a long walk to refresh myself; and in all nature, for instance in trees, I see expression and soul, so to speak. A row of pollard willows sometimes resembles a procession of almshouse men. Young corn has something inexpressibly pure and tender about it, which awakens the same emotion as the expression of a sleeping baby, for instance."[54] Vincent's point of view foreshadowed the experiments of the men who were soon to be his friends: A few years later Gauguin, Anquetin, and Emile Bernard loved to paint the natural features of the Pont-Aven region, such as ragged rocks whose shapes more or less suggested those of the human body, while, inversely, the massive bodies in Cézanne's *Grandes Baigneuses* (1898–1905) in the National Gallery in London showed some of the features of rocks.

Vincent's lively interest in the use of outline also anticipated the Cloisonnist experiments. At that

27
29

time the use of outline formed the basis of Vincent's drawing and constituted its clearly enunciated principle: "In order to take notes from nature, or to make little sketches, a strongly developed feeling for outline is absolutely necessary as well as for intensifying the drawing later.... A landscape study by Roelofs is hanging beside me—a pen drawing, but I cannot tell you how expressive its simple outline is; everything is in it.... And you know from 'Sorrow,' for instance, that I take a great deal of trouble to make progress in that respect. But you will see when you come to the studio that apart from seeking the outline, I have, just like everybody else, a feeling for the power of color."[55]

28 *Fish Drying Barn.* The Hague, May 1882. Crayon, pen and brush with white highlights, 28 × 44 cm. F 938. Rijksmuseum Kröller-Müller, Otterlo.

This was the problem Vincent had to resolve if he wanted to start painting in earnest: He had to reconcile the drawing, the outline representing the permanence of forms, and the fleeting "color effects" that impressed him deeply. However, "color effects" did not yet mean actual color. Vincent was at the stage where he was transcribing his black-and-white work into color: "...while painting, I feel a power of color in me that I did not possess before, things of broadness and strength."[56] Precision was important. The color effects were, above all, light effects. Both the chiaroscuro of his paintings and the swiftness with which he executed them grew directly out of his charcoal drawings. "The problem was—and I found it very difficult—to get the depth of color, the enormous force and solidity of that ground.... But as this effect does not last, I had to paint quickly. The figures were put in at once with

29 *Girl in a Forest.* The Hague, August 1882. Oil on canvas,
39 × 59 cm. F 8. Rijksmuseum Kröller-Müller, Otterlo.

30 *Metairies.* Drenthe, September 1883. Oil on canvas pasted on cardboard, 36 × 55.5 cm. F 17. Rijksmuseum Vincent van Gogh, Amsterdam.

a few strong strokes of a firm brush. It struck me how sturdily these little stems were rooted in the ground. I began painting them with a brush, but because the surface was already so heavily covered, a brush stroke was lost in it—then I squeezed the roots and trunks in from the tube, and modeled it a little with the brush."[57]

His Painting Takes Shape

The speed with which Vincent had acquired technical skill almost exclusively from his drawing brought him to a point of reappraisal: "The reason I enjoy painting so much is not its agreeable aspect, but its throwing light on various questions of tone and form and material. I used to be helpless before them, but now by means of painting I can attempt them."[58] He adopted an impasto method closer to that of the Impressionists than to the glazing used by most painters of the school of The Hague. Although he still retained the rather somber palette of the latter, his growing awareness of the possibilities of paint showed him new expressive potential: the means, for example, in painting a nature study, "to make it so that one can breathe and walk around in it, and to make you smell the fragrance of the wood."[59]

In his desire to make what he saw immediately tangible, Vincent asserted that "drawing... is the backbone of painting, the skeleton that supports all the rest."[60] And in a spirit irresistibly reminiscent of Gauguin, he asked: "What did the old masters use for drawing? Certainly not Faber B, BB, BBB, etc., etc., but a piece of rough graphite. Perhaps the instrument which Michelangelo and Dürer used somewhat resembled a carpenter's pencil. But I was not there to see for myself, so I don't know; I only know that with a carpenter's pencil one can get ef-

fects quite different from those with thin Fabers, etc."[61] He was also well versed in all the tricks of the trade that helped accentuate the "unrefined" side of a technique. For instance, he preferred "the graphite in its natural form to that ground so fine in those expensive Fabers. And the shininess disappears by throwing some milk over it."[62] Or he would say: "One can do great things with charcoal soaked in oil, I have seen Weissenbruch do it: the oil fixes the charcoal and at the same time the black becomes warmer and deeper."[63] Vincent wrote in an almost prophetic manner about one of his first studies in oil: "There is some dune sand in it, and I assure you that this will not be the last one."[64]

When we look at the drawings executed during the years 1882 and 1883, at *Girl Seated by a Cradle* (F 1024), for example, we can see how sensitively Vincent was now able to express his emotions. What a long way he had come in barely three years! And with what meticulous skill he worked on the least drawing, like the one just mentioned, using a whole complex of "quasi-pictorial" methods that led him directly to his first steps in painting. A letter sent to Theo on the eve of 1 January 1883 illustrates this: "But it occurred to me to make a drawing first with carpenter's pencil and then to work in and over it with lithographic crayon, which (because of the greasiness of the material) fixes the pencil, a thing ordinary crayon does not do, or, at least, does very badly. After doing a sketch in this way, one can, with a firm hand, use the lithographic crayon where it is necessary, without much hesitation or erasing. So I finished my drawings pretty well in pencil, indeed, as much as possible. Then I fixed them, and dulled them with milk. And then I worked it up again with lithographic crayon where the deepest tones were, retouched them here and there with a brush or pen, with lampblack, and worked in the lighter parts with white body color."[65] In the same letter Vincent explicitly acknowledged the pictorial equivalence of that type of drawing: "What is called Black and White is in fact *painting in black*, meaning that one gives the same depth of effect, the same richness of

31

31   *Girl Seated by a Cradle.* The Hague, March 1883. Black chalk and crayon highlighted with white, 48 × 32 cm. F 1024. Rijksmuseum Vincent van Gogh, Amsterdam.

tone value in a drawing that ought to be in a painting."[66] He was especially enthusiastic about the deep black crayon he had used for the *Girl Seated by a Cradle* and for his peasant types, because it possessed a "real gypsy soul"[67] and "It has the color of a plowed field on a summer evening!"[68] For working with a brush he concocted a mixture of printer's ink diluted with turpentine that, with the addition of white, created subtle shades of gray.

Fascinated by the "pictorial" possibilities of chiaroscuro, he transformed his studio so that he could vary the lighting of his models simply through a play of shutters that changed the direction and strength of the light. "...When I have seen a little figure in some other house, I can easily reconstruct the effect back home if I pay attention to the way the light strikes it, and regulate my light accordingly."[69]

Under the influence of his friend Van Rappard, who visited him in May 1883, Vincent embarked during the summer on considerably larger drawings, sometimes as much as a meter in length. This enlargement of his drawing format to the size of a painting—he fixed his sheet of paper on a frame for that purpose —shows that he was trying to get to know the difficulties he would encounter when working on a true pictorial space with its own laws. He was encouraged by several Hague painters who had befriended him, especially B. J. Blommers and Théophile de Bock. The latter allowed him to use the pied-à-terre he was renting in Scheveningen, and Vincent told his brother enthusiastically: "I made a few painted studies there, a bit of the sea, a potato field, a field with net menders...."[70]

Assessing the decisive step he had to take, he wrote: "Personally I also feel that having finished those last ten or twelve last drawings, I have reached a point where I must change my course instead of making more in the same way."[71] But the prospect frightened him. Surrounded by painters who were specializing in landscapes, Vincent had come to think more or less as they did: that the first and foremost function of painting was to represent nature.

His initial trials in that vein seemed so clumsy to him compared with the masterly sketches his colleagues dashed off that he suddenly felt unsure of himself. Without even the aid of a drawing, he again was up against those wretched laws of perspective that had given him so much trouble in the past.

This sense of insecurity was so strong that it turned into a malaise for which Vincent grasped the first excuse to hand, a small sibylline phrase of Theo's which he exaggerated out of all proportion: "I can't give you much hope for the future." Vincent convinced himself that this "verdict" referred not so much to the question of money as to his own work, and he suddenly blamed Theo for his physical ill-health: "It may be feverishness or nerves, or something else, I don't know, but I don't feel well."[72] This "something else," the true cause of his illness, was his temporary inability to meet the norms of academic painting as upheld by the painters of the school of The Hague. He was prey to psychosomatic symptoms: "Sometimes it's a kind of dizziness, and at times a headache too. Well, it's nothing but weakness."[73] Somewhat appeased by his brother's profuse reassurances, he blamed his symptoms on lack of money, which often forced him to choose between buying food or buying art supplies. Nevertheless, he harbored thereafter some suspicion towards Theo, which cast a lasting shadow on their relationship.

This was the first occasion on which the close connection between Vincent's work and his health appeared so clearly. There were many more such to come. All followed the same patterns: Contrary to appearances, it was the conditions under which he was working and what he was actually doing that had a direct bearing on his health, not vice versa (which would simply have been cause and effect). When he started to paint, Vincent naturally turned to his favorite subject: nothing gave him greater confidence than the human figure, which he had drawn so often. "I think painting figure studies would help me in a great many ways. I started one of a boy in a potato field, and one in the garden near a fence of plaited rushes."[74] Although very few brush sketches dating from that summer of 1883 have survived, it seems, according to Vincent's accounts, that his progress was satisfactory: "I used to get in a muddle then whenever I lost hold of my sketch while painting; and it took me a long time to make that sketch, so that when I could only have the model for a short time, I made an absolute mess of it. But now I don't care in the least if the drawing is wiped out; and I am now only doing them directly with the brush, and then the form stands out enough for the study to be of use to me."[75]

The figure, on which Vincent concentrated his efforts, was in some ways the *modello* which enabled him to find what he needed in order to pursue his aim: a technical and conceptual focus that would carry through—from preliminary drawing to the actual painting. He explained this quite clearly: "The first two figures I painted this year were done in the way I tried last year, drawing them, and then filling in the outline. That is what I'd like to call the dry manner. The other way is to make the drawing last of all, and first find the tones without caring much about the drawing, only trying to put the tones in their right places; and then gradually make the form and the subdivisions of the colors more exact."[76]

When he reached the stage at which the drawing and colors were less dependent on each other he felt that this "surrounds the figure with more atmosphere," tending to flatten it on the canvas. Landscape, he found, produced a similar "impression" in a natural manner: "What I mean to suggest is that in these studies I believe there is something of the mysteriousness one gets by looking at nature through the eyelashes, so that the outlines are simplified to blots of color."[77] This kind of remark, which shows his awareness of the two-dimensional nature of painting, directly foreshadows the Cloisonnist experiments undertaken some years later by the Pont-Aven painters Anquetin, Emile Bernard, and Gauguin. Vincent was already looking at nature through his lashes, seeing it, just as Anquetin saw it, as a transparency through a colored glass, a landscape with no depth comprised of flat areas of color. At this point he was still a long way from applying his observations in such a radical manner, but at least it gave him some "explanation" of the concepts of Impressionist painting, of which Theo was beginning to tell him without as yet taking them very seriously. By "blots of color" Vincent meant mainly the bold colors of Diaz, or Manet, in whom he was also interested.

To Vincent, painting a landscape meant first and foremost matching himself against the painters of the school of The Hague to which he yearned to belong. This explains his determination to be "recognized" by his cousin Mauve, who was an influential member of that school. To cross this threshold he had to steep himself in nature, to withdraw again far from the city. His friend Van Rappard extolled the virtues of Drenthe, a wild, heather-covered country from which he had just returned full of enthusiasm. There life was less expensive, and more and more painters were going there all the time. That was all the encouragement that Vincent needed; he took out his map of Drenthe. "On it [the map] I see a large white spot without any village names; it is crossed by the Hoogeveen canal, which ends suddenly, and I see the words 'peat fields' on the map, written across the blank space."[78] At once he was imagining not large stretches of heather crossed by canals but all the bustle of the peat fields, which would supply fine live models! He was already wildly excited. But there was a serious decision to be made: he had to choose whether or not to leave Sien and her children whose sole support he was. Thanks to them, he had enjoyed the comforts of family life, the care of a woman, and the affection of children, especially the touching attachment of the youngest who was always clutching his trousers and calling him "Papa." On the other hand, the financial burden of keeping them was becoming unbearable. Sien's health was frail and needed constant attention. Moreover, she was incessantly under the nefarious influence of her mother and brother, who urged her to prostitute herself, and she relapsed in spite of his protection. "The woman," as Vincent called her in the biblical style, dared disobey him! Under the pressure exerted on him by both his father and Theo, who implored him not to marry her, he began to feel that she was ungrateful and did not repay his charitable attitude, and that the risk to his work was becoming too great. But he was ashamed of his weakness and he tried to justify himself.

To begin with he associated Theo directly with his decision: "I should wish it were possible that, instead of sending her out into the street again, we might return her promise to better herself with a cordial pardoning and forgetting."[79] Then he put all the responsibility for their parting on her shoulders, stating that he would not leave her "if she herself does not make it absolutely impossible."[80] Finally he took his courage in both his hands and explained to Sien that they had to separate because of his work but that they would remain "good friends."

In the hope that this would get him more help from Theo, he gave him a formal assurance: "And you may depend on it that whatever may happen to her, I neither can nor ever will live with her again, for she is incapable of doing what she ought to do."[81] The only real regret he felt about Sien was connected with his work, for "...in those rare moments her expression is like that of a 'Mater Dolorosa' by Delacroix or like certain heads by Ary Scheffer."[82]

Drenthe

Vincent's move to Drenthe sprang from the reflex to protect his work and from his concern for the future. At thirty, it was time to think of making a career as a "professional," for a self-taught artist was considered no better than an amateur. In the eyes of the public and the dealers only academic recognition counted, which was provided only by a select group of salons. Theo warmly encouraged Vincent to go to Drenthe, not only because this meant a break with Sien, but because of the "strategic" importance

Vincent attached to the move: "My intention is to make so much progress in painting in Drenthe that when I come back I might be admitted as a member of the Society of Draftsmen. This is again in reference to a second plan to go to England."[83]

Vincent was convinced that in England he would find more outlets for his work than in Holland, especially because of the English love of illustrated papers like the *Graphic* or the *London News*, in which he knew the art was of a high standard. Indeed, he himself collected those kinds of magazines enthusiastically and took a lively interest in lithography, which was well suited to the kind of artwork they published.

"...A woman is sitting peeling potatoes, rather a pretty little figure."[84] This was the first image in Drenthe that made a strong impression on Vincent when he arrived in the small town of Hoogeveen one evening in September 1883. But although he discovered "amazing people," he bore in mind that he must concentrate on painting rather than drawing. Thus he devoted himself intensively to studying the landscape, which offered more scope for expression in painting than did the figure. Vincent noticed that the heather in Drenthe, like the sea, is not "always picturesque; but those moments and effects, too, must be studied if one does not want to be deceived in their real character."[85] Unlike the figure, it gained pictorial force from its lack of picturesqueness so that "painting it in that blazing light and rendering the planes vanishing into infinity makes one dizzy."

Vincent acknowledged this aspect of landscape painting when he wrote to Theo: "I see no possibility of describing the country as it ought to be done; words fail me, but imagine the banks of the canal as miles and miles of Michels or Th. Rousseaus, Van Goyens or Ph. de Konincks."[86] This inability to find words, this "blank" in the description could be expressed in painting only in the "delicate lilac white" of the sky.

In the heart of Drenthe, Vincent discovered the "impressionist" power of the landscape, to which he was highly susceptible, as well as natural effects of whose pictorial equivalent he was deeply aware. Around Nieuw-Amsterdam he painted numerous studies of cottages, *Métairies* (Small Farms) (F 17), packed close together in the hollows of the peat bogs like the birds' nests he had collected as a child. At Zweeloo the gloomy atmosphere of the natural setting, despite its beauty, filled him with anxiety, which was exacerbated still further by his solitude. Added to this was the severe climate—winter was coming—and the suspicion, sometimes amounting to hostility, of the local people. He was often taken for a tramp, and although that was nothing new he found it increasingly difficult to bear. A letter from Theo, who was having financial difficulties and who was even thinking of going to the United States, was the last straw and left Vincent completely demoralized. He wrote: "It's true, it's the same as on a road, one sees the church spire in the distance, but as the ground undulates, when one thinks one has arrived, there is another bit one had not seen at first, but which must still be covered."[87] He made a snap decision to return to the family "nest." But he did not acknowledge defeat and thought of his return home as temporary, even saying that he intended to settle in Drenthe. In fact, he never went back.

His three months' stay in the peat country, although short, was long enough to change his perspective profoundly. The influence of the school of The Hague on his work was muted; his color range became more somber. Most of the painted studies reveal a systematic use of chiaroscuro as a means of expression, a technique he perfected in his depictions of the Drenthe landscapes, of which he wrote, "There are very often curious contrasts of black and white here."[88]

The Brabant Weavers

Vincent arrived in Nuenen during the first days of December 1883. His mental turmoil was such that he overcame his fears of renewing the disagreement with his father, which had kept him away from home. His parents were still unable to understand him, but they welcomed him nevertheless and were willing to try again, even "leaving him entirely free to dress in his odd way," as the Reverend Theodorus told Theo in a letter of 20 December. This laissez-faire atmosphere did not arouse any gratitude in Vincent, however, because he knew that his father did not appreciate his work. In this response he certainly was not motivated by personal pride as Theo alleged, an accusation to which he replied: "I consciously choose *the dog's path through life*; I will remain a *dog*, I shall be *poor*, I shall be a *painter*, I want to *remain human*—going *into* nature."[89] Pride in his work alone determined his attitude, which he explained in the same letter: "I do not speak against Father when I consider his character separately, but I speak against Father as soon as I compare him with the great father Millet, for instance. Millet's doctrine is so great that Father's views appear wretchedly petty by comparison."[90]

Vincent, the spiritual son of Millet, no longer needed a clergyman father to point the way, but he did need effective help, and this he expected his brother to provide. Thus the latter's remonstrances only served to exasperate him, for they sounded just like his father's words all over again. The tone of the exchange grew heated. The dispute between the brothers was interrupted for a short time when Moe had an accident and fractured her pelvis while getting off a train. But it started again in full spate as soon as their mother's life was out of danger. Vincent felt trapped. He had hoped to free himself from his father's authority, thanks to the financial help Theo had promised, and now it was Theo who was trying to take control of him, not only of his life but even of his work. To sort things out, he tried to clarify his position towards his brother: "Now I want to make you a proposal for the future. Let me send you my work, and keep what you like for yourself, but I insist on considering the money I receive from you after March as money I have earned." He added: "I want to feel free with you, but at the same time

32 *Peasant Women in the Fields.* Drenthe, October 1883.
Oil on canvas, 27 × 35.5 cm. F 19. Rijksmuseum Vincent van
Gogh, Amsterdam.

33   *Loom*. Nuenen, May 1884. Oil on canvas, 70 × 85 cm.
F 30. Rijksmuseum Kröller-Müller, Otterlo.

and with *equal* sincerity I want you *to feel free with me.*[91] Vincent was trying to replace his personal dependence on Theo by a business arrangement, which he thought was sealed by Theo's tacit acceptance of three small pictures and nine watercolors Vincent sent him on 13 February 1884. This consignment was followed by a long silence on Theo's part, which was clearly meant as a reproach. This was confirmed when he finally did send an answer, explaining tactfully that Vincent's work was not yet commercial and that he could not offer it to his clients until Vincent had "perfected" it. Vincent was disgusted by his brother's disingenuousness and accused him of only making a pretence of backing him. "You have *never sold a single one for me*—neither for much nor for little—and in fact *you have not even tried.*"[92] He saw quite clearly that, in a way, Theo had been commissioned by the Van Gogh family to make sure that Vincent would not disgrace them, either by living immorally or by exhibiting works that in no way corresponded to the criteria of good taste as postulated by the school of The Hague: "And it has become evident to me that—although you say you leave me absolutely free—as a matter of fact, when for instance I have some affair with a woman which you and others do not approve of, perhaps rightly so, a thing that *once in a while* I do not give a damn about, there comes a little tug at the financial bridle in order to make me feel that it is 'in my own interest' to conform to your opinion."[93] These passionate protests clearly reveal Vincent's sense of helpless bitterness. It was useless for him to cry, "I definitely refuse to become your protege, Theo," and "Better make a break now," for he knew he had not the means to do it. "I do not want to be mixed up in a second series of quarrels (such as I had with *Father No. I*) with *Father No. II. And Father No. II would be you. One is enough.*"[94]

Bound to Theo by the "contract" he had proposed to him, Vincent had to accept Draconian conditions that threatened the very integrity of his work: "Of course I will *send you my work every month.* As you say, that work will be your property then, and I per-fectly agree with you that you have every right to do anything with it; even I couldn't make any objection if you should want to tear it to pieces."[95] Although he was sickened by Theo's lack of faith in his work—on several occasions he wrote to him "We must part company"—he had only one weapon with which to defend himself and that was blackmail, which he employed even to the point of putting his own life at risk. His allusion to the possibility of suicide is scarcely veiled: "If I should drop dead—*which I should not try to evade if it happened, but which I should not seek expressly*—you would be standing on a skeleton, and this would be a damned insecure standpoint."[96] His threat was perfectly clear, and from then on he forced Theo to shoulder his responsibilities by allowing his own mental health to hinge upon his work, the obsessive labor that would gradually burn him up.

There can be no doubt that Vincent felt that his own work had a special affinity to weaving, with the weaver handling his shuttles as the painter handles his brushes. He was fascinated by the complicated machinery of the loom, which stood in the chiaroscuro of the room like a vast spider with the weaver as its unfortunate prey.

To Vincent, this fantastic view was more realistic than an objective description would have been: "Let us say it is only a mechanical drawing—all right, but just put it beside the technical design for a loom—and *mine will be more spectral all the same, you may be sure of that.* As a matter of fact it is no mechanical drawing—or it may be except for a 'je ne sais quoi.' And—if you were to put my study beside the drawing of a mechanic who had designed a weaving loom—mine would express more strongly that the thing is made of oak grimed by sweaty hands; and looking at it (*even if I had not included him in the drawing at all,* or even if I did add his figure out of proportion), you could not help thinking occasionally of the *workman,* whereas absolutely nothing like it would occur to your mind when you looked at the model of a loom drawn by a mechanic."[97] In this letter to Van Rappard, Vincent showed that he

33

did not intend to do a portrait of a weaver, but simply wished to indicate his presence "by putting in some sort of apparition of a weaver, by means of a few scratches and blots, where I had seen it sitting." This procedure seemed so convincing to him that he also used it in his landscapes, at first in drawings like the *Winter Garden* (F 1128) and a *Birch Wood with a Flock of Sheep* (F 1240), "also with a little black

34   *Birch Wood with a Flock of Sheep.* Nuenen, March 1884. Crayon and pen, 39.5 × 54.5 cm. F 1240. Rijksmuseum Vincent van Gogh, Amsterdam.

spook in it, which this time too appears in it not as an example... of the correct drawing of the structure of the human body, but as a contrast," and then in paintings such as *Coming out of Church at Nuenen* (F 25). Corot's "inhabited" landscapes certainly served him as a model, but Vincent revolutionized the drawing of the small figures by stripping them of any narrative, picturesque, or even aesthetic character, in order to give them a deeper meaning: endowing the pictorial space, whether landscape or interior, with a *focus on the human being*. The theme of the weaver at the center of his loom, which largely hides him, illustrates that notion clearly: "...that

35　*Coming out of Church at Nuenen.* Nuenen, October 1884. Oil on canvas, 41 × 32 cm. F 25. Rijksmuseum Vincent van Gogh, Amsterdam.

36　*Ox and Cart.* Nuenen, July 1884. Oil on canvas pasted on board, 57 × 82.5 cm. F 38. Rijksmuseum Kröller-Müller, Otterlo.

little black spook in the background must be the center, the starting point, the *heart* of it, most deeply felt, most elaborately finished, and all the rest must be kept subordinate to it." To Vincent the loveliest landscape would seem incomplete without the presence of man: "Well—first comes the figure; I personally cannot understand the rest without it, and it is the figure that creates the atmosphere."[98] And if he admired the Barbizon landscapists it was because he found "it a mighty clever saying of Israëls," when he remarked of a Dupré, "It is just like 'a picture of a figure.'"

A Realist Palette

The reason why Theo did not show Vincent's work was that it was neither in the Impressionist manner —which was gaining recognition in Paris after five years' hard struggle—nor charming enough to belong to the school of The Hague. Indeed, the darkening of Vincent's palette, which Theo thought excessive, seemed to lead to a monochrome effect as, for instance, in *Ox and Cart* [F 38] or, even more so, in *Poplar Avenue* [F 122], whose dirty tints put off art lovers. Vincent, on the other hand, was convinced that this kind of study marked an advance, a step in a direction similar to Impressionism— which, however, he claimed not to understand very well: "The last thing I made is a rather large study of an avenue of poplars, with yellow autumn leaves, the sun casting, here and there, sparkling spots on the fallen leaves on the ground, alternating with the long shadows of the stems."[99] In doing so he was thinking of Courbet rather than Manet, of whom his brother spoke with admiration, for he himself did "not think he [Manet] can be reckoned among the very first of this century."[100]

37 *Poplar Avenue.* Nuenen, October 1884. Oil on canvas pasted on board, 99 × 66 cm. F 122. Rijksmuseum Vincent van Gogh, Amsterdam.

Theo, who was "well in" in Paris, advised Vincent to paint in light colors and was upset to see him stray away from the mainstream of innovatory trends. To him it seemed that Vincent was doomed to failure, just as he had been during his unfortunate youth; and Vincent's views seemed aberrant: "I think that in a year, if I again spend that year painting much and constantly, my method of painting and my color will change a great deal, and that I shall become darker rather than lighter."[101]

Vincent remained deaf to Theo's advice because he preferred to finish learning all he had to learn rather than throw himself, ill-prepared both theoretically and technically, into the battles of "modernity." Meanwhile, he reminded his brother of some unpleasant facts: "Then, in Daumier's and Millet's younger days, Messrs. G. & Co. were busily occupied with Julien Brochart and *Monsieur* Paul Delaroche—in my eyes not such a very fine *Monsieur* Delaroche, you know."[102] In another letter, he clearly explained his attitude: "When I hear you mention so many new names, it is not always easy for me to understand because I have seen absolutely *nothing* of them. And from what you told me about 'impressionism,' I have indeed concluded that it is different from what I thought, but it's not quite clear to me what it really is. But for my part, I find Israëls, for instance, so enormously great that I am little curious about or desirous for other or newer things."[103]

In 1884 Vincent, self-taught, discovered the works of Charles Blanc, who was well known to the artists of that time. For Theo's benefit, he quoted a passage from *Les Artistes de mon temps* (The Artists of my Time) which justified his use of a dark palette without concern for local color; a passage in which Delacroix was quoted: "There, for instance (he pointed with his finger to the grey and dirty tone of the pavement), is a tone; well, if one said to Paul Veronese: Paint me a beautiful blonde woman whose flesh would have that tone, he would paint her, and the woman *would be blonde in his picture.*" This letter also shows that Vincent had completely assimilated the rules of contrasting colors that

38 *Still Life with Bottles.* Nuenen, November 1884. Oil on canvas, 33 × 41 cm. F 50. Rijksmuseum Kröller-Müller, Otterlo.

39 *Head of a Peasant Woman.* Nuenen, March 1885. Oil ▷ on canvas pasted on board, 45 × 36 cm. F 130. Rijksmuseum Vincent van Gogh, Amsterdam.

Delacroix had seen confirmed in 1839 in a treatise by the physicist Chevreul; a treatise which, in the 1880s, became the reference book of the Impressionists and remained so for following generations until the coming of the abstract painters in the first half of the twentieth century. Thus, according to those rules, "a dark color may seem *light*, or rather give that *effect*; this is in fact more a question of *tone*. But then, as regards the real *color*, a reddish-grey, hardly red at all, will appear more or less red according to the colors next to it. And it is the same with blue and yellow. One has to put but a very little yellow into a color to make it seem very yellow if one puts that color in or next to a violet or lilac tone."[104]

38   In the studies he painted at Nuenen, Vincent set out to "break up" the tones, that is, to contrast complementary colors in order to create luminous effects. But whether the subject was a weaver at work, the head of a peasant woman, a landscape or a still life, the contrasts he achieved remind us of Delacroix's sensual manner of modeling form, a style he shared with such painters as Frans Hals. During a visit to the Amsterdam Museum in October 1885, Vincent discovered the tremendous skill with which the latter had been able to convey differences in texture by means of a "neutral" tone obtained through mixing complementary colors. This reinforced his draftman's instincts, for he was more concerned with problems of form than with those of color. It also explains his persistent use of chiaroscuro, in spite of all of Theo's warnings and complaints that he was painting "too black."

"I think the best way to express form," he told Theo, "is with an almost monochrome coloring, the tones of which differ principally in intensity and in 39   value."[105] The very fine *Head of a Peasant Woman* (F 130) in the Van Gogh Museum in Amsterdam testifies to the artistry with which Vincent conveyed a remarkably vibrant personality. She looks you straight in the eye, and it is difficult to look away. You even feel that you and she are exchanging glances, for her face seems to come towards you, creating the illusion of life. It is an anonymous face; and yet behind the very realistic portrait of a Brabant peasant woman we sense a host of other possibilities. Beneath the flawless folds of the white headdress all faces look alike, but this one, starkly lit, radiates something almost sacred, the feeling Millet had already sought to express.

During this period, color interested Vincent only as a complement to form. He tried to make a given tone contribute as effectively as possible to a form, so that the former would evoke the latter, particularly in the case of blue. He clearly explained his view of its value: "The people here instinctively wear the most beautiful blue that I have ever seen. It is coarse linen which they weave themselves, warp black, woof blue, the result of which is a black and blue striped pattern. When this fades and becomes somewhat discolored by wind and weather, it is an infinitely quiet, delicate tone that particularly brings out the flesh colors. Well, blue enough to react to all colors in which hidden orange elements are to be found, and discolored enough not to jar."[106] It was the function of blue to set off the figure, to point to it lest it should blend into the landscape and be lost in the natural setting. The same kind of blue enables the *Woman Spinning* (F 71) to loom out of the 40 darkness of her room, the peasant woman to stand out against the dark door of her *Cottage at Dusk* 41 (F 83), or the strollers to show up among the tree trunks of the *Poplar Avenue near Nuenen* (F 45). We 43 must remember that this precise use of blue, which Vincent had seen in Millet's *Gleaners*, goes back to the seventeenth century. Poussin's women gleaning in *Summer*, one of those "inhabited" landscapes of the last period of his work (*Four Seasons* series, Louvre, Paris), are wearing blue dresses that stand out against the gold of the corn.

All of Vincent's early paintings, from The Hague period until the Paris period (1886), contain an apparent contradiction, which he attempted to resolve through his use of the palette. Although he was anxious to respect nature as much as possible and to render its effects realistically, the means he used to achieve this aim seem to be inherently opposed to it, for they led away from reality. One of the most obvious examples is his simplification of the palette, which he reduced to a near monochrome, and his failure to respect local color, as he asserted "that a painter had better start from the colors on his palette than from the colors in nature."[107] Vincent undoubtedly was the first "modern" painter *before Cézanne* to declare, as he did in this letter, that "art is a harmony parallel with nature."[e] "Of nature I retain a certain sequence and a certain correctness in placing the tones, I study nature, so as not to do foolish things, to remain reasonable; however, I don't care so much whether my color is exactly the same, as long as it looks beautiful on my canvas, as beautiful as it looks in nature."

Van Gogh has been cast in the role of the ill-starred painter par excellence; it has been assumed that, shut in his "madness," he was "primitive," "crude" and "basic," working with a blind determination and guided only by his instinct. Nothing could be further from the truth. Van Gogh's painting is no less *cosa mentale* (of the mind) than Cézanne's. His correspondence alone is proof of this, proceeding as it does wholly from his work, of which it forms a kind of literary extension. Never has the famous saying of the symbolist Moréas been demonstrated more fully: "to clothe the Idea in palpable form." Vincent often paid tribute to Corot, Millet, Daubigny, Israëls, and Dupré; but when he said, "They follow the color scale in which they started, express their own ideas in color and tone and drawing,"[108] he was actually talking about himself. For it was his great project to let painting not only express an idea but go on to develop it through its own means. He himself clearly wanted to make painting a form of thinking. Admittedly, observation was necessary: "But in the picture I give free scope to my own head in the sense of *thought* ...."[109] Thus he made a clear distinction between the picture and the study, which he considered a simple summary of a subject "where no creative process is allowed, but where one finds food for one's imagination in reality, in order to make it

exact."[110] Painting, on the other hand, used the vocabulary of color, for "*Color expresses something in itself, one cannot do without this, one must use it.*"[111]

Lies More Truthful than Truth

Vincent's concept of painting was based on the principle that the painter must maintain a paradoxical distance in relation to reality, in the sense that all painterly deformations of physical reality (such as not keeping to the local color) are really aimed solely at reproducing that reality. This principle closely links the fundamental structure of the picture with its overall effect: "The best pictures, and, from a technical point of view the most complete, seen from near by, are but patches of color side by side, and only make an effect at a certain distance."[112] Thus the distance at which a combination of juxtaposed patches of color conveys an overall effect is directly proportional to the distance by which the patches are separated on the canvas. It seems extraordinary that, having reached this stage of awareness, Vincent should still have resisted espousing Impressionism—in spite of Theo's pressure!—since between his ideas and theirs there were such strong similarities. Thus his *Poplar Avenue near Nuenen* (F 45) was "pointillist," although the palette was still gloomy and the chiaroscuro a "must." It was on the level of the "idea as color, as shade, and as drawing" wherein lay the difference between Vincent and the Impressionists. Vincent accused them of striving so hard to be modern that they sacrificed a part of reality and showed only a limited aspect of it. He told Theo indignantly: "That's it exactly: They begin to find heresy in every effect against a strong and colored light, in every shadow—they never seem to walk early in the morning or in the evening at sunset—they want to see nothing but full daylight, or gaslight, or even electric light!"[113]

The Impressionism had sanctioned the use of color contrasts and the principle of the optic mix-

◁ 40 *Woman Spinning.* Nuenen, March 1885. Oil on canvas, 43.5 × 34.5 cm. F 71. Rijksmuseum Vincent van Gogh, Amsterdam.

41 *Cottage at Dusk.* Nuenen, May 1885. Oil on canvas, 64 × 78 cm. F 83. Rijksmuseum Vincent van Gogh, Amsterdam.

ture of juxtaposed patches, with which Delacroix had experimented as early as the mid-nineteenth century. Vincent also experimented with it, but cautiously, for he dreaded that the form might disintegrate. Thus in his *Still Life with Open Bible, Candle, and Novel* (F 117) the contrasts of complementary orange and blue colors are circumscribed by the white page. The main subject of Impressionism was landscape, which lent itself best to specifically chromatic experiments without distracting the eye with any narrative interest. Vincent, on the contrary, felt that "Well—first comes the figure; I personally cannot understand the rest without it, and it is the figure that creates the atmosphere."[114] It was the figure that endowed a picture with meaning. What was the point of these Impressionist landscapes? Their "daring" remained purely plastic. Delacroix at least was committed to real life. Didn't he point the way with his *Liberty Guiding the People* (Louvre, Paris) better than Manet with his *Déjeuner sur l'herbe* (Jeu de Paume, Paris), which is confined within an allegory, after the manner of Giorgione's *Concert champêtre?* These people of Manet's, stretched out on the grass, frozen in antique-style poses—to what reality could they testify? Such painting, which was endowed with an aura of scandal because it confronted a naked woman and a clothed man, made no sense to Vincent, because these people were not *doing anything*. In this respect, his confession of faith is very simple: "But I think that however correctly academic a figure may be, it will be superfluous in these days, though it were by Ingres himself (his 'Source,' however, excepted, because that really was, and is, and will always be, something new), when it lacks the essential modern note, the intimate character, the real *action*."[115]

The principle mentioned above of paradoxical distance in relation to reality could be applied perfectly to the depiction of the figure, for when a digger really digs he cannot be represented in a "correctly academic" way, but *must* be deformed on the canvas. Vincent added that "if one photographs a digger, *he certainly would not be digging then*." The

numerous studies of weavers that he did when he first came to Nuenen confirmed him in this view. It was enough for him to indicate the weaver's presence by means of a simple patch of color or silhouette, since all his action went into the loom with which he was closely associated. Vincent thought of the loom as a kind of warping incarnation of the weaver himself at work. This deformation, which painting easily expressed through its own plastic means, suggested the idea of continuity to Vincent and enabled him to define a certain way of showing movement—one that already foreshadowed the ideas of the pioneers of twentieth-century art.

There is no doubt that it was the daily practice of drawing from life that alone could lead Vincent to work out his idea of a realism "something other"—in one of his favorite phrases—than the literal truth. There was not a day when he did not walk through the fields to observe the gestures of a sower here, of a planter there. Carefully watching a peasant reaping (F 1317), he accentuated the disequilibrium of the body, prolonged the twisting movement through the elliptical sweep of the sickles; and yet the whole is in perfect equilibrium. The same applies to a picture of a peasant woman binding a sheaf (F 1264), shown from the front, doubled over right down to the ground, whose arm—though too long by academic standards—offsets the bulk of the rick and of her own body. In the drawing of a peasant woman with a pitchfork (F 1251) the "literal truth" is not respected either, and her bust is shortened in proportion to the lower half of her figure, which conveys the strength of something rooted in the soil, as do her arms holding the fork, which effect the movement. And yet this distortion makes her appear all the more "realistic." Vincent took care always to draw several aspects of the same figure at work, so that he could fix different moments of a movement and, placing them side by side, could reconstruct it in its *continuity*, like a frame-by-frame slow-motion picture.

If we look carefully at the underlying structure of these drawings of the peasants at Nuenen and com-

42   *Still Life with Earthenware Pot and Clogs.* Nuenen, September 1885. Oil on canvas pasted on board, 39 × 41.5 cm. F 63. Rijksmuseum Kröller-Müller, Otterlo.

43 *Poplar Avenue near Nuenen.* Nuenen, November 1885.
Oil on canvas, 78 × 97.8 cm. F 45. Museum Boymans-van
Beuningen, Rotterdam.

44 *The Potato Field*. Nuenen, April 1885. Oil on canvas,
33 × 41 cm. F 129a. Kunsthaus, Zurich.

pare them with those of the Hague or Etten period dating from only two to three years earlier, we will realize how much ground Vincent had covered. Instead of the continuous outline, often hesitant and indecisive, and filled in with a web of fine hatchings that follow it meticulously, that is found in the Hague and Etten drawings, we now see a firm, sustained line, more or less discontinuous, which models the figure and divides the space. Above all, Vincent has eliminated the difference between the outline and the line molding the form; they are one and the same and make up a system of parallel or broken hatchings (depending on their purpose), which build up the movement of the figure. Their junction at various key points of the body (knees, elbows, waist, etc.) gives them play and sets up an overall sense of direction; they sometimes follow the lines of the body so closely under the dress that some of the figures are like studies in anatomy.

46 *Peasant Woman Binding a Sheaf.* Nuenen, August 1885. Black chalk, 45 × 53 cm. F 1264. Rijksmuseum Kröller-Müller, Otterlo.

47 *Peasant Woman with a Pitchfork.* Nuenen, July 1885. ▷ Black chalk, 49.5 × 40 cm. F 1251. Rijksmuseum Vincent van Gogh, Amsterdam.

45 *Peasant Reaping Seen from the Back.* Nuenen, August 1885. Black chalk, 43 × 55 cm. F 1317. Rijksmuseum Vincent van Gogh, Amsterdam.

The studies from life that Vincent did in Antwerp a few months later, in February 1886, were less innovatory because the models held their pose and because Sibert, one of his professors at the academy, corrected him if he ventured to begin with anything other than the outline. But, in studying casts after antique models, he found that his own way of working actually corresponded to that of the Greeks, as he had read in one of Gigoux's works: "The Greeks did not start from the contour, they started from the centers, the nuclei."[116]

In reality the human figure is constantly moving, because it is working most of the time; and so Vincent, who wanted to paint reality and not historical pictures, was bent on expressing movement. He remarked with a hint of sarcasm: "As far as I know there isn't a single academy where one learns to draw and paint a digger, a sower, a woman putting the kettle over the fire or a seamstress. But in every

48   *The Tower of the Cemetery at Nuenen.* Nuenen, May
1885. Oil on canvas, 63 × 79 cm. F 84. Rijksmuseum Vincent
van Gogh, Amsterdam.

49 *Still Life with Open Bible, Candle, and Novel.* Nuenen, October 1885. Oil on canvas, 65 × 78 cm. F 117. Rijksmuseum Vincent van Gogh, Amsterdam.

city of some importance there is an academy with a choice of models for historical, Arabic, Louis XV, in short, *all really nonexistent figures.*"[117]

In 1912 when Marcel Duchamp painted his *Nude Descending a Staircase* (Museum of Art, Philadelphia), he based it on the works of Muybridge, who had isolated successive phases of movement through photography. Vincent's only solution to the problem of rendering motion was to try to capture the rapid succession of postures during a given action. Each drawing consisted of a synthesis of gestures made within a short space of time. Such a drawing could not be academically correct, for it did not represent an immobile figure. He wrote to Theo, who was liable to comment on this, that he yearned.... "to learn to make those very incorrectnesses, those deviations, remodelings, changes in reality, so that they may become, yes, lies if you like—but truer than the literal truth."[118]

Vincent established a universal principle according to which a figure draws its expression and liveliness from faulty rendering and not from a depiction of its literal appearance. He was the first to formulate clearly and apply this idea which led him to deform truth in order to paint reality. This throws some light on the disconcerting remarks he made to his friend Van Rappard: "As for me, what I intend to do —even when I have a much more thorough command of my brush than I have now—is to tell those fellows systematically *that I cannot paint.* Do you hear?"[119] Twelve years later, Paul Gauguin drew the same conclusions from his pictorial experiments in the South Sea Islands. Entitling the large canvas that summed up all that was problematic in his work, *Where Do We Come From? What Are We? Where Are We Going?* (Museum of Fine Arts, Boston), he wrote to Daniel de Monfreid: "The more I see it , the more I become aware of the huge mathematical flaws that I don't want to touch up at any price, it will stay as it is, in the state of a sketch if you like."[f] In the notes he took after *Noa Noa,* quoting Cézanne's famous saying, "One kilo of green is greener than half a kilo," Gauguin used more or less the same words as

Van Gogh when he said that to create the equivalent of nature, "since your canvas is smaller than nature, [you have to] use a green that's greener than nature. This is the truth of the lie."[g] Gauguin was quoting Cézanne, but his thinking must surely have been influenced by his stay at Arles with Van Gogh.

The Potato Eaters

Vincent was painting a series of peasant heads when he heard that his father had died on 26 March 1885. The news did not seem to upset him. In his letter to Theo following this bereavement, he simply said, "I felt the same as you did when you wrote that you could not work as usual the first days; it was the same with me."[120] Pa, the "good shepherd," had long since fallen from the pedestal on which Vincent had placed him in his youth.

The *Still Life with Open Bible, Candle, and Novel* 49 (F 117) reveals Vincent's state of mind at the time, in the purest style of seventeenth-century conceits. The open Bible, from which the young Vincent had learnt so many verses by heart, is confronted with Zola's *Joie de vivre,* a book the Reverend Theodorus thought immoral. The candle, which gives the composition a religious dimension, also suggests desecration, since it places the Bible and Zola's novel on an equal footing. It also lights the gulf that had opened between the son and the father, whom Theo was finally replacing.

From then on Vincent devoted himself entirely to his work. Even Margot Begemann's love was not able to distract him from it. Ten years older than he, she admired the unusual young man who did not hesitate to renounce an easy life for the sake of his art. She valued his courage and his refusal to make concessions to the clergy, who were very careful not to be too literal in their interpretation of the Bible's commandments. Her family, connected to the Van Goghs by a long-standing friendship, dissuaded her from marrying Vincent, and she asked him to wait for two years. But he did not see things in that light and demanded that it should be now or never. There was no way out. Margot tried to commit suicide by swallowing strychnine. The scandal had hastened Pa's death.

Detached from his father's death, indifferent to Margot's declaration of love—the only one he had ever had, now, when it was too late—Vincent continued the studies of heads and hands which he had been doing during the winter. The heads of common people that appeared in the *Graphic* certainly influenced him. Then, too, these parts of the human body are expressive by their very nature and as such had constantly been used by the old masters he particularly admired, Rembrandt, Frans Hals, and Rubens, whose works he regularly went to see in the Antwerp Museum. He wrote, "Rubens is certainly making a strong impression on me; I think his drawing tremendously good—I mean the drawing of heads and hands in themselves. I am quite carried away by his way of drawing the lines in a face with streaks of pure red, or of modeling the fingers of the hands by the same kind of streaks."[121] The *Head of a Peasant Woman* (F 134), for instance, was the product of that technique which Delacroix had already applied in his *Death of Sardanapalus* (Louvre, Paris). Finally, a very practical consideration motivated Vincent to paint some fifty heads. He hoped that this would help him to find work. He had noticed that photography had become very popular and he intended to offer his services to a photographer who needed someone to do coloring and touching up the backgrounds of photographs after studies painted from life.

For the first time Vincent was thinking seriously of executing a large composition, one whose dimensions and underlying idea made it a decisive step at a crucial junction in the artist's work. This series of studies of heads was leading him directly to it. He told Theo: "I am brooding over a couple of larger, more elaborate things, and if I should happen to get a clear idea of how to reproduce the effects I have in mind, in that case I should keep the studies in question here for the time being, because

then I should need them—it would be, for instance, something like this: namely figures against the light of a window. I have studies of heads for it, against the light as well as turned toward the light, and I have worked several times already on the complete figure; spooling yarn, sewing, or peeling potatoes."[122]

One evening when he came back from a long day spent hunting for the "subject," Vincent passed the cottage of the Groot family, whom he knew well, and he decided to stop there for a short rest. He went in. Startled for a moment by the darkness inside, he gradually made out, by the light of an oil lamp hung above the table, the five familiar figures grouped around a dish with steaming potatoes. "Here is my subject," he thought. He had often visited the Groots before, because they were willing to sit for him from time to time for a little money. He had painted the mother on several occasions, and also the son and little Gordina, whose face was not yet marked by hard work. But there, when they were all gathered in the shadows of the confined room, he suddenly found himself plunged into the heart of a "night" à la Ter Borch.

Vincent enthusiastically told Theo of his discovery. "I have just come home from this cottage and have been working at it by lamplight, though I began it by daylight this time. This is what the composition looks like. I painted it on a rather large canvas, and as the sketch is now, I think there is some life in it. Yet I am sure C.M., for instance, would find fault with the drawing, etc. Do you know what a positive argument against that is? That the beautiful effects of light in nature demand a very quick hand in drawing."[123] Although the liveliness of the brush strokes testifies to the speed with which the painting was done, the highly elaborate execution of final painting shows that the composition was worked over several times. Vincent was trying to apply the technical virtuosity he had admired in the works of Frans Hals and Rembrandt. For instance, "in the white...hardly any white has been used, but simply the neutral color, which is made by mixing

50 *Peasant Woman with White Headdress.* Nuenen, January 1885. Graphite and charcoal, 33.5 × 21 cm. F 1184. Rijksmuseum Vincent van Gogh, Amsterdam.

51 *Head of a Peasant Woman.* Nuenen, March 1885. Oil ▷ on canvas pasted on board, 38.5 × 26.5 cm. F 134. Musée d'Orsay, Paris.

◁ 52   *The Potato Eaters* (detail). Cf. ill. 53.

53   *The Potato Eaters.* Nuenen, April 1885. Oil on canvas, 82 × 114 cm. F 82. Rijksmuseum Vincent van Gogh, Amsterdam.

red, blue, yellow, for instance vermilion, Paris blue and Naples yellow. Therefore that color is in itself a pretty dark gray, but in the picture it looks white."[124]

Vincent also was influenced by Rembrandt in his manner of letting faces and hands emerge from the shadows by lighting them from a source set in the center of the picture rather than by the lamp, whose plastic role is purely fictional and constitutes yet another twist of the "literal truth." Finding his first attempt too light, especially the flesh colors, he confided to Theo in the same letter: "I immediately repainted them, inexorably, and the color they are painted in now is like the *color of a very dusty potato, unpeeled of course.* While doing this I thought how perfect that saying of Millet's about the peasants is: 'Ses paysans semblant peints avec la terre qu'ils ensemencent.' [These peasants seemingly painted with the soil they work.]" For it is impossible to un-

52, 53

derstand the *Potato Eaters* (F 82) if we think of them only as a genre scene in the manner of Gérard Dou. Vincent's people are not those cheerful fellows who never seem to have a care in the world except for the occasional bit of licentious behavior. He explained this clearly: "I have tried to emphasize that those people, eating their potatoes in the lamplight, have dug the earth with those very hands they put in the dish, and so it speaks of *manual labor*, and how they have honestly earned their food."[125] The moral value of the picture is obvious. It is addressed especially to town dwellers, who are often ignorant of the conditions of life in the country. This, he thought, was "healthy, especially for city people. Such pictures may *teach* them something."[126] It was a useful lesson for them. In the *Potato Eaters* Vincent at last achieved the pictorial goal he had hitherto been pursuing unsuccessfully along paths that had turned out to be dead ends. In September 1885, he told Van Rappard: "I know too well what my ultimate goal is, and I am firmly convinced of being on the right road after all, to pay too much attention to what people say of me—when I want to paint what I feel and feel what I want to paint."[127]

54   *Brabant Peasant Woman.* Nuenen, May 1885. Pen and wash. Drawing in Letter 409. Rijksmuseum Vincent van Gogh, Amsterdam.

Impelled to bear witness to the poverty of his fellows by the charismatic spirit that had first moved him in the heart of the Borinage, he decided to do a lithograph based on the picture, as he had previously done in the case of *Sorrow.* Thanks to a printer to whose son he had once given a few lessons, he had some twenty copies run off and sent one to Van Rappard, thinking it would please him. Van

Rappard, however, criticized the work harshly. He condemned precisely what had most importance in his eyes, the picture's "gaucheness" and "inaccuracies," such as the distortion of the figure on the left with its excessively long arm, and accused Vincent of carelessness. Furious and upset to see his best friend reacting like a teacher at the Académie des Beaux-Arts, Vincent returned his letter expressing his great surprise, and did not write to him again for a long time.

Winter had come. Darkness fell early over the countryside, which took on an increasingly sinister aspect. Now that his father was dead, the peasants of the area, who were set against him by the Catholic priest, often refused to sit for him for fear of gossip. Schafrath the sexton, who had let him have a room for a studio, had to ask him reluctantly to leave. Added to this were problems connected with the in-

55 *Birds' Nests.* Nuenen, October 1885. Graphite, Drawing in Letter 425. Rijksmuseum Vincent van Gogh, Amsterdam.

56   *The Parsonage*. Nuenen, October 1885. Oil on canvas, 33 × 43 cm. F 182. Rijksmuseum Vincent van Gogh, Amsterdam.

57   *Houses Seen from the Rear*. Antwerp, December 1885.   ▷ Oil on canvas, 44 × 33,5 cm. F 260. Rijksmuseum Vincent van Gogh, Amsterdam.

heritance from his father's will. Vincent quarreled with some of his sisters, and the family atmosphere grew rather tense. Once more, he decided to move on. As usual after a spell of country life, he felt the need to go to the city and be in touch with other painters, making the rounds of the dealers and visiting museums. Since his return from Drenthe, he had in fact dreamt of going to Antwerp, the home of Rubens, where he could enroll for life studies at the Académie des Beaux-Arts. He wanted to acquire a sounder knowledge of anatomy, a science he had hitherto approached only through manuals for artists.

Once again Vincent found himself rejected—both by his family and by Anton Van Rappard, whom he had regarded as his best friend. Another reason for leaving was the need to end his isolation and to escape from a steadily mounting anxiety state from which even the family "nest" provided no refuge. His obsession with birds' nests, which he collected (he sent a whole basketful to Van Rappard, despite

58 *La Grand-Place*. Antwerp, December 1885. Black chalk with white highlights, 22.5 × 30 cm. F 1352. Rijksmuseum Vincent van Gogh, Amsterdam.

their quarrel) and of which he did several studies, reveals his state of mind. Theo was his only support. For fear of losing him too (he had been complaining that business was bad), Vincent reminded him of his promises and responsibilities: "At present I am a tiny vessel which you have on tow, and which at times will seem to you so much ballast. But this—I mean the ballast—you may leave behind by cutting the towrope, if you like.... It may be that there will be a tempest, but even in that case don't count on repairs or provisions, and bear in mind that under the pressure of certain circumstances I may feel obliged to cut the towrope."[128]

Transcending Color

Toward the end of November 1885, Vincent moved to Antwerp, where he stayed at 194 Rue des Images (now Rue Longue-des-Images). On the walls of his small room he pinned a whole set of the Japanese prints that could easily be picked up at the second-hand bookshops in the port. The aesthetic influence of Japanese prints on Western art in the second half of the nineteenth century was considerable. That Vincent was extremely receptive to it is demonstrated in particular by the paintings he did at Arles, since the Japanese prints had the very "faults" of perspective for which he himself was blamed. He was also struck by the various contrasts they presented in their bright colors and flat layout, in their composition, and in the gestures of the figures of all kinds that were portrayed in the numerous genre scenes, such as those by Hiroshige. Walking through the streets of Antwerp, Vincent got the impression that he was seeing a "Japonaiserie": "I mean, the figures are always in action, one sees them in the queerest surroundings, everything fantastic, and at all moments interesting contrasts present themselves."[129] Here again it was movement that intrigued him.

At the Musée des Beaux-Arts, he admired the way Rubens managed to make the flesh of his female figures come alive. That naturally made him think of Delacroix: "What I admire so much in Delacroix, too, is that he makes us feel the life of things, and the expression, and the movement, that he absolutely dominates his colors."[130] Gradually his ideas took shape. He had to learn to draw, like Rubens and Delacroix, in masses instead of outlines, modeling figures entirely through color and thus giving them a life of their own—like the two blonde heads in Rubens' *Saint Theresa in Purgatory*—that transcended color.

Vincent realized that Rubens' palette was infinitely lighter than his own. He too began to use "white tinted with carmine, vermilion, yellow," as in the figure of the *Nurse* (F 174). But while he employed "white with carmine" for flesh, he refused to be tempted by "mother-of-pearl-like combinations" for his landscapes, as can be seen from *Le Quai* (F 211), which remains a harmony in gray.

Vincent worked feverishly. Besides his course at the Académie des Beaux-Arts, where he copied a number of plaster casts of classical sculptures—having overcome the aversion he had shown to this type of study during his lessons with his cousin Mauve—he joined two drawing "clubs," which enabled him to devote his evenings to life studies (forbidden in the official classes). Working at this pace, he learned very fast. "I find here," he declared with satisfaction, "the friction of ideas I want. I get a fresh look at my own work, can judge better where the weak points are, which enables me to correct them."[131]

A sketchbook in the van Gogh Museum in Amsterdam shows a new virtuosity in his line, which is applied like a brush stroke for a sketch, the similarity being enhanced still further by the use of colored crayons. In his fascination with expressing movement, he chose scenes from everyday life, such as a working-class dance in the boatmen's district (he himself was often taken for an Antwerp boatman) where two women carried away in the swirl of the waltz seem to float along without touching the ground.

◁ 59 *Nurse..* Antwerp, December 1885. Oil on canvas, 50 × 40 cm. F 174. Rijksmuseum Vincent van Gogh, Amsterdam.

60 *Le Quai.* Antwerp, December 1885. Oil on board, 20.5 × 27 cm. F 211. Rijksmuseum Vincent van Gogh, Amsterdam.

61   *Women Waltzing at the Dance Hall.* Antwerp, December 1885. Colored crayons, 9 × 16 cm. F 1350b. Rijksmuseum Vincent van Gogh, Amsterdam.

But incessant work and the habit of making do with a piece of bread instead of a meal took their toll, and he fell ill. In February 1886, he told Theo how exhausted he was : "Just think, I went to live in my own studio (in Nuenen) on 1 May and I have not had a hot dinner more than six or seven times since."[132] In his letters to his brother that February, he tried to arouse concern for his health, but though he mentioned gastric trouble and the loss of ten teeth, he said nothing about the syphilis he had contracted in a dockside brothel, though this rather than malnutrition was the chief cause of his ill health. His usual strategy when he was determined to get something out of his brother was to slip continual complaints of this kind in between innocent phrases, so that they stood out all the more. His aim this time was to get Theo to agree to a new proposal, which would be made cautiously at first, then repeated with dogged persistence in a cunning crescendo.

Vincent wanted to join his brother in Paris. In the last fifteen letters from Antwerp, he reverted to the subject no fewer than forty times. The pretext he gave never varied: to work in the studio of Fernand Cormon, an excellent teacher well known for his liberal views. The real reason was less "professional." He wanted to know the truth: Did Theo intend to stand up for his work, or didn't he? What better way of finding out than to go and see for himself?

Theo vainly turned a deaf ear to all this and tried to get him to wait, and with good reason: He was already having difficulty in persuading Boussod and Valadon, his employers, to allow Impressionist works to be shown in the basement of the gallery. He was afraid that the presence of his burdensome brother, with his eccentric ways and excitable nature, might destroy the fragile arrangement he had so far managed to contrive. Moreover, Vincent's proposal to come and live with him was not exactly welcome now that he had grown used to living on his own. Exasperated by Theo's final refusal, Vincent pretended not to understand and decided to force his hand: "I write you once more because at all events my time has almost come to an end, and I have to go back one of these days."

Chapter III   A New Palette

From Light to Color

Vincent presented Theo with a *fait accompli*. One fine morning in early March 1883, a messenger brought the latter a short penciled note: "My dear Theo, Do not be cross with me for having come all at once like this; I have thought about it so much, and I believe that in this way we shall save time. Shall be at the Louvre from midday on or sooner if you like. Please let me know at what time you could come to the Salle Carrée."[1] By arranging to meet his brother in the Salle Carrée at the Louvre, Vincent sought to emphasize the "professional" urgency of the step he was taking. Pending a more satisfactory arrangement, Theo invited him to share his modest apartment in Rue Laval (now Rue Victor-Massé), Montmartre, not far from Cormon's studio, where Vincent duly enrolled. By his own admission Vincent attended Cormon's for barely three months, but while he was there he met those fellow artists who may be said to constitute the "protest movement" against Impressionism, since they all criticized in one way or another the dissolution of form to which that concept of painting had ultimately led. Thus he came into contact with Emile Bernard, Toulouse-Lautrec, Signac, Anquetin, and Gauguin. At the same time, in the basement of the gallery managed by his brother, he had every opportunity of studying at his leisure the works of Monet, Degas, Seurat, and Pissarro. In a letter written (in English) to Levens, an English painter he had known in Antwerp, he remarks: "In Antwerp I did not even know what the impressionists were, now I have

seen them and though *not* being one of the club yet I have much admired certain impressionists' pictures—*Degas* nude figure—*Claude Monet* landscape."[2] At Cormon's studio Vincent continued the life studies and the copies of plaster casts of classical sculptures that had been interrupted at Antwerp. According to Emile Bernard, then aged nineteen, Vincent once aroused the mirth of his codisciples by painting the dark backcloth behind the model a bright color. He was not unduly upset, as he was used to this sort of reaction. But this incident drew Bernard and Van Gogh closer, and soon Vincent was part of the lively group from Cormon's studio who were always ready to sip an absinthe and have a chat at Le Tambourin, a café in the Boulevard de Clichy. This establishment owed its name to the fact that the tables were shaped like tambourines, as can be seen from Vincent's portrait of "La Segatori," the proprietress (F 381). In the background of this portrait, on the right-hand side, can be seen the outline of one of the Japanese prints that Vincent, who found them of great artistic interest, had pinned to the wall. It was in this café that Vincent arranged a group exhibition in the spring of 1887. From this time onwards, he signed his pictures with his first name alone, on the ground that anyone who was not Dutch would find "Van Gogh" difficult to pronounce. By so doing, he got rid of a name that had brought him nothing but bitterness —his father's name, of which he had shown himself unworthy. On leaving Cormon's, he devoted himself for a time almost exclusively to still lifes and landscapes in

94

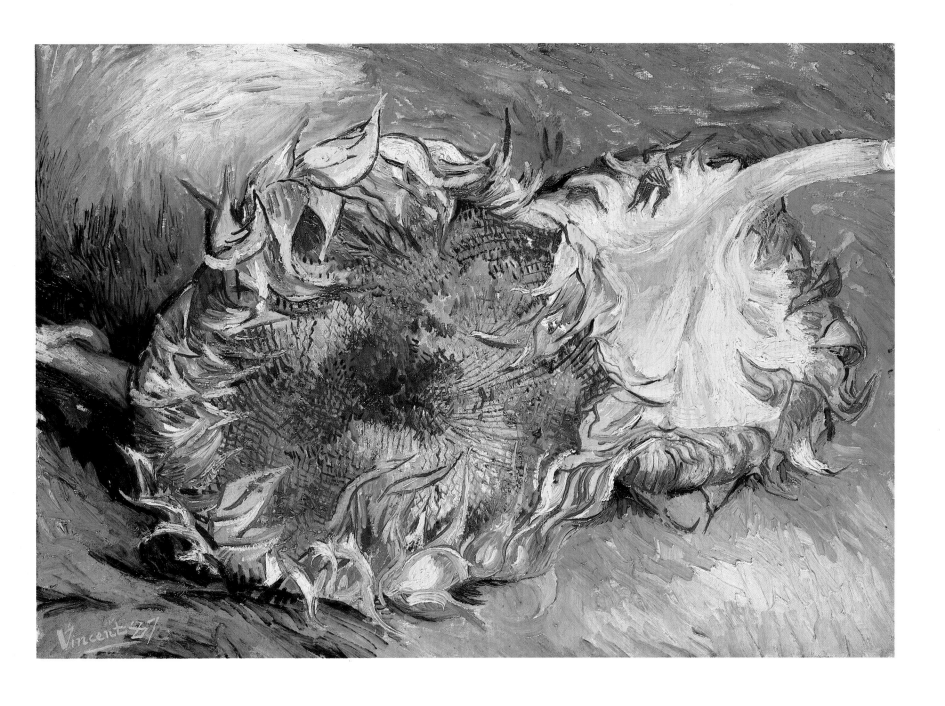

◁ 62 *Woman at Table at the Café Le Tambourin.* Paris, January–March 1887. Oil on canas, 55.5 × 46.5 cm. F 370. Rijksmuseum Vincent van Gogh, Amsterdam.

63 *Cut Sunflowers.* Paris, July–September 1887. Oil on canvas, 43 × 61 cm. F 375. The Metropolitan Museum of Art, New York (Rogers Fund, 1949).

64 *Nude Little Girl Seated.* Paris, April–June 1886. Black chalk, 30.5 × 23.5 cm. F 1367. Rijksmuseum Vincent van Gogh, Amsterdam.

65 *The Roofs of Paris.* Paris, April–June 1886. Oil on canvas, 38.5 × 61.5 cm. F 262. Kunstmuseum, Basle.

66 *Le Moulin de la Galette.* Paris, October–December
1886. Oil on canvas, 38.5 × 46 cm. F 227. Rijksmuseum
Kröller-Müller, Otterlo.

67 *The Hill of Montmartre.* Paris, October–December 1886. Oil on canvas, 36 × 61 cm. F 266. Rijksmuseum Kröller-Müller, Otterlo.

68 *La Guinguette* Paris, October–December 1886. Oil on
canvas, 49 × 64 cm. F 238. Musée d'Orsay, Paris.

69 *The Kingfisher.* Paris, October–December 1886. Oil on canvas, 19 × 26.5 cm. F 28. Rijksmuseum Vincent van Gogh, Amsterdam.

◁ 70 *Cineraria Plant.* Paris, July–September 1886. Oil on canvas, 54.5 × 46 cm. F 282. Museum Boymans-van Beuningen, Rotterdam.

71 *Self-Portrait.* Paris, October–December 1886. Oil on canvas, 39.5 × 29.5 cm. F 178 verso. Gemeentemuseum, The Hague.

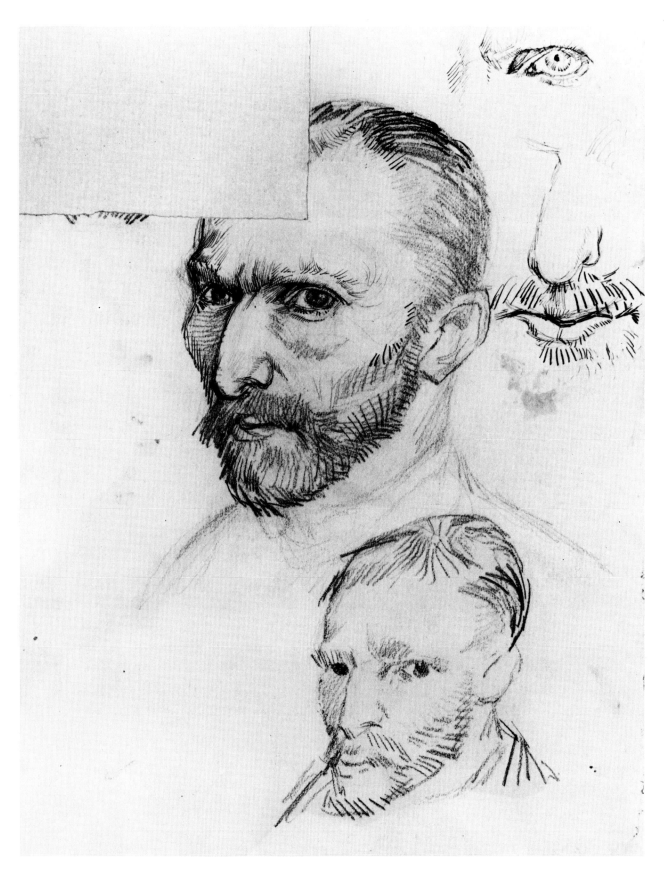

◁ 72 *Self-Portrait with a Gray Hat.* Paris, January–March 1887. Oil on cardboard, 41 × 32 cm. F 295. Stedelijk Museum, Amsterdam.

73 *Two Self-Portraits.* Paris, October–December 1886. Crayon and pen, 32 × 24 cm. F 1378 recto. Rijksmuseum Vincent van Gogh, Amsterdam.

74 *Self-Portrait.* Paris, April–June 1887. Oil on canvas, 41 × 33 cm. F 356. Rijksmuseum Vincent van Gogh, Amsterdam.

75 *Self-Portrait with a Straw Hat.* Paris, July–September ▷ 1887. Oil on cardboard, 41 × 33 cm. F 469. Rijksmuseum Vincent van Gogh, Amsterdam.

76 *Self-Portrait with a Gray Felt Hat.* Paris, winter 1887–
1888. Oil on canvas, 44 × 37.5 cm. F 344. Rijksmuseum Vincent van Gogh, Amsterdam.

77 *Self-Portrait of the Artist at Work.* Paris, winter 1887– ▷
1888. Oil on canvas, 65 × 50.5 cm. F 522. Rijksmuseum Vincent van Gogh, Amsterdam.

order to develop his handling of color. Through his new friends, he discovered the possibilities of a richer palette, and he progressively brightened his range of colors during the year 1886. The *Roofs of Paris* (F 262), a view from Montmartre, are treated in a gray monochrome, but, in the Dutch fashion, there is a good deal of white in the cloud-laden sky. The same applies to the *Moulin de la Galette* (F 227), seen from Rue Girardon, which is yellower in tone, but remains muted despite a very pale sky. The *Hill of Montmartre* (F 266) is more conventional in treatment, rather like the landscapes by painters of the school of The Hague, such as Maris and Mauve, with a color scheme in which green and yellow predominate. On the other hand, in *La Guinguette* (F 238), painted in the autumn, chiaroscuro is combined with Impressionist technique. Here Vincent drew with his brush, dared to insert some touches of bright color, and reintroduced the human figure, simply indicating it by means of little dabs under the arbor. Another example of this mixed technique is to be found in the *Kingfisher* (F 28). This little bird, free as the air and accordingly cherished by the painter, seems to have been the harbinger of his new lightness of touch.

The still lifes painted at this time show the same development in even more definite fashion, particularly the flower pieces. Vincent began a first series of them in May after leaving Cormon's studio, and went on with it until July. In his letter to Levens, he gave the reasons for his choice of subject: "And now for what regards what I myself have been doing, I have lacked money for paying models else I had entirely given myself to figure painting. But I have made a series of color studies in painting, simply flowers, red poppies, blue corn flowers and myosotis, white and rose roses, yellow chrysanthemums—seeking oppositions of blue with orange, red and green, yellow and violet seeking *les tons rompus et neutres* to harmonize brutal extremes. Trying to render intense color and not a grey harmony." This first series of flower pieces is characterized by lightness of touch and bold color contrasts, the effect recalling the bou-

quets of Monticelli, for whom Vincent always had a boundless admiration, rather than those of Renoir or Monet. It is in the second, more limited, series of flower pieces, painted in the summer and early autumn, that his style becomes more personal, even if the colors are not always very bright. The *Cineraria Plant* (F 282) can thus be grouped alongside *La Guinguette* for the way in which the brush strokes draw and model form, more or less ignoring "literal truth." The resultant lack of depth was not greatly appreciated, as is shown by a letter written by André Bonger to Theo, his future brother-in-law, in the summer of 1886. "Taken as a whole, the flowers are gay and colorful; but some of them are flat and I can't convince him of this. He always replies: 'But I wanted to introduce such and such a color contrast.' As if I cared what he wanted to do." This "flatness" of color was among the basic innovations that led over the next decade to a new pictorial language, of which Vincent (albeit posthumously) would be recognized as one of the originators.

During 1887, at the time of these decisive changes in his color range, Vincent produced a series of no less than twenty-two self-portraits. It was as though he felt a need to rediscover himself physically in order to compensate for the transformation of his artistic identity and measure its progress. Dr. Jan Hulsker has observed that, stylistically, these self-portraits fall into pairs, each having at least one variant. He was able to break them down into eight groups that make it possible to follow the evolution of the painter's style as well as that of his appearance.[a] *Self-Portrait* (F 178v), which probably dates from the end of 1886, retains the chiaroscuro of the *Potato Eaters*. On the other hand, the brushwork is "distinguished," as in a portrait by Fantin-Latour, and Vincent himself is dressed with a certain elegance. The preliminary drawing (F 1378) emphasizes the psychological aspect of the portrait. *Self-Portrait with a Gray Hat* (F 295) is still elegant, but the palette is considerably lighter with its delicate harmonies of blue and yellow. The brush strokes tend towards individualization, and the chiaroscuro has totally vanished. This technique is extended in the Pointillism of the background in *Self-Portrait* (F 356), executed in the spring, while the actual face, treated more conventionally, stands out against it. *Self-Portrait with a Straw Hat* (F 469), painted during the summer, expresses the latent peasant in Vincent. The background is sketched in by means of very widely spaced, comma-like strokes, while interwoven parallel strokes are used to model the face. It shows the influence of Emile Bernard and Anquetin, who had finally converted Vincent to the use of pure color and to Divisionist technique. *Self-Portrait with a Gray Felt Hat* (F 344) shows the mastery that Vincent had acquired in the practice of his new technique. This time, as in the works of his Neo-Impressionist friends, strokes of pure color are juxtaposed over the entire surface of the canvas, following the principle of color contrast with complementary blues and oranges. However, there is no question here of attaining the systematic regularity of a Seurat or a Signac. Rather, in its form, direction, and intensity, the brushwork is designed above all to enhance the expressive vitality of the portrait. Thus the dominant strips of blue, counterpointed by touches of orange, form a halo round the face of the artist, in which orange predominates and to which the contrast lends a compelling radiance.

Self-Portrait of the Artist at Work (F 522), dated 1888, was painted just before Van Gogh left for the south of France. From then on, the use of the chiaroscuro would be only a memory. The strokes of pure color express the vibration of light, and in fact constitute its equivalent. In this lay the significance of the new palette so boldly flaunted by Vincent, which prefigured that of the Fauvists at the beginning of the twentieth century. He echoed it in writing in a letter from Arles to his sister Wilhelmina [3]: "In the first place I want to emphasize the fact that one and the same person may furnish motifs for very different portraits. Here I give a conception of mine, which is the result of a portrait I painted in the mirror, and which is now in Theo's possession.

A pinkish-grey face with green eyes, ash-colored hair, wrinkles on the forehead and around the mouth, still, wooden, a very red beard, considerably neglected and mournful, but the lips are full, a blue peasant's blouse of coarse linen, and a palette with citron yellow, vermilion, malachite green, cobalt blue, in short all the colors on the palette except the orange beard, but only whole colors. The figure against a greyish-white wall." The description is followed by this explanation: "And you see—this, in my opinion, is the advantage that impressionism possesses over all the other things; it is not banal, and one seeks after a deeper resemblance than the photographers."

"In Color Seeking Life"

In another letter to Wilhelmina, written in the autumn of 1887, Vincent outlined his conception of art in an apparently lighthearted way. He was always inspired by the same principle: that of effectiveness. Painting in not a "gratuitous act," but consists of giving form to an idea. Two years earlier, at the time of the *Potato Eaters*, his painting had to "smell of bacon, smoke, potato steam," bearing witness to social conditions rather in the spirit of Courbet. Had not Courbet written in 1855, in the preface to the catalogue of his exhibition at the Pavillon in Avenue Montaigne, which was considered as the Realist "manifesto": "What I sought was knowledge, the knowledge that would enable me to interpret the customs, ideas, and appearance of my period as I see it, to be not only a painter but a man, in a word to create living art—that is my aim." During 1887, Vincent discovered that his new palette with its range of pure colors could be more expressive than the old one. To his sister he asserted that "what is required in art nowadays is something very much alive, very strong in color, very much intensified." And he added: "What I think of my own work is this —that the picture I did at Nuenen of those peasants eating potatoes is the best one after all. Only since

◁ 78 *Fritillaries.* Paris, April–June 1887. Oil on canvas, 73.5 × 60.5 cm. F 213. Musée d'Orsay, Paris.

79 *Bouquet of Daisies and Anemones.* Paris, July–September 1887. Oil on canvas, 61 × 38 cm. F 323. Rijksmuseum Kröller-Müller, Otterlo.

80 *Shoes.* Paris, April–June 1887. Oil on canvas, 34 × 41.5 cm. F 333. The Baltimore Museum of Art, Baltimore (Cone Collection).

81 *Still Life with Lemons and Carafe.* Paris, April–June ▷ 1887. Oil on canvas, 46 × 38 cm. F 340. Rijksmuseum Vincent van Gogh, Amsterdam.

82 *Plaster Statuette*. Paris, April–June 1886. Oil on canvas, 41 × 32.5 cm. F 216h. Rijksmuseum Vincent van Gogh, Amsterdam.

83 *Still Life with Plaster Statuette, a Rose, and Two Books of Novellas*. (*Bel-Ami* by Guy de Maupassant and *Germinie Lacerteux* by Jules and Edmond de Goncourt). Paris, winter 1887–1888. Oil on canvas, 55 × 46.5 cm. F 360. Rijksmuseum Kröller-Müller, Otterlo.

then I have lacked the opportunity to pick my models, but on the other hand I got the opportunity to study the question of colors. And when I find the right models for my figures later on, I hope to be able to show that I am after something different from little green landscapes and flowers.... And when I was painting landscapes at Asnières last summer, I saw more color in it than before."[4] Through this new approach, which—he believed—demonstrated a better understanding of life, since it sought to *imitate* it (in the highest sense), Vincent hoped to "attain a certain serenity."

"So as we said at the time: in *color* seeking *life* the true drawing is modelling with color," he wrote to Levens.[5] He attempted to apply this principle in some of the still lifes and landscapes he painted in 1887. Unlike the flower pieces (whose function was purely technical, since they were primarily exercises in the handling of color), these pictures allowed him to explore the expressive possibilities of his new palette by confronting the two most significant aspects of painting: the representation of the subject and the use of color. Vincent was well aware that in this approach to painting the balance was now shifting in the direction of color, which had so long been subservient to drawing. On the other hand, while he appreciated the expressive richness of the Impressionist palette by comparison with the gray tones of the school of The Hague, he was far from approving the use the Impressionists themselves made of it in most cases. In his opinion, they limited themselves to seeking luminous effects or colorful harmonies with purely decorative intent. Impressionist paintings seemed to him to be superficial insofar as they appeared largely to have lost the symbolic depth still to be found in the works of Courbet, Millet, and even Manet, without, however, departing from the illusionist depth of classical perspective. This explains his "resistance" to Impressionism, despite Theo's hints, until his arrival in Paris.

The still lifes of 1887 carry immense symbolic weight. In spirit they are irresistibly reminiscent of

Chardin, in that they depict certain everyday objects which by their extreme poverty make the presence of humanity felt all the more keenly. The *Shoes* (F 333) is a variation of a recurring theme of Vincent's, very close to that of potatoes (which these shoes resemble), and signifies the vital attachment of man to the soil. Harking back to the still lifes of the Nuenen period, the painting's chiaroscuro again reminds us that the artist was a draftsman and lithographer before he returned to painting. A cold light, sustained by a blue background, isolates the shoes with a starkness corresponding to the destitution of their wearer. Even the exposed nails on the upturned shoe allude very clearly to his spiky beard and character.

The *Still Life with Lemons and Carafe* (F 340), also painted that summer, is in quite a different vein. Here the use of chiaroscuro has been replaced by the Impressionist palette, with yellows and vermilions for the fruit and the patterns on the wallpaper, though these are cooled by the bluish green of the cloth. The contrast produces an effect of "white" and even light, which flattens the objects. This impression is enhanced by the parallel verticals of the decorative stripes on the wallpaper in the background, combined with the mural effect of the flat blue expanse of the tablecloth, which takes up almost half the picture surface. This approach is very similar to Cézanne's in his still lifes of the same period, both in the modesty of the means employed and in the defiance of illusionist perspective.

While *Cut Sunflowers* (F 375), painted during the summer, brings in the theme of vanity again, this is less important than the vigor of the sinuous brushwork that models the almost formless mass of the flowers. The contrast between the blue of the background and the yellow of the flowers adds to the morbidity of the overall effect, which is not unlike that produced by the still lifes with skulls painted by

84 *Portrait of Père Tanguy.* Paris, winter 1887–1888. Oil on canvas, 92 × 75 cm. F 363. Musée Rodin, Paris.

85 *Kitchen Gardens of Montmartre.* Paris, April–June 1887.
Oil on canvas, 43 × 80 cm. F 346. Rijksmuseum Vincent van
Gogh, Amsterdam.

86 *View from Vincent's Room, Rue Lepic.* Paris, April–June ▷
1887. Oil on canvas, 46 × 38 cm. F 341. Rijksmuseum Vincent
van Gogh, Amsterdam.

◁ 87 *Banks of the Seine* (detail). Paris, April–June 1887. Oil on canvas, 32 × 45.5 cm. F 293. Rijksmuseum Vincent van Gogh, Amsterdam (The whole picture is reproduced on p. 305).

88 *The Restaurant de la Sirène, Asnières.* Paris, April–June 1887. Oil on canvas, 57 × 68 cm. F 313. Musée d'Orsay, Paris.

89 *Cornfield*. Paris, April–June 1887. Oil on canvas, 54 × 64.5 cm. F 310. Rijksmuseum Vincent van Gogh, Amsterdam.

90 *Underwood.* Paris, July–September 1887. Oil on canvas, 46 × 55.5 cm. F 309a. Rijksmuseum Vincent van Gogh, Amsterdam.

Cézanne almost fifteen years later. We are also reminded of Cézanne in the *Still Life with Plaster Statuette, a Rose, and Two Books* (F 360) dating from the winter of 1887–1888. One of Cézanne's compositions, part of which very much resembles this still life, is again *later* (by some ten years) than Van Gogh's: this is the *Still Life with Plaster Cupid* (Courtauld Institute Galleries, London). In both cases, the plane in which the plaster statuette is placed crosses the picture surface vertically from one edge to the other, forsaking all the rules of illusionist perspective for the "plunging" approach of the Japanese. This "coincidence" shows that Vincent was one of the first Western painters who dared to adopt this approach in such a radical way, without the slightest decorative justification such as one finds in the *Portrait of Père Tanguy*, in which the background consists of Japanese prints.

While the still lifes imposed on Vincent a degree of constraint in their treatment, inducing a certain rigor in the brushwork relative to the form, the landscapes of 1887 allowed the painter much greater freedom. The brushwork is tentative and experimental, adopting in turn all the different techniques and styles flourishing in Paris at the time. In the fluid and delicate *Street Scene in Montmartre* (F 347) Vincent confined himself to acid watercolor tones with blending brush strokes. There is a timid attempt at Pointillism in *Kitchen Gardens of Montmartre* (F 346), where it is restricted to the gardens, to the exclusion of the sky. On the other hand, Pointillist brushwork is resolutely employed over the whole picture surface in —*View from Vincent's Room in Rue Lepic* (F 341).

The gardens of Montmartre with their fresh air made Vincent hanker after the country. The apartment at 54 Rue Lepic to which the two brothers had moved, though certainly bigger than the one in Rue de Laval, was nevertheless not very practical for painting, and this increased Vincent's longing to get out of the city. Ever an indefatigable walker, he went for long rambles in the countryside around Paris, often with his new friend Emile Bernard,

whom he had met at Cormon's. Bernard often invited him to paint at his parents' house in Asnières, where he had built a wooden hut in the garden as a studio. There they both did portraits of Père Tanguy and Vincent started one of Bernard. Then one day, after a row with Bernard's parents, Vincent stormed off with the two canvases, still wet, under his arm. Following Seurat's example, he frequented the Island of La Grande Jatte, sometimes going there with Signac. To memorize his impressions during the day, he would divide a canvas up into a number of compartments in which he could record things directly with his brush. Thus he had a rough outline of the different subjects encountered on his way.

Vincent's brushwork varied considerably in style from picture to picture. Not only was it sometimes Impressionist and sometimes Pointillist, but it would often deliberately diverge from the principles of both schools. Such changes could occur within a single picture. Thus *The Banks of the Seine* (F 293) employs three types of Impressionist brushwork: rectangular, parallel, and edge-to-edge strokes for the water; short, irregular strokes for the vegetation; and fluid, merging strokes for the sky. Much the same phenomenon may be seen in *Restaurant de la Sirène* (F 313), where the almost Pointillist brushwork used for the foliage of the climbing vine contrasts with the straight strokes used for the walls. In *Cornfield* (F 310), the style is Impressionist (apart from the monochrome sky, which is treated more broadly), but depth is impeded. Crossing the canvas from one side to the other, the earth, the wheat, and the sky become virtually three bands of color. Here Van Gogh was paving the way for an artistic equivalence of natural effects that diverges from Impressionism proper. Faced with a subject, he sought to convey the reality of what he saw and to bring out its main lines and its formal structure as simply as possible, choosing the type of brushwork most suited to his purpose. For example, the impression produced by *Underwood* (F 309a) is based on two main components: the foliage filtering the light, the dark line of the trunks traversing the foli-

91   *The Bridge at Asnière.* Paris, July–September 1887. Oil
on canvas, 52 × 65 cm. F 301. E.G. Bührle Collection, Zurich.

age. For the first, the painter chose a counterpoint of short, Pointillist brush strokes, and for the second a thin, continuous line. This structural contrast is enhanced by the colors: the dominant mauve of the trunks cuts across the complementary yellow-green of the foliage.

91 At first sight *Bridge at Asnières* (F 301) seems to adhere faithfully to Impressionist technique. But one need only compare this painting with that on the same subject by Vincent's friend Emile Bernard, who chose the same viewpoint, to appreciate the difference between the two painters. This time, the distinguishing feature is not the brushwork, which is regular and uniform, but the intensity of the color contrasts. Here Vincent pushed the opposition of complementary oranges and blues to the point of frenzy, going beyond Monet's daring *Regatta at Argenteuil* in the use of pure color—witness the scarlet blob of the umbrella—and already anticipating the first Fauvist paintings of Braque and Derain.

92 The Pointillism of *Restaurant Interior* (F 342), however well done, was not handled by Vincent as it would have been by Seurat or Signac. For them, the "dot" was the basic component of a whole pictorial system, whereas Vincent used it only when he needed to convey a particular effect of light. Here, for example, he deployed it on the walls and the floor to give the whole space the same brilliance as the bunches of flowers and the yellow chairs. The resultant surface effect contrasts with the perspective introduced by the tables. However, the Pointillist brushwork stops short at the contours of the objects and at the edges of the doors and the picture on the wall. This decorative adaptation of Seurat's technique, suggesting the patterns on wallpaper, anticipates the *tapisserie* effect of Vuillard's *Interiors*, executed a few years later.

While for Vincent these still lifes and landscapes were primarily stylistic exercises in which he tried out his new palette of pure colors, some of his portraits carried experimentation much further, to the extent of radically upsetting the Impressionist concepts of pictorial space. The various stages of this development can be seen in four portraits he did of women. *Portrait of a Woman in Blue* (F 207 a) is still 96 so much imbued with the spirit of Rubens that Tralbaut had no hesitation in placing it chronologically in the Antwerp period and dating it December 1885. Hulsker puts it forward to January or February 1887. I personally agree with De La Faille's catalogue in plumping for the summer of 1886. All "Ecce Homo"-like expression has disappeared from the sitter's face, although it is still to be found in *Woman of the People* (F 206) and the *Portrait of a Woman* (F 207 a) about which Vincent used the phrase just quoted.[5] Moreover, he appears to allude to the portrait in the letter to Levens, having first emphasized that he had not been doing much figure painting as he had not enough money for models, but just flower pieces, which he considered as exercises: "Now, after these gymnastics I lately did two heads which I dare say are better in light and color than those I did before." The liveliness of the modeling (in a style that is not yet Impressionist) and the sitter's expression of radiant serenity are particulary eloquent evidence that this is one of the portraits in question.[b]

Portrait of a *Woman Seated beside a Cradle* (F 369) 93 is undoubtedly inspired by a picture by Berthe Morisot which is now in the Musée d'Orsay. However, Vincent has placed the emphasis on the sitter, relegating the cradle to the right-hand side. While preserving the artist's individuality, the effect of grace and delicacy and the subtlety of the relationship between the pink ribbon of the woman and the blue ribbon tied to the cradle, combined with the distinction of the fine brushwork, make the picture a worthy rival to the work of the Impressionists on their own ground.

A comparison between the two portraits of La Segatori, with whom Vincent had an affair, eloquently demonstrates his boldness as an artist. The first, usually known as *Woman at Le Tambourin* 62 (F 370), dates from the beginning of 1887. The technique is Impressionist, but the background is treated in "Japanese" fashion, that is divided into parallel

92 *Restaurant Interior.* Paris, April–June 1887. Oil on canvas, 45.5 × 56.5 cm. F 342. Rijksmuseum Kröller-Müller, Otterlo.

133

93   *Woman Seated beside a Cradle.* Paris, January–March 1887. 61 × 46 cm. F 369. Rijksmuseum Vincent van Gogh, Amsterdam.

94   *Italian Woman* (La Segatori). Paris, winter 1887–1888. ▷ Oil on canvas, 81 × 60 cm. F 381. Musée d'Orsay, Paris.

95 *Gypsy Camp.* Arles, August 1888. Oil on canvas, 45 × 51
cm. F 445. Musée d'Orsay, Paris.

bands that undoubtedly represent the Japanese prints fixed to the wall by Vincent. This type of composition is repeated in more radical form in the *Portrait of Père Tanguy*, a small tradesman dealing in artists' colors, who readily extended credit to young painters. The background is made up of Japanese prints arranged vertically in three parallel lines, forming a patchwork of flat colors. This produces an odd effect rather like that of an icon, conferring on Père Tanguy—who richly deserved it—a sort of sainthood. Vincent had copied the cover of *Paris Illustré* for May 1886, a portrait of an actor by Eisen (right) and prints by Hiroshige (plum blossom), Toyokuni III, and Hokusai (left). These prints came mainly from the gallery Samuel Bing had opened a few years earlier at 22 Rue de Provence. They also aroused the enthusiasm of Toulouse-Lautrec, Emile Bernard, and Anquetin, all of whom like Van Gogh deplored the excesses of Pointillism.

However, Van Gogh was the first of them to adopt the style of the Japanese print for a portrait—that of *La Segatori* (F 381), painted in the last few months before his departure from Paris. Its resemblance to the earlier portrait is certainly not very marked. The folk costume has much to do with this. With its geometrical patterns in pure color, which flatten the sitter against the level expanse of golden yellow that forms the background, it is to some extent the painterly *equivalent* of the stage costume of a Japanese actor as generally depicted in the prints. Unbroken contour lines detach the sitter from the background and separate the different parts of the costume in the manner of the print from *Paris Illustré*. Emile Bernard and Anquetin, close friends of Vincent's, must certainly have been particularly impressed by this first Cloisonnist painting.

That Van Gogh had a direct influence on Bernard and Anquetin seems indisputable, even though it has largely gone unnoticed. Vincent definitely completed the portrait with the yellow background in December 1887 and it was on 19 May 1888 that Edouard Dujardin hailed Anquetin's new

Cloisonnist style in the *Revue Indépendante*. As for Emile Bernard, he painted *Breton Women in a Green Field* (Musée Maurice Denis, Saint-Germain-en-Laye) in the spring of 1888 and showed it to Gauguin that summer. Fired with enthusiasm, Gauguin in turn painted *Vision after the Sermon* (National Gallery of Scotland, Edinburgh) and took Bernard's picture to Arles to show it to Vincent. The latter does not seem to have been aware of the part he had just played in developing the new "Synthetist" art, nor was Gauguin, since he gave the credit to Emile Bernard. We shall see later the extent to which Gauguin gradually became aware of it after his stay in Arles. In the meantime, Vincent's reaction upon receiving the self-portraits sent by Gauguin and Bernard from Pont-Aven at the beginning of October showed that he did not feel he was lagging behind them. On the contrary: "I have just received the portrait of Gauguin by himself and the portrait of Bernard by Bernard, and in the background of the portrait of Gauguin there is Bernard's on the wall and vice versa. The Gauguin is of course remarkable, but I very much like Bernard's picture. It is just the inner vision of a painter, a few abrupt tones, a few dark lines, but it has the distinction of a real, real Manet. The Gauguin is more studied, carried further. That, along with what he says in his letter, gave me absolutely the impression of its representing a prisoner. Not a shadow of gaiety. Absolutely nothing of the flesh, but one can confidently put that down to his determination to make a melancholy effect, the flesh in the shadows has gone a dismal blue. So now at last I have a chance to compare my painting with what the comrades are doing."[6]

A peasant in Nuenen, a boatman in Antwerp, and now a painter in Paris, Vincent gladly let himself be led astray by his friends of the "Little Boulevard,"[c] who recognized him as one of themselves. From the Bataille Restaurant in Rue des Abbesses, where he often dined with Theo, the group had migrated to the Tambourin, 62 Boulevard de Clichy, a café where there was sometimes a cabaret in the eve-

94

96 *Portrait of a Woman in Blue.* Paris, January–March 1887. Oil on canvas, 46 × 38 cm. F 207a. Rijksmuseum Vincent van Gogh, Amsterdam.

97 *Still Life with Absinthe.* Paris, April–June 1887. Oil on ▷ canvas, 46.5 × 33 cm. F 339. Rijksmuseum Vincent van Gogh, Amsterdam.

ning. There Vincent had developed a taste for absinthe, a drink forbidden today because it provokes psychotic behavior. He had also developed a taste for the manageress, Agostina Segatori, who from time to time used to dance on the table in colorful costume and who found him charmingly naive. He confided in his sister Wilhelmina as follows: "As far as I myself am concerned, I still go on having the most impossible, and not very seemly, love affairs, from which I emerge as a rule damaged and shamed and little else." He lost his temper easily and sometimes even turned on Theo, accusing him of being too timid to impose his artistic choices on Messrs. Boussod and Valadon. The increasingly frequent scenes between the two brothers were indirectly encouraged by Vincent's friends, who never stopped pestering him to put in a word for them with his brother. Theo suffered greatly as a result. He tried to be patient, but his nerves began to give way. André Bonger, his future brother-in-law, even reports a seizure that left him paralyzed for several hours. Finally, he wrote to Wilhelmina: "Life is almost unbearable. Nobody comes to see me any more as Vincent is always picking quarrels. On top of that, he is so untidy that our apartment is anything but agreeable. I hope he will go off and live somewhere on his own."[d]

Vincent himself was worn out by all this agitation. He felt a deep need for the calming influence of nature, for long rambles in the country. He longed for new landscapes where the sun would shine more brightly than it did in Paris. In the sum-mer of 1886, he had already revealed his plans: "In spring—say February or even sooner I may be going to the South of France, the land of the *blue* tones and gay colors," he wrote to Levens. He also told Wilhelmina of his plans: "It is my intention as soon as possible to go temporarily to the South, where there is even more color, even more sun." One fine day, with the complicity of Emile Bernard, Van Gogh left Paris without warning, just as he had come. Setting out at dawn on 20 February 1888, he arrived in Arles the same evening.

Van Gogh's biographers have often wondered why he chose Arles. It has been suggested that it was on the advice of Toulouse-Lautrec, the scion of an aristocratic family from the South of France. This is possible. The Lautrec family, however came from Albi in the heart of Languedoc, whereas Arles is in Provence. My own theory I find attractive, if unprovable: Could it not have been his mistress, La Segatori, who commended the area to him? In the Japanese-style portrait of which she is almost certainly the subject, her costume is very like that worn by the Gypsies of the time. Might not this "Italian" woman have had something of the Bohemian in her? In that case, when her lover told her he would like to go to a more southerly clime, she might well have told him about Arles and about Saintes-Maries-de-la-Mer, to which Gypsies from all parts of the world make an annual pilgrimage to venerate the relics of Marie Jacobé, Salomé, and Sara. In fact, Vincent often went to paint at Saintes-Maries, where his subjects included a *Gypsy Camp* (F 445).

Chapter IV Between Africa and Japan

First Cloisonnist Experiments

Vincent came to Provence in the depths of winter. In his first letter to Theo, written on the day after his arrival, he said: "And now I'll begin by telling you that there's about two feet of snow everywhere, and more is still falling."[1] But it was nothing like winter in the North. He had gone in the hope of finding a country that already had the flavor of Africa—that quality so dear to Delacroix—and a world of Japanese prints like the ones he had seen at Bing's. He was not disappointed: "And the landscapes in the snow, with the summits white against a sky as luminous as the snow, were just like the winter landscapes the Japanese have painted,"[2] he enthused. This reality wholly justified the use of the Impressionist palette, as he explained to Wilhelmina: "You will understand that nature in the South cannot be painted with the palette of Mauve, for instance, who belongs to the North, and who is, and will remain, a master of the gray. But at present the palette is distinctly colorful, sky blue, orange, pink, vermilion, bright yellow, bright green, bright wine-red, violet. But by intensifying *all* the colors one arrives once again at quietude and harmony. There occurs in nature something similar to what happens in Wagner's music, which, though played by a big orchestra, is nonetheless intimate. Only when making a choice one prefers sunny and colorful effects, and there is nothing that prevents me from thinking that in the future many painters will go and work in tropical countries."[3]

Vincent was now profoundly certain that he was on the right track. His Parisian experiments had shown him that the Impressionist palette, made up of pure colors, enabled painting to become a language in its own right, abstract like music, and capable of fully defining its subject. He realized that, far from being based on fancy, this palette actually had as powerful—if not more powerful—a potential for expression as the chiaroscuro of his earlier Nuenen days. In short, it was a question of his choosing the direction in which Delacroix had led rather than that of Rembrandt, although in fact the two were not mutually contradictory.

Contact with the avant-garde artists convinced him of the truth of his inmost beliefs, which, until then, had not found any echo anywhere. In 1886 and 1887 the works of Gauguin, Emile Bernard, Anquetin or Laval were no more advanced than his. Indeed, the opposite was true. Without being really conscious of it, he had been able to show them the way by daring to paint the portrait of a woman directly on a yellow background, a completely abstract patch of color, in the manner of the Japanese prints.

Vincent took board and lodgings at the Hotel Carrel, 30 Rue de la Cavalerie, in Arles. His room was in the attic story, with a dormer window from which he had a poetic view of the old roofs with their Roman tiles, which he enjoyed drawing. Without delay, he immediately went to work on the neighboring *Charcuterie* (Pork Butcher's) (F 389), 98 outlining directly with his brush in pure colors laid

98 *The Pork Butcher's* (La Charcuterie). Arles, February 1888. Oil on canvas pasted on cardboard, 39.5 × 32.5 cm. F 389. Rijksmuseum Vincent van Gogh, Amsterdam.

99 *Peach Trees in Blossom; "Souvenir de Mauve."* Arles, ▷ March 1888. Oil on canvas, 73 × 59.5 cm. F 394. Rijksmuseum Kröller-Müller, Otterlo.

Souvenir de Mauve
Vincent

down in vertical stripes. This little study on board-canvas is already a Fauvist work before its time, with its contrasts of complementary colors and colors whose vividness is carried to maximum intensity. It is reminiscent of Matisse's *Fenêtres* (Windows). Full of ardor, Vincent took long walks through the countryside. The almond trees were already in bloom, and soon the peach and cherry blossom would be out too. In a letter to Emile Bernard he revealed the feverish enthusiasm that kept him glued to his workplace: "At the moment I am absorbed in the blooming fruit trees, pink peach trees, yellow-white pear trees. My brush stroke has no system at all. I hit the canvas with irregular touches of the brush, which I leave as they are. Patches of thickly laid-on color, spots of canvas left uncovered, here and there portions that are left absolutely unfinished, repetitions, savageries; in short, I am inclined to think that the result is so disquieting and irritating as to be a godsend to those people who have fixed preconceived ideas about technique."[4]

When he had finished a size 20 canvas—"probably the best landscape I've ever done," he wrote to Theo—Wilhelmina sent him an obituary notice on his cousin Mauve, who, he knew, had died on 8 February. He added, "Something—I don't know what—took hold of me and brought a lump to my throat, and I wrote on my picture

99

SOUVENIR DE MAUVE
VINCENT THEO"[5]

Yet the canvas bears only his own signature (F 394). It is likely, as J. Hulsker thinks, that Vincent himself erased Theo's name at his brother's request.

100   Although the *Bridge at Langlois* (F 397) is regarded as one of the most successful works of the Arles period because of the radiant atmosphere evoked 101   by its vibrant colors, it was really the orchard series that gave Vincent his first opportunity to apply the aesthetic principles he'd evolved in Paris on the basis of the Japanese prints. He laid down the broad outlines very clearly to Emile Bernard in the aforementioned letter: "Working directly on the spot all the time, I try to grasp what is essential in the drawing—later I fill in the spaces which are bounded by contours—either expressed or not, but in any case *felt*—with tones which are also simplified, by which I mean that all that is going to be soil will share the same violet-like tone, that the whole sky will have a blue tint, that the green vegetation will be either green-blue or green-yellow, purposely exaggerating the yellows and blues in this case. In short, my dear comrade, in no case an eye-deceiving job." This letter, dated April 1888, bears out what I have said above about the primordial importance of the role Vincent played at the start of the Cloisonnist technique. In fact, it was not until August that Emile Bernard went to Pont-Aven to join Gauguin, who was then applying the same principles in his turn. Vincent's use, from spring 1888, of the continuous outline is also perfectly obvious in the *Cornfield with Irises* (F 409), with its flattened tree trunks and, in the foreground, the irises which are almost reduced to the decorative motif of an embroidered border; while the expanse of the corn and the blue-gray of the sky form two vast patches of color. Thus the whole composition tends to disintegrate into superimposed surfaces separated from one another by large horizontal areas, the gentle slant of the bed of irises paralleled by a line of mixed green-orange brush strokes above, which introduce the plunging perspective typical of Japanese art. No sooner had the picture been finished than Vincent wanted to redo it, as he wrote to Theo: "I'd like to do this study again, for the subject was very beautiful, and I had some trouble getting the composition. A little town is surrounded by fields all covered with yellow and purple flowers; exactly--can't you see it?—like a Japanese dream."[6]

102

Expressing the Essence

While walking along the plateau that held the ruins of the Abbey of Montmajour, Vincent thought of the prophesy Corot had made shortly before his death: "Last night in a dream I saw landscapes with skies

100 *The Bridge at Langlois.* Arles, March 1888. Oil on canvas, 54 × 65 cm. F 397. Rijksmuseum Kröller-Müller, Otterlo.

101 *Orchard in Bloom with the View of Arles* (detail). Arles, April 1889. Oil on canvas, 50.5 × 65 cm. F 515. Rijksmuseum Vincent van Gogh, Amsterdam (The whole picture is reproduced on p. 306).

102 *Cornfield with Irises*. Arles, May 1888. Oil on canvas, 54 × 65 cm. F 409. Rijksmuseum Vincent van Gogh, Amsterdam.

103   *Sunset.* Arles, June 1888. Oil on canvas, 74 × 91 cm.
F 465. Kunstmuseum, Winterthur.

104 *Market Gardens.* Arles, June 1888. Oil on canvas,
72.5 × 92 cm. F 412. Rijksmuseum Vincent van Gogh,
Amsterdam.

all pink, well, haven't they come, those skies all pink, and yellow and green into the bargain, in the impressionist landscapes?"[7] The vision he had on the heights of Montmajour while looking across the countryside went even further. Local color had disappeared definitively, to be replaced by other deep, flat colors, as in Hokusai's landscapes: "Odd, but one evening recently at Montmajour I saw a red sunset, its rays falling on the trunks and foliage of pines growing among a jumble of rocks, coloring the trunks and foliage with orange fire, while the other pines in the distance stood out in Prussian blue against a sky of tender blue-green, cerulean."[8] He felt that the sun could transform Michels and Jules Duprés into Claude Monet, at least! This was the idea behind *Market Gardens* (F 412). Thus he wrote to Theo: "I am working on a new subject, fields green and yellow as far as the eye can reach. I have already drawn it twice, and I am starting it again as a painting; it is exactly like a Salomon Koninck—you know, the pupil of Rembrandt who painted vast level plains."[9] He was dazzled by the result. "Everywhere now there is old gold, bronze, copper, one might say, and this with the green azure of the sky blanched with heat: a delicious color, extraordinarily harmonious, with the blended tones of Delacroix."[10]

When he was securing his easel so that it would not be blown away by the mistral, he thought of the

104

105

◁ 105　*Farmers Working in the Fields.* Arles, April 1888. Reed, 26 × 34.5 cm. F 1090. Rijksmuseum Vincent van Gogh, Amsterdam.

106　*Haystacks.* Arles, June 1888. Oil on canvas, 73 × 92.5 cm. F 425. Rijksmuseum Kröller-Müller, Otterlo.

balance and simplicity of Cézanne's landscapes, proof against the striving for effect generally so much sought after by artists, and exhaling the very essence of form. He felt that his own landscape was close to that "essential" character, as he told Theo: "You will see, however, that there is no attempt at effect. At first sight it is like a map, a strategic plan as far as the *execution* goes." It was precisely this absence of effect that made his paintings so effective. "I went for a walk there with someone else who was *not a painter,* and when I said to him, 'Look, to me that is as beautiful and as infinite as the sea,' he said—and he knows the sea—'For my part I like this *better* than the sea, because it is no less infinite, and yet you feel that it is *inhabited.*'"[11]

Vincent was greatly struck by this remark. "You feel that it is inhabited," is something different from simply "it is inhabited." This meant that, to sense the presence of a human figure, it was not necessary actually to see it in a landscape, but that the view of the colors as determined by the subject was enough. It was not the small figures shown in the picture in the manner of Corot, for instance, that enlivened the landscape, but simply the arrangement of areas

152

◁ 107 *Sower at Sunset*. Arles, August 1888. Reed, 24.5 × 32 cm. F 1441. Rijksmuseum Vincent van Gogh, Amsterdam.

108 *Sower at Sunset*. Arles, June 1888. Oil on canvas, 64 × 80.5 cm. F 422. Rijksmuseum Kröller-Müller, Otterlo.

of color and their contrasts. Vincent found confirmation of this soon afterwards when he did the *Sower* (F 422). This subject—one of the leitmotifs of his work—enabled him to put to full use the pictorial skills he had acquired since the Nuenen period three years previously. He described this to Emile Bernard: "Here is a sketch of a sower: large plowed field with clods of earth, for the most part frankly violet. A field of ripe wheat, yellow ocher in tone with a little carmine. The sky, chrome yellow, almost as bright as the sun itself, which is chrome yellow No. 1 with a little white, whereas the rest of the sky is chrome yellow Nos. 1 and 2 mixed. So very yellow. The Sower's shirt is blue and his trousers white. Size 25 canvas, square. There are many hints of yellow in the soil, neutral tones resulting from mixing violet with yellow; but I have played hell somewhat with the truthfulness of the colors.... The picture is divided in half; one half, the upper part, is yellow; the lower part is violet. Well, the white trousers allow the eye to rest and distract it at the moment when the excessive simultaneous contrast of yellow and violet would irritate it."[12] Vincent gave the same description to Theo, but in fact the sower's trousers are not white but mauve, so that they blend almost wholly into the field. The picture had been reworked, as he explained subsequently. The original subject, the sower, became "transparent" through the contrast of the two surfaces colored with complementary dominant colors, the yellow-green of the sky and the violet-orange of the field. This phenomenon of the "hidden presence" of the figure is somewhat reminiscent of the way the weaver is concealed by his loom and yet "quartered" by it in the four corners of the picture. Here, as Vincent explained to his brother, "You can tell from the simple mentioning of the tones that it's a composition in which color plays a very important part." And it was not by chance that he added a few phrases later, "And so I am almost afraid of it."[13] For the mauve surface of the tilled field occupies more than three-quarters of the space, like a huge shadow cast over the earth. The yellow-violet contrast, in that propor-

tion, is a color transposition of the chiaroscuro in which the peasant must resign himself to live. The *Sower*, by Vincent's own admission, is a failure *as regards the figure* because it is an accessory of the color, which monopolizes all the expressive potential of the picture.

The *Sower* is a fundamental study because it endeavors to define the elements and the means of that transposition. Vincent outlined the problem to Theo: "This is the point. The 'Christ in the Boat' by Eugène Delacroix and Millet's 'The Sower' are absolutely different in execution. The 'Christ in the Boat'—I am speaking of the sketch in blue and green with touches of violet, red and a little citron-yellow for the nimbus, the halo—speaks a symbolic language through color alone. Millet's 'Sower' is a colorless *gray*, like Israëls's pictures. Now, could you paint the Sower in color, with a simultaneous contrast of, for instance, yellow and violet (like the Apollo ceiling of Delacroix's *which is just that, yellow and violet*), yes or no? Why, *yes*. Well, do it then. Yes, that is what old Martin said, 'The masterpiece is up to you.' But try it, and you tumble into a regular metaphysical philosophy of color à la Monticelli, a mess that is damnably difficult to get out of with honor."[14]

The *Sower* occupies a key place in Vincent's work, and he referred to it several times in the course of the correspondence. It was at this point that his painterly balance swung from the world of values to a realm of color, into which he penetrated daily a little more deeply from then on. At that point, the linear perspective became flattened, thrown on to the surface of the canvas, but in parallels, *simplified*; whereas the figure, reduced to a silhouette, faded away discreetly, and then the three black crows appeared, the first heralds of a dark destiny.

Precursor of the Fauvists

In Paris, Vincent had been chiefly preoccupied with his palette and had rather neglected his drawing. He went back to drawing with full vigor in Provence, but in a completely different spirit from that he had felt at Nuenen. In the manner of a Japanese landscapist, he brought out the essential lines of a view he observed by concentrating on the contrasts. The heights of Montmajour with their rugged relief and the ruins of the abbey provided a wealth of views composed of knotty pines and rocky ridges. Trying

the technique of the Oriental masters, he even replaced his pen with a sharpened reed, which enabled him to obtain a broader line. Towards mid-June, in taking leave of a compatriot who was making a short stay with his brother, he wrote: "I have just finished a drawing, even larger than the first two, of a cluster of straight pines on a rock, seen from the top of a hill. Behind this foreground a perspective of meadows, a road with poplars, and in the far distance the town. The trees very dark against the sunlit meadow; perhaps you will get an opportuni-

109   *Rocks.* Arles, July 1888. Crayon, pen, and reed, 49 × 60 cm. F 1447. Rijksmuseum Vincent van Gogh, Amsterdam.

109

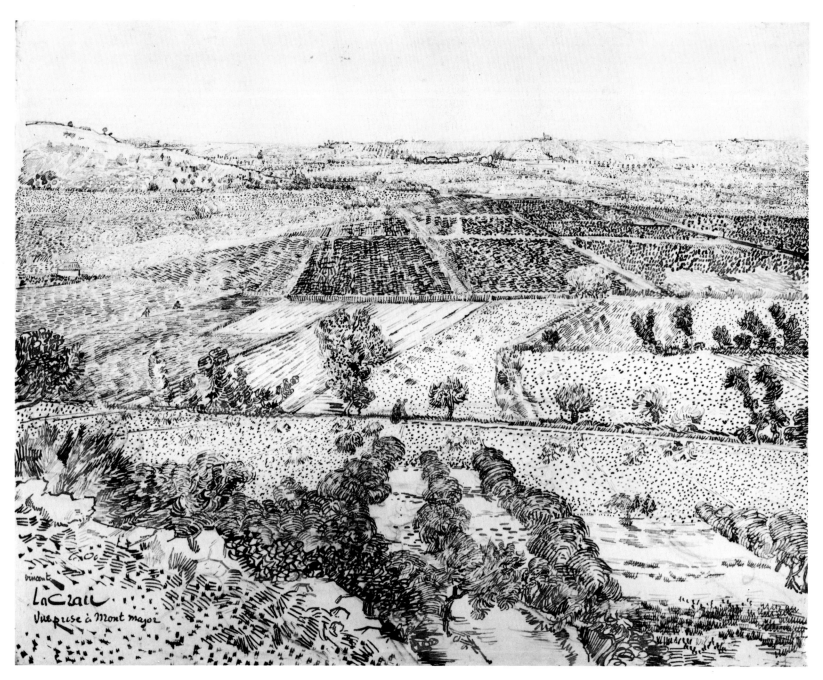

110 *The Plaine de la Crau, Seen from Montmajour.* Arles, July 1888. Black chalk, pen, and red, 49 × 61 cm. F 1420. Rijksmuseum Vincent van Gogh, Amsterdam.

111 *Flower Garden* (detail). Arles, July 1888. Oil on canvas, 72 × 91 cm. F 429. Gemeentemuseum, The Hague (The whole picture is reproduced on p. 305).

ty to see this drawing. I did them with very thick reeds on thin Whatman paper, and in the background I worked with a quill for the finer strokes."[15] Talking about another drawing of the Plain of La Crau, he told Emile Bernard: "It does not have a Japanese look, and yet it is really the most Japanese thing I have done; a microscopic figure of a laborer, a little train running across the wheat field—this is all the animation there is in it."[16] The landscape (F 1420), with a similar composition, shows the extent to which the drawing responded perfectly to this idea, not only in its arrangement as described above but also in its technique. This drawing is not really a sketch but a finished work, executed, be-

156

neath its apparent simplicity, by a variety of sophisticated means: black chalk, pen, reed, black Indian ink, and sepia. Moreover, its muliplicity of means is echoed by its great diversity of line. Each section of the landscape has a specific kind of line adapted to its own character, but chosen also as a contrast to its neighboring sections, as, for instance, the Pointillistic cottages and the parallel curves that form the leaves of the trees. The lines thus also have a pictorial quality resembling brush strokes of color. This plastic equivalence is even more obvious in the drawing Vincent executed after his

painted studies. Thus his *Sailboats* (F 1430b), now in the Pushkin Museum in Moscow, done with a sharpened reed, has a type of line chosen according to pictorial criteria (brush strokes, contrasts) used for paintings.

The same might be said of the *Sower* (F 1441), which takes us back straight to the painting (F 422) we discussed previously, although some of the de-

112

112 *Sailboats at Saintes-Maries*. Arles, August 1888. Reed, 24 × 31,5 cm. F 1430b. Musée d'Art Moderne, Brussels.

113 *Maisons de gardians at Saintes-Maries.* Arles, June 1888. Crayon and reed, 30 × 47 cm. F 1438. Rijksmuseum Vincent van Gogh, Amsterdam.

tails are missing, such as the three crows and the group of houses on the left. This difference between the study painted in June and the drawing executed two months later helps to clarify the idea underlying the latter. By means of the various forms and combinations it uses, the line endeavors to follow the workings of a pictorial brush stroke as closely as possible. Thus we can see that the layout of the mauve strokes in more or less parallel hatchings, or by contrast in fan-form in the foreground, has been followed faithfully in the drawing. Similarly, the dots of the sky or of the upper border of the corn in the *Sower* are mirrored in the pointil-

lism of the line in the drawing. This transcription is characterized by a certain number of constant factors, which constitute a system, as they persist from one drawing to the next—for instance, the combination of five parallel hatchings following an independent direction. This pictorial style was gradually to exert a reciprocal influence on Vincent's painting, making his color stroke increasingly individual until it came to resemble a pen line.

The *Flower Garden* (F 429) is an outstanding example of this development. The brush stroke is systematic, with a certain number of variants that create a stratified layout of colors in the aesthetic style of a Japanese print. Without creating true flat areas, the brush strokes nevertheless determine the planes by colors which are superimposed through the contrasts between adjoining sections. Embodying both

111

drawing and color, the stroke here has become a *symbol* heralding the kind of "pure art" Matisse defined twenty years later. "I cannot copy nature servilely as I have to interpret it and subordinate it to the spirit of the picture. When all my tone relations are achieved, this should create a harmony of living colors similar to the harmony of a musical composition."[a] In a letter to Wilhelmina,[17] Vincent enumerated the flowers that were growing in the garden, for she would not be able to recognize them in the picture. And yet, he explained, reality had been respected, the reality of the visual impression: "Oh, I know very well that not a single flower is drawn completely, that they are mere dabs of color, red, yellow, orange, green, blue, violet, but the impression of all these colors in their juxtaposition is there all right, in the painting as in nature." For this process of simplification, in which color changed form into symbol, could only be justified, in Vincent's view, if it respected reality. In this, his views would always differ from those of Gauguin, who stated: "Art is an abstraction; derive this abstraction from nature while dreaming before it."[b] Reality of what is *seen* on the one hand, but also reality of individual expression—not of dream—is called "suggestive color" and derives from Delacroix and Monticelli. We shall study its characteristics in the portraits.

For Vincent, drawing was also the means of assessing the progress of his work from day to day, a sort of diary to which the letters form the literary portion. From the very start of the correspondence, many of the letters were accompanied by drawings, and sometimes the drawing takes the actual place of writing as a result of some "distraction," as in the letter to Russell[c]: "Well, instead of continuing the letter I began to draw on the very paper the head of the dirty little girl I saw this afternoon whilst I was

114 *View of Saintes-Maries-de-la-Mer.* June 1888. Oil on canvas, 64 × 35 cm. F 416. Rijksmuseum Kröller-Müller, Otterlo.

painting a view of the river with a greenish yellow sky."[18]

Writing, drawing, painting: Vincent was constantly changing from one to the other without noticing, for to him they seemed inextricably linked. In the same letter he remarked, "I spend my time in painting or drawing landscapes or rather studies of color." He saw painting as a continuation of drawing, as he explained to Theo: "Tomorrow I am going to draw, until the paints come. But I have deliberately arrived at the point where I will not draw a picture with charcoal. That's no use, you must attack drawing with the color itself in order to draw well."[19]

Vincent felt that a painting had to have the same characteristics as a drawing. He made a distinction between a "picture" executed in the studio with all possible care, and a "painted study" done on site in the manner of a sketch, even though it might have the same dimensions as a picture (size 25 or 30 canvas). The chief qualities of the latter were its speed of execution, on which the spontaneity of the impression depended, and the simplicity of the means which brought individual expression into play. The connection of this approach with that of Japanese art is self-evident: "The Japanese draw quickly, very quickly like a lightning flash, because their nerves are finer, their feeling simpler," Vincent said. And, talking to Theo, he asked himself indirectly: "I have only been here a few months, but tell me this—could I, in Paris, have done the drawing of the boats *in an hour*? Even without the perspective frame,[d] I do it now without measuring, just by letting my pen go." These were the virtues of that region of the South, he added, that "one's sight changes: you see things with an eye more Japanese, you feel color differently."[20]

In the middle of June, Vincent went to Saintes-Maries-de-la-Mer for the first time to find out to what extent the sea changed his usual way of looking at things. He took the coach following the shores of Lake Vaccarès for some fifty kilometers, crossed the Camargue and admired the herds of white ponies in passing. But he particularly noticed the huts of the keepers and drew the thatched roofs which nearly go down to the ground and which reminded him of the cottages of Drenthe (F 1438). The last time he was to remember them was at Auvers-sur-Oise shortly before his death.

114 Arriving at the small medieval town, he was struck by the equilibrium of its masses, by the harmonious distribution of the houses clustered around the fortified church, by the simplicity of the sharp-ridged volumes such as he had seen in some of the Estaque landscapes painted by Cézanne. He recognized the contrast of the red and orange roofs against the blue sky, and also the flattering effect produced by the extremely bright light. Twelve years earlier Cézanne had already pointed it out to Pissarro: "It's like a playing card. Red roofs against the blue sea ... The sun is so terrible that it seems to turn objects into silhouettes not only in black and white but in blue, in red, in brown, in violet. I may be wrong, but I think this is the antithesis of relief."e

Vincent came to the seaside mainly to observe the color of the sky. "What I should like to find out," he wrote to Emile Bernard, "is the effect of an intenser blue in the sky."21 For the sea itself did not interest him at all. He found that it "has the colors of mackerel, changeable I mean. You don't always know if it is green or violet, you can't even say it's blue, because the next moment the changing light has taken on a tinge of pink or gray."22

115 But the sea is a mirror that adds its own reflection to the blue of the sky. On the beach, at the mouth of the Petit-Rhône, the fishermen had pulled in their boats, whose vivid color stood out strongly against the sky. Vincent accentuated their graceful slender form, which is irresistibly reminiscent of the boats by Hokusai. In the picture, the sea has been reduced to a slim surface. It is significant that Vincent did very few seascapes, and in those that he did, the sea does not really constitute the chief feature in the composition. Cézanne had a similar attitude towards the sea and used it skillfully to break up the aerial perspective in his paintings, and so

had Pissarro, who did pratically no seascapes at all except perhaps rather late in the day. Here they differed from Monet and Sisley, and also from Seurat and Signac, who regarded the study of reflections in the water as one of the main subjects of Impressionism.

Looking at the contrast between the red of the boat in front of him and the blue of the sky, made more luminous by the sea, Vincent thought of something Pissarro had once pointed out to him in Paris, and he reported to Theo: "What Pissarro says is true, you must boldly exaggerate the effects of either harmony or discord which colors produce. It is the same as in drawing—accurate drawing, accurate color, is perhaps not the essential thing to aim at, because the reflection of reality in a mirror, if it could be caught, color and all, would not be a picture at all, no more than a photograph."23

Starry Night

It was 10 June 1888. Night was falling over Saintes-Maries. Vincent had gone down to the beach after reserving a room at the inn. Memories of other twilit evenings came back to him in a rush. He recalled evenings in Ramsgate when, lost in thought, he had wandered along the beach, watching the clouds as they moved across a gray sky. Then there were evenings in Paris, when he was working at Goupil's and liked to stroll along the quays as the street lamps lit up one by one. That evening, on the deserted beach, he once more experienced the same blend of dizziness and serenity. "It was not gay, but neither was it sad—it was—beautiful,"24 he wrote to Theo. This time, silently contemplating nature with a painter's eye, he singled out the forms and colors that would express his emotion: "The deep blue sky was flecked with clouds of a blue deeper than the fundamental blue of intense cobalt, and others of a clearer blue, like the blue whiteness of the Milky Way. In the blue depth the stars were sparkling, greenish, yellow, white, pink, more brilliant, more

115 *Boats on the Beach.* Arles, June 1888. Oil on canvas, 64 × 81 cm. F 413. Rijksmuseum Vincent van Gogh, Amsterdam.

sparklingly gemlike than at home —even in Paris: opals you might call them, emeralds, lapis lazuli, rubies, sapphires. The sea was very deep ultramarine— the shore a sort of violet and faint russet as I saw it, and on the dunes (they are about seventeen feet high) some bushes Prussian blue."[25]

But would he be able to paint it? From that moment on, he had only one dream: to meet the challenge presented by the spectacle of the sea merging with the sky. In a letter to Emile Bernard, he asked: "But when shall I paint my *starry sky*, that picture which preoccupies me continuously?"[26] In order to convey the enchantment of the scene as closely as possible, he considered it essential to follow his usual Impressionist approach, that is, to paint "on the spot" by night, just as he did by day. Only in this way, he felt, could he "bring it off."

The difficulty was obviously how to see clearly enough to distinguish the colors on his palette. This proved a thorny problem. Nevertheless, he decided in mid-July to attack it indirectly by painting, by artificial light, the interior of the "night café" above which he was staying during the preparation of his new abode at 2 Rue Lamartine. Sleeping during the day, he managed to complete the painting in three nights, rejecting the "realistic" chiaroscuro treatment suggested by the presence of the lamps in favor of intense contrasts of pure color: "The room is blood red and dark yellow with a green billiard table in the middle; there are four citron-yellow lamps with a glow of orange and green. Everywhere there is a clash and contrast of the most disparate reds and greens in the figures of little sleeping hooligans, in the empty, dreary room, in violet and blue." He stated very clearly in this letter to Theo, dated 8 September, that this picture was "the equivalent, though different, of the 'Potato Eaters.'" Its whole effect is achieved by color contrasts: "I have tried to express the terrible passions of humanity by means of red and green."[27] A few days later, he added: "In my picture of the 'Night Café' I have tried to express the idea that the café is a place where one can ruin oneself, go mad or commit a crime."

To Vincent, the expressive power of color was as great as that of the text of a novel by—for example— Zola. And it was on this textual quality—defined by the interplay of strokes of color—that he drew "to express, as it were, the powers of darkness in a low public house."[28] With this first night study, he succeeded in going beyond an Impressionist use of his palette to an autonomous form of artistic expression that, by the use of color alone, was able to break away from illusionist perspective. As he wrote to Theo in typical fashion: "It is color not locally true from the point of view of the delusive realist, but color suggesting some emotion of an ardent temperament."[29]

Vincent went one stage further with his second night study, this time painted out of doors, namely *Café Terrace by Night* (F 467). The café was in the Place des Thermes, and he described it to Wilhelmina as follows: "On the terrace there are the tiny figures of people drinking. An enormous yellow lantern sheds its light on the terrace, the house front and the sidewalk, and even casts a certain brightness on the pavement of the street, which takes a pinkish violet tone. The gable-topped fronts of the houses in a street stretching away under a blue sky spangled with stars are dark blue and violet and there is a green tree."[30] A well-known anecdote, rather typical of the South of France, relates that Vincent did this painting by the light of candles fixed to a wide-brimmed felt hat that he wore specially for the occasion. It is thus hardly astonishing that he was referred to as "illuminé" (a French word meaning both "lit up" and "cranky"). The story is a charming one, but there is no evidence to support it. On the contrary, it is clear from the above-mentioned letter that he contented himself with the pale light of the moon and the stars, reinforced to some extent by the lamps that lit the square rather feebly here and there. "Here you have a night picture without any black in it, done with nothing but beautiful blue and violet and green, and in these surroundings the lighted square acquires a pale sulphur and greenish citron-yellow color. It amuses me enormously to paint the night on the spot. They used to draw and paint the picture in the daytime after the rough sketch. But I find satisfaction in painting things immediately. Of course it's true that in the dark I may mistake a blue for a green, a blue-lilac for a pink-lilac, for you cannot rightly distinguish the quality of a hue."[31] Just as *Night Café* (F 463) has its literary equivalent in Zola's *L'Assomoir*, *Café Terrace* has affinities with a novel by Guy de Maupassant, "because the beginning of *Bel Ami* happens to be a description of a starlit night in Paris with the brightly lighted cafés of the Boulevard, and this is approximately the same subject I just painted."[32]

Vincent was nearing his goal. In the same letter, recalling dusk on the beach at Saintes-Maries, he asserted: "At present I absolutely want to paint a starry sky. It often seems to me that the night is still more richly colored than the day, having hues of the most intense violets, blues and greens. If only you pay attention to it you will see that certain stars are citron-yellow, others have a pink glow or a green, blue and forget-me-not brilliance. And without my expatiating on this theme it will be clear that putting little white dots on a blue-black surface is not enough." The view over the Rhone towards the bridge at Trinquetaille offered him a satisfactory subject for a night-piece. Here, at Saintes-Maries where sea and sky merged at twilight, the waters of the Rhone seemed to become one with the sky. This time Vincent felt equal to his task. He no longer hesitated to paint what he saw as he saw it ".... at night under a gas jet. The sky is greenish-blue, the water royal blue and the reflections are russet-green down to greenish-bronze. On the blue-green expanse of sky, the Great Bear sparkles green and pink, its discreet pallor contrasts with the harsh gold of the gas. The colorful little figures of lovers in the foreground."[33]

118, 119   Vincent realized that this *Starry Night* (F 474) was the climax of the painstaking experimental process that began with the *Sower* and was continued in the night pieces. Indeed, on finishing *Night Café*, he de-

clared: "Afterwards, when I have carried these experiments even further, the 'Sower' will still be my first attempt in that style."[34] The first of his twilight scenes, the original version of the *Sower*, is based on a contrast between two tones, which flattens the picture's perspective and concentrates all of its expressive power in the harmony between the two tones, namely yellow and purple. *Night Café* employs more or less the same approach, but the contrasting red and green make up a threefold harmony with yellow. *Café Terrace* is characterized by a color scheme of yellow, orange tones, and blue. In each of the two latter studies, balance is maintained between the three color components. On the other hand, as we saw above, the balance of the *Sower* was achieved only by the addition of a third component, orange, which mitigates the initial tension of the contrast. *Starry Night* takes the same kind of risks as the *Sower* did in its original version, but nevertheless achieves a genuine state of "unstable balance" (as a doctor might put it). Despite appearances, Vincent had very carefully calculated the relative intensities and proportions of the colors in order to produce an overall effect that verges on chiaroscuro without actually succumbing to it. Thus the orange, present in "trace" form, makes the blues vibrate without killing them, while the yellows that lighten them gain an added glitter from a few mauve strokes judiciously placed to form a contrast. The precision of this infinitesimal infusion of simultaneous contrasts is reminiscent of Seurat, whom Vincent admired while rejecting Pointillism. The brushwork is in fact highly individual in the way it adapts itself to the various parts of the composition. In the sky, the repetition of crosswise strokes (and thus of "star" shapes) creates a Milky Way in impasto. Linear horizontal strokes are used to convey the shimmer on the water, and oblique strokes define the piece of land at the bottom of the picture.

There is no trace of illusionist realism in this *Starry Night*. Its depth is metaphysical and has nothing to do with perspective. Vincent confessed as much to Theo: "That does not prevent me from having a

116 *The Night Café*. Arles, September 1888. Oil on canvas, 70 × 89 cm. F 463. Yale University Art Gallery, New Haven, Connecticut (Bequest of Stephen Carlton Clark, B.A. 1903).

117 *Café Terrace by Night*. Arles, September 1888. Oil on ▷ canvas, 81 × 65.5 cm. F 467. Rijksmuseum Kröller-Müller, Otterlo.

terrible need of—shall I say the word?—of religion. Then I go out at night to paint the stars, and I am always dreaming of a picture like this with a group of living figures of our comrades."[35] This passage reveals the meaning of the pair of lovers in the foreground. Superfluous from the purely technical point of view—as was the figure of the *Sower*—self-effacing, even, they mark the presence of humanity in the composition, bringing out by contrast the *inhuman* feeling of the infinite. Like most of the anonymous figures Vincent would paint later on, their significance is essentially symbolic. Veritable fetish images of Vincent himself, they integrate him into the artistic reality of the composition and, to borrow a concept from Japanese Zen, enable him to attain, through painting, the mystic desire of his youth—to assuage his thirst for the absolute.

A field of stars on an azure ground, a celestial vault—from the cupola of the sanctuary to the "starry night"—are the same image of the infinite. It is not, however, an abstract image, since it represents a reaction to the natural scene, as Vincent wrote to Emile Bernard: "Others may have more lucidity than I do in the matter of abstract studies, and it is certainly possible you are one of their number, Gauguin too... and perhaps I myself when I am old. But in the meantime I am getting well acquainted with nature. I exaggerate, sometimes I make chang-

118 *Starry Night*. Arles, September 1888. Pen. Drawing in Letter 553b. Rijksmuseum Vincent van Gogh, Amsterdam.

119 *Starry Night*. Arles, September 1888. Oil on canvas, 72.5 × 92 cm. F 474. Musée d'Orsay, Paris.

es in a motif; but for all that, I do not invent the whole picture; on the contrary, I find it all ready in nature, only it must be disentangled."[36]

Vincent returned to the theme of the *Starry Night* at St. Rémy (F 612) in June 1889. But this time the stars are whirling around as though the sky had been set ablaze by a new Prometheus! We shall consider the significance of this picture later.

"To Express Hope by Some Star"

118, 119 Shortly before painting *Starry Night*, Vincent finished two portraits that are very similar in spirit and already belong to his "nebulous" period: *Portrait of*
121, 120 *Eugène Boch* (F 462) and *Self-Portrait* (F 476). Eugène Boch was a Belgian painter who was then living at Fontvieille about ten kilometers north of Arles. Meeting by chance, the two artists became friends and used to go painting from nature together. Boch willingly agreed to sit for Vincent, but when the latter completed the portrait at the beginning of September, he did so according to a preconceived idea. Writing to Theo in August, he had described a sort of idealized portrait which could only be that of his friend: "I should like to paint the portrait of an artist friend, a man who dreams great dreams, who works as the nightingale sings, because it is his nature. He'll be a blond man. I want to put my appreciation, the love I have for him, into the picture. So I paint him as he is, as faithfully as I can, to begin with. But the picture is not yet finished. To finish it I am now going to be the arbitrary colorist. I exaggerate the fairness of the hair, I even get to orange tones, chromes and pale citron-yellow. Behind the head, instead of painting the ordinary wall of the mean room, I paint infinity, a plain background of the richest, intensest blue that I can contrive, and by this simple combination of the bright head against the rich blue background, I get a mysterious effect, like a star in the depths of an azure sky."[37] The *Portrait of Eugène Boch* occupies a strategic position in Vincent's work, as with it he

turns away from Impressionism to draw his strength from the painting of Delacroix, thereby affirming his convictions as an artist. These are based on the idea of the arbitrary use of color, which becomes more expressive as a result. By revealing to Vincent color contrasts of an extreme intensity, the southern sun had progressively chased the gray tones from his palette, as he explained to Theo: "It is only that what I learned in Paris is leaving me, and I am returning to the ideas I had in the country before I knew the impressionists. And I should not be surprised if the impressionists soon find fault with my way of working, for it has been fertilized by Delacroix's ideas rather than by theirs. Because instead of trying to reproduce exactly what I have before my eyes, I use color more arbitrarily, in order to express myself forcibly."[38]

For Vincent, painting had become an act of faith that took the place of religion. Art was the effective path to salvation, which the artist would have a chance of achieving if he surrendered to poetry. For the artist was one who untiringly pursued the act of creation of Christ, that "*greater artist than all other artists*, despising marble and clay as well as color, working in living flesh. That is to say, this matchless artist, hardly to be conceived of by the obtuse instrument of our modern, nervous, stupefied brains, made neither statues nor pictures nor books; he loudly proclaimed that he made...*living men*, immortals."[39] Needing a devotional image of the artist raised to sainthood by painting, Vincent found the appropriate physical type in Eugène Boch. This "young man with the look of Dante" loved Delacroix; "he even knew the violent cartoon for the 'Bark of Christ,'" dear to Vincent's heart, the latter told Theo: "Well, thanks to him I at last have a first sketch of that picture I have dreamed of for so long––the poet. He posed for me." The *Portrait of Eugène Boch* expresses the wished-for transformation of a man into a poet, of an artist into a star, into a "painter-butterfly" who "would have for its field of action one of the innumerable heavenly bodies, which would perhaps be no more inaccessible to us, after death, than the black dots which symbolize towns and villages on geographical maps are in our terrestrial existence."[40]

Next, just before the *Starry Night*, Vincent painted the *Self-Portrait* (F 476). In a letter to Theo, dated 17 September, he describes it as "a portrait of myself, *almost colorless,* in gray tones against a background of pale malachite."[41] He had also mentioned it to Wilhelmina the previous week: "I also made a new portrait of myself, as a study, in which I look like a Japanese."[42] But it was only at the beginning of October that he indicated its true spirit to Gauguin: "I have a portrait of myself, all ash-colored. The ashen-gray color that is the result of mixing malachite green with an orange hue, on pale malachite ground, all in harmony with the reddish-brown clothes. But as I also exaggerate my personality, I have in the first place aimed at the character of a simple bonze worshiping the eternal Buddha."[43] Vincent represents himself as the humble servitor of a God whose only religion is painting. The lack of color is a sign of transcendence, like the concentric movement of the brush strokes in the "pale malachite" ground which harks back directly to the "pale citron-colored aureole" of a figure of Christ by Delacroix, as described in a letter to Emile Bernard.[44]

At the time of this self-portrait, Vincent was engaged in a number of other works, notably views of the public gardens opposite 2 Place Lamartine, where he had been living since the middle of September. Gauguin was shortly to join him there— Gauguin whom he admired so much that he had "expressly" decorated his room, part of the decoration consisting of these views of the public gardens, rechristened "a poet's garden" in his honor. "And what I wanted was to paint the garden in such a way that one would think of the old poet from here (or rather from Avignon) Petrarch, and at the same time of the new poet living here—Paul Gauguin...."[45] For Vincent, Gauguin was the very incarnation of the poet of whom the portrait of Boch gave only a rough impression— one with whom he would be able to share his most intimate thoughts on painting, those

that even Theo was incapable of grasping: "To express the thought of a brow by the radiance of a light tone against a somber background. To express hope by some star, the eagerness of a soul by a sunset radiance. Certainly there is no delusive realism in that, but isn't it something that actually exists?"[46]

The Painter of the Future

When Vincent first came to Arles he practically abandoned portrait painting except for the portrait of an old Arlesienne woman that he dashed off quickly upon his arrival. Dazzled by the luminosity of the landscape at the time when the fruit trees were in blossom, amazed by the extraordinary transparency of the air, which enabled him to distinguish colors "as far as an hour's distance away," he was entirely absorbed in his palette, striving to heighten the intensity of its contrasts, to set oranges against blues to find golden hues of every subtle shade. He confided his rapture to Emile Bernard: "I work even in the middle of the day, in the full sunshine, without any shadow at all, in the wheat fields, and I enjoy it like a cicada." But he also confessed: "I am forever reproaching myself with not having done any figures here yet."[47] But he did not yet want to go back to doing figures, not until he was sure that he would be able to find a completely new way of expression. Walking through the streets of Arles, he dreamt of the portraits he would be able to do of the lovely women of Arles, some of whom seemed to step right out of a Fragonard or a Renoir. As soon as he was satisfied with his first studies of landscapes, he felt he was entitled to try the figure. There really was a touch of hypocrisy in his letter to Theo when he wrote: "But I don't think that I am the man to do it. I am not enough of a M. Bel Ami for that. But I should be heartily glad if this Bel Ami of the Midi, which Monticelli was not—but was by way of being—whom I feel to be coming, though I know it isn't myself—I should be heartily glad, I say, if a kind of Guy de Maupassant in painting came along

120 *Self-Portrait.* Arles, September 1888. Oil on canvas, 62 × 52 cm. F 476. Fogg Art Museum, Harvard University, Cambridge, Massachusetts (Bequest of the Maurice Wertheim Collection, Class 1906).

121 *Portrait of Eugène Boch.* Arles, September 1888. Oil on ▷ canvas, 60 × 45 cm. F 462. Musée d'Orsay, Paris.

to paint the beautiful people and things here light-heartedly. As for me, I shall go on working and here and there among my work there will be things which will last, but who will be in figure painting what Claude Monet is in landscape? However, you must feel, as I do, that such a one will come. Rodin? He does not work in color, he's not the one. But the painter of the future will be *a colorist such as has never existed*. Manet was working toward it, but as you know the impressionists have already got a stronger color than Manet. But this painter who is to come—I can't imagine him living in little cafés, working away with a lot of false teeth, and going to the Zouaves' brothels, as I do."[48]

When Vincent went to Saintes-Maries-de-la-Mer in the middle of June, about a month after writing these lines, as he told Theo: "Tomorrow I am going to Saintes-Maries on the seacoast to have a look at the blue sea and the blue sky. And to try to get an idea of the figures. For I suppose that all at once I shall make a furious onslaught on the figure, which I seem to be giving a wide berth at the moment, as if I were not interested in it, although it is what I really aim at."[49] He did not find anything that suited him there in the way of figures, but "girls who reminded one of Cimabue and Giotto—thin, straight, somewhat sad and mystic."[50]

On his return, Vincent met a *Zouave* (F 423), Second Lieutenant Milliet, who asked him to give him drawing lessons and agreed to sit for him more or less free of charge. This was the first major portrait Vincent had undertaken since *Père Tanguy*, as he also told Theo: "I have a model at last—a Zouave—a boy with a small face, a bull neck, and the eye of a tiger, and I began with one portrait, and began again with another; the half-length I did of him was horribly harsh, in a blue uniform, the blue of enamel saucepans, with braids of faded reddish-orange, and two stars on his breast, an ordinary blue, and very hard to do. That bronzed, feline head of his with the reddish cap, against a green door and the orange bricks of a wall. So it's a savage combination of incongruous tones, not easy to manage. The

study I made of it seems to me very harsh, but all the same I'd like always to be working on vulgar, even loud portraits like this. It teaches me something, and above all that is what I want of my work."[51] The color is laid on in Cloisonnist flat areas, bounded either by a continuous contour whose orange-tinted line traces the features of the face and the edges of the clothes, or simply by the abrupt contrast of complementary tones like that of the red cap against the green background of the door. The *Zouave*, in fact, inaugurates a new type of portrait combining the psychological qualities of the *Père Tanguy* with the plastic approach we find in *La Segatori*.

We have seen that some compositions were influenced by the contemporary novels Vincent loved: Zola, Flaubert, and Guy de Maupassant for Realism, the Goncourts and Loti for the Japanese touch, and Alphonse Daudet because he felt a certain kinship with Tartarin of Tarascon! One subject may have been suggested by *L'Œuvre*, another by a description from *Bel Ami*. *Germinie Lacerteux* made him "feel color." *Madame Chrysanthème* was the source of "interesting notes on Japan." From it he drew the powerful color of *La Mousmé* (F 431), whose completion he announced to Theo on 29 July: "And now, if you know what a 'mousmé' is (you will know when you have read Loti's *Madame Chrysanthème*), I have just painted one. It took me a whole week, I have not been able to do anything else, not having been very well either.... A mousmé is a Japanese girl—Provençal in this case—12 to 14 years old. That makes two portraits now, the Zouave and her.... The portrait of the girl is against a background of white strongly tinged with malachite green, her bodice is striped blood red and violet, the skirt is royal blue, with large yellow-orange dots. The mat flesh tones are yellowish-gray; the hair tinged with violet; the eyebrows and the eyelashes are black; the eyes, orange and Prussian blue. A branch of oleander in her fingers, for the two hands are showing."[52]

Vincent had hardly finished *La Mousmé* when he started on another portrait, that of the *Postman*

Roulin (F 432) with whom he liked to have a drink and chat of an evening, as is the custom of the people in the Midi. Roulin's open, cheerful character, his proud bearing in his beautiful blue uniform with gold braid, and his trim beard made him an ideal model. He readily agreed to sit for Vincent, and soon his wife and children did so too, including the youngest, who was still in the cradle. At the beginning of August, Theo was told that a new portrait was in progress: "I am now at work with another model, a postman in a blue uniform trimmed with gold, a big bearded face, very like Socrates. A violent republican like Tanguy. A man more interesting than most."[53] Emile Bernard, too, was kept informed: "I have just done a portrait of a postman, or rather even two portraits. A Socratic type, none the less Socratic for being somewhat addicted to liquor and having a high color as a result...what a motif to paint in the manner of Daumier, eh! He kept himself too stiff when posing, which is why I painted him twice, the second time at a single sitting. A blue, nearly white background on the white canvas, all the broken tones in the face—yellows, greens, violet, pinks, reds. The uniform Prussian blue, with yellow adornments."[54] *La Mousmé* and the *Postman* both posed in the same cane chair. Its arms and back fill the space with wide curves which emphasize the rounded shapes of the sitters' arms. M.E. Tralbaut remarks that this "armchair has contributed to a certain 'enlargement of form' which the Fauves—we have it from Picasso—regarded as one of Van Gogh's 'daring experiments' whereas he himself did nothing more than paint the exact reality."[f] True, but it is nevertheless a fact that if Vincent *chose* that armchair it was because of its special shape, to which he adapted the pose of his model. When he says about *La Mousmé* that "the two hands are showing" this means not only that they are in the picture but that they literally form an active part of the composition. The movement of the model's arm forms a continuity with that of the chair, absorbing the whole model in a single arabesque, the "decorative" figure of which Matisse said later: "It is only one

phrase among all the phrases."[g] It is that simplification of the figure into a flattened form giving full play to color from which these portraits draw their power of expression, a method used already by Delacroix and revived by Matisse in treating their common subject, the *Odalisques*.

In August, Vincent did two versions of the *Portrait of Patience Escalier* (F 443, 444), "a sort of 'man with a hoe,' formerly a cowherd of the Camargue, now gardener at a house in the Crau." It is, in a way, a diurnal companion piece to the *Portrait of Eugène Boch*, as he told Theo: "Again, in the portrait of the peasant I worked this way, but in this case without wishing to produce the brightness of a pale star in the infinite. Instead, I imagine the man I have to paint, terrible in the furnace of the height of harvesttime, as surrounded by the whole Midi. Hence the orange colors flashing like lightning, vivid as red-hot iron, and hence the luminous tones of old gold in the shadows."[55] And he added, "Oh, my dear boy...and the nice people will only see the exaggeration as a caricature." The second version (F 444) has a broad, continuous contour which sets off the figure against an abstract background. This simplification creates a real schizogenesis by depriving the model of some of its features, such as the hat, which becomes a flat area of color. Thus part of the figure is "devoured" by the background.

Vincent van Gogh's correspondence testifies to his passionate determination to paint the human figure. He wrote to Emile Bernard: "I want to do figures, figures, and more figures. I cannot resist that series of bipeds from the baby to Socrates, and from the woman with black hair and white skin to the woman with yellow hair and a sunburned brick-red face." But his vehemence is tinged with despair, for he adds, "In the meantime I am mostly doing other things."[56] This paradox can be explained by the recurring periods when lack of confidence sapped his morale. We must remember the early days of his career as an artist. He hardly met with much encouragement. Mauve dropped him, and Tersteeg, his former boss, was even more obnoxious, for he put

122 *The Plowed Field.* Arles, September 1888. Oil on canvas, 72.5 × 92 cm. F 574. Rijksmuseum Vincent van Gogh, Amsterdam.

123 *The Postman Roulin.* Arles, July 1888. Oil on canvas, ▷ 81 × 65 cm. F 432. Museum of Fine Arts, Boston. (gift of Robert Treat Paine 2nd, 1935).

124 *La Mousmé*. Arles, July 1888. Oil on canvas, 74 × 60 cm. F 431. National Gallery of Art, Washington (Chester Dale Collection).

125 *The Zouave*. Arles, June 1888. Oil on canvas, 65 × 54 ▷ cm. F 423. Rijksmuseum Vincent van Gogh, Amsterdam.

126 *Portrait of Patience Escalier*. Arles, August 1888. Oil on canvas, 69 × 56 cm. F 444. Private Collection.

127 *Washerwomen by the Canal*. Arles, July 1888. pen, 31.5 × 24 cm. F 1444. Rijksmuseum Kröller-Müller, Otterlo.

pressure on Theo to abandon his brother. Generally speaking, Vincent's paintings were always condemned for not being "smooth," and people found that *"it was only pictures full of painting."*[57] Thus potential models often refused to sit for someone they considered a common dauber. These criticisms finally undermined his self-confidence. For instance, he humbly agreed with the reproaches his model, the Second Lieutenant Milliet, made about the *Zouave*: "What I have dashed off is very ugly: a drawing of a seated Zouave, a painted sketch of the Zouave against a completely white wall, and finally his portrait against a green door and some orange bricks of a wall." And yet we saw before that he had been pleased with the painting. In the letter to Emile Bernard at the end of June, however, discouragement had gained the upper hand. "It is hard and utterly ugly and badly done.... The figures I do are nearly always detestable in my own eyes, and all the more so in the eyes of others; yet it is the study of the figure that strengthens one's powers most, if one does it in a manner other than the one taught us, for instance, at Mr. Benjamin Constant's."[58] Vincent transferred his ardor to landscape, hoping that it would help him acquire the strength of expression needed for the figure. He wanted to carry on the work of the two fellow countrymen he admired most, Rembrandt and Frans Hals, to become able, as he dreamed, "to make you see the great simple thing: the painting of humanity, or rather of a whole republic, by the simple means of portraiture."[59] From that point of view, his *Self-Portrait*—"almost discolored" —is a real profession of faith, which he also expressed in a letter to Theo: "I want to paint men and women with that something of the eternal which the halo used to symbolize, and which we seek to convey by the actual radiance and vibration of our coloring."[60]

Chapter V   The Studio in the South

Waiting

At the beginning of May, when Vincent told his brother that he had just rented a four-roomed house, he explained how much better this was than living in a hotel, even if it was a little more expensive at first. In reality, when he took that step he had two things in mind: in the short term, to bring together a group of artists, as he had already planned to do in Paris; and in the longer term, to realize a Utopian plan—an association of artists, similar to those that had existed in Holland since the seventeenth century, which "could at least guarantee its members a chance to live and to work," and of which Tersteeg and Theo would be the "expert members."[1] He admired Gauguin, who just then at Pont-Aven was attracting a circle of artists around him, including his friend Emile Bernard, to whom Vincent was singing the praises of the South. He admitted that the cost of living was a little lower in Brittany, but the South had that marvelous sun! Wasn't that irreplaceable? *Here I am in Japan*," he enthused to his sister. "Which means that I have only to open my eyes and paint what is right in front of me, if I think it effective."[2] Didn't it offer wonderful facilities? Why not let the "comrades" share it? "Then, if there were several of us, I am inclined to think one could get more advantageous terms. It might be a real advantage to quite a number of artists who love the sun and colors to settle in the South."[3] And above all, Theo would at last reap the just yield from his "investment." For Vincent never lost sight of the terms of the contract by which he had bound himself voluntarily to his brother. If he shared the house with two or three artists who worked together for Theo in exchange for his support, it would bring him business, at least in the long run. Why, he wondered, couldn't Gauguin come and join him, for a start? He would find a climate that would remind him of Martinique, the country from which he had brought back some really powerful canvases. As it happened, just at that point, in a letter dated 22 May, Gauguin, who was living on credit at the inn of Le Gloanec in Pont-Aven, had asked Theo for help. As soon as Vincent heard about this from his brother, he was full of hope that Gauguin might fall in with his plan. "And this would be the beginning of an association. Bernard, who is also coming South, will join us, and truly, I can see you at the head of an Impressionist Society in France yet. And if I can be of any use in getting them together, I would willingly look upon them all as better artists than I."[4] He immediately wrote to Gauguin to ask how he felt about this possibility, which had nothing but advantages: "I was ill when I came here, but now I am feeling better, and as a matter of fact, I am greatly attracted by the South, where working out-of-doors is possible nearly all the year round.... However this may be, if my brother were to send 250 francs a month for us both, we might share, should you care to come.... And you would give my brother one picture a month; you could do what you like with the rest of your work."[5] Gauguin's reply was ambiguous. He agreed on prin-

128 *A Pair of Clogs.* Arles, March 1888. Oil on canvas,
32.5 × 40.5 cm. F 607. Rijksmuseum Vincent van Gogh,
Amsterdam.

ciple, but in fact he himself was nurturing a plan similar to Vincent's: to start a "Tropics studio" in Martinique with Bernard and Laval and then to raise a capital of six hundred thousand francs to set Theo up as an art dealer in Impressionist pictures. No doubt he was a bit jealous to find Vincent, who was younger than he was—a fact on which he never ceased to harp—trying to establish a "studio in the South" with his brother's money. Vincent, too, he had to admit, was actually closer than he to that "primitive" state he had sought so painfully among the "savages" of Martinique and in the far corners of Brittany; he wrote to his friend Schuffenecker in February 1888: "I love Brittany; here I find the savage, the primitive. When my clogs echo on the granite soil, I hear the dull, muffled and powerful sound I seek in painting."[a]

Out of vanity, Gauguin played hard to get. Theo, in his turn, urged him to go to Arles, for he did not want his brother to be alone during the winter, a time of year when he fell easy prey to depression. Beset by debts, ill, incapable of working most of the time, Gauguin finally accepted the advantageous conditions offered him by the two brothers. He wrote to Vincent: "I fear that your brother, who likes my talents, may be overestimating them. I am a man ready for sacrifice, and I want him to know that whatever he does I will approve of."[b] So as not to lose face in the eyes of his followers, however he told his faithful Schuffenecker at the same time: "Don't worry, however much (Theo) Van Gogh may admire me, he isn't going to undertake to support me in the South for my pretty face. He has studied the form, and like the hard-headed Dutchman he is, he intends to push me as much as possible, and exclusively."[c]

Vincent wanted nothing for himself, since he offered Gauguin, whose strong personality he admired, the position of "studio head." Gauguin was in no hurry to leave Pont-Aven, however, and when Vincent suggested that he might perhaps join him there, he ignored the offer. "And I can't help feeling there is something queer about it,"[6] Vincent said,

adding soon afterwards, "From Gauguin himself not a word for almost a month."[7] But he judged Gauguin's behavior with perfect lucidity: "I feel instinctively that Gauguin is a schemer who, seeing himself at the bottom of the social ladder, wants to regain a position by means which will certainly be honest, but at the same time, very politic. Gauguin little knows that I am able to take all this into account."[8]

While awaiting Gauguin's arrival, Vincent made the house as attractive as possible. The success of his plan, after all, would depend on Gauguin's enthusiasm for the South. Then Emile Bernard and Charles Laval and others would follow, and perhaps even Signac and Seurat—who knew? Having read the description of an "Impressionist house" in the literary supplement of the *Figaro* on Saturday, 15 September, he decided to turn his into an "artist's house." Both from its outside appearance and its interior decoration it could have been christened the "house of contrasts." His first glimpse of it certainly made a decisive impression. He wrote to Theo, shortly after finding it: "It is painted yellow outside, whitewashed inside, on the sunny side. I have taken it for 15 fr. a month."[9] His description to Wilhelmina at the beginning of July was more explicit: "I live in a little yellow house with a green door and green blinds, whitewashed inside—on the white walls very brightly colored Japanese prints, red tiles on the floor—the house in the full sunlight—and over it an intensely blue sky."[10] The *Yellow House* (F 464) constituted a subject par excellence, as he explained to Theo, "in a sulphur-colored sunshine, under a sky of pure cobalt. The subject is frightfully difficult; but that is just why I want to conquer it. It's terrific, these houses, yellow in the sun, and the incomparable freshness of the blue. And everywhere the ground is yellow too." And to justify the picture's contrasts, which the Zouave Milliet had found "horrible," of course, because "exaggerated," he thought "that Zola did a certain boulevard at the beginning of *L'Assommoir*, and Flaubert a corner of the Quai de la Villette in the midst of the dog days at the begin-

129

129 *The Yellow House.* Arles, September 1888. Oil on canvas, 76 × 94 cm. F 464. Rijksmuseum Vincent van Gogh, Amsterdam.

186

130 *Vincent's Room at Arles.* Arles, October 1888, Oil on canvas, 72 × 90 cm. F 482. Rijksmuseum Vincent van Gogh, Amsterdam.

ning of *Bouvard et Pécuchet*, and neither of them is moldy yet."[11] It is worth quoting this passage from Flaubert as an example of the literary character of Vincent's picture, of which we have already spoken earlier: "Beyond the canal, between the houses that separate the work sites, the large pure sky stood out in ultramarine bands and, under the quivering sun, the white façades, the slate roofs, the granite quays, shone dazzlingly."

Before even furnishing the house—he had to wait until he received 300 francs for that purpose on 8 September—he had worked out the decoration of the studio on the ground floor. In the middle of July he outlined the main features to Bernard: "I am thinking of decorating my studio with half a dozen pictures of 'Sunflowers,' a decoration in which the raw or broken chrome yellows will blaze forth on various backgrounds—blue, from the palest malachite green to *royal blue*, framed in thin strips of wood painted with orange lead. Effects like those of stained-glass windows in a Gothic church."[12] This is an echo of the stained-glass decoration of the "Impressionist house." Towards 20 August he announced a program that was twice as ambitious: " If I carry out this idea there will be a dozen panels. So the whole thing will be a symphony of blue and yellow."[13] Thus the interior decoration of the studio picked up the blue and yellow harmony of the outside.

From 8 September on, Vincent prepared the two upstairs rooms. There, too, he wanted to create an effect of contrasts. To begin with, he contrasted the sparseness of his own room with the elegance of Gauguin's, "which I shall try to make as much as possible like the boudoir of a really artistic woman."[14] This subtle idea for Gauguin's room, which might seem surprising at first, is actually capable of a very simple explanation, quite apart from any analytical interpretation. Knowing Gauguin's vanity, Vincent prepared a room worthy of his position as "studio head." At The Hague, he had been struck by the "boudoir" character of some studios belonging to artists who "had made it," like De

Bock, which contained an assembly of casts, drapes, and the most varied ornaments. On the other hand, the only recent examples of luxury he had known at Arles itself were the brothel rooms he visited from time to time. The description of Gauguin's room which he sent to Wilhelmina seems to bear out this interpretation: "However, I want to have the other room nearly elegant with a walnut bedstead and blue coverlet. And all the rest, the dressing table as well as the cupboard, in dull walnut."

In each of the two rooms he introduced a decorative feature that contrasted with the space of the room and its furnishings. For his own, "nothing but straw-bottomed chairs and a table and a bed of unpainted wood. The walls whitewashed, red tiles on the floor. But I want a great wealth of portraits and painted studies of figures in it, which I think I shall do in the course of time." The decor of Gauguin's room was more elaborate: "In this very little room I want to put, in the Japanese manner, at least six very large canvases, particularly the enormous bouquets of sunflowers. You know that the Japanese instinctively seek contrasts.... So it follows, according to the same system, that in a big room there should be very small pictures and in a very little room one should hang many large ones."[15] Though Vincent wanted to impose a deliberate "style" on his house, he was careful to avoid anything excessively precious. He told Theo: "It will have a feeling of Daumier about it, and I think I dare predict it will not be commonplace.... I want to make it really an *artists' house*—not precious, on the contrary nothing *precious*, but everything from the chairs to the pictures having character."[16]

Although we can only try to imagine what Gauguin's room was like, we actually have three pictures of Vincent's, which correspond to the description sent in a letter to Gauguin shortly before his arrival: "Well, I enormously enjoyed doing this interior of nothing at all, of a Seurat-like simplicity; with flat tints, but brushed on roughly, with a thick impasto, the walls pale lilac, the ground a faded broken red, the chairs and the bed chrome yellow, the

130, 131

pillows and the sheets a very pale green-citron, the counterpane blood red, the washstand orange, the washbasin blue, the window green. By means of all these diverse tones I have wanted to express an *absolute restfulness*, you see, and there is no white in it at all except the little note produced by the mirror with its black frame (in order to get the fourth pair of complementaries into it.)"[17] In the original version in the van Gogh Museum in Amsterdam (F 482), the portrait hung above the bed on the right is that of the Zouave Milliet, as mentioned in a letter to Eugène Boch on 4 October[18]: "Your portrait is in my bedroom along with that of Milliet, the Zouave, which I have just finished." In the version at the Musée d'Orsay in Paris, done from memory at St.-Rémy, a portrait of a woman—probably his mother, painted after a photograph—replaces that of the Zouave.

According to a letter sent to Gauguin, the picture *Vincent's Room* was also part of the decoration. Although its exact place has not been given, it is probable that Vincent intended it for his own room. The hypothesis is tempting, for the differences between the picture and the actual space of the room would enable him to create a picture in the new expressive terms of painting. J.L. Ward has pointed to the breaking of the linear perspective along *two* vanishing points, a spatial distortion obtained by a bipositional rotation around a postulat-

130

131 *Vincent's Bedroom.* Arles, October 1888. Pen. Drawing in Letter 554. Rijksmuseum Vincent van Gogh, Amsterdam.

ed central axis.[d] This deformation of the perspective, to which are added the transfer of the local color and the use of "suggestive" color, produces a pictorial space at variance with the natural space. The colors, redistributed and laid on in flat patches, reestablish the picture's equilibrium according to their own laws—those of simultaneous contrasts, as Delacroix had already applied them—which have nothing to do with nature. Although Vincent was deeply attached to nature—he frequently reaffirmed his Impressionist beliefs—without ever falling into the temptation of the fanciful, he felt like Elstir, the painter of *La Recherche*, that "the surfaces and volumes are in reality independent of the names of objects that our memory imposes on them when we have recognized them."[e] We shall see what a long way—despite all appearances—that kind of "abstraction" is from the real abstract concepts of Gauguin's Symbolism, which would have a direct influence on those of the Nabi movement around 1890. As Vincent told Theo, it is in nature that painting finds its "literality": "Is it not emotion, the sincerity of one's feeling for nature, that draws us, and if the emotions are sometimes so strong that one works without knowing one works, when sometimes the strokes come with a continuity and a coherence like words in a speech or letter, then one must remember that it has not always been so, and that in time to come there will again be hard days, empty of inspiration."[19]

Vincent concentrated all his energies on the decoration of Gauguin's room about which he wrote: "I go on painting like a steam engine."[20] For he had a very special motive: "Well, yes, I am ashamed of it, but I am vain enough to want to make a certain impression on Gauguin with my work, so I cannot help wanting to do as much work as possible alone before he comes."[21] A few days before Gauguin's arrival, he repeated this to Theo. It shows how anxious he was not to let himself be overwhelmed by Gauguin's strong personality, although he was awaiting him with growing impatience. As the fourth canvas of the *Poet's Garden* (F 485), which

made up the decoration, was being finished, he was upset because he had not yet received an advance from his brother that would enable him to go on with it: "As that could not be, I have nevertheless pushed what I was working on as far as I could in my great desire to be able to show him something new, and not to be subjected to his influence (for he will certainly influence me, I hope) before I can show him indubitably my own individuality."[22]

In his ambivalent state, half fear, half anticipation, Vincent wanted to "overtake" Gauguin. He aimed at both listening to his advice and showing him the results of his own experiments. He spared no effort to draw the "Master of Pont-Aven" into *his* circle. The top place was reserved for him, gas was laid on so that they would have good light in winter, and once they had had time to settle down, the outlook for work would be most promising. "It is only in the long run that the poetry of this place penetrates.... But I believe after all that once you are here you will be seized like me with a rage for painting the autumnal effects in the intervals between the spells of mistral, and that you will understand why I insisted on your coming here, now that we are having very fine weather."[23] Moreover, Vincent had obtained a promise from Theo—who had just come into a small legacy upon the death of their Uncle Cent—that he would give Gauguin a contract. Gauguin was now at the end of his tether. Although his innate suspicion was aroused by the two brothers' persistence, he could not know that Vincent was planning to immure himself with him "to stand the siege of failure which will last all our lives." His own temperament urged him to fight. He was "hoping for success, he cannot do without Paris, he does not realize the *eternity* of poverty,"[24] Vincent wrote anxiously. For strictly professional reasons, Gauguin had to accept a solution that freed him from material worries, as he explained to Schuffenecker:

132 *Bouquet of Sunflowers.* Arles, August 1888. Oil on canvas, 93 × 73 cm. F 454. National Gallery, London.

"(Theo) van Gogh has just taken 300 francs' worth of my pottery. So I am leaving at the end of the month for Arles, where I think I shall be staying a long time seeing that the aim of my stay is to enable me to work without money worries until I have really been launched."[f] Wasn't it an excellent springboard for his own plans? In fact, he told Bernard: "(Theo) van Gogh hopes to sell all my paintings. If I am so lucky, I shall go to Martinique, I am convinced now that I shall do some fine things there. And if I were to find a larger sum, I would buy a house to found a studio there where all my friends could settle in on practically nothing. I rather agree with Vincent—the future belongs to painters of the tropics that have not yet been painted, and new subjects are needed for the public, the stupid buyer."[g]

Face to Face

On 23 October 1888, Vincent announced to Theo that Gauguin had come. He arrived at dawn, and Vincent, in order not to wake him, went to the famous "night café," where the proprietor recognized him at once, having seen his self-portrait. On the next day they set to work. Vincent wrote: "Gauguin brought a magnificent canvas which he has exchanged with Bernard, Breton women in a green field, white, black green, a note of red, and the dull flesh tints."[25] He made a watercolor copy of it two months later. I have mentioned before just how much that picture owed to Vincent's own work from the time just before he left for Arles. Emile Bernard was struck by the novelty and boldness of his Segatori portrait, treated in the manner of a Japanese print. He realized that his friend Anquetin's experiments had been running along parallel lines. Anquetin had been inspired, according to Bernard himself, by the stained glass on the door of his father's house at Etrepagny. "He noticed that each pane produced a special harmony for each color, a harmony in which all tones, far from being opposed to each other, blended to create a resulting tone.

This was precisely the opposite of the Impressionist theory."[h] Félix Fénéon, the critic, was right about the *Bretonnes* (Breton Women): "With saturated colors Emile Bernard painted Breton women outlined by a design compartmented like a stained-glass window and enveloped in a decor without atmosphere or values."[i] Vincent also had used the stained-glass effect when he did the *Bouquet of Sunflowers* (F 454), as we have seen above.

Gauguin always asserted—with a somewhat suspect insistence, I feel—his superiority over Vincent. Most of the "proofs" he subsequently produced in support of this claim do not really hold water. Thus he wrote, in 1894, in *Avant et Après*: "When I arrived in Arles, Vincent was deep into the Neo-Impressionist school, and he was floundering badly, which made him miserable...."[j] This is totally wrong: Such had not been the case for at least a year. In August, Vincent stated: "Only I am beginning more and more to try a simple technique which is perhaps not impressionistic."[26] *Vincent's Room*, executed in flat tints, proves this, and we know that Gauguin realized it as well. In another letter[27] Vincent stressed the "simple line" of the *Garden*, the way in which his studies were "really done with a single coat of impasto."

Talking about the *Sunflowers*, he pointed out to his brother, "And I must tell you that nowadays I am trying to find a special brushwork without stippling or anything else, nothing but the varied stroke." In the same letter, he also said: "I am now on the fourth picture of sunflowers. This fourth one is a bunch of 14 flowers, against a yellow background, like a still life of quinces and lemons that I did some time ago."[28] Gauguin blithely claimed paternity of that cameo of yellows, although it was actually executed in August, that is, two months *before* his arrival in Arles! And he did not hesitate to assert in his memoirs that Vincent owed everything to him: "I undertook the job of enlightening him, which was easy, for I found a rich and fertile soil.... From that day my Van Gogh made remarkable progress; he seemed to realise all that was in him and from there came a whole series of suns upon suns, in full sunlight."[k] Indeed, the *Sunflowers* made such an impression on Gauguin that he tried continually to obtain them even after the drama that separated the two artists forever. At first Vincent objected: "I think it is rather strange that he claims a picture of sunflowers from me, offering me in exchange, I suppose, or as a gift, some studies he left here. ... But for the moment I am keeping my canvases here and I am definitely keeping my sunflowers in question. He has two of them already, let that hold him."[29] Then he let himself be persuaded, flattered, deep down, by this form of appreciation, remembering too the flattering words which he recounted to Theo: "Besides, you know that Gauguin liked them extraordinarily. He said to me among other things—'That... it's... the flower.'"[30]

In the final analysis we know very little about the communal life of the two artists, except for the very biased account Gauguin gave of it in his memoirs in 1894. At first Vincent gave full vent to his enthusiasm, but his exuberance chilled Gauguin, who wrongly interpreted it as an expression of triumph. The idea that he had let himself be "trapped" by the two brothers began to obsess him. Vincent waited in vain for his companion's comments on the decor of his room, which had been done especially for him and to which Vincent had wholeheartedly devoted himself to the point of exhaustion. There was not a word of encouragement from Gauguin, and yet he could not help admiring the famous *Sunflowers*, which he praised so fulsomely after the event. He was inhibited by his vanity. He did not give recognition to Vincent's art until *after* his stay, when it was easy for him to spread the rumor that the latter owed everything to him. And how easy! People had seen nothing—or almost nothing—of the production of that "studio in the South."

Vincent noticed Gauguin's behavior, but he refused to admit it to himself. It would have meant admitting failure. Gauguin accused him of having lured him with extravagant descriptions of the South, which had made him think he would find something of the atmosphere of Martinique. "I am totally out of my depth in Arles, I find it so small, so mean, the country and the people,"[l] he wrote in December to Emile Bernard. He was much of the same opinion as Signac, who asserted in his *Journal* (Diary): "There is nothing but white in this country. Everywhere the reflected light devours the local colors and turns the shadows into grey. The pictures Van Gogh did at Arles have a marvellous rage and intensity but they do not at all convey the *luminosity* of the South."[m]

After a short, tentative period, the two artists settled down to a sort of "pictorial duel," canvas against canvas, on similar, though not identical, subjects. It is revealing of Gauguin's aggressive temperament that, as he went in for fencing, he brought his mask and gloves to Arles.

Their first encounter in painting took place at the *Alyscamps*, a Gallo-Roman necropolis whose sarcophagi line both sides of an avenue of poplars. At the end of October, Vincent wrote to Bernard: "I myself have done two studies of the fall of leaves in an avenue of poplars, and a third study of this whole avenue, entirely yellow."[31] But that last-named study (F 568), in spite of the dominant yellow, is less innovative than either of the first two. Thus study F 486, for instance, is constructed according to the plunging perspective of the Japanese print. Its frontal aspect is further strengthened by the strict verticality of the curtain of trees, whose trunks—reduced to bands of color flanked by a thick outline—are cut by the borders of the canvas. "The upper part of the picture," Vincent wrote, "is a bright green meadow, and no sky, or almost none."[32] A few years later this method was revived extensively by the Nabis, and then by the Fauvists. Gauguin's composition was a great deal less original. It merely heightened the intensity of the colors while still retaining the Impressionist brush stroke in the form of the fine parallel hatchings so dear to Picasso. The Cloisonnist feature of Vincent's pictures has too often been attributed to the influence of Gauguin's pictures, but we have seen that this

133

133 *Les Alyscamps*. Arles, November 1888. Oil on canvas.
73 × 92 cm. F 486. Rijksmuseum Kröller-Müller, Otterlo.
(The whole picture is reproduced on p. 299).

194

134 *Sower.* Arles, November 1888. Oil on canvas, 32 × 40 cm. F 451. Rijksmuseum Vincent van Gogh, Amsterdam.

cannot be said of the *Alyscamps*. Thus at the end of October 1888, Vincent, far from being Gauguin's pupil, could actually have taught him a thing or two about the subject of synthesis. Study F 486 of the *Alyscamps* is as daring as the *Vision after the Sermon,* which Gauguin did at the beginning of fall, a little before his departure for the South.

It is precisely this picture we think of when we consider the new version of the *Sower* (F 451). There we have the same kind of bent tree, the silhouette of its trunk diagonally across the surface of the canvas; but its role is not at all the same. In Gauguin's composition the tree is a symbolic barrier separating two spaces that have a different meaning, as the artist himself explained to Vincent: "To me, in this picture, the landscape and the struggle (Jacob wrestling with the angel) exist only in the imagination of the congregation, as a result of the sermon. That is why there is a contrast between the people, done naturally, and the struggle in its landscape, not natural and disproportionate."[n] Vincent's composition, on the other hand, has a symbolic meaning that has absolutely nothing to do with dreams or the imagination, but rather sticks closely to nature. It is based on the obvious analogy between the tree and the sower, associated in a trinitarian figure with the sun, the whole suggesting the idea of eternity. On 10 September, Vincent wrote to Theo: "The idea of the 'Sower' continues to haunt me all the time."[33] Around 21 November, he sent him the sketch and a description. "This is a sketch of the latest canvas I am working on, another Sower. An immense citron-yellow disk for the sun. A green-yellow sky with pink clouds. The field violet, the sower and the tree Prussian blue. Size 30 canvas."[34] Later he added: "From time to time there's a canvas which will make a picture, such as the 'Sower' in question, which I myself think better than the first."[35] Vincent was referring to the *Sower* (F 422), the study he did at the beginning of his stay in Arles and which he regarded as a failure. The comparison of the two *Sowers* is edifying. Whereas the naturalistic figure of the first is accessory, the stylized figure

of the second is one of the chief elements in the composition. The yellow-violet contrast creates a symbolic equivalence between the flattened tree and the flattened figure in the foreground, by which they are both rooted in nature. This new *Sower* corresponds to an important phase in Vincent's work because it shows a mastery of a Symbolist way of expression at which *Starry Night* and the *Portrait of Eugène Boch* had only just begun to hint.

This new mastery was undoubtedly the most significant result of Gauguin's influence. On his advice, Vincent began to work from the imagination, a method that was opposed to the naturalism of Impressionist principles. Nevertheless it was in this spirit that he executed the *Memories of the Garden at Etten* (Hermitage Museum, Leningrad) at the end of November. The composition is entirely frontal, set out in compartmented flat areas. There is no sky. In keeping with Japanese aesthetics, the two walking figures are cut at mid-body, and the path behind them winds right up to the top edge of the canvas. "Here you are," Vincent wrote to Wilhelmina. "I know this is hardly what one might call a likeness, but for me it renders the poetic character and the style of the garden as I feel it. All the same, let us suppose that the two ladies out for a walk are you and our mother; let us even suppose that there is not the least, absolutely not the least vulgar and fatuous resemblance—yet the deliberate choice of the color, the somber violet with the blotch of violent citron yellow of the dahlias, suggests Mother's personality to me.... In a similar manner the bizarre lines, purposely selected and multiplied, meandering all through the picture, may fail to give the garden a vulgar resemblance, but may present it to our minds as seen in a dream, depicting its character, and at the same time stranger than it is in reality."[36]

At first Vincent was enchanted by the new possibilities of the abstract methods to which Gauguin seemed to hold the key: He was drawn to the idea that subjects could vary ad infinitum at the whim of his imagination, like dream images suddenly fixed on the canvas as he wished. He wrote to

Theo: "I am going to set myself to work from memory often, and the canvases from memory are always less awkward, and have a more artistic look than studies from nature, especially when one works in mistral weather."[37] Gone was his haggard look, which had resulted from his working outdoors amid gusts of wind. But once his euphoric mood had passed he realized that in breaking his links with nature he would lose that *power* of pictorial expression that he unceasingly sought, and would become incapable of translating "the terrible human passions." For imagination can take great liberty; and especially it has license to erase human misery. When Gauguin painted Breton women harvesting under the Provençal sun, the scene lacked verisimilitude and, as a result, lost the real sense of their hard labor. The plastic innovations of abstraction, on the other hand, were less alluring to Vincent. The frontal composition, for instance, affected the decorative space. This was not to Vincent's taste, as is shown by a letter to Emile Bernard: "As you know, once or twice, while Gauguin was in Arles, I gave myself free rein with abstractions, for instance in the 'Woman Rocking,' in the 'Woman Reading a Novel,' black in a yellow library; and at the time abstraction seemed to me a charming path. But it is enchanted ground, old man, and one soon finds oneself up against a stone wall."[38]

The "strangeness" that Vincent found in Gauguin's art was not due to his attempt to make the subject participate. It was an integral feature of the kind of artistic expression that aims at a symbolic dimension. In one and the same ruling line he integrated the various "distorting" factors: flat areas, contours, plunging perspective, and "suggestive" color. Such was the debt Vincent had always admitted he owed to Gauguin; he wrote to John Russell: "I assure you that I owe much to the things Gauguin told me on the subject of drawing, and I have the highest respect for the way he loves nature."[39] Accustomed to abstractions, Gauguin did not feel at ease when working on site. He saw no need for it, but Vincent, who wanted at any price to show him what he could

do, dragged him to the night café to do the portrait of the proprietress, Madame Ginoux (F 489). Gauguin was still at the sketch stage when Vincent had already finished his picture: "...I have an Arlesienne at last, a figure (size 30 canvas) slashed on in an hour, background pale citron, the face gray, the clothes black, black, black, with perfectly raw Prussian blue. She is leaning on a green table and seated in an armchair of orange wood."[40] This rapidity of execution later, (later, in Letter 573, Vincent shortened the time to three quarters of an hour) was one of the fundamental characteristics of Vincent's technique that, by its very nature, diverged from Impressionist practice and toward synthetist art. It was a technique close to caricature, as Gauguin remarked in a letter to Schuffenecker: "It's funny, Vincent feels this calls for a Daumier here, me, I see a colored Puvis with a mixture of Japan."[o] Both artists derived the same painterly features from the Japanese aesthetic, but they used them differently. Whereas Gauguin evolved an expression of synthesis by "deriving art from nature," Vincent followed an inverse aim by seeking a synthesis of natural expression. He felt very close to the Japanese artist who studies a single blade of grass. "But this blade of grass leads him to draw every plant and then the seasons, the wide aspects of the countryside, then animals, then the human figure." And he exclaimed, "Oh! someday I must manage to do a figure in a few strokes."[41] The *Portrait of the Postman Roulin* had already been done in that spirit, as is shown in a letter to Theo of 5 August: "I have kept the big portrait of the postman, and the head which I included was done at a *single sitting*. But that's what I'm good at, doing a fellow roughly in one sitting. If I wanted to show off, my boy, I'd always do it, drink with the first comer, paint him, and that not in water colors but in oils, on the spot in the manner of Daumier."[42]

Vincent used the same method for the *Dance Hall at Arles* (F 547), a composition with numerous figures in which the influence of *Breton Women in the Meadow* by Emile Bernard—of which he had done a copy—is obvious. Gauguin had brought the picture

135 *L'Arlésienne, Mme Ginoux.* Arles, November 1888. Oil on canvas, 93 × 74 cm. F 489. Musée d'Orsay, Paris.

136 *The Dance Hall at Arles* (detail). Arles, December ▷ 1888. Oil on canvas, 65 × 81 cm. F 547. Musée d'Orsay, Paris (The whole picture is reproduced on p. 306).

198

to Arles to use as a model for his *Vision*. In the *Dance Hall* Vincent showed in his turn that he had mastered the lesson perfectly. But his interpretation was closer to the ideas of Toulouse-Lautrec than those of Gauguin. We need only compare the *Dance Hall* with *La Danse au Moulin Rouge* (Musée d'Orsay, Paris) to see this, although Lautrec would not have ventured such a radical frontal treatment before 1890. From 1888 on, Vincent pushed the Cloisonnist method to its utmost limits of distortion to express the formless reality of the crowd and the anonymity of those that made it up. It was a subject he had already treated at The Hague in 1882, in a watercolor showing a crowd of people gathered outside the office of the *Loterie Nationale* (State Lottery) (F 970).

Gauguin felt that Vincent's ideas were not logical. He could not understand how Vincent was able to paint in the synthetist manner, using both contour and flat areas, and yet at the same time retain his naturalist notions. Vincent showed great humility toward his companion and pretended to follow his advice, but in reality his chief aim was to demonstrate the value and originality of his own experiments. Although both behaved with good will in everyday matters, the lack of understanding between the two arists was bound to grow worse. As early as December, Gauguin told Emile Bernard: "Vincent and I generally disagree, especially on painting. He admires Daumier, Daubigny, Ziem and the great (Théodore) Rousseau, all of them people I can't stand. And he, for his part, loathes Ingres, Raphael, Degas—all people I admire; I reply, Boss, you're right, for the sake of peace. He likes my pictures very much, but while I am doing them he always finds that I am wrong in this or that."[p] Contrary to what Gauguin always claimed, his own art did not remain uninfluenced by Vincent's work. This is confirmed by a letter from Schuffenecker to Gauguin, dated 11 December, published by J. Rewald: "On Saturday I went with my wife to Goupil to see your latest canvases. I am absolutely enthralled. This lot is even more beautiful than your dispatch from Brittany, more abstract and more powerful. What stupefies me most is the fecundity and wealth of your production."[q] The rivalry between the two artists may have been exhausting, but it was certainly also stimulating.

The Drama of the Severed Ear

Gauguin and Van Gogh were moving in opposite directions, and yet there is an odd resemblance between their works. This was just where the danger lay. Gauguin, who did not understand Vincent's work, "undertook the task of enlightening him," as he was accustomed to do with his disciples in Pont-Aven. Gauguin's forceful personality has become legendary. Vincent himself tells us that Emile Bernard was frightened of doing his portrait. So it is hardly surprising that Vincent, in spite of his resistance, was unsettled by the authoritarian advice of the "master of Pont-Aven." In December he wrote to Theo: "Gauguin, in spite of himself and in spite of me, has more or less proved to me that it is time I was varying my works a little. I am beginning to compose from memory...."[43] What he did not immediately realize was that Gauguin was about to make him repudiate his faith in nature. The maneuver was all the more skillful for being concealed in a dialectic about the principles of Japanese art, whose importance was acknowledged equally by the two artists. But whereas Gauguin saw it simply as a new plastic system, Vincent realized its spiritual implications. When writing to his brother, he wondered aloud: "Come now, isn't it almost a true religion which these simple Japanese teach us, who live in nature as though they themselves were flowers?"[44]

"He is romantic and I am rather inclined to a primitive state,"[r] Gauguin wrote to Bernard about Vincent, who was no less primitive! Which of them was the greater primitive? He who put on clogs in Pont-Aven and dreamt of "living as a native" in Martinique, or he who painted clogs in Arles while imagining that he was in Japan? Their two separate

200

137 *Breton Women* (after E. Bernard). Arles, December 1888. Aquarelle, 47.5 × 62 cm. F 1422. Civica Galleria d'Arte Moderna, Milan.

concepts of nature confronted each other, wholly irreconcilable, like night and day. This was the meaning behind the two companion pieces which Vincent executed at the beginning of December: *Vincent's Chair* (F 498) and *Gauguin's Armchair* (F 499). In fact, he wrote to Theo: "Meanwhile I can at all events tell you that the last two studies are odd enough. Size 30 canvases, a wooden rush-bottomed chair all yellow on red tiles against a wall (daytime). Then Gauguin's armchair, red and green night effect, walls and floor red and green again, on the seat two novels and a candle."[45] When Theo acknowledged the receipt of these two canvases among a rather large batch, on 22 May 1889, he "forgot" the armchair and mentioned only the chair: "Certainly there is none of the beauty which is taught officially in them, but they have something so striking and so near to truth."[46]

Vincent remembered an illustration in the *Graphic* by Luke Fildès, The *Empty Chair,* on the day when the latter visited Charles Dickens and heard of his death. He had written to Theo: "Empty chairs—there are many of them, there will be even more."[47] An image of grief by its very nature, the image of his father's departure in Amsterdam, which left him "as miserable as a child," the image of Pa's death linked with his own death by the shared pipe lying abandoned on the chair. A still life, in short, that is immediately reminiscent of the still life with flowers and a pipe in the foreground—a rough sketch of it accompanied a letter sent to Theo just after the pastor's death. Behind the chair, a wooden box filled with sprouting onions bears the signature "Vincent," a reminder of the funerary inscription on the coffin of the stillborn "first Vincent."

In painting his chair, his own "absence," as a pendant to Gauguin's, Vincent achieved his resurrection. His poor chair is a creature of light. The intensity of the yellow note, emphasized by the vibrant blue of the contour, marks the painting of the future painted "in such a way that everybody, at least if they have eyes, would see it."[48] Whereas the elegant armchair is bathed in full chiaroscuro.

Vincent now accepted that double death. Vincent II, the resurrected Vincent I, had replaced Pa with Theo, who became Pa II in his life. Theo sent him Gauguin, to whom he offered the "director's" armchair of the studio in the South. But Gauguin could not care less about understanding his "pupil" and began to "enlighten" him in his own manner, "in spite of him, in spite of me," Vincent said, although he accepted Gauguin's advice with a great show of humility. "I always think my artistic conceptions extremely ordinary when compared to yours," he told him. "I have always had the coarse lusts of a beast. I forget everything in favor of the external beauty of things, which I cannot reproduce, for in my pictures I render it as something ugly and coarse, whereas nature seems perfect to me."[49] Moreover, he had less and less confidence in Gauguin, as he hinted to Theo: "On various occasions I have seen him do things which you and I would not let ourselves do, because we have consciences that feel differently about things. I have heard one or two things said of him, but having seen him at very, very close quarters, I think that he is carried away by his imagination, perhaps by pride, but... practically irresponsible."[50] Vincent may have become aware of Gauguin's unscrupulousness. For instance, the way he appropriated Emile Bernard's *Breton Women in the Meadow* without ever acknowledging what he owed to it was really shocking, so much so that we would not know anything about it if Emile Bernard had not defended himself and accused Gauguin, in an article in the *Mercure de France* of June 1895, of having "plagiarized" him.[5] After the *Breton Women* it was the turn of Vincent's *Sunflowers*. And we know that in spite of the latter's protests, "he has two of them already, let that hold him,"[51] Gauguin's obstinacy got him his way.

The portrait of *Vincent Painting Sunflowers* (van Gogh Museum, Amsterdam) executed by Gauguin at the beginning of December, testifies to that state of mind. He hid Vincent's picture and appropriated the bunch of sunflowers, which he then interpreted very much as Vincent had done. According to

Gauguin, Vincent hardly recognized himself and said: "It's me all right, but me gone mad." And at St.-Rémy he added, "but it was really me, very tired and charged with electricity as I was then."[52] In his memoirs, Gauguin admitted: "Between two people, him and me, one all volcano, the other also boiling, but inside, a kind of battle was brewing." He tells us that Vincent reacted violently when he saw his portrait. "That evening we went to a café. He took a light absinthe. Suddenly he threw his glass and its contents at my head. I dodged, and taking him by the arm, I left the café, crossed Place Victor Hugo, and a few minutes later Vincent found himself on his bed where he fell asleep within a few seconds and did not wake up until next morning."[1] The following morning Vincent hardly remembered anything of the incident and begged his companion to forgive him. The latter actually accepted the apology, but at the same time he warned Vincent that he was writing to Theo and tell him that he was returning. "You are leaving?" Vincent asked. "Yes," Gauguin replied. At that point "he immediately tore this phrase from a newspaper," Gauguin told Emile Bernard, "and pressed it into my hand: *The murderer has fled.*'"

Vincent's allusion must be taken *literally*. The murder of which he accused Gauguin had been perpetrated on his painting and on himself. The portrait of *Vincent Painting Sunflowers* proves it. Gauguin had shattered his concepts of painting, stolen his sunflowers, and driven him "mad." Once he had committed this crime, all he could do was to flee; but, of course, an excessively precipitate departure would incriminate him further. To distract Vincent, he suggested a trip to Montpellier to visit the Musée Fabre and see the Delacroixs and Courbets in the famous Alfred Bruyas collection—Vincent insisted on calling it "Brias." There he stopped in front of Delacroix's portrait of his patron, of which he gave Theo a disturbing description: "In the portrait by Delacroix he is a gentleman with red beard and hair, uncommonly like you or me, and made me think of that poem by Musset,

partout ou j'ai touché la terre
un malheureux vêtu de noir
auprès de nous venait s'asseoir,
qui nous regardait comme un frère.

[Wherever I touched the earth—a miserable fellow in black sat down close to us, and looked at us like a brother.] It would have the same effect on you, I'm sure." Vincent gave free interpretation of *La Nuit de Décembre* (December Night). As Viviane Forrester said, in Vincent's mind Musset's "I" had become "we." And he persisted: "Tell Degas that Gauguin and I have been to see the portrait of Brias by Delacroix at Montpellier, for we have the courage to believe that *what is is*, and the portrait of Brias by Delacroix is as like as you and me as another brother."[53] Musset's poem is strangely apt. It was December. The Delacroix awoke the "first Vincent," the "double" that bound the two Van Gogh brothers to each other. In the same letter, Gauguin was compared to both Rembrandt and Delacroix and described as "The Traveler" or as "The Man Come from Afar," the subject of a famous painting by Courbet, *Bonjour Monsieur Courbet*, which was also in the Bruyas collection and which later inspired Gauguin's *Bonjour Monsieur Gauguin* (Museum of Modern Art, Prague). Rembrandt, Delacroix, Courbet, three masters whom Vincent admired and of whose stature he believed Gauguin was. Gauguin's wide currency among the painters of the "Little Boulevard" and the circle that had formed around him spontaneously at Pont-Aven encouraged him to hope so. Wasn't it his, Gauguin's, vocation to carry the torch of a new art? After all, what did it matter if the flame had gained brightness from Bernard's and Anquetin's Cloisonnism and from Vincent's yellow?

Gauguin was only a bird of passage in the studio in the South. He had to pursue his mission in other places, pass the torch which burnt in the armchair painted by Vincent into other hands. "I owe much to Paul Gauguin," Vincent repeated in his letter to Albert Aurier, the critic, in the middle of February 1890, thanking him for his article in the *Mercure de*

◁ 138 *Vincent's Chair*. Arles, December 1888. Oil on canvas, 93 × 73.5 cm. F 498. National Gallery, London.

139 *Gauguin's Armchair*. Arles, December 1888. Oil on canvas, 90.5 × 72 cm. F 499. Rijksmuseum Vincent van Gogh, Amsterdam.

France. Then he went on: "A few days before parting company, when my disease forced me to go into a lunatic asylum, I tried to paint 'his empty seat.' It is a study of his armchair of somber reddish-brown wood, the seat of greenish straw, and in the absent one's place a lighted torch and modern novels. If an opportunity presents itself, be so kind as to have a look at this study, by way of a memento of him; it is done entirely in broken tones of green and red."[54] A funerary image, *Vanity*, a still life meant to be a substitute for Gauguin, was the middle of a series of three still lifes with candles. The first one, *Still Life with Open Bible, Candle and Novel* (F 117), shows Vincent's progress from his father's religion, the Bible, to his own, art. The third was *Still Life with Drawing Board* (F 604) in which he assembled, on one and the same plane, that of the table, all the items that were on the *Armchair*—the candle and the book—and on the *Chair* or beside it—the pipe and tobacco as well as the onions. The green jar, whose handle, the symbol of union, is "opened" by the top edge of the picture, clearly shows that the collaboration between the two artists was coming to a close. Finally, two objects that did not figure in either of the companion pieces have a special meaning. The hammer, near the candle, could be used as a weapon—by Gauguin, the "murderer"—and the bottle which, responding to the vertical of the candle in the composition, is a reference to Vincent's fondness for absinthe, a very classic way of drowning one's sorrows. In the right-hand corner, a letter, lying upside down in the manner of seventeenth-century paintings and addressed to the author, suggests Theo's presence, whereas the sprouting onions in the center remind us that the shadow of the "first Vincent" hovers over their lives. All the protagonists were now in position for the coming drama. The real drama was being played out on canvas, that battlefield of painting where the "terrible human passions," red against green confronted each other: The "happening" which took place one December evening just before Christmas was only its sad reflection. It was the battle which Gauguin—like

Delacroix in his Chapelle des Anges of the Church of St.-Sulpice—showed in the *Vision* when Jacob wrestles with the angel. A conflict that is eternally reenacted, as Antonin Artaud judged, "to the day when the violet light of the rush armchair finally submerges the picture. And we cannot fail to notice that crack of lilac light that devours the bars of the large grim armchair, of the old old armchair with the green straw, although one might not see it at once. For its center is somehow elsewhere and its source oddly obscure, like a secret to which Van Gogh alone had kept the key."[u]

Perhaps that secret was the "high yellow note" that Gauguin discovered in its nascent state in the *Sunflowers*, and through which Vincent asserted he was carrying on what Monticelli had begun. For Monticelli "is a painter who did the South all in yellow, all in orange, all in sulphur. The great majority of the painters, because they aren't colorists in the true sense of the word, do not see these colors there, and they call a painter mad if he sees with eyes other than theirs."[55] And it was with Gauguin that Vincent wanted to "saunter in the Cannebière" in Marseilles, dressed like Monticelli "with an enormous yellow hat."

The "high yellow note" of *Vincent's Chair*, a complement of the violet light of Gauguin's *Armchair*, surely had the power to revive a language that had gradually been lost to painting since the time of the Primitives. Delacroix had already rediscovered it, as Vincent remarked, in *Christ in the Boat on Lake Gennesaret*. "He—with his pale citron-colored aureole—luminously asleep against that patch of dramatic violet...."[56] After all, Vincent himself said that Delacroix's *Christ in the Boat* enabled him to do the *Sower* (F 422) with a simultaneous contrast of yellow and violet. "The masterpiece is up to you,"[57] he told Theo. The first *Sower* was a "failure." Vincent felt very lonely at the end of June, when the initial exuberance of the first few months had passed. V. Forrester has noticed a significant lapsus. When quoting Delacroix's study, he wrote "sea" instead of "lake." On the other hand, the second *Sower*, executed in November, achieved its aim. It was no longer a study. Gauguin's reassuring presence had enabled him to do a canvas "which will make a picture."[58]

To assuage the anguish he felt when Gauguin announced that he was leaving, Vincent reverted to a millenary rite. He painted a protective idol, *La Berceuse* (Augustine Roulin), a generously shaped mother goddess. Seated in an armchair, she occupied the "empty place" left by Gauguin. This first version of a series of five (F 504) directly preceded the first crisis, which struck him down at the end of December. A letter sent to Theo on 28 January 1889 traced its genesis after the event: "I have just said to Gauguin about this picture that when he and I were talking about the fishermen of Iceland and of their mournful isolation, exposed to all dangers, alone on the sea—I have just said to Gauguin that following those intimate talks of ours the idea came to me to paint a picture in such a way that sailors, who are at once children and martyrs, seeing it in the cabin of the Icelandic fishing boat, would feel the old sense of being rocked come over them and remember their own lullabys." Madame Roulin sat for him a second time. But the gentleness that shines from the portrait (F 503) is succeeded by the severity of the second (F 504), an idealized face vaguely resembling that of Moe, done after a photograph which Vincent did not find lifelike. The rectangular arms of the chair stress the rigidity of the figure. *"Now, it may be said that it is like a chromolithograph from a cheap shop.* A woman in green with orange hair standing out against a background of green with pink flowers. Now these discordant sharps of crude pink, crude orange, and crude green are softened by flats of red and green." Through Gauguin, Vincent became aware of the "abstract" reality in painting which the latter defined as "the tongue of the eye that listens," equivalent to music.

Beneath its resemblance to a "chromolithograph from a cheap shop," *La Berceuse* reverberates with the "terrible human passions" to the tune of red and green. The comforting chant is in reality a prayer of incantation. The gravity of her face and the frontal treatment of her body evoke one of the figures sculpted on the frieze of a paleo-Christian sarcophagus in the necropolis of the Alyscamps, or one of the apostles above the lintel on the porch of the cathedral of Saint-Trophime in Arles. The instructions Vincent sent to Theo on how to show the *two* proofs of *La Berceuse* executed to date, in the middle of a friezelike arrangement consisting of several canvases, bears this out: "I picture to myself the same canvases between those of the sunflowers, which would thus form torches or candelabra beside them, the same size, and so the whole would be composed of seven or nine canvases."[59]

Like the figure of a saint, *La Berceuse* carries her attribute in her hand, a piece of rope which at once identifies her indisputably as an allegorical representation of Moe: not the consoling mother, as Vincent claimed to see her, but the accusing mother of his childhood, the mother who never forgave him for taking the place of the "first Vincent." The piece of rope is, first of all, a symbol of the umbilical cord, the bond of sympathy that once had bound Vincent and his mother, and which was cut by the "first Vincent's" death; it is also symbolic of the bond that closely united Vincent and his brother, the cable with which Vincent's "tiny vessel" was towed by Theo's big ship. Moe threatened to break that tie by separating them through a woman, Jo Bonger, whom she felt Theo must marry. "....it has been our mother's wish," Vincent reminded him.[60] Later he added, "Now that you are married, we don't have to live for great ideas any longer, but, believe me, for small ones only."[61]

In painting *La Berceuse*, Vincent himself severed the cord binding him and his brother, and at the same time named the one he blamed for his act. Theo had been warned since September 1885: "It may be that there will be a tempest, but even in that case don't count on repairs or provisions, and bear in mind that under the pressure of certain circumstances I may feel obliged to cut the towrope."[62] Vincent suspected Theo of sending Gauguin to him

140 *Portrait of Augustine Roulin*. Arles, December 1888.
Oil on canvas, 55 × 65 cm. F 503. Oskar Reinhart Collection,
Winterthur.

141 *La Berceuse* (Augustine Roulin). Arles, December ▷
1888. Oil on canvas, 92 × 73 cm. F 504. Rijksmuseum
Kröller-Müller, Otterlo.

208

142   *Still Life with Drawing Board.* Arles, January 1889. Oil
on canvas, 50 × 64 cm. F 604. Rijksmuseum Kröller-Müller,
Otterlo.

so that he would be able to cut the lifeline without too much remorse. But Gauguin was oddly like Tartarin of Tarascon, the hero of Alphonse Daudet's book, and Vincent himself was like Tartarin's companion, who was roped to him and who in the Alps cut the rope as he fell so as not to drag the other into the abyss. Such was the comparison Vincent cited to Theo in his letter of 17 January 1889, as an explanation of the drama that had just taken place: "Has Gauguin ever read *Tartarin* in the Alps, and does he remember Tartarin's illustrious companion from Tarascon, who had such imagination that he imagined in a flash a complete imagery of Switzerland? Does he remember the knot in a rope found high up in the Alps after the fall? And you who want to know how things happened, have you read *Tartarin* all the way through? That will teach you to know your Gauguin pretty well."[63]

In leaving him, Gauguin cast Vincent adrift. The Provençal Japan became a mirage and the South a desert. It was the death knell of his grand design, of which he had been able to write to his friend Emile Bernard at the beginning of his stay in Arles: "More and more it seems to me that the pictures which must be made so that painting should be wholly itself, and should raise itself to a height equivalent to the serene summits which the Greek sculptors, the German musicians, the writers of French novels reached, are beyond the power of an isolated individual; so they will probably be created by groups of men combining to execute an idea held in common."[64]

Vincent could not help resenting Gauguin for having jeopardized the studio in the South. But at the same time he probably never really believed that he would leave, for he knew that Gauguin needed Theo's subsidies as desperately as he did himself. He simply despaired of finding in Gauguin the partner with whom he could "execute an idea held in common." He told Theo: "Our arguments are terribly *electric*, sometimes we come out of them with our heads as exhausted as a used electric battery."[65] In fact, Gauguin put off his departure, as

he informed Schuffenecker: "Unfortunately I am not coming yet. My situation here is very awkward; I owe a lot to (Theo) Van Gogh and Vincent, and in spite of some disagreements I can't be angry with a kind heart who is sick, who is suffering and needs me. Remember the life of Edgar [Allan] Poe, who, as a result of worries and a nervous condition became alcoholic. One day I shall explain it all fully to you. In any case, I am staying here, but my departure is on the cards."[v] Vincent, in his turn, told Theo on 23 December: "I think that Gauguin was a little out of sorts with the good town of Arles, the little yellow house where we work, and especially with me. As a matter of fact, there are bound to be grave difficulties to overcome here too, for him as well as for me. But these difficulties are more within ourselves than outside. Altogether I think that either he will definitely go, or else definitely stay."[66]

The alternative was cruel. Obsessed by Gauguin's threatened departure, Vincent got up during the night to make sure he was still there. Both were under tremendous nervous strain. Vincent resorted increasingly to absinthe and tobacco, for "the only thing to bring ease and distraction, in my case and other people's too, is to stun oneself with a lot of drinking or heavy smoking."[67] Absinthe, the use of which is now prohibited because it is thought to cause psychotic behavior, further undermined Vincent's constitution, which was already weakened by years of undernourishment and repeated fasts. Gauguin was worried about Vincent's condition, but did not realize how serious it had become. Instead of reassuring Vincent and responding to his distress signals with encouragement, he shut himself into a reproachful silence and adopted a conspicuously standoffish attitude.

In the evening of 23 December,[w] Gauguin decided to take a short, solitary walk after dinner, to get away from Vincent's usual noisy scenes. This was the beginning of the real drama. The two witnesses we have differ greatly about the actual course of events. Gauguin's account, which dates from 1903, is far too biased to be entirely credible, for all the circumstances he recounts combine to exonerate him. Taken all together, in fact, they plead "legitimate defence." "I had already crossed almost the whole of Place Victor Hugo when I heard a familiar little step behind me, quick and jerky. I turned round at the very moment when Vincent threw himself at me, an open razor in his hand. I must have given him a terribly commanding look, for he stopped, and bowing his head, he turned running for home."[x] The second testimony comes from a letter from Emile Bernard to Albert Aurier, the critic, dated 1 January 1889: Emile Bernard quoted Gauguin's own words, as he had just returned to his friend Schuffenecker in Paris: "I ran to see Gauguin, who told me this: 'The night before I left Vincent ran after me—it was night—I turned round, for he had been very odd for some time and I was suspicious. He said to me, 'You are taciturn, but I'll be the same.' I went to sleep at the hotel, and when I came back the whole of Arles was in front of our house. The police arrested me, for the house was full of blood. This is what happend: Vincent came home after I had left, took the razor, and cut his ear clean off.'" This impartial account by Emile Bernard definitively clears Vincent of an attempted assault on Gauguin, whom Bernard in turn accused of "abandoning a person in danger."

According to the rest of Gauguin's account—which we have no reason to doubt—"Van Gogh came home and immediately cut off his ear flush with his head. It must have taken him some time to stop the bleeding, for on the next day numerous wet towels were spread all over the flagstones of the two ground floor rooms. The two rooms and the little staircase leading to our bedroom had been soiled with blood. When he was fit to go out, his head buried in a Basque beret pulled right down, he went straight to a house where you can find women when you are away from home and gave the doorkeeper his ear, nicely cleaned and put into an envelope. 'Here, take this,' he said, 'in memory of me,' then fled and returned home, where he went to bed and slept."[y]Although all testimonies are agreed on the nature of Vincent's sinister gift to the brothel of Arles, they do however vary regarding in the details of the exchange. Was it the whole ear or only the lobe? A detail, no doubt, but a bloody detail! *Le Forum Republicain* of 30 December, a Sunday paper, was not explicit on this point in its local news: "Last Sunday, at 11.30 at night, one Vincent Vaugogh [*sic*], a painter, a native of Holland, presented himself at brothel No I, asked for one Rachel, and gave her...his ear, saying, 'Keep this object carefully.' Then he disappeared." The policeman on duty that evening recalled—admittedly a bit belatedly, in 1929: "Passing the brothel No I run by a certain Virginie..., the girl in question (Rachel), her pseudonym Gaby, it was she herself in the presence of the Madam that gave me a paper...saying, 'Here is what the painter gave us.' I questioned her a little, I realized it was a parcel and that it contained an entire ear."[z] Dr. Rey, the intern at the Arles hospital where Vincent was taken the following day, was of the same opinion. In fact, Vincent must have cut off a good half of the external ear, like Sergeant Radoub in Victor Hugo's *Quatre-vingt-treize*—a novel that influenced him considerably—who had half his ear shot off. The size of the bandage shown on the — *Self-Portrait* executed in January 1889 (F 527) confirms this.

The reason for this self-mutilation was twofold. This was Vincent's way of cutting the cord, since Gauguin remained "deaf" to his arguments and Theo preferred Jo to him. It is somewhat disturbing to note that the end of rope in the hands of the *Berceuse* has the strange outline of an ear. This act also expressed his autistic wish to immerse himself in painting, to cut off anything that could distract him from it. This, too, was the meaning of Matisse's famous recommendation to his pupils, in 1908, advising them to cut out their tongues!

143

143 *Self-Portrait with Bandaged Ear.* Arles, January 1889. Oil on canvas, 60 × 49 cm. F 527. Courtauld Institute Galleries, London.

Chapter VI   Mad About Painting

Adrift

Gauguin took flight from Arles like a man who had something on his conscience. When he was questioned by the police, his reactions were those of a guilty man. "The gentleman in the bowler hat said to me point-blank, in a terribly severe tone, 'Sir, what have you done to your friend?' 'I don't know....' 'Oh, yes, you know very well, he is dead.'

I wouldn't wish a moment like this on anyone, and it took several minutes for me to be able to think and to quieten my wild heartbeat. Anger, indignation, and grief too, and embarrassment at all those looks that bored into me were stifling me, and I said, stammering, 'All right, Sir. Let's go up and we'll discuss it there.'

Vincent was lying curled up in his bed, completely wrapped in the sheets: he seemed lifeless. Gently, very gently, I felt the body, and its warmth showed that it must be alive. At that, all my wit and strength returned. Almost whispering, I said to the police superintendent: 'Sir, would you wake this man very gently and, if he asks for me, tell him I have left for Paris: it might upset him to see me.' "[a]

When he awoke, Vincent asked for Gauguin insistently. But his companion in the yellow house—the man who, a few months later, had the temerity to paint himself as Christ in the *Garden of Olives*!—had deserted him. Even so, Vincent was not angry with him. What use would that be? He knew that Gauguin had left, in spite of the financial advan-

tages he had enjoyed there, because the "pupil" had proven as gifted as the "master," if not more so. Gauguin was a good teacher, as was shown by his decisive influence on Sérusier and the Nabis, and Vincent enjoyed hearing how he ordered them about—"By God, the mountains were blue, were they? Then chuck on some blue and don't go telling me that it was a blue rather like this or that, it was blue, wasn't it? Good—make them blue and it's enough!"[1]—advice that Vincent did not need, but that Gauguin nevertheless insisted on drumming into him.

Theo must have been horrified by the violence of Vincent's first attack. When Vincent was taken to hospital, Theo hastened to his bedside, but he did not stay long. In fact, his visit was so brief that Vincent barely remembered it. He wrote to him on 2 January: "Now let's talk about our friend Gauguin. Have I scared him? In short, why doesn't he give me any sign of life? He must have left with you."[2] Theo must have recognized in his brother the symptoms of that hereditary epileptic illness from which, he knew, both he and their sister Wilhelmina also suffered. He returned quickly to Paris, so as not to reveal his own anxiety, knowing at this point that his own days were numbered too.

Was Vincent "abandoned" by his brother? On the face of things, we might well think so. Only the postman Roulin and the Reverend Salles stayed by Vincent's side. The latter even expressed his indignation at Theo's seeming indifference, since he was slow to do anything about Vincent's increasingly critical condition. After a fresh stay in the hospital between the 6th and 18th February 1889, during which Vincent complained of being persecuted, he was able to return home and resume his work, thanks to the solicitude of the intern, Dr. Rey. But he was beset by fresh difficulties, for rumors had arisen locally that he was a "dangerous lunatic." It was whispered in Arles that the man with the cut ear hit children and caught girls by the waist. Didn't he look like a convict? How could he be allowed to roam free? The people of Arles worked each other up into a state of panic: Wasn't that so-called painter actually some kind of sorcerer? Who had ever seen

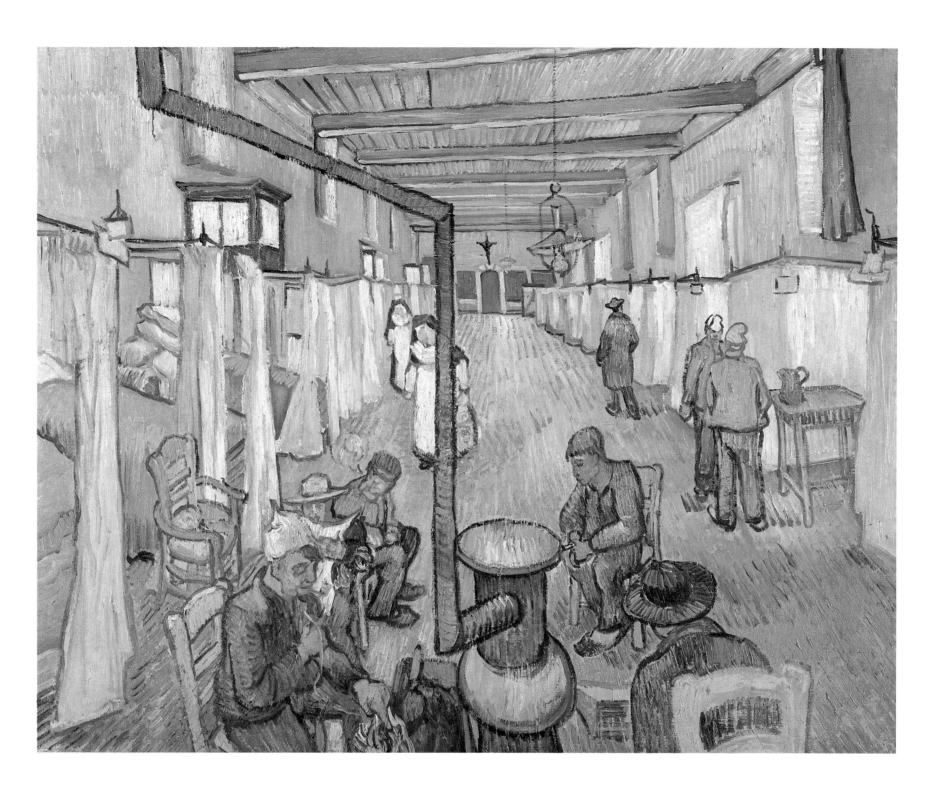

◁ 144 *Enclosed Field with Sower in the Rain.* St.-Rémy, March–April 1890. Black chalk, 24 × 27.5 cm. F 1551. Rijksmuseum Vincent van Gogh, Amsterdam.

145 *The Dormitory at the Hospital of Arles.* Arles, April 1889. Oil on canvas, 74 × 92 cm. F 646. Oskar Reinhart Collection, Winterthur.

217

anyone paint at night? Some of the villagers—about thirty, in fact, not eighty as has been stated—signed a petition to have Vincent committed, a measure the mayor hastened to implement in order to please his electors. On 26 February the police superintendent took Vincent by force to the hospital, where he was confined without being allowed to work, read, or even smoke. Not surprisingly, he had another attack that left him in a state of depression until the end of March. During this time he was unable to write, and Theo was kept informed of his condition by the Reverend Salles. But the pastor did not know that Theo

146 *Farm in the Snow and Peasants.* St.-Rémy, March–April 1890. Crayon, 31.5 × 23.5 cm. F 1593. Rijksmuseum Vincent van Gogh, Amsterdam.

himself was suffering from nervous attacks, shorter no doubt, but no less violent. Theo seized the opportunity to ask Signac, who was making a trip to the South, to visit Vincent. Vincent was greatly pleased by this: "I found Signac very quiet, though he is said to be so violent; he gave me the impression of someone who has balance and poise, that is all. Rarely or never have I had a conversation with an impressionist so free from discords or conflict on both sides."[3] Together they broke open the doors of the yellow house, which had been sealed by the police, to look at Vincent's pictures. But Vincent was still unstable. "Suddenly he wanted to gulp down a whole liter of turpentine which was on the table in the room. It was time to go back to the hospice."[b]

Vincent was very lucid about the true causes of his condition: "M. Rey says that instead of eating enough and at regular times, I kept myself going on coffee and alcohol. I admit all that, but at the same time it is true that to attain the high yellow note that I attained last summer, I really had to be pretty well keyed up.... But all I want to say is that this is a thing above the mere question of illness and health.... And that is what the first and last cause of my aberration was. Do you know those words of a Dutch poet's—'I am attached to the earth by more than earthly ties.'"[4] This passage is vitally important if one wishes to reach an understanding of Vincent's condition at that time. It enables us to see that Vincent's "drifting" from one attack to the next was the superficial aspect of a partly unconscious process, which imposed its rhythms ruthlessly and against which Vincent rebelled spasmodically. We have seen above that the *Berceuse* is one of the key figures in Vincent's work. This is shown clearly by the conditions under which its five versions were executed. The attack of Christmas 1888 interrupted work on the first, and the other four were executed during short periods of respite: the first two (F 505 and F 506) in January, and the last two (F 508 and F 507) in February and March 1889, respectively.

Thus, at the very moment when Vincent achieved a mastery of his art that enabled him to consider

147   *The Courtyard of the Hospital at Arles.* Arles, April 1889. Oil on canvas, 73 × 92 cm. F 519. Oskar Reinhart Collection, Winterthur.

himself the equal of the "master of Pont-Aven"—so that he even could write to Theo, "in my opinion he is worth more as a man than as an artist,"[5]—the *Berceuse* loomed up, the figure of the maternal interdict, holding Vincent and Theo, bound, at either end of the rope.

Both of the brothers were struggling to free themselves, each in his own way, from the guilt their mother attached to them for the death of the first-born Vincent, to whom the second Vincent was referring when he cried, "I am attached to the earth by more than earthly ties." This was the true nature of the pact that linked them so closely to each other, both straining toward the same goal, but threatened by the Widow who was poised to thwart their endeavors.

If we look carefully at the way the *Berceuse* holds the cord, we notice that in the second version (F 505) she holds it oddly between the index finger and the long finger in an eloquent "scissor" position, a strangely apt illustration of the two brothers' situation at that time. Their paths were diverging: Theo was wholly absorbed by his forthcoming marriage on 17 April, and Vincent was doubly imprisoned in his cell and in his hallucinations. Nonetheless, they both had the same unconscious inner aim: to bring back the absent Vincent. Whereas Vincent was realizing a work that would immortalize the name Vincent, which he had chosen as his sole signature, Theo was trying to procreate a "third Vincent" of flesh and blood. A veritable race against time began between them. Which of them would be able to satisfy Moe's wish? Would it be the immortality of the name, or the living flesh? "Who will lift the stone from the tomb for us?"

Vincent had only one choice: "Now if I recover, I must *begin again*, and I shall not again reach the heights to which sickness partially led me."[6] But when he tried to distract himself at the "Folies Arlésiennes," he was plagued by hallucinations of mother figures. Thus, in the "mystic crib" he discovered an "old peasant woman, just such another as Mme. Tanguy, with a head of silex or flint, dishonest, treacherous, silly," who "began to sing in her quavering voice, and then the voice changed, changed from the voice of a witch to that of an angel, and from an angel's voice to a child's, and then the answer came in another voice, strong and warm and vibrant, the voice of a woman behind the scenes."[7] Vincent's anxiety at the prospect of being unable to fulfill his mother's expectations drove him to despair. This was the meaning of the leitmotif that echoed from one letter to the next in the guise of a plaint: "I am only good for something intermediate, and second-rate, and self-effaced."[8] He felt

148 *Fountain in the Asylum Garden.* St.-Rémy, May 1889. Black chalk, pen, and reed, 49.5 × 46 cm. F 1531. Rijksmuseum Vincent van Gogh, Amsterdam.

149 *The Asylum Garden.* St.-Rémy, May 1889. Black chalk, ▷ pen, and aquarelle, 63 × 45 cm. F 1535. Rijksmuseum Vincent van Gogh, Amsterdam.

that his whole life was pointless, and that he had to resign himself to it, as he told Theo. "I will not deny that I would rather have died than have caused and suffered such trouble. Well, well, to suffer without complaining is the one lesson that has to be learned in this life."[9] So that it was not without a shudder that Vincent found he had been vouchsafed a reply to his hidden complaint a few days later, an echo of his own fate, which made a profound impression on him since he quoted it a number of times: "Quite accidentally I found in an article in an old newspaper some words written on an ancient tomb in the country between here and Carpentras. Here is this very, very, very old epitaph, say dating from the time of Flaubert's *Salammbô*. 'Thebe, daughter of Thelui, priestess of Osiris, who never complained of anyone,'"[10] he told Theo on 29 March. It was the reply of a priestess from a cult of the resurrection! And after all, wasn't Vincent achieving the resurrection of painting itself through the use of the "high yellow note" and contrasts of pure colors?

A man wholly confused in mind and spirit by his attacks, in despair over the shipwreck of his studio in the South, and apprehensive because of Theo's silence, Vincent nevertheless managed to be reborn from chaos and to achieve masterpieces. As if by some process of osmosis, his painstakingly elaborated pictorial contrasts imprinted a syncopated rhythm on his life. "I have had in all four great crises," he wrote to Wilhelmina, "during which I didn't in the least know what I said, what I wanted and what I did. ... Notwithstanding this I am working, and I have just finished two pictures of the hospital, one of a ward, a very long ward, with rows of beds with white curtains, in which some figures of patients are moving [F 646]. ... And then, as a pendant, the inner court [F 519] ... However, three gloomy black tree trunks pass through it like serpents, and in the foreground four big dismal clusters of somber box shrub. It is probable that people here won't see very much in it, but nevertheless it has always been my great desire to paint for those who do not know the artistic aspect of a picture."[11]

The Splash of Black

Vincent no longer felt strong enough to live alone. "Beginning again that painter's life I have been living, isolated in the studio so often, and without any other means of distraction than going to a café or a restaurant with all the neighbors criticizing, etc., *I can't face it....*"[12] He felt he would rather join the Foreign Legion than return to such a life. On the advice of the Reverend Salles he asked Theo to have him confined in the asylum of St.-Rémy-de-Provence on the condition that he would be allowed to go on painting there. Theo did not need any urging to agree to the request; he replied immediately, on 24 April: "If, however, there was no hidden meaning in what you said when you wrote me, I think you are quite right in going to St.-Rémy."[13]

Vincent's decision to go, which he carried out on 8 May, left Theo's hands free to carry out his marriage plans. Vincent was aware of this. He had written to Theo on 29 April[14]: *Then one thing that gave me great pleasure was your saying that Mother looks as if she were growing younger. Naturally, very soon, or even now already, her mind will be running on seeing you with a child.* That child, with whom his sister-in-law Jo was pregnant—as she told him, rather abruptly, on 5 July—would be none other than the "third Vincent," so much dreaded by the second. This news triggered off a fresh attack, Vincent's first at St.-Rémy.

At first he tried to reassure himself, without much confidence, by replying: "As for being godfather to a son of yours, when to begin with it may be a daughter, honestly, in the circumstances I would rather wait until I am away from here. Then Mother would certainly rather set her heart on its being called after our father."[15] Here was Pa rehabilitated, to serve Vincent's purpose, in a desperate reaction, although Vincent knew very well that this was not what Moe wanted.

No doubt it was in anticipation of this inevitable event that he chose to be placed under supervision, to be protected from his self-destructive impulses, as he hinted to his brother: "If I were without your friendship, they would remorselessly drive me to suicide, and however cowardly I am, I should end up by doing it." And he quoted the example of Monticelli: "You can be fairly sure that the Marseilles artist who committed suicide did not in any way do it as the result of absinthe, for the simple reason that no one would have offered it to him and he couldn't have had anything to buy it with."[16] Vincent no longer considered himself wholly responsible for his acts, so dependent was he on Theo. He was terrified at the thought that Theo might no longer be able to subsidize him because he had to bring up the "third Vincent." He saw his work as the only reason for his existence. "I am absent-minded and could not direct my own life just now."[17] Not now, not ever. He was stalked by the idea of suicide, which he might commit if, alone and defenceless in the fields, he were seized by a rather more violent attack than usual. It needed no more than just one horrible hallucination. Only just one of those strange voices, a "maternal" voice, to come and swell his guilty feelings beyond what he could bear.

Was Vincent epileptic? This was the view of Dr. Peyron, the head of the asylum, and was entered in the records of admissions. More recent medical interpretations, although more sophisticated, do not really teach us any more. Thus Dr. Russell R. Monroe has made a connection between Vincent's various psychotic reactions—self-mutilation, swallowing paints or kicking the warder, Poulet—and the neurophysiological "short-circuits" that accentuated his schizoid tendencies.[c]

Madness? Even today this word is used unanimously in describing Vincent, shut in an asylum, that "menagerie" where the food was so foul that he contented himself with bread and soup, and where the night was broken by screams. It was a different world, but Vincent was not its prisoner. He escaped into his pictures. The first-floor cell that he used as a studio was well equipped with iron bars, and yet in *Entrance to the Asylum* (F 1530) the sinister

bars have mysteriously disappeared. Some of his finest landscapes were done in that room. "Through the iron-barred window," he told Theo, "I see a squarefield of wheat in an enclosure, a perspective like Van Goyen, above which I see the morning sun rising in all its glory."[18] This was the *Field of Unripe Corn at Sunrise* (F 720): "In the foreground a field of wheat ruined and hurled to the ground by a storm. A boundary wall and beyond the gray foliage of a few olive trees, some huts and the hills. Then at the top of the canvas a great white and gray cloud floating in the azure. It is a landscape of extreme simplicity in coloring too. That will make a pendant to the study of the 'Bedroom' which has got damaged."[19]

Shutting himself up behind the bars of the asylum enabled Vincent to shut himself up in painting. *The Cup in the Madhouse*, a lithograph after Delacroix, recalled his experience, as did the *Round of Prisoners* (F 669) after Gustave Doré. The iron bars outlined squares in the space, "framed" the surfaces which he only had to recompose on the canvas. In fact, after his first attack, six weeks of madness at St.-Rémy, he felt no urge to leave his room at once, as he explained to Wilhelmina: "It is splendid weather outside—but for a long time—two months to be exact—I have not left my room; I don't know why. What I need is courage, and this often fails me. And it is also a fact that since my disease, when I am in the fields I am overcome by a feeling of loneliness to such a horrible extent that I shy away from going out. ... Only when I stand painting before my easel do I feel somewhat alive."[20]

To Vincent the landscape inhabited by man was a fragment of the universe, a "piece of nature," as the Impressionists liked to say, limited by the field of vision as is the pictorial field of a picture. Inversely, the latter, as the artist's means of expression, had a visual impact through which it acted on the human unconscious by modifying its "landscape." But whereas Gauguin, Emile Bernard, and the Nabis did not hesitate to stray from nature to draw man out of his miserable reality, Vincent sought in nature pre-

150 *Entrance to the Asylum.* St.-Rémy, October 1889. Gouache, 61.5 × 47 cm. F 1530. Rijksmuseum Vincent van Gogh, Amsterdam.

151 *Vincent's Room at the Asylum.* St.-Rémy, October 1889. ▷ Gouache, 61.5 × 47 cm. F 1528. Rijksmuseum Vincent van Gogh, Amsterdam.

cisely the features that would help man transcend it. This aim he had followed through his choice of subject and his use of style and symbol, in a stubborn search for truth, lasting almost ten years, and guided by the forceful models he found in Millet, for the symbol, and in Delacroix, for the style. With what deep humility he copied them, even when he was already their equal! With what near-religious fervor he set to work! "And I must tell you," he wrote to Theo, "—and you will see it in 'La Berceuse,' however much of a failure and however feeble that attempt may be—if I had had the strength to continue, I should have made portraits of saints and holy women from life."[21] This break with the mother, which the *Berceuse* shows symbolically, is expressed in the *Pietà* after Delacroix, through a certain violence in the gesture of her open arms letting go of the still warm body of her son (F 630).

154

Disabled by his long attacks, Vincent was driven to what he himself called, by analogy with music, "interpretation." "I let the black and white by Delacroix or Millet or something made after their work pose for me as subject. And then I improvise color on it...searching for memories of *their* pictures—but the memory, 'the vague consonance of colors which are at least right in feeling'—that is my own interpretation. ... And then my brush goes between my fingers as a bow would on the violin, and absolutely for my own pleasure."[22] On 19 September, seven of Millet's ten versions of *Work in the Fields* were finished after engravings by Jacques-Adrien Lavieille that Theo had sent. To the copies were added "repetitions" of his own subjects, recent ones like the *Bedroom* (F 483) and *L'Arlésienne, Madame Ginoux*, or old ones like the *Sower*, the *Potato Eaters*, and *Old Man Holding His Head in His Hands* (F 702). This "going back on himself" corresponded more or less to Vincent's periods of depression. His use of familiar subjects was the means by which he regained control and got a grip on himself before continuing his work. Significantly, the pictures he chose to represent mark stylistic accomplishments and bear the stamp of the "I".

155

It was at St.-Rémy that Vincent forged the style that became famous after his death and which the Expressionists adopted at the beginning of the twentieth century. It was the seal of an intimate agreement between the subject and its representation: an "agitated" style, as is shown by the *Mountain Landscape* (F 611) executed from his window, and born, by a strange paradox, when the painter himself remained more or less immobile, seated behind the double screen of the window bars and his easel, or perhaps in the immediate vicinity of the asylum, in the shadow of that huge, dark monastery. This style has often been cited as conspicuous proof of his "madness," and yet his famous brush strokes—applied in swirling curves that finally set the whole pictorial space ablaze, in colors that flew like sparks from his incendiary palette during the mistral weather, as if they had been thrown on the canvas in a rage—were actually applied with deliberate care. What Vincent tells us about his way of working is quite unambiguous: "What a queer thing the *touch* is, the stroke of the brush. In the open air, exposed to the wind, to the sun, to the curiosity of people, you work as you can, you fill your canvas anyhow. Then, however, you catch the real and essential—that is the most difficult. But when after a time you again take up this study and arrange your brush strokes in the direction of the objects—certainly it is more harmonious and pleasant to look at, and you add whatever you have of serenity and cheerfulness."[23]

158

At first sight, Vincent's brush strokes do not seem "natural." Yet they spring directly from observation of nature, and especially of the characteristic features of the Provençal landscape: the surging cornfields, the cypresses buffeted by gusts of wind, the knotty olive trees and the bent pines, and the shaggy Alpilles with winding slopes, dominated by day by the intense glare of the sun and at night by the glow of a sky spanned by shooting stars. In the "extreme simplicity" of all these forms, Vincent captured a Promethean sweep.

Starry Night (F 612) was one of the first examples

156, 157

of the application of this unifying principle, which led to the development of an entire elliptical complex, almost abstract in its impression. The immobile sparkle of *Starry Night*, which was painted from nature by the light of a street lamp, gave way to the flares of St.-Rémy. The cypresses and hills are treated in flat patches, in the Japanese manner, like the scenery in a theater, so as to increase the crushing effect of the sky, which occupies two-thirds of the surface of the canvas. The excessively pointed spire of the church and the slate-blue roofs might be regarded as memories of the North, harbingers of the homesickness that overwhelmed Vincent at the approach of winter as he feared a new attack. In the upper-right-hand corner of the sky, the moon and the sun form an eclipse, showing the basic principle of contrast, yin and yang, uniting light and darkness, yellow and violet. The cypresses and the stars are joined in the same cosmic vision drawn, in that apocalyptic night, by the infinite movement of the white spiral which is no less than the diurnal version of the Biblical column of fire, the cloud that guided the Israelites in the desert on their road to salvation.

By introducing the idea of movement, Vincent's composition directly heralded those of the pioneers of abstract art at the beginning of the twentieth century. The simultaneous *Formes circulaires, Sun-Moon* (1913) by Robert Delaunay, and Kupka's *Compénétrations* (1911) now seem to be a disturbing confirmation of Vincent's clairvoyance. Georges Yakulov's "theory of the suns" was probably founded on similar ideas. Based on the study of the relationships between colors–light and the solar prism, it brings into play the special movement of the spiral. To Yakulov, "the sun is the power that makes colors move around it, like the planets, giving to each its own rhythm..."[d]

At the same period, a rather less obvious parallel, the work of the Lithuanian painter Ciurlionis, takes on a new meaning that is also derived from musical metaphors. In his fantastic landscapes trees and clouds often merge into each other, earth and sky meet. Helmholtz, a physicist and contemporary of Van Gogh defined the instant of maximum energy or *Vortex* in his work on electric phenomena, and especially the nerve impulse, which might be represented as the swirl of a continuously rotating liquid mass in motion. An assiduous reader of all the newspapers he could lay hands on, Vincent may have been interested in the scientific articles that featured regularly at a time when electricity still retained all its mystery in the eyes of the public. He may even have borrowed more specialized magazines from Dr. Peyron, a former ship's doctor and the only person with whom he could launch into one of those long discussions so dear to the people of the South.

1889 was the year of the World's Fair, when the Eiffel Tower and the Galerie des Machines, a brilliant demonstration of the new potential of iron and glass, were contemporaneous with the archaeological reconstruction of ancient buildings. Vincent mentioned his interest in the Egyptian artists, "tillers of the soil, worshippers of the sun," who, he told Theo, "having a *faith*, working by feeling and by instinct, express all these intangible things—kindness, infinite patience, wisdom, serenity—by a few knowing curves and by the marvelous proportions."[24] When doing the cypresses he thought irresistibly of Egyptian art. "The cypresses are always occupying my thoughts, I should like to make something of them like the canvases of the sunflowers, because it astonishes me that they have not yet been done as I see them. It is as beautiful of line and proportion as an Egyptian obelisk. And the green has a quality of such distinction. It is a splash of *black* in a sunny landscape, but it is one of the most interesting black notes, and the most difficult to hit off exactly that I can imagine. But then you must see them against the blue, *in* the blue rather."[25] This was the "black note" which Albert Aurier, the critic, acknowledged in his article in the *Mercure de France* as a color. Undoubtedly Vincent was touched by this judicious remark, for it was *Cypresses* that he sent to Aurier with the following lines: "The study I have

159

227

152 *The Field of Unripe Corn at Sunrise.* St.-Rémy, June
1889. Oil on canvas, 72 × 92 cm. F 720. Rijksmuseum
Kröller-Müller, Otterlo.

153 *Cornfield at Noon.* St.-Rémy, September 1889. Oil on canvas, 74 × 92 cm. F 618. Rijksmuseum Vincent van Gogh, Amsterdam.

◁ 154   *La Pietà* (after Delacroix). St.-Rémy, September 1889. Oil on canvas, 73 × 60.5 cm. F 630. Rijksmuseum Vincent van Gogh, Amsterdam.

155   *Woman Binding Sheaves* (after Millet). St.-Rémy, September 1889. Oil on canvas, 43.5 × 33.5 cm. F 700. Rijksmuseum Vincent van Gogh, Amsterdam.

◁ 156 *Starry Night* (detail). Cf. ill. 157.

157 *Starry Night.* St.-Rémy, June 1889. Oil on canvas, 73 × 92 cm. F 612. The Museum of Modern Art, New York.

158 *Mountain Landscape.* St.-Rémy, June 1889. Oil on canvas, 70.5 × 88.5 cm. F 611. Ny Carlsberg Glyptotek, Copenhagen.

159 *Cypresses.* St.-Rémy, June 1889. Oil on canvas, 92 × 73 ▷ cm. F 620. Rijksmuseum Kröller-Müller, Otterlo.

set aside for you represents a group of them in the corner of a wheat field during a summer mistral. So it is a note of a certain nameless black in the restless gusty blue of the wide sky, and the vermilion of the poppies contrasting with this dark note."[26]

There was no question of the artists of the "Little Boulevard" being admitted to the Centennial Exhibition at the World's Fair. Roger Marx, the critic, had already had difficulties in getting Monet, Manet, and Pissarro accepted. Nor did Gauguin and his companions have the means to have their own pavilions built inside the grounds of the fair, as Courbet and Manet had done on an earlier occasion. It was Schuffenecker, that faithful friend, who saved the day in the nick of time. He succeeded in persuading one Volpini, the proprietor of a large café near the official section of the Beaux-Arts, to allow them to exhibit their canvases on the café walls in the place of the big mirrors he had ordered but which had not been delivered in time for the fair. Vincent, however, did not take part in this scheme. Theo objected to it, for he was furious when he found out that Gauguin was planning to show only six of his brother's canvases, as against the ten of his own and of Guillaumin's, Schuffenecker's and Bernard's. Hurt by this injustice and by the ingratitude of Gauguin, for whom he had done so much, Theo wrote to his brother: "At first I had said you would exhibit some things too, but they assumed an air of being such tremendous fellows that it made one sick.... It gave one somewhat the impression of going to the Universal Exhibition by the back stairs."[27] Vincent, for his part, felt no resentment against Gauguin, although the latter clearly wanted to accord him only second-rate status in the exhibition. Apparently Vincent did not understand Theo's attitude fully, but he trusted him and backed his view. The only place where some of his canvases hitherto had been seen was outside Père Tanguy's shop, and at the annual exhibition of the *Indépendants*, where a very few of his canvases had been shown during the previous year. So he was delighted to accept an invitation from Octave Maus to take part in the salon of the XX in Brussels in January 1890, together with Cézanne.

Dormant Sensibility

"We must get our eyes accustomed," Vincent often said, in order to sharpen our own sensibility. So that the *Cypresses* would "stand" in spite of the winds that tossed them incessantly, he "worked their foregrounds with thick layers of white lead, which gives firmness to the ground."[28] The sun "aroused" the perception of their color on the retina, and its intense light increased the contrasts, while the continuously blowing wind provided a sense of constant motion to their forms. This sense of vitality is conveyed strikingly in the *Yellow Corn* (F 615) in which the "agitated" brush stroke is adapted to each feature of the landscape. Vincent said that he was looking for all that was restful and calm in nature. When he read a Shakespeare play, for instance, he immediately felt the need to go and look at a blade of grass, a pine twig, or an ear of corn to calm himself. In painting it was as if the pictorial distortion he imprinted on the landscape released his excessive nervous tension and transferred a corresponding emotional power to the picture.

There is no doubt that, from this point of view, painting was beneficial, but it is equally certain that Vincent's intensive activity, the scale of his emotional "investment" and his excessive repetition of the creative act were bound to produce periods of severe depression and finally lead to those terrible, dreaded attacks. "I am working like one actually possessed," he told Theo," more than ever I am in the dumb fury of work. And I think that this will help cure me. Perhaps something will happen to me like what Eug. Delacroix spoke of, 'I discovered painting when I no longer had any teeth or breath left,' in the sense that my distressing illness makes me work with a dumb fury—very slowly—but from morning till night without slackening—and—the

160   *The Yellow Corn*. St.-Rémy, June 1889. Oil on canvas, 73 × 92 cm. F 615. National Gallery, London.

161   *Poppy Fields.* St.-Rémy, June 1889. Oil on canvas 71 × 91 cm. F 581. Kunsthalle, Bremen.

secret is probably this—work long and slowly." *Yellow Corn* was a revealing reversion to the Northern palette with its colder, more acid tones, which expressed the homesickness that preceded his attacks. "What I dream of in my best moments is not so much striking color effects as once more the half tones."[29] The cooling of the palette that accompanied his eloquent pictorial distortion was a sign of the depression he suffered as an effect of his creative activity.

A number of canvases painted between June and December 1889 are of this kind, with a preponderance of earthy colors, muted by mauves. These were mainly olive fields (such as F 585 and F 710), whose "lines are warped as in old wood," and mountain landscapes (e.g., F 724 and F 622), and also the *Entrance to a Quarry* (F 744) and his penultimate *Self-Portrait* (F627). "I rather like the 'Entrance to a Quarry,'" Vincent explained to his brother, "—I was doing it when I felt this attack coming on—because to my mind the somber greens go well with the ocher tones; there is something sad in it which is healthy, and that is why it does not bore me. Perhaps that is true of the 'Mountain' too. They will tell me that mountains are not like that and that there are black outlines of a finger's width.... Altogether I think nothing in it *at all* good except the 'Field of Wheat,' the 'Mountain,' the 'Orchard,' the 'Olives' with the blue hills and the portrait and the 'Entrance to the Quarry,' and the rest tells me *nothing*, because it lacks individual intention and feeling in the lines. Where these lines are close and deliberate it begins to be a picture, even if it is exaggerated. That is a little what Gauguin and Bernard feel, they do not ask the correct shape of a tree at all, but they do insist that one can say if the shape is round or square—and honestly, they are right, exasperated as they are by certain people's photographic and empty perfection."[30]

Although the forceful continuous contour outlining the rocks and tree trunks in these pictures was also used by Gauguin and Bernard, Vincent applied it in a notably different manner. While they imposed "abstract" forms taken from their imaginations, he always sought the line that was synthesized directly from his observations of nature. Numerous drawings testify to his love for nature, and its freshness and truth of expression are to be found in his paintings too. Both *Pine Trees against the Light* (F 652) and F 657, *Road Menders,* with its centuries-old plane trees which to this day line the road to St.-Rémy, are wonderful examples of this. No wonder he grew angry when he saw the rendering of natural features by Gauguin and Bernard in their *Christ in the Garden of Olives,* "with nothing really observed," he thought[31]: "...our friend Bernard has probably never seen an olive tree. Now he is avoiding getting the least idea of the possible, or of the reality of things, and that is not the way to synthesize."[32] And a little later he added, about his own olive fields: "Of course with me there is no question of doing anything from the Bible—and I have written to Bernard and Gauguin too that I considered that our duty is thinking, not dreaming, so that when looking at their work I was astonished at their letting themselves go like that."[33] He even wrote to Bernard at the beginning of December to express his criticism, saying that "one can try to give an impression of anguish without aiming straight at the historic Garden of Gethsemane; that it is not necessary to portray the characters of the Sermon on the Mount in order to produce a consoling or gentle motif." In his view, Millet had proved it. "The Bible! The Bible! Millet, having been brought up on it from infancy, did nothing but read that book! And yet he never, or hardly ever, painted Biblical pictures."[34]

Admittedly, Vincent had done a few Biblical scenes, but these were "interpretations" done after Rembrandt, that is, the *Raising of Lazarus* (F 677); or after Delacroix, like *La Pietà*, and the *Good Samaritan* (F 633, Rijksmuseum Kröller-Müller, Otterlo).

At the end of 1889, Vincent's landscapes strangely came to resemble those of Cézanne. As early as 1876 the latter had said at L'Estaque: "There are subjects that would need three or four months of work, and they could be found, for the vegetation there does

162 *Olive Field.* St.-Rémy, June 1889. Oil on canvas, 72 × 92
cm. F 585. Rijksmuseum Kröller-Müller, Otterlo.

163 *Olive Fields.* St.-Rémy, November 1889. Oil on canvas, 74 × 93 cm. F 710. The Minneapolis Institute of Arts, Minneapolis (The William Hood Dunwoody Fund).

164   *View of the Alpilles.* St.-Rémy, June 1889. Oil on canvas,
59 × 72 cm. F 724. Rijksmuseum Kröller-Müller, Otterlo.

165 *Mountains.* St.-Rémy, July 1889. Oil on canvas, 73 × 93 cm. F 622. The Solomon R. Guggenheim Museum, New York (The Justin K. Thannhauser Collection).

166 *Entrance to a Quarry*. St.-Rémy, October 1889. Oil on canvas, 60 × 72.5 cm. F 744. Rijksmuseum Vincent van Gogh, Amsterdam

167 *Self-Portrait*. St.-Rémy, September 1889. Oil on canvas, ▷ 65 × 54 cm. F 627. Musée d'Orsay, Paris.

244

◁ 168 *Pine Trees against the Light.* St.-Rémy, November 1889. Oil on canvas, 92 × 73 cm. F 652. Rijksmuseum Kröller-Müller, Otterlo.

169 *The Road Menders.* St.-Rémy, December 1889. Oil on canvas, 74 × 93 cm. F 657. The Cleveland Museum of Art, Cleveland (Gift of the Hanna Fund).

not change. These are the olive trees and the pines which always keep their foliage. The sun is so terrible that I think objects stand out in silhouettes not only in black and white but in blue, red, brown, and violet. I may be wrong, but I think that this is the antithesis of form."e He preferred pines to olive trees, which were a new subject in Vincent's view, as he wrote to Emile Bernard: "The olive trees here, old man, would be the very thing for you ... they are silver against a soil of orange and violet hues, under the large white sun. ... In the first place there is something of Corot in that silvery gray, and this especially no one has done yet, whereas several painters have got their apple trees, for instance, and their willows right."[35]

In Cézanne's work, the tree trunks are outlined with a discontinuous contour, which permits "passages" from one colored plane to another, and they form the skeleton of a homogeneous pictorial structure. In Cézanne's earliest picture of the *Montagne Saint Victoire* (1885–1887), he distorted the "natural" view of the landscape to substitute his own "inner view." As Liliane Brion-Guerry said: "The mass of Saint Victoire rises, haunting, as if it occupied the foreground of the landscape in reality, whereas if the painter had followed the classic laws of perspective, it would appear at the back of the composition as a low hill."f This kind of pictorial language, combining the patch of color with the form of the masses to create an autonomous means of expression, was also used by Vincent, but to the point of dissociating the two component parts. Hence, in the last resort, form became less descriptive than meaningful, a step toward a notably greater symbolic content in the picture.

The fact that, Vincent had "experienced" distortion during his attacks, in a manner of speaking, certainly assisted that process. He confided to Wilhelmina: "During the attacks I experience this to such a degree that all the persons I see then, *even if I recognize them,* which is not always the case, seem to come toward me out of a great distance, and to be *quite different* from what they are in reality."[36]

Man Walking among Trees (F 742), an expression of Vincent's apprehensions about solitude, combined the flattened forms of the outlined tree trunks, the twisted mass of the foliage in the center of the picture, and the tiny silhouette of the figure, with whom Vincent identified himself and who, by way of contrast, is made to appear much farther away, than the trees. He told Theo: "I am trying as much as possible to simplify the lists of paints—therefore I very often use the ochers as I did in the old days. I know quite well that the studies in the last package, drawn with such great shadowy lines, were not what they ought to have been; however I beg you to believe that in landscape I am trying to mass things by means of a drawing style which tries to express the interlocking of the masses."[37]

Oddly enough, it was Cézanne who, from 1890 on, continued his research in that direction, although he had advised Emile Bernard "to turn his back on Gauguin and Van Gogh." His numerous studies of rocks in the woods have a frontal treatment and effect of mass that recall *Entrance to a Quarry*, which Vincent described to Bernard: "...pale lilac rocks in reddish fields, as in certain Japanese drawings. In the design and in the division of the color into large planes there is no little similarity to what you are doing at Pont-Aven."[38] Whereas the power of synthesis of the *Ravine* (Les Peiroulets) (F 661) found during the same period an echo in Cézanne's *Sainte Victoire*.

Since the beginning of September, Vincent had suggested to Theo on several occasions that he wanted to leave St.-Rémy and come back to the North. Both of them thought that Pissarro might lodge him at Eragny-sur-Epte, near Gisors. But, on 4 October, Theo wrote to his brother that this solution could no longer be considered, since Pissarro's wife objected. Nevertheless, Pissarro had advised Vincent to get in touch with a certain Dr. Gachet, a homeopathic physician living at Auvers-sur-Oise and a spare-time painter under the pseudonym of Paul Van Ryssel. This was a distinct possibility, especially since Dr. Gachet was already looking after

170 *The Raising of Lazarus.* St.-Rémy, May 1890. Oil on canvas, 48.5 × 63 cm. F 677. Rijksmuseum Vincent van Gogh, Amsterdam.

171 *Man Walking among Trees.* St.-Rémy, November 1889.
Oil on canvas, 46 × 51 cm. F 742. Rijksmuseum Kröller-
Müller. Otterlo.

172 *The Ravine* (Les Peiroulets). St.-Rémy, December 1889. Oil on canvas, 72 × 92 cm. F 661. Rijksmuseum Kröller-Müller, Otterlo.

173 *Siesta* (after Millet). St.-Rémy January 1890. Oil on canvas, 73 × 91 cm. F 686. Musée d'Orsay, Paris.

174 *The Red Vineyards at Arles* (detail). Arles, November ▷ 1888. Oil on canvas, 75 × 93 cm. F 495. Pushkin Museum, Moscow (The whole picture is reproduced on p. 306).

Manet, Monet, Renoir, and Sisley, among others. On the other hand, he advised against Brittany, which "had something of the cloister," and would thus hardly be much of a change from the atmosphere of Saint Paul of Mausole. In January, however, Vincent wrote to Gauguin to ask him if he could come to Pont-Aven, but the latter declined, and in order to keep him far away suggested—with a certain amount of insolence—that he should go to Antwerp and found a studio there in his, Gauguin's, name.

While Vincent was seriously considering settling in Antwerp, with the consent of Dr. Peyron, three things happened simultaneously: He received an enthusiastic review by Albert Aurier, which ap-

174 peared on 18 January; he heard that his *Red Vineyards* (F 495) (Pushkin Museum, Moscow), which had been exhibited at the XX, had been sold; and above all, he had news of the birth of the "third Vincent," born on 31 January. He wrote to his mother, on 15 February, to disclaim all responsibility for the choice of the baby's name, repeating what he had already told his brother: "I should have greatly preferred him to call the boy after Father, of whom I have been thinking so much these days, instead of after me; but seeing it has now been done, I started right away to make a picture for him, to hang in their bedroom, big branches of white almond blossom against a blue sky."[39] Vincent did not breathe a word of this project to Theo. It was a surprise, a christening present for his godson, a "funny" picture, to use one of his favorite expressions; for on

175 that abstract blue background the *Flowering Almond Tree Branches* (F 671) "float" in total weightlessness. No trunk attaches them to the ground. The branches have been cut, or cut out by the rectangle of a window. They were probably painted from indoors, to be framed and hung on the wall as were the locks of hair of the "first Vincent."

Branches cut off in flower, the *Raising of Lazarus*: the stone had been lifted from the tomb, and a few days later, Vincent suffered the longest attack he had ever had, from which he emerged only intermittently and which kept him confined at St.-Rémy until mid-May. On 29 March, Theo and Jo wrote to him for his birthday. Theo told him about meeting Dr. Gachet, "a man of understanding" who, he mentioned in passing, bore a physical likeness to his brother. But Vincent was in no state to reply, and the correspondence between the two brothers was interrupted until around 20 April. The break had occurred just when the *Flowering Almond Tree Branches* was being executed. "My work was going well," he explained to Theo when at last he was better, "the last canvas of branches in blossom—you will see that it was perhaps the best, the most patiently worked thing I had done, painted with calm and with a greater firmness of touch. And the next day, down like a brute!"[40]

Vincent was now determined to leave the South as quickly as possible to try to erase the terrible memories that tormented him. He was convinced that in the North he would get better more quickly. "I think of it as a shipwreck," he wrote at the beginning of May.[41] His "tiny vessel" was sinking, swallowed by the waves. In his painting there were no more horizons, no more stars, only the surging ridge of the thatched roofs under a vast, cloud-swept sky, the landscapes of his *Souvenirs of the North* (F 675), which had surfaced to ease his appre-176 hension. He told his mother and his sister Wilhelmina: "I continued painting even when my illness was at its height, among other things a memory of Brabant, hovels with moss-covered roofs and beech hedges on an autumn evening with a stormy sky, the sun setting amid ruddy clouds."[42]

Vincent felt he must at all costs wipe out the sinister visions of his solitude like the *Two Peasant Wo-*177 *men Digging in a Snow-Covered Field* (F 695), bent in their futile effort to break through the hard frost of the soil. These poor souls, whom he often drew without faces, were deformed by their obscure labor as he was by his—were swept away by a destiny of mechanical work. "The brush strokes come like clockwork," Vincent had remarked about his own work.[43] And he had made so many self-portraits! So he persisted in telling Theo that he wanted to go

175 *Flowering Almond Tree Branches.* St.-Rémy, February 1890. Oil on canvas, 73 × 92 cm. F 671. Rijksmuseum Vincent van Gogh, Amsterdam.

176 *Souvenirs of the North.* St.-Rémy, March–April 1890.
Oil on canvas pasted on wood. 29 × 36.5 cm. F 675. Rijksmuseum Vincent van Gogh, Amsterdam.

177 *Two Peasant Women Digging in a Snow-Covered Field.* St.-Rémy, March–April 1890, Oil on canvas, 50 × 64 cm. F 695. E.G. Bührle Collection, Zurich.

178   *Meadow with Dandelions.* St.-Rémy, May 1890. Oil on canvas, 72 × 90 cm. F 676. Rijksmuseum Kröller-Müller, Otterlo.

179   *Walk in the Moonlight amidst Olive Trees.* St.-Rémy, ▷ May 1890. Oil on canvas, 49.5 × 45.5 cm. F 704. Museu de Arte, São Paulo.

◁ 180 *The Road with Cypresses.* St.-Rémy, May 1890. Oil on canvas, 92 × 73 cm. F 683. Rijksmuseum Kröller-Müller, Otterlo.

to Auvers, to Dr. Gachet: *"I think the best thing will be for me to go myself to see this doctor in the country as soon as possible."*[44] As if to convince his brother that he was completely recovered, he began to paint the most serene subjects. Large bouquets of flowers, roses and *Irises* (F 678), a smiling *Meadow with Dandelions* (F 676), and some real allegories of happiness and the joy of living, like the *Walk in the Moonlight amidst Olives* (F 704) and the *Road with Cypresses* (F 683). "At present all goes well," he assured Theo, "the whole horrible attack has disappeared like a thunderstorm and I am working to give a last stroke of the brush here with a calm and steady enthusiasm."[45]

184
178
179
180

"We Can Only Make Our Pictures Speak"

"For myself I can see from afar the possibility of a new art of painting, but it was too much for me, and it is with pleasure that I return to the North,"[46] Vincent told Isaacson, one of the very few people, besides Albert Aurier, to appreciate his work.

When he arrived back in Paris on the morning of Saturday, 17 May, he surprised Jo, who was expecting to see a frail invalid, by his robust looks, decisive manner, and cheerful expression. "He is completely well and even seems a lot stronger than Theo," she remarked.[8] Vincent stayed only three days with his brother and sister-in-law, spending most of the time looking again at his canvases, which cluttered up the small apartment, stored even under the furniture. Anxious to get back to painting, he went to Auvers on 21 May, and decided to settle not at the inn recommended by Dr. Gachet but at the café kept by the Ravoux family in Place de la Mairie, where the room was only half the price.

Full of ardor, Vincent set to work at once. "Auvers is decidedly very beautiful," he exclaimed happily, feeling his mastery returning. This is shown by his first series of landscapes, that is, *Cottages at Cordeville* (F 792), whose sure and forceful brush strokes and brilliant colors testify to the skill he had acquired in the South. "It is as I thought," he wrote to Theo, "I see more violet hues wherever they are."[47] He also did several studies of *Dr. Gachet's Garden.* But it was with *Church at Auvers* (F 789) that he reached his summit.

181–183
185
186
187
189

He had not achieved such fullness and power of expression for a long time. Yet the work also had an unequalled serenity, juxtaposing the "synthetist" patches of contoured color with deliberate accents of his vibrant brush stroke, which in the foregrounds had the almost Pointillist character it had shown in the brilliant Arles landscapes of 1888. Vincent gave Wilhelmina an eloquent description: "I have a larger picture of the village church—an effect in which the building appears to be violet-hued against a sky of simple deep blue color, pure cobalt; the stained-glass windows appear as ultramarine blotches, the roof is violet and partly orange. In the

181 *The Old Vineyard.* Auvers-sur-Oise, May 1890. Crayon and aquarelle, 43.5 × 54 cm. F 1624. Rijksmuseum Vincent van Gogh, Amsterdam.

◁ 182   *Bouquet of Flowers.* Auvers-sur-Oise, June 1890. Oil on canvas, 42 × 29 cm. F 764a. Rijksmuseum Vincent van Gogh, Amsterdam.

183   *Roses and Anemones.* Auvers-sur-Oise, June 1890. Oil on canvas, 51 × 51 cm. F 764. Musée d'Orsay, Paris.

◁ 184 *Still Life: Irises.* St.-Rémy, May 1890. Oil on canvas, 92 × 73.5 cm. F 678. Rijksmuseum Vincent van Gogh, Amsterdam.

185 *A House with Two People.* Auvers-sur-Oise, June 1890. Oil on canvas, 38 × 45 cm. F 806. Rijksmuseum Vincent van Gogh, Amsterdam.

186 *Cottages at Cordeville.* Auvers-sur-Oise, May 1890. Oil
on canvas, 72 × 91 cm. F 792. Musée d'Orsay, Paris.

187 *Dr. Gachet's Garden.* Auvers-sur-Oise, May 1890. Oil ▷
on canvas, 73 × 51.5 cm. F 755. Musée d'Orsay, Paris.

266

188   *Portrait of Dr. Gachet.* Auvers-sur-Oise, June 1890. Oil
on canvas, 68 × 57 cm. F 754. Musée d'Orsay, Paris.

189   *The Church at Auvers.* Auvers-sur-Oise, June 1890. Oil ▷
on canvas, 94 × 74 cm. F 789. Musée d'Orsay, Paris.

foreground some green plants in bloom, and sand with the pink glow of sunshine on it. And once again it is nearly the same thing as the studies I did in Nuenen of the old tower and the cemetery, only it is probable that now the color is more expressive, more sumptuous."[48]

188 The *Portrait of Dr. Gachet* was executed at the same time. The same blue is there. Vincent was trying to re-launch his grand design, always returned to and always interrupted for lack of models or by his not being "ready." Each time he resurrected the project, he asked his brother for the Bargue manual in order to improve himself further. "What impassions me most," he repeated, "—much, much more than all the rest of my metier—is the portrait, the modern portrait. I seek it in color, and surely I am not the only one to seek it in this direction. I *should like*... to paint portraits which would appear after a century to the people living then as apparitions. By which I mean that I do not endeavor to achieve this by a photographic resemblance, but by means of our impassioned expressions—that is to say, using our knowledge of and our modern taste for color as a means of arriving at the expression and the intensification of character."[49]

Indeed, he did paint a whole series of portraits over the month of June. But most of them were ra-
190 ther hastily dashed off studies, like the *Two Children* in bonnets (F 783) painted in "compartments" with the help of a wide and curving purplish outline.
191 This is not true, however, of the portrait of *Marguerite Gachet at the Piano* (F 772), a canvas whose elongated format recalls the Japanese kakemonos. In this picture Vincent evolved an aesthetic of flat space which he had not attempted so definitely since the portrait of *La Segatori* and which yields nothing to the Nabi portraits by Vuillard. The use of a decorative Pointillism for the background, divided horizontally into two parts; the pose of the model, seated in profile; and the huge white flat area produced by her dress, which partially hides the stool and is integrated in the plane of the canvas, all contribute to the creation of what Matisse would later call a "de-

corative figure on an ornamental ground": a human figure painted like an object, capable of distortion, integrated in an autonomous plastic space.

Taken in the horizontal sense, in the manner of a makemono, this format, which is twice as long as it is wide (around 102 ×50 cm), is particularly well suited to landscapes, especially those that have either distant views or, on the contrary, only foregrounds. Photography, which the painters of that period—especially the Impressionists and the Nabis—liked to practice, might have had something to do with the choice. Vincent regularly used photographic reproductions, both of works by Delacroix or Millet that he had used as models, and of his own works, to send to his friends and ask for their opinions. At The Hague he had already witnessed the popularity of photography. Undoubtedly the phenomenon made a deeper impression on him than he would admit because of its inherent framing and focusing capabilities. Thus the *Roots and Tree Trunks* (F 816) 193 with their twisting lines fascinated him, so that he showed them in close-up. But in *Daubigny's Garden* 194 (F 777)—"one of my most purposeful canvases," he told Theo—the ground actually curves in the manner of the "wide angle," with the various features of the landscape set out along it. "To the left a green and lilac bush and the stem of a plant with whitish leaves. In the middle a border of roses, to the right a wicket, a wall, and above the wall a hazel tree with violet foliage. Then a lilac hedge, a row of rounded yellow lime trees, the house itself in the background, pink, with a roof of bluish tiles. A bench and three chairs, a figure in black with a yellow hat and in the foreground a black cat. Sky pale green."[50]

The same lengthwise format determines the characteristics of two canvases which mark the end of Vincent's life: the *Field under a Stormy Sky* (F 778) and *Crows over the Cornfields* (F 779). Never before had Vincent achieved such intense expressiveness through such sober means. Thus the *Field under a* 196 *Stormy Sky* displays the simplicity of a canvas divided into two planes, the sky and the earth, depicted by a palette restricted to two primary colors, blue

190   *Two Children*. Auvers-sur-Oise, June 1890. Oil on canvas, 51.5 × 51.5 cm. F 783. Musée d'Orsay, Paris.

◁ 191 *Marguerite Gachet at the Piano*. Auvers-sur-Oise, June 1890. Oil on canvas, 102 × 50 cm. F 772. Kunstmuseum, Basle.

192 *Mademoiselle Gachet in her Garden*. Auvers-sur-Oise, June 1890. Oil on canvas, 46 × 55 cm. F 756. Musée d'Orsay, Paris.

le jardin de Daubigny

◁ 193 *Tree Trunks and Roots.* Auvers-sur-Oise, July 1890. Oil on canvas, 50.5 × 100.5 cm. F 816. Rijksmuseum Vincent van Gogh, Amsterdam.

◁ 194 *Daubigny's Garden.* Auvers-sur-Oise, July 1890. Oil on canvas, 56 × 101.5 cm. F 777. Kunstmuseum, Basle (on loan to the Rudolf Staechelin'sche Familienstiftung).

195 *Poppy Field.* Auvers-sur-Oise, June 1890. Oil on canvas, 73 × 91.5 cm. F 636. Gemeentemuseum, The Hague.

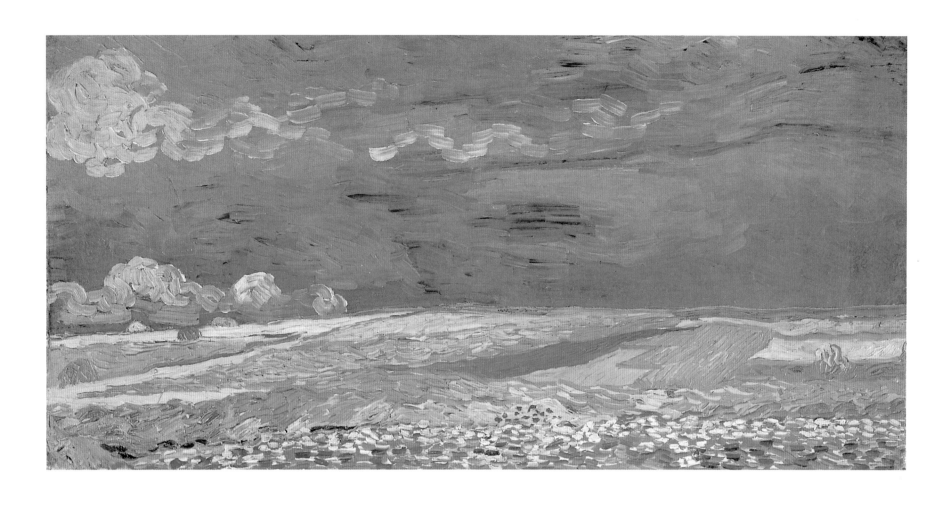

196   *The Field under a Stormy Sky.* Auvers-sur-Oise, July
1890. Oil on canvas, 50 × 100 cm. F 778. Rijksmuseum Vincent van Gogh, Amsterdam.

and yellow, and the resultant secondary color, green. The short, incisive brush strokes are essential to the pictures, creating and animating the surfaces according to their direction and juxtapositions.

198, 199 *Crows over the Cornfields* entirely dispenses with aerial perspective, which still had lingered in the previous picture. In an absolutely frontal treatment the ears of corn form a compact mass produced by the thick crossed tangle of strokes applied with a restrained vehemence, a life-giving gust that bends them from left to right. The mud path in blood-red, emphasised by a wide green border, desperately hugs the "large patch of yellow," which it cannot cross. The picture is divided rigidly by the flat areas of color thus formed, the only link between them being provided by the foreboding diagonal flight of crows.

These two paintings reveal the grave worries that beset Vincent at the beginning of July. Theo was having serious difficulties at his job and was even thinking of leaving Goupil, but this was not possible, for he had *three* people to keep: his wife, his son, and his brother. One Sunday when Vincent was visiting Paris, they discussed this depressing situation. Vincent returned to Auvers that same evening distressed and in confusion, in his own words, not knowing if his monthly payments would still be made to him as before. He was also very anxious about his nephew's state of health, for the infant had been ill—yet another worry: "Since you were good enough to call him after me, I should like him to have a soul less unquiet than mine, which is foundering. ...I feel exhausted," he added. "So much for me—I feel that this is the lot which I accept and which will not change. ... And the prospect grows darker, I see no happy future at all."[51] A few days later, these feelings still persisted: "Back here, I still feel very sad and continued to feel the storm which threatens you weighing on me too." Somewhat reassured by a more cheerful letter from Jo, he went back to work—"though the brush almost slipped from my fingers"—and executed the two dramatic *Cornfields* in one sitting. "They are vast fields of wheat under troubled skies, and I did not need to go out of my way to try to express sadness and extreme loneliness. I hope you will see them soon—for I hope to bring them to you in Paris as soon as possible, since I almost think that these canvases will tell you what I cannot say in words, the health and restorative forces that I see in the country."[52,h]

"There Is No End to Sorrow"

In an attempt to overcome the sense of apprehension that again gripped him at the thought of the burden he was to his brother and the futility of his efforts to lighten it, Vincent began to paint frenziedly, as he had done in the last days at St.-Rémy. Then he had written that he was working "like one actually possessed." At Auvers his working became really diabolical. During the last seventy-one days of his life, Vincent executed over eighty canvases; that is, more than one a day! And sometimes he worked on several simultaneously.

The solitude in which he shut himself to suspend time and escape mundane worries became total. Disappointed in Dr. Gachet, he broke off all relations with him. (Even when he had first arrived at Auvers his impression had been rather reserved: "I have seen Dr. Gachet, who gives me the impression of being rather eccentric, but his experience as a doctor must keep him balanced enough to combat the nervous trouble from which he certainly seems to me to be suffering at least as seriously as I," he had written to his brother.)[53]

Vincent quickly saw a parallel between his own behavior and that of Dr. Gachet, a man in his sixties who could have been his father. The doctor's Flemish origins and red hair, which earned him the nickname Dr. Saffron, accentuated the resemblance between the two down to the most minute physical features. A spare-time painter to boot, the doctor seemed to Vincent like a double, a new substitute for his father and brother, rolled into one. "I have found a true friend in Dr. Gachet," he told

Wilhelmina, "another brother, so much do we resemble each other physically and also mentally."[54] His *Portrait of Dr. Gachet*, started at the beginning of June, was done with that idea in mind and based directly on his penultimate self-portrait (F 627), as he told Theo: "I am working at his portrait, the head with a white cap, very fair, very light, the hands also a light flesh tint, a blue frock coat and a cobalt blue background, leaning on a red table, on which are a yellow book and a foxglove plant with purple flowers. It has the same sentiment as the self-portrait I did when I left for this place."[55]

It seems that the relationship between the two men was always rather strained, in spite of some early enthusiastic remarks of Vincent's. He could not fail to be faintly suspicious of the sometimes excessive friendliness with which he was treated. For example, the doctor felt obliged to invite his "protege" to "four- or five-course dinners, which is as dreadful for him as for me."[56] But this obviously was not the cause of the gradual cooling of their friendship, nor was it the explanation generally put forward that Vincent was angry because of a picture by Guillaumin, *Nude Woman on a Bed* (Musée d'Orsay), which the doctor did not have framed.

A "sacrilege" on a different scale, more difficult to understand, may have been the cause of their split. In his first visit Vincent must have noticed that the doctor had a great many Impressionist canvases by Cézanne, Guillaumin, Monet, and Renoir, most of them gifts received in return for medical treatment. He also knew, or soon realized, that Gachet himself was an amateur painter under the pseudonym of Paul Van Ryssel. At first these facts, added to their personal similarities which he had already noticed, made the doctor's understanding and lively encouragement seem natural to him. Vincent told Wilhelmina about his first portrait of the *Arlésienne* (F 543), which he had seen again at Theo's: "My friend Dr. Gachet is *decidedly enthusiastic* about the latter portrait of the Arlésienne, which I have made a copy of for myself—and also about a self-portrait, which I am very glad of, seeing that he will urge me to paint figures, and I hope he is going to find some interesting models for me to paint."[57]

But he also must have realized, bit by bit, that the good doctor applied his artistic talents chiefly to copying the works of his Impressionist friends, over his own signature. There are several examples of this in the Musée d'Orsay in Paris. It is possible that Vincent began to suspect that the encouragement he received was not as disinterested as it had seemed at first. This appeared to be confirmed by the enthusiasm with which Dr. Gachet spoke of his portrait, about which, Vincent said, he was "absolutely *fanatical*." We may conclude that the doctor's behavior finally irritated Vincent, who still retained bitter memories of the passionate insistence with which Gauguin had appropriated his *Sunflowers*.

In mid-July, he told Theo frankly: "I think we must not count on Dr. Gachet *at all*. First of all, he is sicker than I am, I think, or shall we say just as much, so that's that. Now when one blind man leads another blind man, don't they both fall into the ditch? I don't know what to say. Certainly my last attack, which was terrible, was in a large measure due to the influence of the other patients, and then the prison was crushing me, and old Dr. Peyron didn't pay the slightest attention to it, leaving me to vegetate with the rest, all deeply tainted."[58]

Dr. Gachet's attitude seems very strange in retrospect. Antonin Artaud, who had experienced a "confinement" similar to Vincent's, did not hesitate to hold the doctor largely responsible for Vincent's suicide, and blamed him for having sent him "to bury himself in a landscape in order to escape the evil of thinking."[i] In his loneliness, Vincent saw his subjects rise up in front of him like insurmountable walls, brutally hostile, walls which color turned into flat areas, impasto surfaces contained in an outline but nevertheless moving according to the currents set in motion by the brush strokes. In vain he sought in *Thatched Roofs at Chaponval* (F 780) the reassuring image of the "nest" capable of protecting him from the threat of a fresh attack. "Consoling" painting was no more. Although *Crows over the Cornfields*

197 *Thatched Roofs at Chaponval.* Auvers-sur-Oise, July
1890. Oil on canvas, 65 × 81 cm. F 780. Kunsthaus, Zurich.

198 *Crows over the Cornfields* (detail). Cf. ill. 199.

199 *Crows over the Cornfields.* Auvers-sur-Oise, July 1890. Oil on canvas, 50.5 × 100.5 cm. F 779. Rijksmuseum Vincent van Gogh, Amsterdam.

200   *The Staircase at Auvers,* Auver-sur-Oise, July 1890. Oil
on canvas, 51 × 71 cm. F 795. The St. Louis Art Museum, St.
Louis, Missouri.

was not his last picture, it was nonetheless his last *painted* cry of revolt.

His pathological agitation came back, along with the threat of a new attack, as the agitated brush strokes and the twisted outlines of the *Staircase at Auvers* (F 795) testify. In despair, Vincent tried to apply Dr. Gachet's advice, painting "calmly" so as not to tire himself too much; but the results, a few rather bleak cornfields, desolated him. On 20 July, Theo wrote to his wife, who was in Holland: "If only he did not become melancholy, if only a new attack wasn't in the offing, everything seemed to be going so well."[j] And yet, even so, how much he managed to convey through those cornfields! Even at St.-Rémy, shut in his cell, he had only to see the corner of a landscape through the iron bars of his window to draw reverberating yellow harmonies from it. And when by chance the frail silhouette of a reaper came into his field of vision, far away against the light, he would suddenly grow excited and tell his brother: "For I see in this reaper—a vague figure fighting like a devil in the midst of the heat to get to the end of his task—I see in him the image of death, in the sense that humanity might be the wheat he is reaping. So it is—if you like—the opposite of that sower I tried to do before. But there's nothing sad in this death, it goes its way in broad daylight with a sun flooding everything with a light of pure gold."[59]

Vincent was thinking of the art of the "ancient Japanese." What power of expression in their least prints, and what skillful observation! What a formidable lesson they had taught him: how to look at a blade of grass, a pine twig, an ear of corn! And the question of that "devil of yellow," of painting "full of sulphur," exploding like a challenge to the grayness of the salon—didn't it have to be asked? And what if all these efforts, all that painful self-denial, were to be annihilated forever by an incurable hereditary disease? How many more of these horrible attacks could he bear?

On 25 July 1890, Theo wrote to Jo: "I have a letter from Vincent that I find wholly incomprehensible. When will a better day dawn for him too?"[k] Vincent was losing his grip. Theo was farther away from him than ever, entirely monopolized by the "third Vincent," who had been very ill and was still frail. Vincent remembered what he had told his sister Wilhelmina just a year ago: "What else can one do, when we think of all the things we do not know the reason for, than go look at a field of wheat?"[60] All the pictures Vincent painted *after* the *Crows over the Cornfields* are fields of wheat. But it did not bring him peace. On the contrary, for some days he had been incapable of finishing the canvases that were still in the state of rough sketches. Vincent knew that this invariably happened when an attack was approaching. This thought petrified him. One day, when he discovered where Ravoux hid his revolver, he took it and decided to keep it, even when going out to paint outdoors. When the unbearable hallucinations came to overwhelm him, he would at least have a means of cutting short his suffering.

July 27. Night fell. Vincent had not come in for dinner. Then he suddenly did come in, staggering, and without saying a word went past the astonished Ravouxs. Worried, Ravoux went up to the dormer room where Vincent lodged and found him stretched out, fully dressed, on his narrow iron bed, grimacing with pain, his hand clenched on his chest. "I missed myself," he said curtly, revealing a spreading blood stain on his chest. Ravoux immediately sent for the village doctor, Dr. Mazery, as well as for Dr. Gachet. Was it so difficult to extract the bullet? Did they think that there wasn't any hope? Whatever the case, they confined themselves to putting on a light dressing. Vincent was stifling in the torrid atmosphere, burning with a high fever. Hirschig, the painter, who had witnessed his tragic arrival, heard him cry: "Isn't there anyone to open my stomach?" Then Vincent fell into a near coma, watched over by the Ravouxs. In the morning the pain was deadened, and he smoked a pipe. The police, who had been informed, questioned him. Why had he tried to commit suicide? Where had he obtained the weapon? He replied that his actions concerned no one but himself, no more; and the gendarmes had to content themselves with that laconic statement.

Theo could not be informed until the gallery opened. As soon as he arrived, the two brothers were left alone together until the end, on Tuesday, 29 July, at around one o'clock in the morning. Theo remembered then what Vincent had said at the bedside of their dying father: "Dying is difficult, but living is even more difficult." He gave an account of the last moments to their sister Elisabeth in a letter dated 5 August: "He himself wanted to die. When I was with him and tried to convince him that we would cure him and that we hoped he would be spared further attacks, he replied: 'There is no end to sorrow.' I thought then that I understood what he meant. He was very calm. Soon afterwards he was shaken by a fresh spasm and, a minute later, closed his eyes."[1]

When Theo closed his brother's eyes, he found an unfinished letter addressed to himself.[61] This posthumous message contains some phrases that sound like a testament. "There are many things I should like to write to you about, but I feel it is useless. ....Since the thing that matters most is going well, why should I say more about things of less importance? My word, *before we have a chance to talk busi-ness more collectedly, we shall probably have a long way to go.* ...Well, the truth is, we can only make our pictures speak. ...Well, my own work, I am risking my life for it and my reason has half foundered because of it—....but que veux-tu?"

Seated on the solitary straw chair in the dim light of the small room, Theo closed his own eyes. Haunting images came to him: Vincent walking through the fields, feeling deep in his pocket the reassuring weight of the revolver. Violent mid-July thunderstorms had delayed the harvest. Behind the cemetery, a mud path led deep into the cornfields. Out of sight, surrounded on all sides by this flood of yellow, buffeted by the gusts of wind, Vincent must have felt that he was disintegrating in the heart of a maelstrom. The path led nowhere. The waving corn blotted out even the line of the horizon—exactly as in the *Crows over the Cornfields*. Vincent was walking through his own picture. "That's it." At last. A strange lightheadedness overcame him. Not some horrible hallucination, but an extraordinary sense of buoyancy. The sun was setting. His fingers brushed over the glossy barrel of the revolver. A slight pressure on the trigger, now. "Well, the truth is, we can only make our pictures speak." It was so *simple*. Over to the "third Vincent."

Appendix

Notes

Introduction

a. Elisabeth du Quesne-Van Gogh, *Souvenirs personnels de Vincent van Gogh* (Personal memories of Vincent Van Gogh) (1910), translated by G. and B. Zurcher, Paris, 1982, p. 68.
1. Letter 309.
2. Letter 43.
3. Letter 605.

Chapter I

a. J.-P. Sartre, *L'existentialisme est un humanisme* (Paris: Nagel, 1970), p. 57.
b. Charles Bargue, painter and lithographer, (Paris? – Paris, 1883), *Exercice au fusain pour préparer à l'étude de l'académie d'après nature*, (Paris: Goupil & Cie, 1871), 60 plates.
c. M. E. Tralbaut, *Van Gogh le mal aimé*, (Lausanne: Edita, 1969), p. 56.
d. The first embodiment of the ideal woman was Eugénie Loyer (often called Ursula!), the image of the heartless beauty.

1. Letter 12.
2. Letter 3.
3. Letter 9.
4. Letter 9a.
5. Letter 11a.
6. Letter 20.
7. Letter 25.
8. Letter 26.
9. Letter 39.
10. Letter 41.
11. Letter 30.
12. Letter 42.
13. Letter 50.
14. Letter 67.
15. Letter 110.
16. Letter 111.
17. Letter 37.
18. Letter 41.
19. Letter 65.
20. Letter 67.
21. Letter 68.
22. Letter 69.
23. Letter 69a.
24. Letter 72.
25. Letter 79.
26. Letter 82.
27. Letter 92.
28. Letter 93.
29. Letter 103.
30. Letter 104.
31. Letter 95.
32. Letter 115.
33. Letter 101.
34. Letter 95.
35. Letter 111.
36. Letter 69.
37. Letter 124.
38. Letter 126.
39. Letter 126.
40. Letter 126.
41. Letter 131.
42. Letter 134.
43. Letter 136i.
44. Letter 127.
45. Letter 136i.
46. Letter 135i.
47. Letter 135i.
48. Letter 136i.
49. Letter 138.
50. Letter 140i.
51. Letter 140i.
52. Letter 143.

53. Letter 145.
54. Letter 146.
55. Letter 146.
56. Letter 147.
57. Letter 150.
58. Letter 169.
59. Letter 140.
60. Letter R 2.
61. Letter 150.
62. Letter 150.
63. Letter 150.
64. Letter 165.
65. Letter 149.
66. Letter R 1.
67. Letter 153.
68. Letter 154.
69. Letter 164.
70. Letter 193.
71. Letter 164.
72. Letter 156.
73. Letter 164.
74. Letter 117.
75. Letter 165.
76. Letter 166.
77. Letter 166.

Chapter II

a. The old men from the almshouse.
b. Elisabeth du Quesne-Van Gogh, *Souvenirs...*, op. cit., p. 21
c. Henri Matisse, "Propos recueillis par Maria Luz," XXth century, No. 2, January 1952; cf. *Ecrits et propos sur l'Art,* (Paris: Hermann, 1972), p. 248.
d. Emile Bernard, "Sur Paul Cézanne," *Conversation avec Emile Bernard,* (Paris: Michel, 1925), p. 99.
e. Paul Cézanne, Letter to Joachim Gasquet, Le Tholonet, 26 September, 1897; cf. *Correspondance,* (Paris: Grasset, 1978) p. 262.
f. Paul Gauguin, Letter to Daniel de Monfreid, Tahiti, March 1898; cf. *Oviri, Ecrits d'un Sauvage,* (Paris: Gallimard, coll. Idées, 1974), p. 217.
g. Paul Gauguin, *Diverses Choses* (1896–1898); cf. *Oviri...,* op. cit., p. 177.

1. Letter 142.
2. Letter 142.
3. Letter 139.
4. Letter 164.
5. Letter 165.
6. Letter 167.
7. Letter 166.
8. Letter 169.
9. Letter 241.
10. Letter 218.
11. Letter R 12.
12. Letter 242.
13. Letter 181.
14. Letter 180.
15. Letter 652.
16. Letter 221.
17. Letter 251.
18. Letter 174.
19. Letter 178.
20. Letter 185.
21. Letter 193.
22. Letter 219.
23. Letter 215.
24. Letter 189.
25. Letter 191.
26. Letter 181.
27. Letter 201.
28. Letter 204.
29. Letter 198.
30. Letter 201.
31. Letter 201.
32. Letter 218.
33. Letter 181.
34. Letter 185.
35. Letter 261.
36. Letter 262.
37. Letter 172.
38. Letter 191.
39. Letter 170.
40. Letter 190.
41. Letter 251.
42. Letter 178.
43. Letter 235.
44. Letter 189.
45. Letter 192.
46. Letter R 17.
47. Letter 218.
48. Letter 177.
49. Letter 220.
50. Letter 182.
51. Letter 218.
52. Letter 221.
53. Letter 241.
54. Letter 242.
55. Letter 221.
56. Letter 225.
57. Letter 228.
58. Letter 227.
59. Letter 227.
60. Letter 224.
61. Letter 195.

62. Letter 195.
63. Letter 195.
64. Letter 224.
65. Letter 256.
66. Letter 256.
67. Letter 272.
68. Letter R 30 March 1883.
69. Letter 269.
70. Letter 301.
71. Letter 303.
72. Letter 302.
73. Letter 308.
74. Letter 305.
75. Letter 308.
76. Letter 308.
77. Letter 309.
78. Letter 316.
79. Letter 314.
80. Letter 317.
81. Letter 319.
82. Letter 314.
83. Letter 319.
84. Letter 323.
85. Letter 325.
86. Letter 330.
87. Letter 339.
88. Letter 331.
89. Letter 347.
90. Letter 347.
91. Letter 360.
92. Letter 359.
93. Letter 358.
94. Letter 358.
95. Letter 364.
96. Letter 355a.
97. Letter R 44.
98. Letter 394.
99. Letter 383.
100. Letter 355.
101. Letter 383.
102. Letter 362.
103. Letter 371.
104. Letter 370.
105. Letter 394.
106. Letter 394.
107. Letter 429.
108. Letter 405.
109. Letter 403.
110. Letter 403.
111. Letter 429.
112. Letter 431.
113. Letter 414.
114. Letter 394.
115. Letter 418.
116. Letter 447.
117. Letter 418.
118. Letter 418.
119. Letter R 43.
120. Letter 397.
121. Letter 439.
122. Letter 396.
123. Letter 399.
124. Letter 405.
125. Letter 404.
126. Letter 404.
127. Letter R 57.
128. Letter 419b.
129. Letter 437.
130. Letter 439.
131. Letter 447.
132. Letter 449.

Chapter III

a. Jan Hulsker, *The Complete Van Gogh* (New York: Abrams, 1980), p. 262.
b. The other head is certainly that of the *Bearded Man* (F 209).
c. This is opposed to the "painters of the great boulevard," that is, the Impressionists, who exhibited their paintings at the Goupil Gallery (run by Theo) on the Boulevard Montmartre.
d. Theo Van Gogh to his sister Wilhelmina, Paris 1886–1887; see *Verzamelde Brieven van Vincent van Gogh* (Amsterdam, 1952–1954), vol. I, Introduction, p. xxxviii.

1. Letter 459.
2. Letter 459a.
3. Letter W 4.
4. Letter W 1.
5. Letter 459a.
6. Letter 545.
7. Letter W 4.

Chapter IV

a. Henri Matisse, "Notes d'un peintre," *La Grande Revue,* vol. 52, 25 December 1908; see *Ecrits*, op. cit., pp. 46–47.
b. Paul Gauguin, Letter to Schuffenecker, Pont-Aven, 14 August, 1888; see *Oviri*, op. cit., p. 40.
c. John Russell (1858–1931), an Australian painter whom Vincent met at Cormon's and who stayed with Gauguin at Pont-Aven.

d. He is speaking of a perspective frame.

e. Paul Cézanne, Letter to Camille Pissarro, L'Estaque, 2 July, 1876; see *Correspondance*, op. cit., p. 152.

f. Marc Edo Tralbaut, *Vincent van Gogh,* (Lausanne: Edita 1969), p. 228.

g. Henri Matisse, "Entretiens avec Dorothy Dudley, The Matisse Fresco in Merion," *Hound and Horn*, 7, No. 2, 1934; see the *Ecrits*, op. cit. p. 142, no. 6.

1. Letter 463.
2. Letter 463.
3. Letter W 3.
4. Letter B 3.
5. Letter 472.
6. Letter 487.
7. Letter 489.
8. Letter 492.
9. Letter 496.
10. Letter 497.
11. Letter 509.
12. Letter B 7.
13. Letter 501.
14. Letter 503.
15. Letter 498a.
16. Letter B 10.
17. Letter W 7.
18. Letter 501a.
19. Letter 539.
20. Letter 500.
21. Letter B 6.
22. Letter 499.
23. Letter 500.
24. Letter 499.
25. Letter 499.
26. Letter B 7.
27. Letter 533.
28. Letter 534.
29. Letter 533.
30. Letter W 7.
31. Letter W 7.
32. Letter W 7.
33. Letter 543.
34. Letter 533.
35. Letter 543.
36. Letter B19.
37. Letter 520.
38. Letter 520.
39. Letter B 8.
40. Letter B 8.
41. Letter 537.
42. Letter W 7.
43. Letter 553a.
44. Letter B 8.
45. Letter 544a.

46. Letter 531.
47. Letter B 7.
48. Letter 484.
49. Letter 498a.
50. Letter B 6.
51. Letter 501.
52. Letter 514.
53. Letter 516.
54. Letter B 14.
55. Letter 520.
56. Letter B 15.
57. Letter 524.
58. Letter B 8.
59. Letter B 13.
60. Letter 531.

Chapter V

a. Paul Gauguin, Letter to Schuffenecker, Pont-Aven, February 1888; cf. *Oviri*, op. cit., p. 40.

b. Paul Gauguin, Letter to Vincent Van Gogh, Pont-Aven, September 1888; quoted by John Rewald, *Post-Impressionism*, (Paris: Albin Michel, 1961), p. 136.

c. Paul Gauguin, Letter to Schuffenecker, Quimperlé, 16 October 1888; cf. *Oviri*, op. cit., p.44.

d. J. L. Ward, "A Reexamination of Van Gogh's Pictorial Space," *The Art Bulletin*, December 1976, pp. 593–604.

e. Marcel Proust, *A la recherche du temps perdu*, Gallimard, Pléiade, ed. 1954, vol. I, p. 835.

f. Paul Gauguin, Letter to Schuffenecker, Quimperlé, 8 October 1888; cf. *Oviri*, op. cit., p. 42.

g. Paul Gauguin, Letter to Emile Bernard, Pont-Aven, October 1880; cf. *Oviri*, op. cit. p.43

h. Emile Bernard, "Louis Anquetin," *Gazette des Beaux-Arts*, February 1934, p. 113.

i. Félix Fénéon, *Le Chat Noir,* 23 May 1891.

j. Paul Gauguin, "Souvenirs sur Vincent Van Gogh (winter 1894)," *Avant et Après*, (Iles Marquises: Atuana, 1903); cf. *Oviri,* op. cit., pp. 293–294.

k. Cf. Note j. Paul Gauguin, Letter to Emile Bernard, Arles, s.d. [December 1888]; cf. *Oviri*, ibid., p. 45.

l. Paul Signac, *Journal*, Saint-Tropez, 29 September 1894; cf. Extraits, *Gazette des Beaux-Arts*, July–September 1949.

m. Paul Gauguin, Letter to Vincent Van Gogh, Pont-Aven, September–October 1888; cf. *Oviri*, op. cit., p. 42.

n. Paul Gauguin, Letter to Schuffenecker, Arles, December 1888; cf. *Oviri,* ibid., p. 45.

o. Paul Gauguin, Letter to Emile Bernard, Arles, s. d. [December 1888]; cf. *Oviri*, ibid.

p. Emile Schuffenecker, Letter to Paul Gauguin, 11 December 1888; original document, published by John Rewald, *Post-Impressionism,* op. cit., pp. 151–152.

q. See *Verzamelde Brieven.* op. cit., vol. IV.

r. Gauguin defended himself against Emile Bernard's accusation after a lapse of four years; cf. Letter to Maurice Denis, s.d. [June 1889]; cf. *Oviri,* op. cit., p. 225.

s. Paul Gauguin, *Avant et Après*; cf. *Oviri,* ibid., p.295.

t. Letter from Gauguin to Bernard, quoted by the latter in a letter to Albert Aurier, Paris, 10 January 1889; published by John Rewald, *Post-Impressionism,* op. cit., p.153.

u. Antonin Artaud, "Van Gogh le suicide de la société" (1947), *Oeuvres complètes,* vol. XIII, (Paris: Gallimard 1974), p. 30.

v. Paul Gauguin, Letter to Schuffenecker, Arles, end of December 1888; cf. *Oviri,* op. cit., p. 46.

w. According to *Le Forum Républicain,* dated Sunday, 30 December 1888, the event took place "Last Sunday at 11.30 o'clock in the evening...," that is, 23 December and not the 24th as usually has been stated.

x. Paul Gauguin, *Avant et Après,* cf. *Oviri,* op. cit. pp. 295–296.

y. Emile Bernard, letter to Albert Aurier, Paris, 1 January 1889; published by John Rewald, *Post-Impressionism,* op. cit., p. 156.

z. Letter of 11 September 1929, quoted by V. Doiteau and E. Leroy, in "Vincent van Gogh et le drame de l'oreille coupée," *Aesculape,* July 1936.

1. Letter 468.
2. Letter W 7.
3. Letter B 2.
4. Letter 493.
5. Letter 494a.
6. Letter 522.
7. Letter 523.
8. Letter 538.
9. Letter 480.
10. Letter W 7.
11. Letter 543.
12. Letter B 15.
13. Letter 526.
14. Letter 534.
15. Letter W 7.
16. Letter 534.
17. Letter B 22.
18. Letter 553b.
19. Letter 504.
20. Letter 535.
21. Letter 544.
22. Letter 556.
23. Letter B 22.
24. Letter 524.
25. Letter 557.
26. Letter 526.

27. Letter 541.
28. Letter 527.
29. Letter 571.
30. Letter 573.
31. Letter B 19a.
32. Letter 559.
33. Letter 535.
34. Letter 558a.
35. Letter 560.
36. Letter W 9.
37. Letter 561.
38. Letter B 21.
39. Letter 623a.
40. Letter 559.
41. Letter 542.
42. Letter 525.
43. Letter 563.
44. Letter 542.
45. Letter 563.
46. Letter T 9.
47. Letter 252.
48. Letter 526.
49. Letter 544a.
50. Letter 571.
51. Letter 571.
52. Letter 605.
53. Letter 564.
54. Letter 626a.
55. Letter W 8.
56. Letter B 8.
57. Letter 503.
58. Letter 560.
59. Letter 574.
60. Letter 572.
61. Letter 590.
62. Letter 419b.
63. Letter 571.
64. Letter B 6.
65. Letter 564.
66. Letter 565.
67. Letter 507.

Chapter VI

a. Paul Gauguin, *Avant et Après*; cf. *Oviri,* op. cit., p. 297.

b. Letter from Paul Signac to Gustave Coquiot, quoted by G. Coquiot, *Vincent van Gogh,* (Paris: Ollendorff, 1923), p. 194.

c. Russell R. Monroe, "The Episodic Psychoses of Vincent Van Gogh," *The Journal of Nervous and Mental Disease,* Baltimore, 1978.

d. Georges Yakoulov, "La definition de soi," *Notes et document,*, published by the Société des amis de Georges Ya-koulov, May 1967, p. 15.

e. Paul Cézanne, Letter to Camille Pissarro, L'Estaque, 2 July 1876; cf. *Correspondance*, op. cit., p. 152.

f. Liliane Brion-Guerry, *Cézanne et l'expression de l'espace,* (Paris: Flammarion, 1950). p. 193, no. 47.

g. Johanna van Gogh-Bonger, *Verzamelde Brieven*, "Intro-duction," op. cit. Vol.I, pp. XLVI–XLVII.

h. Jan Hulsker thinks that *Crows over the Cornfields* (F 779) is not the picture referred to in Letter 649, first because, in his view, there is a contradiction between the "vast fields of wheat under troubled skies" and the frontal treatment of the picture, which he thinks also could not be described as showing what is "healthy and restorative in the country" because of the presence of the crows. I do not agree with these arguments because I think it was the essence of Vincent's art precisely to express the feel-ing of vastness through one plane, and to introduce the crows to show what is "healthy and restorative in the country" by contrast, an allegory of his own threatened life.

i. Antonin Artaud, *Van Gogh le suicide de la société*, op. cit., p. 32.

j. Theo van Gogh to Jo, Paris, 20 July 1890; *Verzamelde Brieven,* "Introduction," op. cit., Vol.I, p. XLVIII.

k. Theo Van Gogh to Jo, Paris, 25 July, 1890; ibid.

l. Elisabeth du Quesne-Van Gogh, *Souvenirs*, op. cit., p. 87.

1. Letter 607.
2. Letter 567.
3. Letter 581.
4. Letter 581.
5. Letter 623a.
6. Letter 570.
7. Letter 574.
8. Letter 581.
9. Letter 579.
10. Letter 582.
11. Letter W 11.
12. Letter 585.
13. Letter T 5.
14. Letter 587.
15. Letter 599.
16. Letter 588.
17. Letter 586.
18. Letter 592.
19. Letter 594.
20. Letter W 14.
21. Letter 605.
22. Letter 607.
23. Letter 605.
24. Letter 594.
25. Letter 596.
26. Letter 626a.
27. Letter T 10.
28. Letter 596.
29. Letter 604.
30. Letter 607.
31. Letter 615.
32. Letter 614.
33. Letter 615.
34. Letter B 21.
35. Letter B 20.
36. Letter W 15.
37. Letter 613.
38. Letter B 20.
39. Letter 627.
40. Letter 628.
41. Letter 630.
42. Letter 629a.
43. Letter 630.
44. Letter 632.
45. Letter 633.
46. Letter 614a.
47. Letter 636.
48. Letter W 22.
49. Letter W 22.
50. Letter 651.
51. Letter 648.
52. Letter 649.
53. Letter 635.
54. Letter W 22.
55. Letter 638.
56. Letter 638.
57. Letter W 22.
58. Letter 648.
59. Letter 604.
60. Letter W 13.
61. Letter 652.

Vincent's Distinctive Hand

The whole of Van Gogh's output was painted in eight years—an extremely short time in which to produce more than 800 pictures. This brevity makes it possible for us to consider his work as a whole from beginning to end. Such an overall view reveals the lightning speed with which his concepts changed, which was expressed in the diversity of his brushwork. At first his strokes were blended in the style of the great Dutch masters of the seventeenth century, an example of this being *Still Life with Bottles* (ill. 38), where the strokes emphasize the contrasts of light that give the objects volume. The bottles, primarily cylindrical forms, are involved in an interplay of light and shade that recalls some of Chardin's still lifes as well as Zurbaran's *bodegones*. In Vincent's *Potato Eaters* (ill. 53), inanimate objects have been replaced by figures. But while his brushwork remains the same, its power is multiplied tenfold, sculpting the figures' faces and hands, and deepening their wrinkles to the point of caricature.

During his first four years of painting (1882–1886) Van Gogh developed a style with values very similar to those of his drawings. The touches of color in his paintings were muted, and it was only towards the end of this period that his palette lightened under the influence of Rubens, whose works he learned to admire during his stay in Antwerp. To this development was added, in autumn of 1885, a growing curiosity about the Impressionists of whom Theo talked so enthusiastically, to the extent

Still Life with Bottles (detail, see ill. 38).

that early in March 1886 Vincent suddenly found it imperative to go to Paris. *Poplars Avenue near Nuenen* (ill. 43) bears witness to his interest in the new technique of which—by his own admission—he knew very little. In fact, though his brush strokes were reduced to thin strips to represent the ground and even to dots to represent the foliage of trees or bushes, they show none of the special characteristics of Impressionist brushwork. Thus the resultant landscape—monochrome of browns broken only by the vivid blue of the smock worn by the little figure—reminds us of Corot rather than Pissarro.

During the whole of Vincent's first period of artistic development, that is, up to his first sojourn in Paris, his drawing was of much greater importance than his painting. We have seen how the practice of drawing was more than a mere exercise for him. He devoted himself to it exclusively during these years of apprenticeship, and even afterwards he always took recourse in drawing when there was some "pictorial" obstacle to be overcome. A new stage in his development was almost always marked by a return to drawing. In fact, his drawings form the very backbone of his achievement. He first produced drawings with some regularity during his second visit to England, following his break with art dealing. It is interesting to note that these drawings made their appearance in his earliest letters to Theo. Subsequently he got into the habit of making more or less elaborate sketches in his letters in order to illustrate some of his descriptions. Sometimes the drawings replaced the text altogether. In a letter to Russell, written in Arles in June 1888, Vincent confessed to having interrupted the letter to draw the head of a little girl on the same paper. All through the course of his career, his correspondence—like "bone-marrow"—supplied him with features that would strengthen his work: for the drawings accompanying his letters—or sent separately—gain progressively in "painterly" significance, as we have seen. Until the Parisian period, this development is apparent in his use of watercolor washes and highlights. Then, during his

stay in Arles, Vincent—using pen or reed—developed a graphic system of equivalence with painting that is manifest in the interplay of brush strokes. His drawing gives his work its coherence. It spanned the gap between writing and painting, permitting endless transitions from one to the other. By establishing a relationship between the letters and the pictures, it ensured a double circulation for Vincent's ideas. This literary deployment of his work comes out in his painting, creating a kind of "pictorial handwriting" whose significance goes far beyond the concept of "style."

During his brief career as a painter, Vincent produced groups of assorted paintings in the same "handwriting." To measure the effect of each artistic "script," he returned to certain themes time and again in the course of his experiments. The theme of the sower, for example, marks the acquisition and organization of new means of expression, from the time of his first stiff and awkward drawings, through the lingering Impressionism of the vision of the *Sower* (F 422, ill. 108), which is almost effaced by the blinding contrast of the red and yellow strokes, to the synthetist manifestation of the *Sower* (F 451, ill. 134) with which he replaced the haunting shade of Millet's *Sower*. His use of the self-portrait proceeded similarly: It enabled Vincent to perfect his technique and to confirm his mastery of an idiom learnt under the influence of Signac, Pissarro, and Emile Bernard. In Paris he witnessed the beginning of a transition in his painting from a pictorial world of halftones to a universe of colors whose intensity he would gradually increase under the southern sun. The twenty-odd self-portraits he executed in the summer of 1887, mostly one right after the other, show his progress with the "shortened" Impressionist brush stroke. The fact that the portraits were painted so close together creates an effect of accelerating stylistic development. The flossiness of the first portraits is replaced by a finer,

Avenue of Poplars near Nuenen (detail, see ill. 43).

294

Daisies and Anemones (detail, see ill. 79).

lighter texture, with delicate brush strokes that reach a peak of refinement in *Self-Portrait with a Gray Hat* (ill. 72). A similar delicacy is found in many of the flower pieces painted at the same period, such as *Daisies and Anemones* (ill. 79), which is specifically Impressionist. *Self-Portrait with a Gray*

Felt Hat (ill. 76) shows how Vincent had now utilized his brush not so much to follow the contours of the face as to depict the planes offered by its different parts. Strongly individualized, with a dominant contrast of two complementary colors, orange and blue, the strokes radiate from the center of the portrait, Vincent's eyes endowing his gaze with magnetism. At Arles Vincent used the same procedure in *Night Café* (ill. 116) to express the radiance of the oil lamps, and at St.-Rémy, in *Starry Night* (ill. 157), to express the twinkling of the stars and the whirling passage of a comet through the sky.

The portrait of Augustine Roulin (*La Berceuse*) (ill. 141) gave rise to a series of five portraits, which are almost identical save for the different positioning of the hands in the first. We have already examined in depth the significance of these portraits. All that need be said here is that, in these frontal portraits in which the Japanese manner reigns supreme, Van Gogh using only areas of flat color like those in a print, succeeds in expressing a vibrant sense of the sitter's identity.

While Vincent knew the rules of the orthodox Pointillism of Seurat and Signac, as can be seen from *View from Vincent's Room, Rue Lepic* (ill. 86), he was not interested in this fashionable new technique of the 1880s for its own sake, but for the new possibilities it could open up for him. Indeed, he was very quick to shake off the constraints of the system of regular dots, while retaining its principle of contrasting complementary colors. In what might be called a "composite" style, the *Banks of the Seine* (ill. 87) superimposes the various techniques practiced by Vincent: blending brush strokes, reminiscent of Mauve, for the sky; Pointillist brushwork for the foliage; and narrow horizontal strokes for the water. In *Restaurant Interior* (ill. 92), Pointillist brushwork is no longer used systematically. The space of the room remains strongly framed by the outlines of the doors delimiting the walls and by those of the tables

View from Vincent's Room, Rue Lepic (detail, see ill. 86). ▷

Italian Woman (La Segatori)(detail, see ill. 94).

and chairs, which maintain the room's full depth. Nevertheless, the role of the brushwork is to confer unity by flattening the spatial references on the surface of the canvas. Under the influence of Japanese prints, which Vincent collected, the brushwork structures the space by means of increasingly differentiated colored planes. It creates patches of flat color, often outlined, as in the portrait of the Italian woman (*La Segatori*) (ill. 94), where the decorative border, cut off halfway around the picture, enhances the effect of a popular print, while applying the principles of Japanese perspective. The *Pork Butcher's* (ill. 98), one of the first pictures he painted in Arles, follows the same principles. The colored patches are arranged geometrically in parallel lines or secants. A similar device is used to represent the parallelism of the tree trunks forming the avenue at the Roman burial ground of the *Alyscamps* (ill. 133).

By the autumn of 1888, Vincent had examined and experimented with the various components of the Impressionist style, mingling and using them as he pleased according to his needs. This was undoubtedly one of the main reasons why the Impressionists of his generation failed to welcome him to their ranks: Basically, they were irritated by his failure to conform and by the impossibility of giving him a precise place within the Impressionistic milieu. Above all, they considered that his way of doing things demonstrated a lack of maturity combined with downright clumsiness. Even Theo, despite the help he provided out of a sense of family duty rather than conviction of Vincent's talent, was saddened by it. Gauguin would probably never have come to Arles if not compelled by his financial difficulties, for he expected more from the promises held out by Theo than from the company of Vincent, whom he considered to be more than a pupil. And yet

The Alyscamps (detail, see ill. 133).

Gauguin was certainly the first to discover the surprising reality: By his own efforts, Vincent had succeeded in perfecting an enormously effective pictorial technique. He found Vincent to be a man who lived in his work at least as much as he did himself. It was more than his pride could stand. After his paternalistic attitude had triggered the drama that enabled him to end his stay for reasons acceptable to Theo, Gauguin fled like a thief in the night, taking with him the secret of the *Sunflowers* (ill. 132), which he was able to put to profitable use.

We must go back to the *Sunflowers* to understand the lesson that Gauguin had learned in spite of himself. Yellow flowers in a yellow vase against a yellow background: It is an image that is in the nature of a manifesto. When he painted it, Vincent was thinking of Monticelli, "a painter who did the South all in yellow, all in orange, all in sulphur,"[a] who had opened his eyes to the expressive power of color, which far surpasses the reality of normal vision. "The great majority of the painters, because they aren't colorists, in the true sense of the word, do not see these colors there, and they call a painter mad if he sees with eyes other than theirs," he wrote to Wilhelmina in October 1888.[b] Never had any Impressionist raised color to such a pitch of intensity. Long before the Fauvists, Vincent invented a special kind of monochrome in which the values were based on brilliant tones rather than dull grays. In so doing, he succeeded in taking into account the expressive power of line, drawing attention to form without in any way depriving himself of the expressive power of color. Moreover, it is not so much the objective form or its outline that emerges from this treatment as the graphic dimension of a "pictorial handwriting" that transcends it. With the *Sunflowers*, Vincent rediscovers the vivacity and biographical immediacy of his drawings, by painterly means alone.

As regards Vincent's work, the whole story of the "Studio in the South" can be summed up as a constant see-saw between two extreme concepts of painting—line and color—which somehow had to

Mountains (detail, see ill. 165).

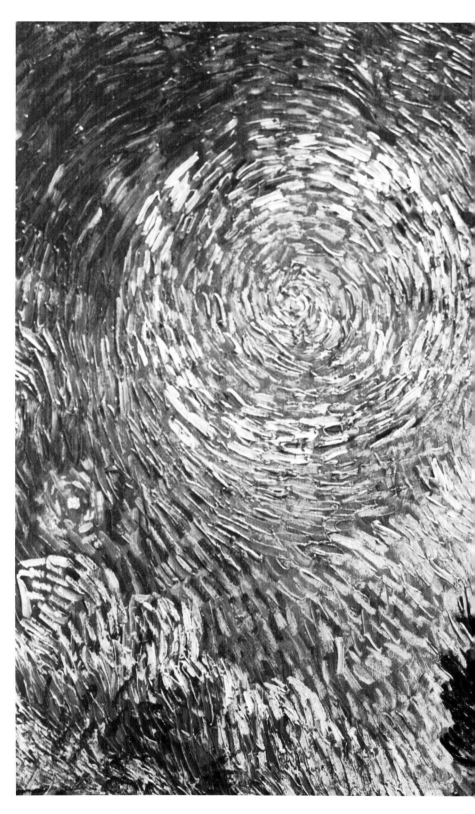

Road with Cypresses (detail, see ill. 180).

be accommodated in the same canvas without sacrificing either to the other. It was from this standpoint that he considered the *Sower* (F 422, ill. 108) as a failure. Cézanne had written to Pissarro from

L'Estaque on 2 July 1876: "I may be mistaken, but it seems to me that it is the very antipodes of relief."[c] Twelve years later Vincent strikingly confirmed this: "No stippling, no hatching, nothing, only flat colors in harmony" was how he described his painting of his bedroom (ill. 131) in a letter to Theo.[d]

In St.-Rémy, where he was more isolated than ever, Vincent saw the contorted landscape of the Alpilles and the gnarled trunks of the olive trees as the expression of a universal dynamic principle governing all things and all beings, from a blade of grass to the stars. For a time the violent contrasts of complementary colors in his work disappeared. Whatever the subject, whether *Olive Fields* (ills. 162 and 163), cornfields as in *Yellow Corn* (ill. 160) or *Cornfield at Noon* (ill. 153), the *Entrance to a Quarry* (ill. 166), a *Road with Cypresses* (ill. 180), a *Self-Portrait* (ill. 167), or even a *Pietà* (after Delacroix), (ill. 154), his brushwork became uniformly sinuous. It blurs the outlines of the forms and casts them, relatively undifferentiated, into a space without depth where they are caught in the same arabesque—that of the sky in *Starry Night*, a gigantic ellipse metaphorically summing up Vincent's life, which had been littered with failures since childhood.

His color regained its brilliance with his arrival at Auvers-sur-Oise. Nevertheless, the sinuous distortions in his paintings persisted, the areas of flat

Pietà (detail, see ill. 154).

Dr. Gachet's Garden (detail, see ill. 187).

color reappeared. *Portrait of Dr. Gachet* (ill. 188) and The *Church at Auvers* (ill. 189) are splendid examples of this. He had succeeded in painting in a way that was quite independent of illusionist representation. In *Dr. Gachet's Garden* (ill. 187) where the eye has some difficulty in penetrating the scene, and even more radically in *Crows over the Cornfields* (ill. 199), the colored brush strokes are in the nature of ciphers that make up a sign-language. Apart from their difference in color, the crows are not structurally distinct from the ears of corn over which they fly. As they penetrate the leaden blue of the sky, they lose even this specific quality and gradually disappear from sight.

Notes

a. Letter W 8.
b. Ibid.
c. P. Cézanne, *Correspondance*, op. cit., p. 152.
d. Letter 555

Chronology

1851 Marriage of the Reverend Theodorus Van Gogh, at Groot Zundert, a small village in Brabant near the Belgian frontier, to Anna Cornelia Carbentus, the daughter of a bookbinder at the Court.

1852 30 March: Vincent Willem, the "first Vincent" is still-born.

1853 30 March: Birth of Vincent Willem, the "second Vincent."

1857 1 May: Birth of Theo.

1866 Vincent is entered for the secondary school at Tilburg.

1868 Vincent returns to Zundert. His studies are interrupted.

1869 From 1 August employed by the Goupil & Co. art gallery, on the recommendation of his uncle Vincent, a shareholder of the firm, and admitted as a clerk in the branch at The Hague.

1871 Theodorus Van Gogh is appointed to Helvoirt

1872 August. Beginning of the correspondence between Vincent and Theo, who was studying at Oisterwijk at the time.

1873 1 January. Theo also joins the staff of Goupil & Co., at their Brussels branch.
May. Vincent is sent to the London branch. He boards with the Loyers and falls in love with his landlady's daughter, Eugénie. First unhappy love affair.
November. Theo replaces Vincent at The Hague.

1874 October. Vincent is sent provisionally to the head office of the Goupil art gallery in Paris, until December, then returns to London.

1875 May. He is definitively appointed to the Paris office. He loses interest in his work, however, neglecting it to devote himself to the study of the Bible and to visiting museums and art galleries.
October. The Reverend Theodorus is transferred to Etten, near Breda.

1876 1 April. Vincent is forced to hand in his resignation to Messrs. Boussod and Valadon, the successors of Goupil.
17 April. He settles in Ramsgate, near London, and works as assistant teacher in Mr. Stokes' small school.
July. Becomes assistant preacher to the Reverend Jones at Isleworth. In December returns home to his parents.

1877 Vincent is employed at the Blussé & Van Braam bookshop in Dordrecht, but is considered unsatisfactory. He begins to draw frequently.
9 May. His father agrees to let him follow his religious vocation and sends him to Amsterdam to study for the entrance examinations to the University Theology course. He stays with his uncle Johan, the director of the shipbuilding yards. Despite all of his efforts, he fails.

1878 July. Unable to enter holy orders, Vincent sets his heart on becoming an evangelist. Refused by the School of Laeken because of his temperament, which is considered too "impulsive," he leaves in despair for the mining region of the Borinage.

1879   January. Finally appointed for six months at Wasmes, near Mons, Vincent devotes himself to alleviating the misery of the miners. But his zeal is judged "excessive" by his superiors and he is forced to leave his post. In August he settles in Cuesmes where he tries to continue his mission, meanwhile devoting himself increasingly to drawing.

1880   October. Encouraged by Theo, who starts to help him financially, Vincent leaves for Brussels to attend the courses at the Académy des Beaux-Arts. He meets the painter Anton Van Rappard, who becomes his friend.

1881   12 April. He leaves for Etten to see Theo there and then decides to stay. Van Rappard pays him a visit. The two men work together. During the summer, Vincent gets to know his cousin Kate Vos and falls in love with her, but she rejects his advances.
Second rejection. He draws enthusiastically, however.
28 November. His cousin Anton Mauve, one of the chief leaders of the School of The Hague, puts him up until Christmas. Thanks to Mauve's advice, Vincent executes his first studies in oil, and figures in watercolors.
25 December. After a serious quarrel with his father about his slackness in religious observance, he suddenly leaves Etten on the 31st and returns to The Hague.

1882   January. Supported by Theo's financial help and by lessons from Mauve, who also lends him money, he executes numerous aquarelles. But he refuses to work from plaster molds, which leads to a quarrel with Mauve in spite of Vincent's admiration for him.
He draws numerous figures of working-class people from life and forms a relationship with one of his models, Clasina Maria Hoor-

nik, called Sien, who soon comes to live with him together with her two children. In June, he is admitted to the Hague hospital for gonorrhoea. His father visits him, as does his former chief at Goupil's, H. G. Tersteeg, who disapproves vehemently of his new career.
4 August. The Reverend Theodorus Van Gogh settles with his family at Nuenen.
Vincent devotes himself increasingly to oil painting and executes his first landscapes in this medium. He also does his first lithographs and takes a passionate interest in the English periodical The *Graphic*.

1883   11 September. Under pressure from Theo, Vincent breaks with Sien and goes to Drenthe, a peat country in the northeast area of the Netherlands. He considers settling there, but soon feels that the solitude is too much for him, and at the beginning of December he returns home to his family at Nuenen.

1884   17 January. Vincent's mother breaks her leg while getting off a train. To distract her while keeping her company, he draws the small Protestant church bordered by trees.
In spring, Vincent set up his studio at Schafrath's, the Catholic sacristan. During the summer Margot Begemann, a neighbor, falls in love with him and, faced with opposition from the two families, tries to commit suicide. Vincent is shaken, but not deeply hurt. He executes six decorative panels for the dining room of the Eindhoven goldsmith, Hermans, and even gives a few painting lessons, especially to Kerssemakers, a tobacco merchant. He executes numerous studies of weavers and peasants at work. Van Rappard pays him two visits.

1885   January–February. Vincent plans to paint some fifty heads before the end of the winter.
26 March. Death of the Reverend Theodorus Van Gogh. Despite their differences, Vincent is deeply affected by his father's death.

Banks of the Seine. Cf. ill. 87

April–May. He devotes himself entirely to his first large oil painting, The *Potato Eaters,* of which he makes a lithograph. The latter is the cause of his quarrel with Van Rappard, which leads to a breach between them in spite of their friendship of five years' standing. In September, the Catholic priest accuses him of being the father of a child born to Gordina de Groot, one of his models. Left without models, he paints mostly still lifes and birds' nests.

October–November. After a three-day visit to the Rijksmuseum in Amsterdam, where he is particularly fascinated by the works of Rembrandt and Frans Hals, he decides to go to Antwerp.

1886 Vincent revels in the contrasts afforded by city life. At the book stalls in the port he discovers Japanese prints and starts to collect them. He is deeply impressed by Rubens's paintings and this leads him to use brighter colors, like carmine and cobalt. He also studies the laws of colors, which had already fascinated Delacroix.

18 January. He registers at the Académie des Beaux-Arts, where he meets the English painter Levens, who does his portrait. Disap-

pointed once more by academic teaching, he leaves Antwerp at the beginning of March to join his brother in Paris, intending to study with Cormon in Montmartre.

April–May. He meets Emile Bernard, John Russell, Louis Anquetin, and Henri de Toulouse-Lautrec. He also makes contact with Camille Pissarro, Paul Signac, and Paul Gauguin.

1887 Spring. Vincent has a few canvases permanently exhibited at Père Tanguy's, the color dealer in Rue Clauzel. He organizes the first exhibition of the "painters of the Little Boulevard," with Gauguin, Bernard, Anquetin, and Lautrec, at the Au Tambourin café, Boulevard Clichy.

1888 20 February. Vincent leaves Paris for Arles to found an "artist's colony," of which Gauguin is to be the head. He rents the "yellow house," 2 Place Lamartine, and explores the region: Saintes-Maries-de-la-Mer, Montmajour and the plain of the Crau. He also does portraits and night scenes.

20 October. Arrival of Gauguin. After an initial period of friendly collaboration, the rela-

Flower Garden. Cf. ill. lll.

The Red Vineyards at Arles. Cf. ill. 174.

The Dance Hall at Arles. Cf. ill. 136.

tionship between the two artists deteriorates.

December. Theo announces his engagement with Jo Bonger.

23 December. The drama breaks out: Vincent attacks Gauguin, then cuts part of his own ear off with a razor. Gauguin takes flight the next morning. Vincent is taken to hospital, in the care of Dr. Rey, the resident. Theo comes to see him, but leaves again very soon.

1889   7 January. In spite of his insomnia and headaches Vincent is able to return to his studio, helped by the postman Roulin and the Reverend Salles. In the middle of January, Theo announces his marriage with Jo.

6–18 February. *Second attack.* Subsequently, Vincent paints in his studio during the day but returns to the hospital in the evening.

26 February. A petition signed by some of his neighbors accusing him of disturbing the public order, forces the mayor to have him shut up again. *Third attack.*

24 March. Signac visits Vincent. He now lives at the asylum.

17 April. Theo's wedding.

21 April. Vincent asks Theo to have him confined at the asylum of St.-Rémy, run by Dr. Peyron.

8 May. Vincent arrives at St.-Rémy. He immediately starts painting enthusiastically in the garden and the surroundings.

End of May. Theo refuses to let Vincent take

Orchard in Bloom with the View of Arles. Cf. ill. 101.

part in the exhibition organized by Gauguin in the Café Volpini.

5 July. Announcement of Jo's pregnancy. Certain that the child will be a boy, she tells Vincent that she intends to name it after him.

8 July. After a visit to Arles, he is struck by a *fourth attack*, which lasts until mid-August, with some remissions. He is invited to take part in the exhibition of the XX in Brussels.

22 December. He hears that Jo's confinement is approaching.

24 December. *Fifth attack.*

1890 January. Albert Aurier's article, "Les Isolés," appears in the *Mercure de France*. At the XX, Vincent's canvases attract attention. Lautrec challenges De Groux to a duel for speaking insultingly of them. The *Red Vineyard* is sold to Anna Boch for 400 francs.

23–30 January. *Sixth attack.*

31 January. Birth of the "third Vincent."

February. *Seventh attack*, which lasts until mid-April, with periods of remission. According to a warder, Vincent tries to swallow paints.

19 March. He exhibits ten canvases at the *Indépendants.*

17 May. Vincent leaves St.-Rémy for Paris.

21 May. He goes to stay at the Ravoux's café at Auvers-sur-Oise, where he is watched over by Dr. Gachet.

27 July. Vincent's suicide: He shoots himself in the chest, but does not die at once.

29 July. Vincent dies at dawn.

30 July. Burial in the cemetery of Auvers.

October. Theo goes mad. Jo takes him back to Holland.

1891 January. Gauguin opposes a retrospective of Van Gogh's works, planned by Bernard.

21 January. Death of Theo. (He has been buried alongside Vincent since 1914.) Homage to Vincent Van Gogh at the XX, in February; at the *Indépendants* in March, and at the Galerie Le Barc de Boutteville in April.

1901 First major retrospective of Vincent Van Gogh, at the Galerie Bernheim-Jeune in Paris (seventy-one works).

1907 29 April. Death of "Moe," Vincent and Theo's mother, at Leyden, aged 88.

Family Tree of Vincent Van Gogh

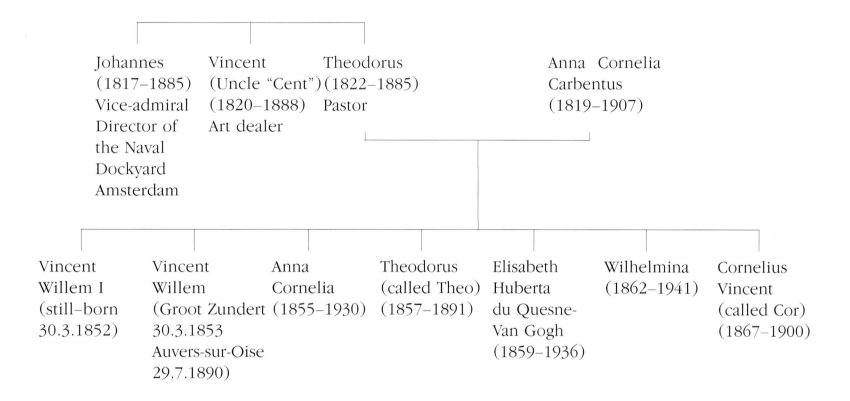

Johannes
(1817–1885)
Vice-admiral
Director of
the Naval
Dockyard
Amsterdam

Vincent
(Uncle "Cent")
(1820–1888)
Art dealer

Theodorus
(1822–1885)
Pastor

Anna Cornelia
Carbentus
(1819–1907)

Vincent
Willem I
(still–born
30.3.1852)

Vincent
Willem
(Groot Zundert
30.3.1853
Auvers-sur-Oise
29.7.1890)

Anna
Cornelia
(1855–1930)

Theodorus
(called Theo)
(1857–1891)

Elisabeth
Huberta
du Quesne-
Van Gogh
(1859–1936)

Wilhelmina
(1862–1941)

Cornelius
Vincent
(called Cor)
(1867–1900)

Bibliography

(listed in chronological order of titles)

I   Descriptive Catalogues

Faille, J.-B. de la, *L'œuvre de Vincent van Gogh,* catalogue raisonné, 4 vols., G. van Oest, Paris-Brussels, 1928.

Faille, J.-B. de la, *Les faux van Gogh,* G. van Oest, Paris-Brussels, 1930.

Scherjon, W., *Catalogue des tableaux de Vincent van Gogh décrits dans ses lettres—périodes Saint-Rémy et Auvers-sur-Oise,* Société d'Editions A. Oosthoek, Utrecht, 1932.

Scherjon, W., and de Gruyter, W.J., *Vincent van Gogh's Great Period: Arles, Saint-Rémy and Auvers-sur-Oise,* De Spieghel, Amsterdam, 1937.

Faille, J.-B. de la, *The Works of Vincent van Gogh, His Paintings and Drawings,* Meulenhoff, Amsterdam; Reynal in association with William Morrow, New York, 1970.

Hulsker, J., *Van Gogh en zijn weg,* Meulenhoff, Amsterdam, 1977; English translation, *The Complete Van Gogh, paintigs, drawings, sketches,* Harry N. Abrams, New York, 1980.

II   Letters

The Complete Letters of Vincent van Gogh. With reproductions of all the drawings in the correspondence, 3 vols., Thames and Hudson, London, 1958, reprinted 1978.
Letter excerpts from THE COMPLETE LETTERS OF VINCENT VAN GOGH by New York Graphic Society Books/ Little, Brown and Company are reprinted by permission of Little, Brown and Company.

III   Principal Exhibition Catalogues

Exposition Van Gogh au Panorama à Amsterdam, 1892– 1893, organized by Johanna Van Gogh-Bonger. Preface by R.N. Roland-Holst. 104 pictures and drawings.

Exposition Vincent Van Gogh, Galerie Bernheim-Jeune, Paris, 15–31 March 1901. Preface by J. Leclercq. 65 pictures and 6 drawings.

Exposition Van Gogh, Galerie Bernheim-Jeune, Paris, January 1908. 100 pictures.

Vincent van Gogh – Gemälde, Galerie Paul Cassirer, Berlin, January 1928. Preface J.-B. de la Faille. 92 pictures.

Vincent van Gogh, Museum of Modern Art, New-York, 1935. Catalogue designed by Alfred H. Barr, Jr.

Vincent van Gogh, Museums voor Schoone Kunsten, Luik, Bergen; Paleis voor Schoone Kunsten, Brussels, October 1946–January 1947. Preface by E. Langui. 171 works.

Vincent van Gogh, Musée de l'Orangerie, Paris, January– March 1947. Preface by R. Huyghe. 172 pictures and drawings.

Catalogue of 270 Paintings and Drawings of Vincent van Gogh belonging to the Collection of the State Museum Kröller-Müller, Otterlo,1952; new edition, Otterlo, 1959.

Vincent van Gogh, City Art Museum, Saint Louis; Philadelphia Museum of Art; Toledo Museum of Art, October 1953–April 1954. Preface by V.W. van Gogh. 181 works.

Van Gogh et les peintres d'Auvers-sur-Oise, Orangerie des Tuileries, Paris, November 1954–February 1955. Prefaces by P. Gachet and G. Bazin. Notes by A. Châtelet.

Vincent van Gogh, Stedelijk Museum, Amsterdam, summer 1955. Preface by V.W. van Gogh. 243 pictures and drawings mostly from the V.W. van Gogh collection.

Vincent van Gogh – Leben und Schaffen, Dokumentation, Gemälde, Zeichnungen, Villa Hügel, Essen, October-December 1957. Preface by M.E. Tralbaut.

Vincent van Gogh, Musée Jacquemart-André, Paris, February–May 1960. Documentation by M.E. Tralbaut. Preface by L. Hautecœur.

Van Gogh Self-Portraits, Marlborough Fine Art Ltd., London, 1960. Essays by A.M. Hammacher and O. Kokoschka.

Van Gogh's Sources of Inspiration: 100 Prints from His Personal Collection, The Brooklyn Museum, Brooklyn, 1971. Introduction by J. Miller.

Vincent van Gogh, Orangerie des Tuileries, 21 December

1971–10 April 1972. Collection of the Rijksmuseum Vincent van Gogh, Amsterdam. Introduction by H. Adhémar.

Vincent van Gogh and the Birth of Cloisonism, Toronto, Art Gallery of Ontario and Amsterdam, Rijksmuseum Vincent van Gogh, 1981. Text by B. Welsh-Ovcharov.

Vincent van Gogh in Arles, Metropolitan Museum of Art, New York, 18 October–30 December 1984. Text by R. Pickvance. French translation by Solange Schnall, *Van Gogh en Arles.* Foreword by J.-M. Rouquette, Skira, Geneva, 1985.

IV   Souvenirs and Memoirs

Gauguin, P., *Avant et après,* Iles Marquises, Atuana, 1903; Kurt Wolff, Munich, 1914; G. Crès, Paris, 1924; see *Oviri, Ecrits d'un sauvage,* Gallimard, coll. Idées, Paris, 1974.

Du Quesne-Van Gogh, E. H., *Persoonlijke Herinneringen aan Vincent van Gogh,* J. F. Van der Ven, Baarn, 1910; Piper Verlag, Munich, 1911; Houghton Mifflin, Boston, 1913; French translation by Gwénolée and Bernard Zurcher, *Vincent van Gogh, Souvenirs personnels racontés par sa sœur,* Hazan, Paris, 1982.

Mendes de Costa, N. B., "Persoonlijke Herinneringen aan Vincent van Gogh," *Algemeene Handelsblad,* 2 December 1910.

Bernard, E., *Lettres de Vincent van Gogh à Emile Bernard,* Vollard, Paris, 1911.

Van Gogh-Bonger, J., Preface to *Vincent van Gogh, Brieven aan zijn Broeder,* Mij. voor Goede en Goedkoope Lectuur, Amsterdam, 1914.

Bernard, E., "Souvenirs de Van Gogh," *L'Amour de l'Art,* vol. V, December 1924, pp. 393–400.

Hartrick, A.S., *A Painter's Pilgrimage Through Fifty Years,* University Press, Cambridge, 1939.

Carrié (née Ravoux), A., "La femme en bleu revient à Auvers," *Les Nouvelles Littéraires,* 12 August 1954.

Ravoux, A., "Souvenirs sur le séjour de Vincent van Gogh à Auvers-sur-Oise," *Les Cahiers de Van Gogh,* no. 1, s.d. [1956], pp. 7–17.

Gachet, P., *Deux amis des impressionnistes: le docteur Gachet et Murer,* Editions des Musées nationaux, Paris, 1956.

V   Some Studies on Vincent's Behavior

Jaspers, K., "Strindberg und Van Gogh: Versuch einer pathographischen Analyse unter vergleichender Heranziehung von Swedenborg und Höderlin," *Arbeiten zur angewandten Psychiatrie,* vol. V., E. Bircher, Berne, 1922.

Leroy, E., "Le séjour de Vincent van Gogh à l'asile de Saint-Rémy-de-Provence," *Aesculape,* vol. XVI, May–July 1926.

Doiteau, V., and Leroy, E., *La folie de Vincent van Gogh,* Editions Aesculape, Paris, 1928.

Bataille, G., "La mutilation sacrificielle et l'oreille coupée de Vincent van Gogh," *Documents,* vol. II, no. 8, 1930.

Beer, F.J., *Essai sur les rapports de l'art et de la maladie de Vincent van Gogh,* Thesis, University of Strasbourg, 1936.

Doiteau, V., and Leroy, E., "Vincent van Gogh et le drame de l'oreille coupée," *Aesculape,* vol. XXVI, July 1936.

Mauron, C., "Notes sur la structure de l'inconscient chez Vincent van Gogh," *Psyche,* vol. VIII, nos. 75–78, January–April 1953.

Gastaut, H., "La maladie de Vincent van Gogh envisagée à la lumière des conceptions nouvelles sur l'épilepsie psychomotrice," *Annales médico-psychiatriques,* 1956, vol. 114, p. 196–238.

Nagera, H., *Vincent van Gogh: A Psychological Study,* prefaced by Anna Freud, International Universities Press, New York, 1967; French translation, *Vincent van Gogh: Etude psychologique,* Buchet-Chastel, Paris, 1968.

Destaing, F., "Le soleil et l'orage ou la maladie de Van Gogh," *La Nouvelle Presse médicale,* 23 December 1972, vol. I, no. 46, pp. 3141–3143.

Lubin, A. J., *Stranger on the Earth: A Psychological Biography of Vincent van Gogh,* Holt, Rinehart & Winston, New York, 1972.

Monroe, R. R., "The Episodic Psychoses of Vincent van Gogh," *The Journal of Nervous and Mental Disease,* 1978, vol. 166, no. 7, pp. 480–488.

VI   Principal Biographies

Aurier, A., "Les isolés: Vincent van Gogh," *Mercure de France,* January 1890.

Mirbeau, O., "Vincent van Gogh," *L'Echo de Paris,* 31 March 1891.

Bernard, E., "Vincent van Gogh," *La Plume,* 1 September 1891.

Meier-Graefe, J., *Vincent van Gogh,* R. Piper & Co., Munich, 1910; English translation by J. H. Reece, *Vincent van Gogh,* The Medici Society, 2 vols., London, 1922.

Coquiot, G., *Vincent van Gogh,* Ollendorff, Paris, 1923.

Piérard, L., *La vie tragique de Vincent van Gogh,* G. Crès, Paris, 1924.

Fels, F., *Vincent van Gogh,* Floury, Paris, 1928.

Florisoone, M., *Van Gogh,* Paris, 1937.

Schapiro, Meyer, *Vincent van Gogh,* Harry N. Abrams, New York, 1950.

Rewald, J., *Post-Impressionism: From Van Gogh to Gauguin,* Museum of Modern Art, New York, 1956; French translation by Alice Rewald, *Le Post-Impressionnisme de Van Gogh à Gauguin,* Albin Michel, Paris, 1961.

Huyghe, R., *Vincent van Gogh,* Flammarion, Paris, 1958.

Elgar, F., *Vang Gogh,* Hazan, Paris, 1958.

Tralbaut, M.E., *Van Gogh: Eine Bildbiographie,* Kindler Verlag, Munich, 1958.

Badt, K., *Die Farbenlehre Van Goghs,* DuMont Schauberg, Cologne, 1961.

Leymarie, J., *Qui était Vincent van Gogh?,* Skira, Geneva, 1968.

Hammacher, A.M., *Genius and Disaster: The Ten Creative Years of Vincent van Gogh,* Harry N. Abrams, New York, 1969.

Keller, H., *Vincent van Gogh: The Final Years,* Harry N. Abrams, New York, 1969.

Tralbaut, M. E., *Van Gogh le mal aimé,* Edita, Lausanne, 1969.

Leprohon, P., *Vincent van Gogh,* Editions Corymbe, Cannes, 1972.

Hulsker, J., *Van Gogh door Van Gogh,* Meulenhoff, Amsterdam 1973.

Welsh-Ovcharov, B.M., *Van Gogh in Perspective,* Prentice-Hall, Englewood Cliffs, N.J., 1974.

Welsh-Ovcharov, B.M., *Vincent van Gogh: His Paris Period, 1886–1888,* Editions Victorine, Utrecht N.J. and The Hague, 1976.

Secretan-Rollier, P., *Van Gogh chez les gueules noires,* L'Age d'Homme, Lausanne, 1977.

Forrester, V., *Van Gogh ou l'enterrement dans les blés,* Le Seuil, Paris, 1983.

VII   Miscellaneous

Doiteau, V,. "La curieuse figure du Dr. Gachet," *Aesculape,* vol. XIII, 1923 and vol. XIV, 1924.

Gelder, J. G. van, "De Genesis van de Aardappeleters (1885) van Vincent van Gogh," *Beeldende Kunst,* vol. XXVIII, no.1, 1942, pp. 1–8.

Seuphor, M., "Vincent van Gogh: esquisse pour un portrait spirituel," *Tout Dire,* 1945, pp. 195–210.

Langui, E., "Vincent van Gogh, la technique," *Les arts plastiques,* 1947, vol. I, pp. 29–38.

Artaud, A., "Van Gogh le Suicidé de la Sociéte," Editions K., Paris, 1947; *Œuvres Complètes,* vol. XIII, Gallimard, Paris, 1974.

Buchmann, M., *Die Farbe bei Vincent van Gogh,* Bibliander Verlag, Zurich, 1948.

Cooper, D., "The Yellow House and Its Significance," Gemeentemuseum, The Hague, *Mededelingen,* 1953, vol. VIII, nos. 5–6, pp. 94–106.

Aigrisse, G., "L'évolution du symbole chez Van Gogh", *Psyché,* 1954, vol.IX, no. 92, pp. 310–318.

Leymarie, J., "Symbole et réalité chez Van Gogh", Gemeentemuseum, The Hague, *Mededelingen,* 1954, vol. IX, nos. 1–2, pp. 41–49.

Tralbaut, M. E., "Van Gogh's Japanisme," Gemeentemu-seum, The Hague, *Mededelingen,* ibid., pp. 6–40.

Cooper, D., *Drawings and Watercolors by Vincent van Gogh,* MacMillan, New York, 1955.

Blum, H. P., "Les chaises de Van Gogh," *Revue française de Psychoanalyse,* 1958, vol.XXI, no.1, pp. 82–93.

Graetz, H. R., *The Symbolic Language of Vincent van Gogh,* McGraw-Hill, New York, 1963.

Meerloo, J. A. M., "Vincent van Gogh's Quest for Identity," *Nederlands Kunsthistorisch Jaarboek,* 1963, vol. XIV, pp. 183–197.

Roskill, M. W., "Van Gogh's Blue Cart and His Creative Process," *Oud Holland,* 1966, vol. LXXXI, no.1, pp. 3–19.

Joosten, J., "Van Gogh publicaties," *Museumjournaal,* 1969–1970, vol. XIV–XV; see also *Bulletin du Rijksmuseum Vincent van Gogh,* Amsterdam, 1970–1976, vol. I–IV.

Roskill, M. W., *Van Gogh, Gauguin and the Impressionist Circle,* New York Graphic Society, Greenwich, Connecticut, 1970.

Wylie, A., "An Investigation of the Vocabulary of Line in Vincent van Gogh's Expression of Space," *Oud Holland,* 1970, vol. LXXXV, no.4, pp. 210–235.

Heelan, P.A., "Toward a New Analysis of the Pictorial Space of Vincent van Gogh," *The Art Bulletin,* vol. LVI, December 1972, pp. 478–492.

Rewald, J., Theo van Gogh, Goupil and The Impressionists," *La Gazette des Beaux-Arts,* vol. LXXXI, January 1973, pp. 1–64.

Ward, J.-L., "A Reexamination of van Gogh's Pictorial Space," *The Art Bulletin,* vol. LVIII, December 1976, pp. 593–604.

Châtelet, A., "Le dernier tableau de Van Gogh," *Archives de l'Art français,* 1978, pp. 439–442.

Martin Heidegger et les souliers de Van Gogh. Martin Heidegger: "L'origine de l'œuvre d'art." Meyer Schapiro: "La nature morte comme objet personnel." Jacques Derrida: "Restitutions de la vérité en peinture"; *Macula,* nos. 3 and 4, 1978, pp. 4–37.

Stark, D., "Charles de Groux's Le Bénédicité: A source for Van Gogh's Les mangeurs de pommes de terre," *La Gazette des Beaux-Arts,* vol. XC, May–June 1982, pp. 205–208.

VIII   General Bibliography

Chevreul, E., *De la loi du contraste simultané des couleurs et de l'assortiment des objets colorés considérés d'après cette loi, dans ses rapports avec la peinture* (1839); Imprimerie nationale, Paris, 1889 (2nd ed.).

Signac, P., *D'Eugène Delacroix au néo-impressionnisme,* Floury, Paris, 1911.

Denis, M., *Théories (1890–1910). Du Symbolisme et de Gauguin vers un nouvel ordre classique,* Bibliothèque de l'Occident, Paris, 1912; Rouart and Watelin, Paris, 1920.

Morice, C., *Quelques Maîtres modernes,* Société des Trente, Albert Messein, Paris, 1914.

Bernard, E., *Conversation avec Emile Bernard,* Michel, Paris, 1925.

Cézanne, P., *Correspondance* (1858–1906), Grasset, Paris, 1937; 1978 (2nd ed.).

Dorival, B., *Les étapes de la peinture contemporaine,* vol. I, Gallimard, Paris, 1943.

Brion-Guerry, L., *Cézanne et l'expression de l'espace,* Flammarion, Paris, 1950.

Proust, M., *A la recherche du temps perdu,* Gallimard, coll. Pléiade, Paris, 1954.

Hoog, M., "La composition de G. Yakoulov," *Notes et Documents,* Société des Amis de Georges Yakoulov, Paris, May 1967.

Shattuck, R., *The Banquet Years: The Origins of the Avant-Garde in France, 1885 to World War One,* Vintage, New York, 1968.

Sartre, J.-P., *L'existentialisme est un humanisme,* Nagel, Paris , 1970.

Jaworska, W., *Paul Gauguin et l'Ecole du Pont-Aven,* Ides et Calendes, Neuchâtel, 1971.

Marcadé, V., *Le renouveau de l'art pictural russe,* L'Age d'Homme, Lausanne, 1971.

Matisse, H., *Ecrits et propos sur l'art,* compiled by Dominique Fourcade, Hermann, Paris, 1972.

Luthi, J.-J., *Emile Bernard cet initiateur,* Caractères, Paris, 1974.

Clay, J., *De l'Impressionnisme à l'Art Moderne,* Hachette, Paris, 1975.

Index

Africa 141
Albi 140
Amsterdam 13, 16, 20, 46, 93, 202
   Nieuw-Amsterdam 59
Anquetin, Louis 50, 57, 97, 115, 137, 141, 192, 203
Antwerp 78, 92, 93, 97, 293
Arles 9, 43, 82, 93, 115, 137, 140, 144, 171, 192, 193, 200, 207, 211, 215, 216, 261, 294, 296, 298, 299
Artaud, Antonin 206, 278
Asnières 122
Aurier, Albert 203, 212, 227, 254, 261, 291
Auvers-sur-Oise 9, 162, 248, 261, 277, 301
Avignon 171

Balzac, Honoré de 36
Barbizon 20, 67
   School 20
Bargue, Charles 20, 26, 270
Bernard, Emile 50, 57, 97, 115, 130, 132, 137, 140, 141, 144, 154, 156, 162, 164, 168, 170, 171, 175, 182, 183, 185, 188, 192 193, 197, 200, 202, 203, 211, 212, 223, 236, 239, 248, 291, 294
Bing Gallery 141
Bing, Samuel 137
Bingham 20
Blanc, Charles 67
Blok, bookseller 34
Blommers, B. J. 56
Blussé & Van Braam 15
Boch, Eugène 170, 189
Bock, Théophile de 56, 188
Bonger, André 114, 140
Bonger, Jo 207, 212, 261, 277, 283

Borinage 20, 35, 40, 88
Boussod 13, 14
Boussod and Valadon 14, 140
Brabant 59–67, 70, 254
Breitner, George-Henri 40
Breton, Jules 20
Brion-Guerry, Liliane 248
Brittany 183, 185
Brochart, Julien 67
Brussels 17, 20, 21, 236
Bruyas, Alfred 203
Buddha 171

Camargue 161
Cassagne 25
Cent (Uncle Vincent) 11, 15, 38, 190
Cézanne, Paul 50, 71, 82, 122, 130, 152, 162, 236, 239, 248, 278, 300
Chardin, Jean-Baptiste 31, 122, 293
Chevreul, Eugène 70
Charivari 40
Cimabue (Cenni di Pepi) 174
Ciurlionis, Constantin 227
Cloisonnism 50, 57, 137, 141–144, 174, 193, 200, 203
Constant, Benjamin 182
Coquiot, Gustave 35
Cor (Uncle Cornelius, called C.M.) 16, 31, 33, 46, 83
Cormon, Fernand 97, 130, 289
Corot, Jean-Baptiste Camille 17, 63, 71, 144, 152, 248 294
Courbet, Gustave 50, 67, 115, 122, 203
Courrières 20
Crau, Plain of La 156, 175
Cuesmes 20

Daubigny, Charles 17, 71, 200
Daudet, Alphonse 174, 211

Daumier, Honoré 22, 40, 67, 175, 188, 197, 200
Degas, Edgar 97, 200, 203
Delacroix, Eugène 58, 67, 74, 83, 93, 141, 150,154, 161 170, 171, 175, 190, 203, 206, 226, 236, 239, 270, 301
Delaroche, Paul 67
Delaunay, Robert 227
Diaz (de la Pena), Narcisse 57
Dickens, Charles 34, 202
Dordrecht 15
Doré, Gustave 223
Dou, Gérard 88
Drenthe 9, 57, 58–59, 92, 162
Duchamp, Marcel 82
Dujardin, Edouard 137
Dupré, Jules 43, 67, 71, 150
Dürer, Albrecht 55

Eisen 137
Elisabeth, Vincent's sister 39, 284
Elstir 190
England 58, 294
Eragny-sur-Epte 248
Estaque, L' 162, 239, 300
Etten 15, 17, 22, 25, 39, 78

Fantin-Latour, Ignace Henri Jean Théodore 114
Fauvism, Fauvists 132, 144, 193, 299
Fénéon, Félix 192
Figaro, Le 185
Fildès, Luke 34, 202
Flaubert, Gustave 174, 185, 188
Fontvielle 170
Forrester, Viviane 203, 206
Forum Républicain, Le 212
Fragonard, Jean-Honoré 171
Frère 31

Gachet, Paul, Dr. 248, 261, 270, 277, 278, 283
Gauguin, Paul 43, 50, 55, 57, 82, 97, 137, 141, 144, 161, 168, 171, 183, 185, 188, 189, 190, 192, 193, 196, 197 f., 200, 202f., 206, 207, 211, 215, 223, 239, 248, 278, 289, 291, 299
Gavarni 22, 40
Germany, German 211
Gigoux, Jean 78
Ginoux, Madame 197
Giorgione 74
Giotto 174
Gladwell, Harry 12 f.
Gogh, Theo van 9, 17, 18, 20, 27, 33, 34, 35, 36, 38, 39, 40, 42, 43, 56, 57, 58, 59, 62, 67, 70, 71, 82, 88, 96, 97, 122, 140, 144, 154, 161, 162, 164, 165, 171, 174, 175, 182, 183, 190, 192, 193, 196, 202, 207, 211, 215, 218, 220, 222, 254, 277, 278, 283, 289, 294, 299, 300
Goncourt, Edmond 174
Goncourt, Jules 174
Goupil Gallery 12, 14, 20, 34, 38, 162, 200, 277, 289
Goyen, Jan Josephszoon Van 58, 223
Grande Jatte, Island of 130
Graphic, The 34, 58, 83
Greece, Greek 78, 211
Groot familiy 83
    Gordina de 83
Guillaumin, Armand 236, 278

Hals, Frans 70, 83, 182
Helmholtz, Ferdinand 227
Herkomer, Hubert 34
Hiroshige 93, 137
Hirschig, Anton 283
Hokusai 137, 162
Hol, Frank 34
Holbein, Hans 20
Honthorst 9
Hoogeveen 57
Hoornik, Clasina, Maria 35, 36, 38, 39, 43, 58
Hugo, Victor 212
Hulsker, Jan 114, 132, 144, 292

Impressionists 97, 130, 132, 141, 164, 170, 270, 278, 293
    Neo-Impressionists 115, 192
Ingres, Jean Auguste Dominique 25, 200

Isaacson, J. J. 261
Isleworth 14
Israëls, Jozef 17, 71, 154

Japan, Japanese 93, 130, 132, 137, 141, 144, 155, 156, 161, 171, 174, 188, 193, 196, 197, 200, 211, 227, 248, 270, 283, 296, 298
John 21
Jones, Reverend 14, 15
Jongkind, Johann-Barthold 11

Kee (Vos) 27, 29, 31, 35
Koninck, Philippe de 58
Koninck, Salamon 150
Kupka, Frantisek 227

Laeken 17
Landelle, Louis 36
Laval, Charles 141, 185
Lavater and Gall 21
Lavieille, Jacques-Adrien 226
Levens, H. M. 97, 114, 122, 140
London 11, 12
    National Gallery 50
    London News 34, 58
Loti, Pierre 174
Loyer, Eugéne 11, 12, 287
Louis XV, King 82

Maaten, Van der 17
Manet, Edouard 57, 67, 122, 137, 174, 236, 254
Margot (Begemann) 82
Maris, Jacob 17, 114
Maris, Wilhelm 17, 114
Marseilles 206, 223
Martinique 183, 185, 193, 200
Marx, Roger 236
Matisse, Henri 42, 144, 175, 212, 270
Maupassant, Guy de 165, 171, 174
Maus, Octave 236
Mauve, Anton 26, 29, 31, 33, 34, 36, 38, 39–43, 57, 93, 114, 141, 175, 296
Mazery, Dr. 283
Mendes da Costa 16
Mercure de France, Le 203 f.
Michel, Georges 20, 58, 150
Michelangelo Buonarroti 55
Michelet, Jules 12
Millais, John-Everett 17
Millet, Jean-François 26, 34, 59, 67, 70, 71, 88, 122, 154, 226, 239, 270, 294

Milliet, Second Lieutenant 182, 185, 189
Moe, Vincent's mother 59, 207, 222
Monet, Claude 97, 114, 132, 150, 162, 174, 236, 254, 278
Monfreid, Daniel de 82
Monticelli, Adolphe 114, 154, 161, 171, 206, 223, 299
Montmajour 144, 150, 155
Montpellier 203
Moréas, Jean 71
Morisot, Berthe 132
Moscow 158
Musset, Alfred de 203
Muybridge, Eadweard 82

Nabis 43, 190, 193, 215, 223, 270
Naples 88
Netherlands 43, 58, 150, 183, 283
Nuenen 9, 40, 70, 74, 96, 137, 141, 154, 155

Paris 12, 20, 43, 46, 67,70, 88, 96, 137, 140, 154, 161, 162, 165, 183, 189, 190, 212, 215, 277, 278, 294
    Clichy 137
    Drouot 12
    Eiffel Tower 227
    Galerie des Machines 227
    Louvre, Musée du 12
    Luxembourg, Musée du 12
    Montmartre 12, 97, 114, 130
Paris Illustré, Le 137
Pas-de-Calais 20
Patterson 39
Peyron, Dr. 223, 227, 254, 278
Picasso, Pablo 193
Pissarro, Camille 97, 162, 236, 248, 294
Poe, Edgar Allan 211
Pont-Aven 57, 137, 144, 183, 185, 190, 200, 203, 220, 248, 254, 289
Pointillism 130, 132, 137, 159, 165, 261, 270, 296
Poussin, Nicolas 50, 70
Provence 141, 154
Puvis de Chavannes, Pierre 197

Rachel 212
Radoub, Sergeant 212
Ramsgate 13, 162
Raphael 200
Rappard, Anton Van 21, 25, 26, 43, 56, 57, 82, 88 f., 92
Ravoux family 261, 283

Ravoux, father 283
Rembrandt, Harmenszoon van Rijn 9, 17, 83, 88, 141, 150, 182, 203, 239
Renan, Ernest 12
Renoir, Auguste 114, 171, 254, 278
Revue Indépendante, La 137
Rewald, John 200
Rey, Dr. 212, 216
Roche, Edmond 12
Rodin, Auguste 174
Roelofs, Willem 21, 51
Roozendaal 23, 25
Rossetti, Christina 13
Roulin, Madame 207
Roulin, postman 215
Rousseau, Thédore 58, 200
Rubens, Peter Paul 83, 92, 93, 132, 293
Russell, John 161, 197, 289
Russell, R. Monroe, Dr. 223
Ruysdael, Jacob van 17
Ryssel, Paul Van 248; *see* Gachet

St. Francis of Assisi 19
St.-Rémy-de-Provence 10, 40, 42, 203, 222, 223, 226, 227, 239, 248, 254, 277, 283, 296, 301
Saintes-Maries-de-la-Mer 140, 161, 162, 165, 174
Salles, Reverend 215, 218, 222

Schafrath, sexton 89
Scheffer, Ary 17, 58
Schenkweg 34
Schmidt 20
Schuffenecker, Emile 185, 192, 197, 200, 212, 236
Segatori, Agostina 140
Sérusier, Paul 215
Seurat, Georges 97, 130, 132, 162, 185
Shakespeare, William 36, 236
Sien: *see* Hoornik
Signac, Paul 97, 115, 130, 132, 162, 185, 218, 294
Sisley, Alfred 162, 254
Socrates 175
South Sea Island 82
Steen, Jan 31
Stokes, teacher 13
Stricker, clergyman 16, 17

Tanguy, Madame 220
Tanguy, Père 137, 175, 236
Tartarin de Tarascon 211
Ter Borch 83
Tersteeg, H. B. 11, 20, 27, 33, 34, 36, 38, 40, 175, 183
The Hague 11, 33, 35, 43, 46, 55, 56, 59, 70, 78, 188, 200, 270
    School 62, 67, 114, 122

Theodorus, Reverend 59, 82
Toulouse-Lautrec, Henri de 97, 137, 140, 200
Tralbaut, Marc Edo 17, 132, 175

United States 59

Vaccarès, Lake 161
Valadon: *see* Boussod
Veronese, Paolo 67
Volpini 236
Vuillard, Edouard 270

Wagner, Richard 141
Walker 34
Ward, J. L. 189
Wasmes 19
Weissenbruch, Johannes 17, 55
Wetherall, Elizabeth 14
Wilhelmina, Vincent's sister 115, 140, 141, 144, 161, 185, 196, 215, 222, 223, 248, 254, 278, 299

Yakulov, Georges 227

Ziem, Félix 200
Zola, Emile 36, 82, 164, 165, 174, 185
Zweeloo 59

Index of Van Gogh's Works

The numbers in italics refer to the captions. The letter F refers to the *Catalogue raisonné* by De la Faille.

A House with Two People (F 806) 261; *185*

A Pair of Clogs (F 607) *128*

Asylum Garden, The (F 1535) *149*

At the Coalmines (Letter 126) 18; *4*

Banks of the Seine (F 293) 130, 296; *87*

Barn with the Mossy Roof, The (F 842) 23; *9*

Birch Wood with a Flock of Sheep (F 1240) 63; *34*

Birds' Nests (Letter 425) 93; *55*

Bleaching-Ground at Scheveningen, The (Letter 220) 43; *25*

Boats on the Beach (F 413) 162; *115*

Bouquet of Daisies and Anemones (F 323) 296; *79*

Bouquet of Flowers (F 764a) *182*

Bouquet of Sunflowers (F 454) 192, 193, 202, 206, 278, 299; *132*

Brabant Peasant Woman (Letter 409) *54*

Breton Women (F 1422) 197, 202; *137*

Bridge at Asnière, The (F 301) 132; *91*

Bridge at Langlois, The (F 397) 144; *100*

Café Terrace by Night (F 467) 164, 165; *117*

Church at Auvers, The (F 789) 261, 302; *189*

Churches of Petersham and Turnham, The (Letter 82) *3*

Cineraria Plant (F 282) 114; *70*

Coming out of Church at Nuenen (F 25) 63; *35*

Cornfield (F 310) 130; *89*

Cornfield at Noon (F 618) *153*

Cornfield with Irises (F 409) 144; *102*

Cottages at Cordeville (F 792) 261; *186*

Cottages at Dusk (F 83) 70; *41*

Courtyard of the Hospital at Arles, The (F 519) 222; *147*

Crows over the Cornfields (F 779) 270, 277, 278, 283, 284, 302; *198, 199*

Cut Sunflowers (F 375) 122; *63*

Cypresses (F 620) 227; *159*

Dance Hall at Arles, The (F 547) 197, 200; *136*

Daubigny's Garden (F 777) 270; *194*

Diggers (F 829) *7*

Dormitory at the Hospital of Arles, The (F 646) 222; *145*

Dr. Gachet's Garden (F 755) 261, 301, 302; *187*

Enclosed Field with Sower in the Rain (F 1551) *144*

En route (Letter 140) 22, 26; *11*

Entrance to a Quarry (F 744) 239, 248, 301; *166*

Entrance to the Asylum (F 1530) 223; *150*

Farm in the Snow and Peasants (F 1593) *146*

Farmers Working in the Fields (F 1090) 150; *105*

Field of Unripe Corn at Sunrise, The (F 720) 223; *152*

Field under a Stormy Sky, The (F 778) 270; *196*

Fish Drying Barn (F 938) 43, 46; *28*

Flower Garden (F 429) 159; *111*

Flowering Almond Tree Branches (F 671) 254; *175*

Fountain in the Asylum Garden (F 1531) *148*

Fritillaries (F 213) *78*

Garden of the Carpenter and the Laundry, The (F 939) 43; *26*

Gauguin's Armchair (F 499) 202, 206; *139*

Girl in a Forest (F 8) 50; *29*

Girl Seated by a Cradle (F 1024) 55, 56; *31*

Good Samaritan (F 633) 239

Great Lady, The (Letter 185) 35, 36; *17*

Gypsy Camp (F 445) 140; *95*

Haystacks (F 425) *106*

Head of a Peasant Woman (F 130) 70; *39*

Head of a Peasant Woman (F 134) 83; *51*

Hill of Montmartre, The (F 266) 114; *67*

Houses Seen from the Rear (F 260) 57

In Front of the Wood Fire 22

Italian Woman (La Segatori) (F 381) 137, 174, 270, 298; *94*

Kingfisher, The (F 28) 114; *69*

Kitchen Gardens of Montmartre (F 346) 130; *85*

La Berceuse (F 504) 207, 296; *141*

La Berceuse (F 505) 218, 220

La Berceuse (F 506) 218

La Berceuse (F 507) 218

La Berceuse (F 508) 218
La Grand-PLace (F 1352) 58
La Guinguette (F 238) 114; *68*
La Mousmé (F 431) 174, 175; *124*
La Pietà (F 630) 226, 239, 301; *154*
L'Arlésienne (F 543) 278
L'Arlésienne, Mme Ginoux (F 489) 197, 226; *135*
La Segatori: see *Italian Woman* (F 381)
Le Moulin de la Galette (F 227) 114; *66*
Le Quai (F 211) 93; *60*
Les Alyscamps (F 486) 193, 196, 298, 299; *133*
Les Alyscamps (F 568) 193
Loom (F 30) *33*

Mademoiselle Gachet in her Garden (F 756) *192*
Maisons de Guardians at Saintes-Maries (F 1438) 162; *113*
Man Walking among Trees (F 742) 248; *171*
Marguerite Gachet at the Piano (F 772) 270; *191*
Market Gardens (F 412) 150; *104*
Meadow with Dandelions (F 676) 261; *178*
Men and Women Going to the Mines (F 831) *6*
Metairies (F 17) 59; *30*
Miner Shouldering A Spade (F 827) *5*
Miners Returning Home (F 832) *8*
Miners' Wives (F 994) 42; *22*
Mountain Landscape (F 611) 226; *158*
Mountains (F 622) 239, 300, 301; *165*

National Lottery, The (F 970) 40, 200; *21*
Night Café, The (F 463) 165, 296; *116*
Nude Little Girl Seated (F 1367) 64
Nurse (F 174) 93; *59*

Old Almshouse Man (F 962) 42; *24*
Old Man Holding His Head in His Hands (F 702) 226
Old Vineyard, The (F 1624) 261; *181*
Olive Field (F 585) 239, 301; *162*
Olive Fields (F 710) 239, 301; *163*
On the Beach (F 4) 50; *27*
Orchard in Bloom with the View of Arles (F 515) 144; *101*
Ox and Cart (F 38) 67; *36*

Parsonage, The (F 182) *56*
Peach Trees in Blossom (F 394) 43, 144; *99*
Peasant Reaping, Seen from the Back (F 1317) 74; *45*
Peasant Seated by the Fire (F 868) 26; *15*
Peasant Seated by the Fire (Letter 150) 26; *16*
Peasant Woman Binding a Sheaf (F 1264) 74; *46*
Peasant Woman with a Pitchfork (F 1251) 74; *47*
Peasant Woman with White Headdress (F 1184) 83; *50*
Peasant Women in the Fields (F 19) *32*
Peasants at Table (F 1588) 42; *23*
Pine Trees against the Light (F 652) 239; *168*
Plaine de la Crau, The (F 1420) 156; *110*
Plaster Statuette (F 216h) *82*
Plowed Field, The (F 574) 171; *122*
Poet's Garden (F 485) 190, 192
Poplar Avenue (F 122) 67; *37*
Poplar Avenue near Nuenen (F 45) 70, 71, 294; *43*
Poppy Fields (F 581) *161*
Pork Butcher's, The (F 389) 141, 198; *98*
Portrait of Augustine Roulin (F 503) 207; *140*
Portrait of a Woman in Blue (F 207a) 132; *96*
Portrait of Dr. Gachet (F 754) 270, 278, 302; *188*
Portrait of Eugène Boch (F 462) 170, 175, 196; *121*
Portrait of Patience Esaclier (F 444) 175; *126*
Portrait of Patience Escalier (F 443) 175
Portrait of Père Tanguy (F 363) 130, 137, 174; *84*
Postman Roulin, The (F 432) 174–175, 197; *123*
Potato Eaters, The (F 82) 9, 88, 114, 115, 164, 226, 293; *52, 53*
Potato Field, The (F 129a) *44*

Raising of Lazarus, The (F 677) 239, 254; *170*
Ravine, The (F 661) 248; *172*

Red Vineyards at Arles, The (F 495) 254; *174*
Restaurant de la Sirène, The (F 313) 130; *88*
Restaurant Interior (F 342) 132, 296; *92*
Road Menders, The (F 657) 239; *169*
Road with a Row of Willows and a Roadsweeper (F 1678) 26; *10*
Road with Cypresses, The (F 683) 261, 300, 301; *180*
Rocks (F 1447) 155; *109*
Roofs of Paris, The (F 262) 114; *65*
Roses and Anemones (F 764) 261; *183*
Round of Prisoners (F 669) 223

Sailboats at Saintes-Maries (F 1430b) 158; *112*
Self-Portrait (F 178 verso) 114; *71*
Self-Portrait (F 356) 115; *74*
Self-Portrait (F 476) 170, 171; *120*
Self-Portrait (F 627) 239, 278, 301; *167*
Self-Portrait of the Artist at Work (F 522) 115; *77*
Self-Portrait with a Gray Felt Hat (F 344) 115, 296; *76*
Self-Portrait with a Gray Hat (F 295) 114, 296; *72*
Self-Portrait with a Straw Hat (F 469) 115; *75*
Self-Portrait with Bandaged Ear (F 527) 212; *143*
Shoes (F 333) 122; *80*
Siesta (F 686) *173*
Sorrow (F 1655) 35, 39, 42, 43, 88; *18*
Souvenirs of the North (F 675) 254; *176*
Sower (F 451) 196, 206–207, 294; *134*
Sower (F 830) 26; *12*
Sower (F 856) 26; *13*
Sower (F 862) 26; *14*
Sower at Sunset (F 422) 154, 158, 159, 196, 206, 226, 294, 300; *108*
Sower at Sunset (F 1441) 154, 158, 159; *107*
Staircase at Auvers, The (F 795) 283; *200*
Starry Night (F 474) 10, 165, 170, 171, 196, 296, 301; *119*
Starry Night (Letter 553b) 170, 171; *118*
Starry Night (F 612) 170, 226, 227; *156, 157*
Still Life: Irises (F 678) 261; *184*
Still Life with Absinthe (F 339) 140; *97*

Still Life with Bottles (F 50) 293; *38*

Still Life with Drawing Board (F 604) 206; *142*

Still Life with Earthenware Pot and Clogs (F 63) *42*

Still Life with Lemons and Carafe (F 340) 122; *81*

Still Life with Open Bible, Candle, and Novel (F 117) 74, 82, 206; *49*

Still Life with Plaster Statuette, a Rose and Two Books of Novellas (F 360) 130; *83*

Street Scene in Montmartre (F 347) 130

Study of Hands (F 1360) Frontispiece

Sunset (F 465) *103*

Thatched Roofs at Chaponval (F 780) 278; *197*

Tower of the Cemetery at Nuenen, The (F 84) *48*

Tree Trunks and Roots (F 816) 270; *193*

Two Children (F 783) 270; *190*

Two Peasant Women Digging in a Snow-Covered Field (F 695) 254; *177*

Two Self-Portraits (F 1378 recto) 114; *73*

Underwood (F 309a) 130; *90*

View from the School Window (Letter 82) *2*

View from Vincent's Room, Rue Lepic (F 341) 130, 296; *86*

View of the Alpilles (F 724) 239; *164*

View of Saintes-Maries-de-la-Mer (F 416) 162; *114*

Vincent's Bedroom (F 483) 226

Vincent's Bedroom (Letter 554) 188; *131*

Vincent's Chair (F 498) 202, 206; *138*

Vincent's Room at Arles (F 482) 188, 189, 192; *130*

Vincent's Room at the Asylum (F 1528) 223; *151*

Walk in the Moonlight amidst Olive Trees (F 704) 261; *179*

Washerwomen by the Canal (F 1444) *127*

Winter Garden (F 1128) 63

Woman at Table at the Café Le Tambourin (F 370) 97, 132; *62*

Woman Binding Sheaves (F 700) 226; *155*

Woman of Scheveningen (F 871) 40; *19*

Woman of the People (F 206) 132

Woman Reading a Novel 197

Woman Rocking 197

Woman Seated Beside a Cradle (F 369) 132; *93*

Woman Spinning (F 71) 70; *40*

Women Repairing Nets in the Dunes (F 7) 42

Women Waltzing at the Dance Hall (F 1350b) *61*

Workmen at Their Task (Letter 190) 40; *20*

Yellow Corn, The (F 615) 236, 239, 301; *160*

Yellow House, The (F 464) 185; *129*

Zouave, The (F 423) 174, 182; *125*

Acknowledgments

I should like to thank all those who have helped in the production of this book. I am especially grateful for the kindness of Mr. Michel Hoog, head curator of the museums of the Orangerie and the Palais de Tokyo, who has enabled me to undertake this fascinating work. My thanks, too, to Frédéric Berthet, the writer, who has often been kind enough to offer advice and criticism during our fruitful discussions. To my wife, Gwénolée, I should like to express my thanks for her continuous help and for her unfailing tender encouragements. Finally, my very special thanks to my collaborators at the Office du Livre: Madame Ingrid de Kalbermatten, and Messrs Dominique Guisan and Marcel Berger.

Photo Credits

The author and the publishers wish to thank all those who have supplied photographs for this book. The numbers refer to the plates.

The photo research for this book was done by Ingrid de Kalbermatten.

A. C. L., Brussels 112
Archivio Fotografico dei Civici Musei, Milan 137

The Baltimore Museum of Art, Baltimore 80
The Cleveland Museum of Art, Cleveland 169
A. C. Cooper Ltd., London 126
Walter Dräyer, Zurich 91, 177
Fogg Art Museum, Cambridge, Massachusetts 120
Gemeentemuseum, The Hague 71, 111, 195
Giraudon, Paris 143
Hans Hinz, Allschwil 65, 174, 191, 194
Kunsthalle, Bremen 161
Kunsthaus, Zurich 44, 197
Kunstmuseum, Winterthur 103
The Metropolitan Museum of Art, New York 10, 63
The Minneapolis Institute of Arts, Minneapolis 163
Musée Rodin, Paris 84
Museu de Arte, São Paulo 179

Museum Boymans-van Beuningen, Rotterdam 43, 70
The Museum of Modern Art, New York 156, 157
Museum of Fine Arts, Boston 123
The National Gallery, London 132, 138, 160
National Gallery of Art, Washington, D.C. 124
Ny Carlsberg Glyptotek, Copenhagen 158
Oskar Reinhart Collection, Winterthur 140, 145, 147
Réunion des Musées Nationaux, Paris 51, 68, 78, 88, 94, 95, 119, 121, 135, 136, 167, 173, 183, 186, 187, 188, 189, 190, 192
Rijksmuseum Kröller-Müller, Otterlo 5, 6, 7, 8, 9, 13, 14, 15, 22, 26, 28, 29, 33, 36, 38, 42, 46, 66, 67, 79, 83, 92, 99, 100, 106, 108, 114, 117, 127, 133, 141, 142, 152, 159, 162, 164, 168, 171, 172, 178, 180
The Solomon R. Guggenheim Museum, New York 165
Stedelijk Museum, Amsterdam 1, 2, 3, 4, 11, 12, 16, 17, 18, 19, 20, 21, 23, 24, 25, 30, 31, 32, 34, 35, 37, 39, 40, 41, 45, 47, 48, 49, 50, 52, 53, 54, 55, 56, 57, 58, 59, 60, 61, 62, 64, 69, 72, 73, 74, 75, 76, 77, 81, 82, 85, 86, 87, 89, 90, 93, 96, 97, 98, 101, 102, 104, 105, 107, 109, 110, 113, 115, 118, 122, 125, 128, 129, 130, 131, 134, 139, 144, 146, 148, 149, 150, 151, 153, 154, 155, 166, 170, 175, 176, 181, 182, 184, 185, 193, 196, 198, 199
The St. Louis Art Museum, St. Louis, Missouri 200
Yale University Art Gallery, New Haven 116